"Scotland seems to be producing some
pretty good novelists these days and,
on the evidence of FROM SCENES LIKE
THESE, Gordon M. Williams promises to be
among the best of them. . . . What impresses
most is the harsh authenticity, its ability to
get physical details pinned down and
brought into vivid focus, its refusal to
whip up more drama and violence than the
events actually contain . . . Williams gets
across the pains and perplexities of
adolescent desire, guilt and aspiration
convincingly and without literary frills"

New Statesman

By the same author
in Mayflower Books

THE CAMP
THE MAN WHO HAD POWER OVER WOMEN

From Scenes
Like These

Gordon M. Williams

A Mayflower Paperback

FROM SCENES LIKE THESE
Gordon M. Williams

Mayflower Paperbacks are published
by Mayflower Books,
3 Upper James St., London, W. 1.
Made and printed in Great Britain by
C. Nicholls & Company Ltd.,
The Philips Park Press, Manchester

TO RALPH SAUNDERS

From scenes like these old Scotia's grandeur springs,
That makes her lov'd at home, rever'd abroad;
Princes and Lords are but the breath of kings,
"An honest man's the noblest work of God";
And certes, in fair virtue's heavenly road,
The cottage leaves the palace far behind;
What is a lordling's pomp? a cumbrous load,
Disguising oft the wretch of human kind,
Studied in arts of hell, in wickedness refined.

O Scotia! my dear, my native soil!
For whom my warmest wish to Heaven is sent,
Long may thy hardy sons of rustic toil
Be blest with health, and peace, and sweet content!
And O! may Heaven their simple lives prevent
From luxury's contagion, weak and vile!
Then, howe'er crowns and coronets be rent,
A virtuous populace may rise the while,
And stand a wall of fire around their much-lov'd isle.

O thou! who pour'd the patriotic tide,
That stream'd thro' Wallace's undaunted heart,
Who dar'd to, nobly, stem tyrranic pride
Or nobly die, the second glorious part;
(The patriot's God, peculiar Thou art,
His friend, inspirer, guardian and reward!)
O never, never Scotia's realm desert;
But still the patriot, and the patriot bard
In bright succession raise, her ornament and guard!
                Robert Burns (*The Cottar's Saturday Night*)

CHAPTER ONE

It was still dark, that Monday in January, when the boy, Dunky Logan, and the man, Blackie McCann, came to feed and water the horses, quarter after seven on a cold Monday morning in January, damn near as chill as an Englishman's heart, said McCann, stamping his hobnail boots on the stable cobbles.

Dunky Logan rested his old bicycle against the stable wall, then hung the gas-mask case, containing his sandwiches and vacuum flask on a nail. The slack sleeves of his grimy fawn pullover hung down over his hands, stretching inches beyond the elastic cuffs of his green zip-jerkin. Even on a morning like this it would have been unthinkable to wear gloves. Only nancy boys wore gloves. He'd pulled down his pullover sleeves to protect his fingers from the freezing metal of his bicycle handlebars. Even in the stable the air was cold. It rasped on the back of his throat. His mother had got him out of his warm bed in the kitchen at half-past six. There was still a strong sensation of porridge at the back of his mouth, even although he'd been chewing bacon rind since he'd got up from the kitchen table and pedalled up the hill from the old tenement in Shuttle Place through the Darroch Council house scheme, teeth working on the rubbery wad of rind, eyes on the frosty road for bricks or broken bottles, one hand on the handlebars, the other in his trouser pocket. At that time in the early morning the sloping streets of the Darroch scheme were almost empty. Men who worked in factories and engineering shops were only thinking about getting up. It made him feel tough and hard being a farmworker who had to be yoked by the time other men were only crawling out of their beds.

He'd cycled up the road which led from the edge of the sprawling scheme to the farm, along the edge of the field which lay between the back gardens of the houses and the railway embankment. The harsh blue sodium lights of the scheme streets ended at the railway bridge, a dank vault from whose iron rafters hung silvery icicles. It had to be very cold before the drips from the underside of the bridge froze up.

The farm steading stood on the left of the road past the bridge, its buildings low, black silhouettes against the faint

7

light from the low moon. Dismounting, he could see from the yard somebody moving about in the farmhouse kitchen, Willie Craig, no doubt.

Once he and McCann had been inside the stable for a few moments it felt warmer, horse-dung warm, the three Clydesdales snorting and pulling at their ropes to see what was moving behind them in the darkness. McCann blew on his fingers and rubbed them in his armpits. He reached up for the paraffin lamp, striking two matches before he got a light. The black wick smoked into a ring of smelly flame. One of the horses blew steamy air out of flared nostrils, like a dragon in a storybook. Dunky rubbed his eyes with his knuckles. He could have slept for another two or three hours, no bother. Monday was always the worst day for getting up, especially in the winter. Monday was the worst day all round, the start of another five and a half days of work, back to the stable and its mess of sharn and straw and old harness and broken tools, a place that would be tidied up only when they'd finished lifting and pitting the potatoes, if it was ever tidied up at all.

McCann hung the lamp on an old saddle-post beside the small, cobweb-layered window.

"Come on then, Smallcock," he said, his voice hoarse and impatient, not at all friendly. "Get among they beasts, a bit of work'll soon warm ye up. In ye go, they won't eat you."

McCann still didn't like him, even after three weeks' working at Craig's farm. Three weeks! It didn't seem more than a day or two since he'd been sitting in school waiting desperately for the Christmas holidays, to be finished at last with the daftness of lessons and homework, the whole silliness of being a schoolboy. Three weeks! He was still not used to the big horses, big brutes they were, only it wouldn't do to let McCann see him look nervous about going into the stalls. McCann could be very coarse. Some of them called him Blackie, or Black McCann, partly because he had jet-black hair and a blue chin, but more because of his moods. Nobody knew what caused his bad spells but when they came on two fields was a good distance to have between McCann and yourself. He was twenty-four, McCann, a fully-grown man. He had a funny sense of humour, too, even when he wasn't in a bad mood. He knew Dunky was scared of going into the stalls beside the horses and he took a great delight in rubbing it in.

"The weather forecast says it's going to rain by dinnertime," Dunky remarked as he took the corn-pail to the big

8

kist, trying to make McCann think he wasn't concerned about feeding the horses.

"More'n likely," said McCann, standing against the end wall for a run-off. "Ye'd better get a move on, Auld Craig'll be wanting to make an early start."

He fed the mare first, the smallest of the three horses but still a good two inch taller at the rump than himself, a light brown horse with neat, white-mopped feet and a white nose. In the morning they got just enough corn to keep them going all day, just enough to stop them from starving for grass when they were yoked.

Her long, hard-boned head swung round to meet him, soft lips pulled back from old-yellow teeth as she tried to guzzle corn out of the pail. He tipped it into the earthenware trough. As he left the stall he gave her rump a friendly pat, partly because he liked her for being tame and partly to show Mc-Cann he was in control of the situation. She was a nice horse, female, soft, not dangerous. McCann leaned on the broom handle, dark eyes looking for signs of nervousness.

"Nothing to it, lad," he said, grinning, sleep-puffed eyes giving him an air of added malice. Now for Big Dick, the middle horse, biggest of the three, a dark brown gelding who normally played up like a thoroughbred stallion. Big Dick stood across his stall diagonally, head in one corner, hind-quarters blocking his entrance. As he approached the stall, hoping the horse would move over of its own accord, McCann lifted the broom handle and gave Big Dick a meaty smack on the haunch. The horse sidled abruptly, at the same time lashing out a hind-leg in a bad-tempered swipe.

"There, that's how to treat the buggers," said McCann, grinning.

It was a dirty trick to play, for Big Dick was bad-tempered enough without hitting him. McCann was trying to push him into a fight, he knew that well enough. Well, he was no mug. If they hadn't been alone he'd have taken his chance, probably swung the bucket into Blackie's face, hoping to crack him on the shebonk. If McCann kept this up they would have a fight, but he wasn't going to risk it when they were alone. For some reason he felt it would be embarrassing, just the two of them. Fighting was silly. It seemed more natural to fight when there were other men there, quite apart from the fact that the others would stop the fight before McCann could ruin him for life.

He could feel the great weight of Big Dick moving beside

9

him in the stall. He kept his eyes on the horse's head, which was raised above its wooden hayrack, ears alert for trouble, eyes waiting for some excuse to swing over and flatten him again the solid, greasy boards of the stall partition, ready to bear down on his boots, metal-shod hooves bashing down with the force of a ton or more of Clydesdale. Big Dick was as chancy a bastard to deal with as McCann. On his very first day at the farm (not counting previous years when he'd worked there during school holidays and had only been the boy) he'd watched McCann going over Big Dick with the stiff wire brush and the horse had taken a casual side-kick at Blackie, casual in the way of a bad horse, a sort of half-interested gesture just to let you know peace has not been declared. Blackie had jumped away, feeling his shin, swearing something awful, although Dunky was sure he hadn't really been touched. Saying he'd worked horses all his life, he knew what to do with them, Blackie had hammered the toe of his boot into Big Dick's right hindleg, above the hoof, jumping clear at the same time. That was the good thing about industrial boots, McCann had said, viciously, they had fine steel-plated toe-caps for lashing into the evil bastard and showing him who was boss.

The horse breathed in steamy snorts, pent-up air released in abrupt, almost warning rushes. There was a slight suggestion of pawing the ground in the nervous movements of his forefeet. Even in the middle where his back slumped the brute was taller than he was. The great head swung down and round as he lifted the pail to the trough. He felt like dropping it and running, but sooner or later he *had* to get used to the bastard. The edge of the pail bumped against the bones of its head. He felt the power of it. A dribble of corn fell on the straw. He forced himself nearer the trough, feet tingling in anticipation of its hooves. Then the grains tipped out of the bucket and Big Dick fell to munching. He was out of the stall, safe, much to McCann's disappointment, no doubt.

"He's all right once he gets used to you," he remarked.

"Don't kid me on, Smallcock," said McCann. "Ye're scared to death o' the beast, aren't ye, scared of a bluddy horse."

"Is that a fact?" he said, as cheekily as was safe with McCann. He filled corn for the third horse, old Charlie, a tired old beast who hardly had the energy to lift his tail for a shite, let alone kick you. When he did try his hand with McCann he would definitely get a hammering, he wasn't near as strong

10

as a man, but as long as Donald Telfer and Young Willie and Coll were there they'd stop Blackie before it got too bad. It was some kind of custom. In factories, they said, new apprentices always got some sort of roughing up from the men, like an initiation test. Until McCann had a chance to give him a hammering – or rub his face in cow-shite – he wouldn't leave him alone. The very thought of it made him clench his teeth. His heart seemed to be beating against the skin of his chest. He'd had hundreds of fights but they were with boys his own age. McCann would try to knock his head off.

Mattha McPhail the knee-padder was next to arrive in the stable.

"Aye aye there," was all he said to McPhail. He didn't like the wee dirty man with the fallen mouth where his teeth were missing (he kept his dentures for Saturdays) and the filthy white silk scarf knotted over his adam's apple. Mattha McPhail was actually quite pleased to be known as the knee-padder. Knee-padding was his game, he always said, as though it was much the same as being a Baptist or a greyhound fanatic. He did it in parks and woods and up on the Braes on Sundays in good weather, crawling about on his knees in bushes to watch courting couples on the job. Only once had he been caught, he always boasted; some guy had happened to look up at the least expected moment and lost his stroke as he saw Mattha's ferrety wee face peering at him from the whins. This guy had chased McPhail halfway to Kilmarnock, shouting the odds about kicking his features out of the back of his head, but McPhail was too fly to be caught. In any case, he said, he always had an answer if he *was* caught, the secret was to take your breeks down when you were slinking about in the bushes, then if you were nabbed you just said you'd crawled in for a quick shite.

"I know why you take your trousers down, you wee scunner," Telfer would say. "Ninety-nine change hands one hundred, ye mean, ye dirty old tosser."

McPhail saw no insult in being called a masturbator, knee-padding was a great laugh all round, nothing to be ashamed of, why should it, it was his game, that was all.

Dunky felt glad he was no longer a casual and classed with McPhail, who was hired for the potatoes and the harvest, not much of a worker, always nipping off to go up to Kilcaddie Labour Exchange for his burroo money, hoarse-voiced and shifty, officially unemployed and still drawing dole money

11

from the burroo, he said with pride, after seven whole years.

"Holy Mary mother of Jesus it's colder'n a nun's bum," was McPhail's greeting.

"Ye're early this mornin'," said McCann, still playing about at sweeping the stable floor. "Was something wrang wi' ye, couldn't ye sleep?"

Dunky took the other broom and swept horse shite and sharn up the gutter which ran the length of the stable. Auld Craig, the farmer, hated anybody to look idle. It was Blackie's job to get the three horses yoked into the three carts, as long as he was shoving shite about the old man wouldn't shout at him. Auld Craig thought all townees (which meant anybody who didn't actually have dung on his boots) were idle scum out to rob him. Dunky liked to imagine the farm was under siege, what with the burgh housing scheme advancing up the hill towards the railway line and the new school taking up half the field on the other side of the embankment and talk of an annexe to the school to be built on the rest of the railway field, not to mention the factory going full blast on the west side of the farm; and there was talk that it would need to expand. Apart from all that, scallywag kids from the scheme were always burning down Craig's haystacks or chasing his cows or stealing his hens or playing in his corn.

He didn't consider himself a scheme kid and yet he lived in the town, so he wasn't one or the other. Like young Jim Hawkins, able to talk to both Long John Silver and Squire Trelawney, was one of his dafter notions. It was just as bloody well nobody knew how many daft notions he actually had. Sometimes he thought he might be a bit soft in the head. Ever since he could remember he'd had these funny ideas running about his brain, sort of play-acting; if he wasn't going to Hollywood and picking up Rhonda Fleming at a dance he was playing for Scotland at Hampden, the very first left-back who put the hems on Stanley Matthews. Or he was a *real* gangster who came back to Kilcaddie from Chicago and when the hard neds of the King Street gang came into a café he stood up, all silent and casual, telling them quietly to beat it ... he'd noticed that the more he stayed at the silly school the dafter these notions had become. He'd wanted to get a job, be a hard case, a real working man, not a silly schoolboy whose brain was affected by too many pictures. He wanted Craig to treat him like one of the men, he wasn't really afraid of Craig, not the way he used to be afraid of his father before he'd been paralysed, no, not afraid. It was easier to do your work – more than your share if necessary – than be shouted at by Craig. One day he might be a hard enough case to laugh back at the old man, the way Telfer did when he got a telling off. One day ... he couldn't risk it, he wasn't like Telfer, he was scared of the sack, really scared. Getting the sack would be a disgrace, something terrible, something you'd be ashamed to go home and tell your mother.

The stable sharn was solid and heavy against the stiff-bristled broom. McCann was gassing to McPhail when Young Willie came into the stable. He put his whole weight behind the brush, counting on Willie seeing that he was working.

"For God's sake, McCann, ye lazy hooring shite, ye've no' got they horse yokit yet, what the hell d'ye think this is, the civil service? Damn ye tae hell, McCann, ye idle shite."

Young Willie they called him, although he was over fifty. The hardest-working man on the place, bar none. The Craigs were between housekeepers and he'd have been up for hours, feeding the beasts in the byre, feeding the hens, milking their two cows, making his own breakfast. The men said his roaring meant nothing, he only did it to show his old man he could run the farm.

McCann replied to Willie's bawling with his usual gesture of impudence, pivoting slightly on his toes to stick out his arse, making a farting noise with his lips. In a bad mood he was as likely to have gone into a sulk for the whole day. McCann could get away with it, he was young and strong and possessed all his wits, a rare combination for farm wages of seven pounds fourteen shillings a week. The factory paid a basic eleven with bags of overtime. Dunky imagined that Craig put up with McCann because he couldn't get any better, which McCann knew full well, saying in times of argy-bargy that if they didn't treat him decent he'd just as soon fuck off to the factory, or maybe join the police.

Young Willie went into Big Dick's stall and loosed the tether rope, holding his mane till he had the rope halter over him. Big Dick stamped a bit but young Willie could manage him. Dunky liked Young Willie. There was something comic about him, even the shape of his body, his short, bow legs and thick, squat trunk making him look short, when in fact he was as tall as McCann. He had big eyes which seemed to be trying to pop out of deep, lined sockets. He cut his own red hair, cropping it short with kitchen shears. He hadn't shaved for a day or two, his shirt was near rotten under his filth-shiny waistcoat and his right eye was red with a weeping cold. His mouth had fallen – he said gums were just as good as Government teeth.

"Get out, ye brute!" Willie roared as Big Dick shied at the low stable door. Outside it was lighter, the highest part of the sky bright with a rosy glow. McPhail and McCann pulled the shafts of the high-backed, two-wheel cart down on either side of the horse and they yoked him in for the day's work. Dunky held the reins while they brought out the other horses.

The first tattie-howkers were coming into the yard for their eight o'clock start and he hoped they didn't think he was just the boy given the reins to hold because he wasn't fit for anything else. Somebody had to hold Big Dick, especially in the morning when he felt frisky. As if he cared what that bunch thought, a raggle-taggle collection of women and girls and school-kids, some in woollen balaclava helmets, some in men's overcoats which hung down their shins, some in wellington boots with the tops turned down, some in ordinary street shoes. They were just casual labour, a scruffy lot taken on for the tattie-howking. They made him feel like one of the real men.

That was another daft notion which made him wonder if he was normal, the idea he had that all sorts of people, some he knew and some he didn't, were watching him wherever he was. Sometimes he talked to them, in his head. How would Craig's farm look to them, he wondered – *them* in this case being a vague conglomeration of town people, schoolteachers, girls who'd been in his class, guys he knew in football teams. Like an old dump, he had to admit it, a sharny old relic hanging on against the creep of the town, its steading here and there resembling an abandoned ruin, low stone walls sprouting weeds, the cartshed, the byre, the small barn, the big corrugated iron barn open on one side and one end, the tumbledy house in which there were stone floors and no carpets and three dogs and no hot water and two men who hadn't swept the floor since the last housekeeper left before Christmas and who wouldn't sweep a floor till the new housekeeper appeared, the black midden, the yard, all loose stones and puddles and frozen mud and bits of rotting wood and the mad black dog chained to an iron stake by a leaky kennel, chained there winter and summer, hail or snow, no wonder it was mad, poor brute, a blunt black dog which raced to the end of its

14

chain when anybody walked across the yard, barking like a maniac, standing on hind legs, neck so calloused it no longer felt the choking pull of the chain, a dog that would tear your heart out if the chain ever broke. Out of all this Auld Craig had made, the men said, more money than the provost of Kilcaddie, and the provost owned three chemist's shops, so he was really rich.

Auld Craig reminded Dunky of the evil old uncle in *Kidnapped*, so mean and terrible he was; the corn in the loft above the small barn was typical, the old man happy to have it piled loose on the floor, not caring a tuppenny bun if his three horses had to eat as much rat shite as grain. The chances were, the men said, he was only hanging on until the factory or the council gee-ed up their offering price for the rest of his land. Not a penny was ever spent on building repairs. Willie patched up the fences himself. If a window was broken the most that happened was a bit of sacking was nailed over the space. The old man, the men said, was stashing away his cash for his retirement. McCann's big joke was that on his nine-tieth birthday (nor far away, they said) the old bastard would celebrate by lashing out two whole shillings for his first bus ride to Glasgow.

By eight they were ready to leave the yard for the tattie field, Donald Telfer leading the way with the Fordson tractor, the refugee-like howkers trailing behind the three carts. McCann led with Big Dick, Blackie McCann standing on the sloping floor of the high-walled cart, being carried above the black hedges of the unmade track road that led through Craig's hillside. Young Willie came next, walking at the head of the young mare, not interested in cutting a flash figure like McCann. He stood in the third cart with McPhail and Daftie Coll from Oban. Coll, the highland man, had a fat, open face which was always grinning away at something or another, looking back now at the stumbling pack behind them.

"Aye aye then," he shouted, lifting off his cloth cap with thumb and index finger of his right hand and stroking grizzled hair with the three free fingers, his voice the high pitched sing-song of the highland cheuchter. "It's a fine fresh day for you all, eh? Never mind, missus, the cold air will be killing all your wee bugs."

A woman shouted something back at Coll, her voice the flat, abrasive accent of Kilcaddie, the kind of voice that came best out of the side of the mouth. There were about a dozen women and girls from the scheme, and twenty or so school-kids let off by the Education for tattie-howking – in the national interest. One and sixpence an hour! He had been a school-howker, he was glad he worked horse now, these kids actually thought it was better than school, grovelling about on their knees in cold, wet earth, hands so numb you'd think they'd been pulverised by a hammer.

Charlie's broad rump swung from side to side, his front hooves stamping down on frozen tracks, hind legs moving in a different way, the lower hocks coming forward uncertainly, shaking, almost like a cat picking a reluctant way through water. The iron-rimmed wheels trundled over stones and frozen mud ridges and crunched the ice on small puddles. The axle creaked. The hawthorne hedges were bare and black.

"D'ye hear their new housekeeper's comin' the day?" said McPhail.

"She won't last any longer than the last one," said Coll. Dunky liked to hear Coll speak. Highlanders used a precise sort of English, they'd all been used to speaking the Gaelic and had learned English like a foreign language. Coll knew another highlander who maintained the stretch of railway siding which ran past the farm to the factory. If Coll saw him walking by on the embankment he'd shout something to him in Gaelic. It sounded like gibberish.

"It's supposed to be raining later the day," he said, wanting to join in the man's talk. The sky was now high and dull with just a streak of blue to the west, which might mean that the weather was breaking over the Atlantic, a wind getting up to bring rain clouds over the hills towards Kilcaddie. There were hills on all sides except the east, where even now he could see the black smoke hanging over Glasgow.

They turned into the field, the horse knowing the way so well he hardly had to use the reins at all. Old Charlie had been coming this way for eleven years and he wasn't a young horse when Craig had bought him, McCann said.

Telfer was yoking the mechanical digger shaft into the iron triangle-bar under the spring seat of the tractor. Coll and McPhail vaulted down from the cart. He stayed on board until he reached the far end of the field. Telfer the tractorman was as fair and open-faced and cheery as McCann was black. Just to watch Telfer swinging his leg over the tractor seat made him feel young and awkward and shabby, Telfer alone

16

of the men didn't wear a cloth cap. He had curly yellow hair and instead of sharny old flannel shirts and greasy jackets and mouldy pullovers he wore a white undervest (back to front so that it showed white at the neck, the way the Canadians who played ice-hockey at Ayr wore their vests, or the way soldiers did in American films), a clean grey shirt and brown leather jerkin with no collar. He had blue denim trousers and working the tractor he could get away with wearing ordinary shoes. Dunky preferred the weight of his boots (an old pair of his father's) but there was no doubt that in boots your socks formed hard wrinkles under the foot, especially when they were a size too big.

"Look out, you people," Telfer shouted as he swung the tractor and digger round towards the end of the drill, "this machine's built for speed."

He had a funny way of sitting on the sprung-seat, twisted round almost sideways, smoking a cigarette – which none of the other men did. The big tyre treads threw up small dollops of black earth. Telfer grinned at the howkers, no doubt looking for some bit that might be game for a ride one of these nights, creep back down to the hay-barn when the Craigs were in the house, that was Telfer! Trying to look gruff and manly, Dunky jumped down from the cart. It wasn't so easy if you were only fifteen and hardly needing to shave. It was all right for Telfer, he seemed to think work was all a great joke.

"Keep them at it, McCann," Young Willie shouted as he and Coll and McPhail headed off towards the tattie pits at the far end of the next field. Telfer started up the drill. The whirling spokes of the digger's wheel threw dirt and tatties and half-withered shaws against a mesh-net hanging from a bar. The net let through the earth but dropped the potatoes in a more or less straight line about a yard wide.

The howkers had split up, two or three to each section of about ten to fifteen yards. When the digger passed through their section they either bent their backs over the line of potatoes, or got their knees down on bits of sacking which they dragged along as they threw tatties into their coracle-shaped wire baskets, each holding about forty pounds of potatoes. Some of the women wore old aprons over their coats. They were from the poor end of the scheme and some of them probably had just the one coat.

He led Charlie to the first filled baskets. He was getting hardened to it now, after more than a week among the tatties,

17

Bend, hands under either end of the basket, brace the stomach muscles, up with it in one movement, shift the angle of the elbows, push up, drop one end into the cart. Throw the empty basket on the ground. Bend, both hands up, twist elbows, push, and let the yellow potatoes rumble onto the wooden floor of the cart. It was easy at the beginning, when the potatoes were below the top of the cart walls, he could get a basket up onto the edge and then let them drop in. He threw down the second basket and walked to Charlie's head. His fingers were numb, but they'd warm up by the end of the first drill. Two more baskets. The short walk forward. Three baskets this time. Don't hurry, the secret was to take it at a steady pace. Try to look flash now and you'll be knackered by teabreak. A piece of earth fell onto his face. He rubbed at it with the sleeve of his old jerkin. Halfway down, his stomach muscles beginning to make themselves felt, he passed Telfer on his way up to the head of the next drill.

"Aye, aye," Telfer shouted, "You still think it's better'n school?"

"Oh aye," Dunky shouted back. Two more baskets. Up with the bastards, throw the empties down, don't waste time, ten drills to go before teabreak. The cart began to fill up. He had to throw each new basket-load into the middle so that the potatoes would be evenly distributed. The big iron-rimmed wheels sank into the soft earth. Charlie had to jerk the cart forward after each stop. His arms began to ache. The secret was to swing them about a bit as you walked between the waiting pairs of howkers. Now the load was a yellow pyramid appearing above the walls of the cart. He had to push the last two baskets up to the top of the heap. The thing was to take it steady. Try to hurry and you'd let a load fall back on the ground – that would look very silly. By now McCann was leading Big Dick down the second drill. He put his hand on Charlie's nose strap and led him to the gate. If they worked it right there was always one cart out of the field, at the pits, one being filled, and one empty, ready to take up the next drill. McCann, being stronger, was supposed to do most of the loading, with him leading them to the pits. The cart rumbled up the slight bump at the gate and they were onto the track road. He kicked earth off his boots. At the pits the three other men were waiting by the long, low trench. They let him back Charlie towards the pit, and when it was in position they unyoked the cart shafts and got their shoulders under the shafts and held them steady as the cart tipped up and back. Then they pulled down the shafts and he left them to heap the yellow Golden Wonders into a continuous pyramid. They spread a layer of straw over the sloping pile and shovelled earth on top and banged it down with their spades, sealing the tatties off from the frost until it was time to open the pits and weigh them into bags for the potato merchant.

Back in the field McCann was already walking away from Big Dick's load towards the mare and the empty cart.

"Where've ye been, for Jesus' sake?" he shouted. "Gie that lazy brute a kick on the arse if he'll no' get a move on."

He went back to the pits with the second load, walking a good two feet clear of the horse's stamping fore-hooves, his own boots continually picking up an extra sole of black, cloying earth. With a full load even Big Dick had no chance of playing up, but on the way back with an empty cart, seeming to know that it was only a boy at his head, he decided to move along at a brisk rate, now and then throwing up his head when something unseen to Dunky excited him.

This time McCann was still loading. He took Dick to the end of the third drill, tying the rope reins tight to the shaft so that the horse wouldn't stand on them, which would cause more excitement. The short rest only made his arms ache more as he started to throw in the baskets, this time doing it with even more care, in case a potato flew up and startled the horse. He didn't joke with the howkers. He was too young to treat them the way McCann did, like a lot of half-witted scum. The older women had terrible sharp tongues. Bend, grip, up, twist, push, throw down the empty, bend, grip, up, twist, push ... each time he took the horse forward he felt the cold air rasping into his heaving lungs, but his hands were getting warm. Black and warm.

On this trip he had a look at the factory, away down the hill towards the railway line. It had two large hangar-type sheds, huge buildings still painted with wartime camouflage, green and brown in irregular blotches. Around the big sheds were smaller buildings, and at one end a mountain of scrap. They pounded this down for melting with a huge iron ball dropped from a crane. And the two-storey office block where, said Telfer, there was enough talent to drain the balls of King Farouk. Telfer knew all about the women in the factory office, don't worry, he'd rammed a few of them, don't worry.

By nine o'clock the sky was streaky, smears of blue among

19

high drifting cloud. It seemed to be getting warmer, although that might be just from working. At half-nine the factory hooter would go for teabreak, vacuum flasks brought out of old gas-mask cases, sandwiches eaten under a hedge, sitting on dry sacks. He was famished already. He had bacon and cheese today. He was coming back from the pits with old Charlie, standing on the bumping cart floor, when he spotted Auld Craig's head moving above the hedges.

"Girrup, Charlie," he said, flicking the rope-reins on the horse's sagging back. Charlie raised his head and pricked his ears, but his step slowed back to normal in a matter of yards. He was willing enough, but the muscle had gone. His head dropped again, his great hindquarters rolling slowly, the cart creaking and jerking along the slowly-melting ruts.

Auld Craig followed him into the field on his bike, boots sticking out at right angles, his hodden grey suit hanging in loose folds now that he was eighty-five or so and shrinking. Maybe he'd be away to the far end of the field before the old man said anything, he was a fearful man to speak to, a terrible bent old man with light blue eyes that only occasionally allowed themselves to be seen through great grey eyebrows and heavily-bearded cheekbones. He jumped off the cart to tie Charlie to a post. From the horse's head he could watch the old man get off his bike, a favourite performance among the men.

Auld Craig let the bike and himself fall to one side, making a scrabbling sort of mad jump to free his old bowed legs from the falling frame, at the same time waving his arms, getting his left boot caught, half stumbling, finally jumping clear and taking a kick at the bike.

"MAAYYYAH!" was what his oath sounded like, the bellow of an old sheep. Dunky walked up the drill with the mare. Telfer was now at the far end, six drills dug now, little bursts of smoke pop-popping from the tractor's thin, upright exhaust pipe.

"MCCANN DAMN YE!" Auld Craig damned most people before he spoke to them.

"CRAIG!" McCann roared back, grinning at the boy from the shelter of the horse. McCann was very impudent, as long as the old man was a good distance away.

"COME HERE DAMN YE MAN!"

Dunky tied the mare's reins to the rear of Big Dick's cart and took over from McCann, who walked down the drill towards the old man. He took a firm hold on the rope so that it pressed hard on Dick's soft mouth. It was a good moment for Big Dick to be well under control. A bad horse was nothing compared to Auld Craig.

"You've got an easy time of it, huvn't ye?" said a woman howker, her face streaked with dirt, a balaclava helmet covering her hair, a woman who could have been anything from twenty to fifty.

"How's that, missus?" he said. Up with the basket, up to the top of the load, almost on tip-toe, arms and shoulders lead-filled.

"Ach, he's only a wean," her mate said. "He's no up to real toil."

"A wean?" he said. Everybody thought everybody else's job was easier than their own. Howking was dirty and cold, but it wasn't heavy, just a bit sore on the back. "Is that a fact?"

He'd thought he'd have time to give a bit of patter to the one or two good-looking girls, not a chance. He was breathing heavy again. What the hell would he do when the front cart was full? Bring the mare round in front? No, Big Dick wouldn't like that. He'd have to lead the horse forward and then walk back to the second cart. Wasting valuable time! Craig would notice that. Bend, grip, up, back sore, twist, hands raw against the wire, push, stay up you bastards. It must be giving him good muscles, what Baldy Campbell said he needed for football, more weight and strength. He took off his green zipper jerkin and tied its sleeves round the shaft. The elbows of his pullover were ragged holes. Under that he wore an old, collarless shirt of his father's. Crows and gulls were all about now, whirling in the sky, zooming down in flocks behind the tractor. The gulls were moving inland, they'd been told at school, more food. Watch out, birdies, he thought, ye cannae steal Auld Craig's valuable worms and expect to live.

"HEY YOU BOYYY, COME HERE!" Aye aye. Trouble. He hung the mare's reins over the shaft and led Big Dick's load down towards the two men. Here and there was a Golden Wonder the howkers had missed. If Auld Craig saw them there would be ructions. Valuable tatties!

"We're not needin' the three horse," the old man said, staring at his boots. "Gin dinnertime take that old beast back to the stable. Two cairts is enough. And cut out that chatterin' to the girls, I'm no' peyin' ye to dae your winchin' here. Get

21

a move on, damn ye, if it turns out wet we'll be buggert."

"Aye, right, Craig," he said. That was the proper way to address the farmer, although it sounded strange to call the old man by his surname. Willie had explained to him that his father was entitled to be called Craig – he was *the* Craig. Only men who didn't own land needed to be called Mister. Even Willie called his own father Craig.

"Hrrmmph." The old man cleared his throat and spat a lump of catarrh the size of a penny. Then he squinted through his eyebrows. "Is this suiting you better than being a scholar, Logan?"

"Oh aye," he said, grinning. Craig must like him. He walked back to the two carts. It was very strange how the old man changed accents. Sometimes he spoke to you in broad Scots, sometimes in what the schoolteachers called proper English. They were very hot on proper English at the school. Once he'd got a right showing up in the class for accidentally pronouncing butter "bu'er". Miss Fitzgerald had gone on (him having to stand in front of the class) about the glottal stop being dead common and very low-class, something that would damn you if you wanted a decent job. A decent job – like a bank! His mother spoke proper English, but then she was hellish keen on proving they were respectable. His father spoke common Kilcaddie, which he knew his mother didn't like. When the Craigs spoke broad it wasn't quite the same as common Kilcaddie – some of their expressions sounded as though they came straight out of Rabbie Burns! Telfer had a Kilcaddie accent, but he pronounced all his words properly, no doubt from seeing too many pictures. McCann spoke very coarse and broad, but there was something false about him, as though he put it on deliberately.

He still spoke the school's idea of proper English, he knew that all right because every time he opened his mouth he could hear himself sounding like a real wee pan-loaf toff. (Maybe that was what annoyed McCann?) Why did Auld Craig and Willie change about? Did it depend on what they thought of you? He remembered Nicol the English teacher saying that broad Scots was pronounced very much like Anglo-Saxon or middle English or some such expression. If that was so why did they try and belt you into speaking like some English nancy boy on the wireless? He'd asked Nicol that and Nicol said right or wrong didn't come into it, proper English was what the school had to teach you if you weren't going to be

22

a guttersnipe all your life. Was it being a guttersnipe to talk your own country's language? It would be a lot healthier if folk spoke one way. Sometimes you hear them say "eight" and sometimes "eicht", sometimes "farm" and sometimes "ferm". Sometimes "ye" and sometimes "youse" and sometimes "yese" and sometimes "you". Sometimes "half" and sometimes "hauf". Was it your faither or your father? Your mither or your mother? He felt he was speaking to his audience again. You see, if school was any use it would teach you things like that, not just jump on you for not talking like a Kelvinside nancy boy. Why teach kids that Burns was the great national poet and then tell you his old Scots words were dead common? What sounds better – "gie your face a dicht wi' a clootie" or "give your face a wipe with a cloth"? One was Scottish and natural and the other was a lot of toffee-nosed English shite.

"See me, I'm Peter Cavanagh, the man with a million voices," he said to Big Dick as they walked along the track road to the pits. "Gi'es a len' o' yur pen, hen? What was that my good man? Sorry, lady, give us a wee loan of your fountain pen, madam. Otherwise Ah'll melt ye. And here is that ancient man of the moment, that crazy comic from Kilcaddie, Sir Crawly Craig, what song are you giving us the night, Sir Crawly – what's that, 'gin lowsing ye'll ging for a wee donner doon the heather'? Very nice, I hope it isn't dirty."

Coming back from the pits he passed old Charlie, now tied to the fence, head down looking for grass. Eleven years working for Craig, he deserved a rest. On the last time down the drill he'd had to kick him on the leg to get him moving. One of the howker women said it was disgraceful, kicking a dumb animal.

"It's him or me," he'd said, trying to make her laugh. She didn't see the joke, ignorant old bag. Did she think he liked putting the boot on a horse – like McCann? He liked the old horse, he hadn't really tried to hurt him – just wake him up. Everybody had to work. Work or want. Kids got belted at school, horses got belted on a farm. But only if they wouldn't work.

Big Dick had lost a bit of steam now.

"Come on, you evil bugger," he said, leading him forward down the drill, speaking softly so that the howkers wouldn't hear. "Let's see how strong you think you are."

They'd have to go faster now, with only the two carts and three men waiting at the pits. Still, it was a decent thought of the old man to let old Charlie stop working, his insides might have collapsed. Poor old devil, he'd earned his rest out on the grass. He hadn't really enjoyed kicking him. He wasn't like McCann.

As he came back into the field from his next trip to the pits he felt cheerful enough to bend down and pick up a stone. Once you'd got through the first hour or so of Monday morning you began to get used to it all again. He waited till he was within range of a bunch of strutting crows. They fluttered into the air but his savagely-thrown stone landed harmlessly on the ground.

Then the factory hooter went for half-past nine and tea-break. Only the tip of his nose was cold now,

CHAPTER TWO

On the bus from Beith to Kilcaddie, Mary O'Donnell took the seat behind the driver's cab, downstairs at the front of the bus. There was a woman in the window seat. Mary O'Donnell sat on the outside, her stiff left leg sticking out into the gangway. She didn't care if people looked at it. She'd passed the girlish stage of being embarrassed by the wasted leg and its apparatus of metal rods which ran from a hip support down to a metal and leather knee grip and then down either side of shrivelled bone and flesh to turn at right angles into holes bored in the thick heel of her dumpy black shoes.

The red, double-decker bus was fairly full, wives going shopping in Kilcaddie or Ayr, a soldier in uniform, two men in soft hats, a few farmers on the way to Paisley market. The inside of the bus was warm, almost steamy. It was beginning to thaw outside, the black hedges looked damp and the fields cold and uninteresting. The road rolled over featureless hills, down through barren villages. She was looking forward to living near Kilcaddie. It was a real town, more than fifty thousand people, they said, with picture houses and big shops – a Woolworths *and* a Marks and Spencers. Her family back home in Sligo didn't understand why she preferred to live away in Scotland, working as housekeeper to dour Scots farmers. They thought it was all slaving away in cold old farmhouses. They didn't know the half of it, thank God.

As Kilcaddie drew near fields gave way to detached houses of dark red brick and then to semi-detached bungalows and then to good-class tenement houses, three and four storeys high, with shops on the ground floor. She'd been four and a half years with Stephenson, the Beith farmer. If it hadn't been for that stuck-up bitch who'd married Stephenson's son she'd be there yet, mistress of the house! When she'd left Sligo they'd all warned her how hard it was in Scotland, how mean the tight-fisted Protestants could be. Oh, sure, they were mean and dour all right – if you didn't know how to handle them. The old man Craig had come the mean trick at her interview.

"I cannae pay ye the full five pounds a week," he'd said, hairy-faced old monument that he was. "There's a lot o' jobs a limpy cannae do. I'll give ye four and your board,"

25

"And there's just yourself in the house?" she'd replied. There were more important things in life than a Scots pound note.

"No, there's Willie, my son," he'd said. "That's all, just the two of us."

"Oh well, I'll take four pounds," she'd said. "But if I'm satisfactory you'll make it up?"

"Hrrmmph," the old man had replied.

Buttoning up her heavy, meal-coloured coat, she watched as the bus came towards Kilcaddie Cross, a wide shopping street cutting across the main Glasgow road. As the bus drew in to the stop, she got up and limped along the gangway, ignoring the faces. The young conductor bent down to lift her suitcase out from the luggage space under the stairs. Mary O'Donnell didn't think much of a man who'd take a woman's job on the buses.

"I'll manage, thank you," she said, not smiling, taking the case out of his hand. With one bad leg she was a better man than his sort.

On the four corners of the Cross stood small groups of idling men, no matter that it was Monday morning, a working day. She didn't like the looks of them, a scruffy lot, a lot of them fairly young, all with hard faces, eyes like rats. She knew what their type would be thinking and saying: *A good-looking piece, pity about the gamey leg, ach, who cares about their legs, she'd rattle good as anything, I'd do a turn with her any day, rather ride her than a tramcar.* She'd heard it all.

At the local bus stop she put down the case. Across the wide street she saw well-dressed women going in and out of a good class tearoom. Town women, fancy hats and high heels and nylon stockings. To her eye the solid greys and blacks of Kilcaddie's buildings seemed almost glamorous. Picture houses that weren't country fleapits. Here and there a shop with a newly-modernised front. From the bus stop she could see the town war memorial, two kilties with hanging heads on a granite plinth. Around the Cross, at least, Kilcaddie looked solid and well-off, real money in its granite-fronted banks.

The local bus turned away from the Cross through streets of shops and pubs and big stores, their windows bright against the grey gloom of the morning. In small shops heavily-laden women queued for butcher meat and bread and fish; dark-fronted pubs were already open at half-past ten, their shadowy

interiors hidden behind swing doors and opaque glass, sometimes even stained glass; then it began to climb streets where
older tenements stood side by side with brick sheds, timber
yards, warehouses, small engineering works. In Sligo she'd
always thought of Scotland as heather and mountains and
shining lochs, but in these cold, windy streets people seemed
to walk with their shoulders hunched, shabby people whose
children had dirty faces, only the occasional young man walking with his head up.

The housing scheme marked an abrupt change from the
old town, wider streets lined by three-storey blocks faced in
grey roughcast and roofed with red tiles. Most of the garden
spaces in front of the houses were unkept, rough grass criss-
crossed by hard-tramped earth paths, battered privet hedges
with gaps wide enough to take motor cars. Washing hung in
balconies. Here and there a paling-fence lolled over onto the
pavements; a motor-bike without wheels stood by one of the
open block entrances. In Scotland, she knew, the working
folk didn't care how their houses looked, inside or out. They
talked about bog Irish, but they were rougher than any folk
she'd known back home. These were good houses, but most
of them didn't care.

The rain had started by the time the conductress told her
they were at the stop for the farm road. With the case banging against the calf of her good leg, she pulled up her collar
and crossed the road. Big drops fell from a low sky, a bitter
wind getting up from the west. She walked with a roll, stiff
left leg going forward, body leaning over as the iron took the
weight, right leg forward in a long step. The sooner she was
settled into the farm the better. Didn't even think of her having to change buses and walk nearly a mile. Hard. Well, they
were making a mistake if they thought she wasn't just as hard
as they were. . . .

The rain came on heavier and after looking several times at
the sky to the west, Willie decided it was going to be too wet
to carry on working. It wasn't for the howkers he stopped –
wet tatties were liable to go rotten in the pit. He and McPhail
and Coll heaped earth over the last load. In the other field
McCann threw a tarpaulin over the half-filled cart and he
and Dunky led the three horses back to the farm, following
behind the racing howkers. Rain, the curse of Scotland,
Dunky thought, feeling quite cheery at the break they'd get,

27

By the time they'd got the horses in the stable and rubbed them down with sacks it was hammering down in sheets. Young Willie went away to the house, walking at his normal pace, rain or no rain.

"Hey, Smallcock," said McCann, "you've to come over with us to the byre, we're to do a bit of muckin' out, keep ye from getting lazy."

They ran through the bouncing rain, past the cartshed where the howkers sheltered in a rabble. Inside the byre door Telfer was lighting a cigarette, blond hair streaked and flattened, raindrops on his red face.

"This weather's lousy," he remarked and McCann and he ran through the door. "Ice in the morning, rain at dinnertime, snow by night no doubt. Just look at it, pishing down."

"It's better in Canada, of course," said McCann, banging his cap against his trousers legs. He pronounced it to rhyme with Granada, the way the more ignorant scheme folk did. Dunky knew this was McCann's way of taking the piss out of Telfer – who lived in the scheme and was never tired of talking about the great life overseas in Canada.

"Anywhere's better than rain like that," Telfer said, bitterly. He drew on his fag. "I'm tired of bloody rain all the time, sick and tired of it. One good week, that was all we had last summer, one stinking lousy week. Christ, it never stops in this place. I can't remember a bloody time in this town when it wasn't bloody raining. You get your shoes ruined and your suits ruined, ten to one if you walk out the door with the sun shining you'll be soaked before you reach the gate. You can't take a woman a walk but it comes down like buckets. It affects people, you know. That's why they're all such miserable gets in this dump. They've been rained on all their stupid lives, and they haven't got the imagination to get out of it. Rain, rain, rain – it gets in your brain."

Neither of the men made a move towards the two lines of cattle. Dunky supposed they were to muck them out, fork out deep layers of manure, not the two milkers, Willie always did them, but the store bullocks, fat-backed black crosses brought into the byre for the worst of the winter, solid-flanked beasts who stood on a packed layer of their own skitter trodden into straw. Well, he wasn't going to start if the two men didn't, he wasn't that daft about work.

"Where wid we be without rain, eh, ever thought o' that?" asked McCann. "Things wouldnae grow without it."

28

"Who cares whether things grow or not? People, that's what matters. Give them one solid month of sunshine, you'd see the change. They'd be a different race altogether." Telfer blew smoke towards the downpour. The blue cloud was slashed to nothing by the slanting drops. McCann stood behind him. He wouldn't be all that keen on mucking the byre either, he liked to think he was the horseman about the place. Daftie Coll did most of the mucking out. Cattle were beneath McCann.

"On ye go, Smallcock," he said, turning on Dunky. "Let's see ye do some fancy work with a fork, did they teach ye that in yur school, eh? Or would ye rather have a handful o' cowshite round yur balls?"

He had a funny look in his eyes. Once, when he'd been just a boy at the tatties, Dunky had seen McCann – who was then too important to notice him – take the trousers off some young bloke who'd been cheeky. After a lot of kicking and struggling he'd rubbed tractor oil on his arse. He wasn't going to have that. He pretended not to hear. He walked up the middle of the byre to where there was a four-pronged grape lying against a half-filled wheelbarrow. If McCann came near him he'd shove the tines into his throat. McCann walked a couple of steps after him. What he wanted was for Telfer to join in. One man roughing up a boy wasn't such good fun. With two of them it could be made to look like horse-play.

Dunky picked up the grape and made a move into the nearest stall, touching the shiny black back of a bullock with the grape handle. He saw McCann coming nearer. If the grape didn't work he'd break McCann's shinbone with the toe of his boot. That was one thing you learned playing football. In a way he was beginning to look forward to getting it over with, hammering or not. It had to come sometime.

"Hey, look what's coming into the yard," Telfer shouted from the door of the byre. Dunky stood still, elbows pressed against solid, beef-covered ribs. McCann hesitated. "It's the housekeeper woman," Telfer said.

They stood in the doorway. Through rain which came up off the mud and stones in a fine white spray they saw the limping woman carry her suitcase, one strand of red hair falling from under her tight headscarf. Dunky stood on tip-toe to look over the men's shoulders. He'd kept hold of the grape, in case McCann wasn't interested in what Telfer had seen.

"She's a bloody limpy dan!" McCann looked astonished.

The woman came up the middle of the yard, alongside the midden.

Telfer put his hands to his mouth.

"Hey, watch the dog, missus," he shouted. His voice didn't carry far through the bucketing rain. Dunky saw her look up to see where the voice had come from. She kept on walking. Telfer waved at her.

"Go over the other side," he shouted, "the dog's in the –"

She was almost at the end of the midden when the black dog came roaring out of its kennel. It was fly enough, Dunky realised, to stay inside till potential victims were in chain-range. Its mad barking roared round the whole yard, frightening the steers who jumped and shook their chains, big eyes raised above the concrete stall partitions.

Mary O'Donnell tried to swing the case round to protect her from the dog. Telfer ran out of the byre, shouting, but the dog was on her, leaping up at her chest, ears flat back on its blunt head. The weight of its paws landed on the suitcase. Mary O'Donnell fell backwards, sitting on the mud with her left leg sticking out at a right angle, the case on her lap.

Telfer reached the dog before it could get at her.

"Gerrout, ya dirty brute!" he roared. Dunky watched him draw back his right boot and swing it into the dog's ribs. The kick sent the dog sprawling on its side. It started screaming with pain, an unnatural, high-pitched yelping. Telfer ran at it, boot poised again. The dog scrabbled away on its stomach and then scurried for its kennel, still howling like a mad thing. Telfer turned to the woman.

"Are you all right?" he asked. "Come on, get up before you're soaked through."

Her eyes staring, Mary O'Donnell was too shaken to move. Telfer bent down and pulled her to her feet.

"Can you manage to the house?" he asked, picking up her case.

"I'm not helpless," she said. Telfer thought she was going to cry. He didn't like to take her arm. She started walking towards the yard-door of the house. He walked beside her, suitcase in one hand, the other hovering near her elbow in case she stumbled. He banged on the door.

"Hey, Willie, your housekeeper's here," he shouted, giving her a smile, both of them standing under the shelter of the little porch. "Welcome to Buckingham Palace."

When Willie came to the door, he handed him the suitcase,

"She just about got killed by that brute dog," Telfer said. "You want that animal hung, it'll tear somebody's throat out."

"I'm all right," she said. "It just caught me off my balance."

"Ye'd better come in," said Willie. "You get on wi' the byre, Telfer."

Telfer came slowly back through the rain, seemingly not caring.

"A bloody cripple, that's about Craig's mark," McCann said, bitterly. "I bet he's peyin' her half wages. What the hell's use is a limpy dan housekeeper?"

Dunky watched Telfer push back his hair. He wished he'd been the one who'd run out in the rain. Telfer had looked like a real hard man.

"She's Irish," Telfer said. "That black bugger would have had her throat out. I should've cracked its bloody neck for it. I will, one of they dark nights. Hey, Blackie, did you get a good look at her?"

"Ach," said McCann, "she's a limpy. Whut good's a fuck'n cripple?"

"She's a bloody smasher," Telfer said. "I felt the tits on her when I picked her up!" Without warning he picked up an armful of straw and rammed it into McCann's face. "She's a bloody lovely bit of stuff, you miserable get. And I'm the brave boy that saved her life! Just watch me, you buggers."

McCann cursed as he pulled straw out of his shirt. As Dunky began forking solid cow-shite he didn't know whether he was more jealous of Donald Telfer for having saved the woman or for having covered Blackie McCann in straw. It was all right if you were a man.

When it came to half-past twelve they left the byre and went across the yard to the stable. On Mondays he did not go home for dinner. His mother gave him two extra sandwiches so that she could get on with the washing. He remembered the smell of Mondays. Bleach, ammonia, worst of all on days when it rained and the shirts and pyjamas and towels and even sheets hung wet and cold from the pulley in the kitchen. Wet Mondays were the worst – the washing had to dry inside the house and he couldn't get out to play football in the street or catch newts in the ditch beside the railway embankment. Now he'd never have to worry about being in the house on washing day. He was a working man.

He gave each horse a twist of hay. Coll went home for

his dinner, to the old cottages farther up the hill. So did Mc-Phail, Christ knew what kind of mansion Mattha went home to, he had five or six full-grown sons, according to the knee-padder they were so rough they hardly let him inside his own house. The women howkers either walked home in the rain or stayed in the cartshed with their sandwiches – their "pieces", jam and white bread. An Education bus took the schoolkids to the canteen at the scheme school. Craig should have given them hot soup, by regulation, but he was excused this because he had no housekeeper. Telfer was always asking Willie what kind of scoff he and the old man cooked up for themselves and Willie always said fried eggs and tatties, but none of the men ever went in for meals with the Craigs to find out. The house might be a bigger mess than the steading, but it was the farmer's house and they were just the men, and a few hesitant paces into the kitchen was as far as they penetra-ted. In one way Dunky resented this. Ever since he'd even thought about things like that he'd thought it wrong that some people should be better than others. That's what they were taught in the Sunday School – yet when he told his mother what he thought she said the Bible wasn't to be taken literally! Of course, she'd say they were as good as the Craigs and bet-ter than Telfer or McCann – and that made him glad he was one of the men to be kept out of the farmhouse. Maybe his family was a bit more – well, respectable, decent, whatever word his mother used, than the Telfers or the McCanns, but all he wanted was to be exactly like them. His mother was kid-ding herself on. Just because Grandpa Aitchison had owned his own shop! It reminded him of the Academy, having to wear a school tie, as if that dump was any better than ordinary schools. The first time he even remembered knowing about this sort of thing was coming home from the Sunday School, he must have been about four or five, he wasn't even going to school. To reach their church you had to go through one of the worst slum dumps in Kilcaddie, Bell's Place. The kids there never had shoes – they certainly didn't go to the same Sunday School as he did! One morning he'd been coming home on his own and a gang of boys from Bell's Place were playing football with a tin can – in bare feet. He'd wanted to play with them but one of them called him a toff. They'd pointed to his cap – a new one, he remembered it as clearly as anything, stupid bloody thing with a wee cloth button on the top and a skip, grey to match his suit. He'd taken it off and thrown it over a wall – to show them he hated it. He *thought* he could remember them letting him play after that, but maybe he'd invented that part later on to prove to Alec, his pal, that he'd always been a bit of a Communist. What he did remember was getting the belt from his father for losing the cap, a real belting with the old razor-strop.

McCann and Telfer and he ate their pieces in the dusty harness room at the end of the stable, sprawling on a wooden floor covered with white plaster dust and rat droppings, heads resting against rotten plaster walls which had disintegrated here and there to reveal the lathwork strips.

"No' be lang noo' fore we're finished the tatties," said Mc-Cann. Telfer winked at Dunky.

"No' lang the noo, Jock, eh, hoots mon – where d'yah dig up all that Harry Lauder patter, eh?" McCann's face darkened, blushing under his heavy growth.

"I speak natural like," he said. "Better'n tryin' to sound like some yankee fly boy."

McCann ripped into his sandwiches, not biting so much as tearing and cramming. Telfer had cheese on brown bread. His big thing about Canada was written all over him, one leg drawn up, white socks, even the way he held his bread. To Dunky, the Craigs seemed like something out of the past, even Young Willie, who'd been to the Academy. McCann was just plain, ordinary coarse. But Telfer was a big-timer, well-known in the scheme, notorious, almost. His father was away in England somewhere living with some fancy woman. Telfer's mother was a big dyed blonde, a fast piece, as they said. The Telfers had drinking parties in their house – which, said Dunky's mother, showed you what a fast crowd they were. She was always on the lookout for any sign that "her wee boy" was getting too friendly with Telfer. He was Not A Good Influence.

"Ah talk normal," McCann said. "No' like you, Telfer, you're jist a picture fiend, yur heed's full o' fairy tales from Hollywood. Ah bet ye thought ye were right gallus, yah big-time idiot, out there in the yard wi' that limpy dan."

"She's all right, that one," Telfer said. "What did you think of her, Dunky?"

"No' bad." McCann made the inevitable sneering face.

"Him! He wouldnae ken whit tae dae wi' a wumman if she lay doon and pit her legs roon his neck."

Dunky wanted to change the subject, knowing how long

33

McCann could keep up that particular line of attack. Whatever the reason, he seemed to get on Blackie's nerves, just by being there.

What was it about guys like Blackie? Kilcaddie was full of them, tetchy bastards with hair-trigger tempers, guys who'd put a broken bottle in your face just for looking at them, guys who went to dances hoping for fights, guys who went on to a football pitch ready to break somebody's leg. He'd been a bit of a fighting cock himself, when he was younger. Once, when Shuttle Place had a lot more houses than it did now, they'd been playing football in the street with a composite-rubber imitation cricket ball and some guys from the scheme had run away with it. Guys? None of them could have been much more than five or six, including himself. The Shuttle Street boys had chased the Darroch scheme boys the length of Dalmount Drive before the scheme boys had stopped running. He could still feel the temper he was in at that moment when he grabbed one of them and dragged him to the pavement and sat on his chest and grabbed his hair and banged his head on the asphalt, banging and shouting, trying to kill him. Six years old! A man had dragged him off the other boy, a man in a boiler suit with dirty hands. He said he was going to get the police. They'd all run away and hidden in the coal yard, going home, eventually, in dread of a belting, only to find that the man hadn't called the bobbies and nobody knew anything about it.

So why had *he* stopped being like that? Was it because he'd gone to the Academy where, as his mother said, he mixed with a decent class of boy? Softies, to be exact. No, he'd had fights at the Academy. Was it the summer he'd been evacuated to Portpatrick, just after the Clydebank blitz when everybody thought the Germans were going to bomb the whole Glasgow area to smithereens? He'd gone to a village school there for a term. The country boys were bigger, they wore tackety boots, they had red faces . . . no, he couldn't remember having any fights down there. Was it because he was a coward? How did you know if you were a coward – it was natural to feel a bit scared before you went into a fight, that was half of the reason you tried to kill the other guy, in case he turned out to be stronger than you were.

Why, then? One part of him would have jumped like a shot at the chance of parting McCann's hair with a fifty-six pound weight, maybe he would have to some time, but the part of him that *considered* things found the idea disgusting. He didn't mind roughing up guys in a game of football, that was natural, the harder a player you were the more respect you got. But not fighting. Maybe it was from the same daftness that gave him his funny ideas? At school he could not remember any occasion when he'd been in agreement with the rest of the class. When everybody else wanted to be a Cavalier he'd found himself liking the idea of Cromwell and the Round-heads, because they seemed more like ordinary people. When they'd reached the '45 Rebellion he was on the side of the Lowlanders who'd more or less ignored Prince Charlie's army. Funny about that, he didn't care all that much for the Jacob-ites when he read about them operating in Scotland, but as soon as they were over the border into England he found him-self wishing they'd gone on south from Derby and taken Lon-don. It was the same with football. He'd never really *liked* Rangers, although he was a Protestant. Celtic had always seemed more friendly, somehow. Look at Charlie Tully. Ran-gers went in for strength, like granite. Charlie Tully had bowly legs and was bald and didn't look strong enough to beat car-pets yet he had more personality in his little finger than Ran-gers had in their whole team. Charlie Tully would jink towards the Rangers defence – you'd need guts to take on big George Young and Willie Woodburn and Sammy Cox and Jock Tiger Shaw – and when they came at him, ready to hammer him into the ground, he'd bamboozle them, pointing the way he pre-tended to pass the ball, sending them chasing in the wrong direction, or running on without the ball but still pretending to dribble so cleverly they'd follow him, trying to make a tackle.

Yet despite all that, as soon as Scotland played England he thought of Waddell and Young and Woodburn as heroes – because they were Scottish then, not Rangers. Instead of being giants from Ibrox Park they became part of your own coun-try taking on the might of England. That was the greatest thing he could imagine in the whole world, being picked against England – he'd *die* for Scotland.

It was just a pity that the Scottish selectors were blinded by Glasgow Rangers. Great players with small clubs didn't stand a chance of being picked for Scotland if there was some six-foot Tarzan at Ibrox Park. Rangers didn't even play like real Scots yet they dominated the whole game because they had the big money. Hibs played like Scots, tricky, clever, artistic – yet Gordon Smith, the great Gay Gordon who could do *anything* with a ball, hardly ever got capped for Scotland. Willie McNaught was the classiest left-back in the game, but because he played for Raith Rovers he never got a look in. Jimmy Mason of Third Lanark, small and round-shouldered and insignificant till he got on the ball, had helped Scotland beat England three-one at Wembley – but how many caps did he get after that?

So, he was chronically on the side of the small guy against the big guy. So what had that to do with not liking, or understanding, nature's hard cases? Was it just another of his silly-boy imaginings that he sometimes wondered if he belonged to a completely different race? Maybe aye, maybe hooch aye, as Grandpa Logan used to say. There was a man from another race, all right. According to his father, Grandpa Logan was such a nutcase he'd registered as a conchie in the First World War – knowing full bloody well they didn't take men whose right hands were carved out of wood and hidden under black leather gloves. Maybe he was a nutcase throwback to Grandpa Logan? That wasn't a very cheery prospect, all he wanted was to be like everybody else.

"Wasn't that funny, Auld Craig stopping Charlie working in the middle of the morning?" he said, hoping the other two could talk about horses without arguing.

"He's done," said McCann. "Craig was feart he couldnae walk to the knackers. He's about twenty year, that auld wreck."

"I'd shoot the lot of them," said Telfer. "Machinery, that's what you need on farms these days. One tractor'll do the work of the three of them."

"Bugger off," said McCann. "Give me a horse onytime. When does it break doon, eh?"

"It's the modern way," said Telfer. "Farmers with sense are getting machinery instead of horse. Craig's just too shiting miserable, that's his trouble."

McCann spat. Dunky untied his bootlaces, finger nails picking painfully at the hard, wet knots.

"Horses are natural about a ferm," said McCann. "People are jist following a craze for machinery. Ye'll niver beat horse."

Dunky took off his boots. He pulled at his stiff, woollen socks to straighten out wrinkles on the soles. His feet were cold and wet. He lay back, head on the wall, aches in the small of his back and his arms. His trousers were wet. McCann and Telfer weren't interested in anything he had to say. He stared round the harness room. It was festooned with old sets of harness hanging from saddle trees, black leather dry and cracked through years without oil, brass-work covered in green mould and white dust. Lying about on the floor were weights for filling potato bags, fifty-six pounders like four-sided, flat-topped pyramids, circular two-pounders like coins giants used in ancient days. The window was thick with spiders' webs, successive layers solidified in a dusty curtain (what did they catch?). On wet days the men had cut daft messages and drawings in the plaster ... *The Pope's a Pape ... D. Telfer, gentleman farmer ... Oor Wullie pongs ... Scotland the grave ... Mrs Mcann hubba-hubba ...* Blackie said he wouldn't lower himself to scratch that one out. His mother was twice married, her first man killed when a cattle float had crushed him against a byre wall. Blackie hated the second, a foreman at a big market garden out at the Brig, only a few years older than Blackie, they said, nobody ever getting Mc-Cann to tell them why he stayed on in the same house. ... *Women's knickers ... Ride em cowboy ...* there were swear words and scratchy drawings meant to be cocks and balls and women's fuds and doos, why men drew these on the wall he didn't know, unless it was just another form of madness.

". . . you work Craig's horses all your natural for all I care," Telfer was saying. "Seven quid a week and all the shite you can eat – that's not my idea of living. Soon's I've got the cash I'm off, Canada, that's the place, work a tractor on a big wheat farm for a coupla years, save all you can, buy a place of your own, two hundred acres, that's just a croft over there, land's cheap, you go far enough into the wilds and the government gives you land for frees. They're desperate for skilled men, everybody knows that."

"Skillt?" said McCann. "Who's fuck'n skillt aboot here, eh?"

Telfer grinned at Dunky, who could just see him, perched on a big combine in a field as big as a shire. He agreed with everything Telfer said. He wanted to ask McCann why he kicked his horses if he liked them so much. Blackie threw the dregs of his tea across the dusty floor.

"Aye, it's all going tae hell now," he said, a surprising touch of sadness in his voice. "They used tae have six horse here and four hired men bar Willie and his brother George. Where the factory is they had three big fields, I remember ma Daddy takin' me roon by on a Sunday. They'll be nae ferming at a' soon, jist factories and corporation houses. All this fuck'n machinery, it's spoilin' everythin'."

Telfer snorted.

"Sooner the better. That George was the clever one, away tobacco-farming in Rhodesia. Hey, I wonder what they cut at the harvest, Player's Full Strength?"

Telfer got up for a run-off down a hole in the floorboards. Dunky bent over his knees, tying his laces. He'd liked to have seen Telfer's weapon, just to find out how small his own really was by comparison. He could smell the piss and see its steam and spray, but he kept his eyes on the floor.

Young Willie came into the harness room five minutes before the half hour, his usual time. They wouldn't make a move till the factory hooter went at half-past one, gone were the days when Auld Craig's fob watch was the only timer on the farm, as Willie told them when they complained, that old watch went hellish fast near yoking and hellish slow before lowsing.

"Hey, Willie, how's the housekeeper doing?" asked Telfer, grinning over his shoulder, the stream of water still spattering into the hole in the floor. That was another thing he didn't have in common with most blokes, all this pissing and spitting, pissing on the terraces at football matches (all they said was "Hey, Jimmy, mind yur back" and got it out, even in a crowded ground), against walls and up closes – at school in Miss Peacock's class they used to crawl under desks and piss down a knothole. Spitting was another thing – when he was about four they'd had spitting matches in Shuttle Street and he'd gone home covered in the stuff. Everybody in Kilcaddie had catarrh and everybody spat, all the time, out of habit. A guy called Shanky had once spat in the High Street and said proudly, "They'll skid on that all day." Spitting and pissing were as common as breathing.

"Niver you mind about the housekeeper, Telfer," said Willie. Dunky got to his feet. Willie was always good for a laugh, a mad bugger but good-natured. He got away with saying things that coming from anybody else would start a fight. Sometimes he'd go up to McCann and stare in his face, close-up, and shout so loud you could hear him two parks away, "Ah hear ye're no good with wimmin, McCann, is that right what they tell me, ye're no' up to it?" His big eyes would open

38

wide, white all round the pupils, roaring out his daft nonsense, staring into your face and then turning away and shrieking with glee. A mad bugger. Once he'd read in the papers about a Glasgow woman asking for a divorce because her man had run off with a fancy woman, described as "pretty, dark-haired Irish Kitty Daly." Something about this tickled Willie and for weeks afterwards he'd come up to you in the fields, eyes opening wide, staring into your face and roaring out "pretty, dark-haired Irish Kitty Daly." Nobody knew what he was getting at.

"It's a good job you're Craig's son, Willie," Telfer would say. "If you were just a common shite like the rest of us you'd be in a padded cell."

It was still coming down in buckets when the hooter blew, a deep, hooting wail which was exactly like the sirens in the war, when they'd run down to the brick shelters in the street and spend the night drinking cocoa out of flasks, listening to the crump-crump of the big bombs and the lighter bangs of the ack-ack and the droning of the planes. Funny about those times in the shelter, looking back they were about as happy as any times he could remember. Everybody laughed and joked and shared their sandwiches and cocoa. Grown-ups told funny stories and joked about for the benefit of the kids. James Mason hid in a shelter like theirs in the film *Odd Man Out*, when he was bleeding. Most of these families had gone away from Shuttle Place now that it was being demolished. Funny to think you remembered all these people and would probably never see them again.

"It'll be damn wet up the braes the night," Telfer said, looking out. "I'll need a tent and a groundsheet."

This was his subtle way of letting them know he had a big date. If anybody was impressed they didn't show it.

"You are a ravishing scoundrel, Donald Telfer," said Willie, speaking deliberately as though mimicking something he'd heard on the wireless. "That's what you are, Telfer, a ravishing scoundrel. You tell the wimmin you're an agricultural student with a college degree, Donald Telfer, I'll tell you the only letters you'll ever have after your name, Donald Telfer – s.s. Shite Scraper, that's the only degree you've got, Telfer, ye dirty ravisher."

"Women like a bit of fancy patter," Telfer said. He fingered Willie's shirt. "I'll tell you something, friend, you'll never get into bed with the housekeeper wearing a rotten old rag like that.'

39

"Niver you mind about the housekeeper, you ravishing scoundrel, you'll no' be getting up to any of your agricultural student tricks with her."

"Oh," said Telfer, winking heavily at the other two," I see, you fancy her yourself, eh? Willie's got a hard-on for her. That didn't take long. I suppose you and Auld Craig'll be mounting her in turns the night?"

Dunky noticed that McCann turned away as though angry about something.

"Hey, Willie," Telfer went on, "when *did* you last change that stinking shirt?"

It was a frequent question, a regular joke, Willie always having the same answer:

"Whit dae ah need tae change the bugger for, there's nuthin' wrang wi' it?"

"Most people change when they're dirty," Telfer said. "You're not supposed to keep a shirt on your back till it falls off in bits."

"Ach, Telfer, we don't all want tae look like nancy boys," said Young Willie. "Hey, Blackie, tell they howkers we're feenished for the day. You, Logan, pit a halter on that old beast and tak' him doon the road tae Cairney's, ye know whaur they are, don't ye?"

"You want the boy to die of pneumonia?" Telfer said. "Take him yourself, you lazy old fart, it's pishing down."

"It'll dae his dandruff the world o' good," said McCann.

Dunky ignored McCann's remark. He wanted to take the horse through the scheme, that would be something.

"I'll be all right," he said. "I'll take the oilskin."

"There's an old bunnet o' mine in the kitchen," Willie said. "Ask the housekeeper for it."

"Will I put a blanket over his back?" he asked Willie. It was said on impulse, without thinking how silly it would sound.

McCann laughed.

"What's he needin' a blanket fur?" he said. "Ye think he's goin' tae the Royal Highland Show?"

Putting on the yellow oilskin cape, cracked along the lines of its folds, Dunky put a rope halter on old Charlie and led him out of the stable and round the small barn to the kitchen. A drain was choked and water was spreading across the yard.

Dunky led the horse up to the porch. He was excited – and

40

a bit nervous – about having to speak to the crippled house-keeper. Telfer would have known what to say – all he could do was be serious, try not to give her the idea he was daft. When the door opened she looked out at the boy and the horse with a funny, almost bad-tempered expression on her face. She was wearing a brown cardigan. She had big tits. Her eyes were greenish, her hair red. Dunky tried to speak like a a man of the world.

"Hullo, Willie says you've to give me his old bunnet."

She looked at him as though he might be trying to hide something from her.

"Wait here," she said. What the hell did she think he was likely to do, walk Charlie into the kitchen? She came back to the door, the cap held out at arm's length. "There you are," she said, pushing it at him. He thought he could smell her. He'd felt the same way when he'd finally summoned up the courage to go up to girls and ask them to class parties. Like a criminal. His eyes couldn't help travelling down from her breasts to the gamey leg. "Have a good look while you're at it," she said. He blushed. He couldn't think what to say. She shut the door in his face.

The cap was far too big for him, never mind, so were his boots. Jesus Christ, he was a right galumph all right, he'd forgotten to bring his bike!

"Did ye get wet, poor wee bairn?" McCann sneered as he went into the stable. He ignored that.

"Face the oncoming traffic," Telfer shouted after him as he walked away, horse rope in his right hand, fingers of the left hand splayed over the centre-piece of the handlebars. Telfer watched him from the door, a skinny lad in a daft cap down to his ears, walking with a decrepit old horse whose belly looked ready to sink to the ground. Telfer wondered if he'd ever looked as gormless as that. He lit a cigarette and wondered what repair job on the tractor he could invent to keep him out of the byre.

In the house Mary O'Donnell sat down again at the kitchen table, taking a piece of paper from the pocket of her apron. Checking that day's date from the newspaper, she counted on her fingers. Eleven days overdue now and still no period. Curse her bloody bad luck, four and half years with Stephenson and she'd been landed with it in her last month. Kicked her out just in time, that stuck-up bitch. Nothing like this would ever catch *her* out, not that hard-faced cow. Oh no, it never happened to women like her, they had brains like counting machines. They were all hard, hard as stone, the old ones and their sons and their women. Compared to them she was just trash, a nobody, a bedmat for as long as it suited the old devil then – out.

Maybe it was a punishment for her own sinful weakness, maybe she deserved to be treated like trash, maybe that's all she'd ever been good for, since the day she was born. But it wasn't going to happen to her child. It was going to get a fair chance, if she had to lie and cheat and murder for it. Nobody was going to treat it like trash. Her fists clenched on the table, she stared at the meaningless headlines of the newspaper. Her child was going to have a proper father and a proper home and a proper upbringing, she didn't care what she had to do, she'd give her child a proper life. They thought they were hard and mean, but she'd show them.

CHAPTER THREE

The dog barked at him from the door of its kennel as he led Charlie across the yard. Dunky kicked a stone at it, but its momentum was lost in a puddle. Craig knew what he was doing, having the brute in the yard, nobody could get near the steading without the dog making a din. (But how was Donald Telfer able to creep in at night to shag his big lumbers in the barn? Donald Telfer could do anything.) Rain drove down on the puddles, running off the peak of Willie's cap, cracking against the oilskin, washing down his face. They turned on to the road, Charlie walking with a sad attempt at a swing, clopping along in bucketing rain, poor old devil. Was the new housekeeper watching from one of the house windows? Why had she been so bad-tempered with him? Was she really thinking – *who is that hard-looking lad, I must get to know him better?* Rhonda Fleming – that's who she was like, with the red hair and the severe expression. Why did a lot of really beautiful women always have that bad-tempered look about them? He could imagine taking her up the town to the flicks and the neds at the Cross sneering at her out of the side of the mouth, *who's the geek with the limpy lumber?* and he'd go across to them, all calm and cold eyes, *you speaking to me, mac?*

The part of the scheme nearest the farm was known as The Jungle, the hard man's area. Here, it was well known, they kept coal or greyhounds in the bath. One family, the Sweeneys, had been kicked out by the Corporation housing factor because they'd taken big hammers and knocked down the wall between the kitchenette and the living-room, to save them the bother of walking through the lobby.

"They're just scruffs," his mother said about the Jungle folk. "It's a disgrace, there's plenty of money for drink and radiograms but the children don't even have shoes."

The main scheme road ran for more than a mile between the big blocks, four storeys high, some with as many as five separate close-entrances. The biggest block, known as the Queen Mary, had six closes. Dalgetty's double-decker buses which ran from the scheme were called The Yellow Peril, their drivers being notorious speed merchants. He could vaguely

43

remember them when they had open tops. There had been a murder once in the Jungle, an axe murder. McCann said he wouldn't live in the scheme, he called them razor-slashers and Irish scum, but this was just to get at Telfer, who always laughed it off saying the deadliest razor he'd seen was the one his mother used to shave her oxters.

He walked with the horse near the kerb, the rope hanging loosely in his right hand. He wouldn't have fancied walking Big Dick through the scheme, the very sight of a yellow peril bus made him turn side-on and kick out like hell. He talked to Charlie when there was nobody in sight, not that many folk were out in that weather, an occasional wifey hurrying home, a few school-dodgers playing headies up a close, occasionally a couple of men standing at a close-mouth, just smoking and gassing away the afternoon, their blue smoke rising into the rain, me who watched him go by, an event in their lives. Rainwater gurgled along the gutter, making triangular dams where a drain was choked, dammed by bricks and sludge and paper. Charlie's hair hung down his nose and neck, black wet plaits, natural oil being washed away. Now and then he lowered his head and gave it a great, spluttering shake. Poor old brute, done his eleven years' toil and all he got was a long walk in the rain to Cairney's. In England, he'd read, they did put old horses out to grass, but they could afford to be soft in England. Craig didn't have spare fields for old horses, even if he'd ever had such an idea, which was unlikely.

"Ach, you're probably better out of it anyway," he said. "Think of me, I'm just starting."

White faces peered at them through the steamy windows of a bus, its inside lights already on at two in the afternoon. Aye, have a good look, people, he said to himself, it's just a daftie from the farm and a ruined nag. They'd be jealous underneath. Not many blokes of his age got to march a horse about the town, better than working in a stupid office. He should have got up on Charlie's back, ha ha, they'd have a right laugh at that, say he was playing cowboys and Injiens, just like a big saft wean.

At the far end the scheme street turned left into a cul-de-sac. He took Charlie and the bike between three stone pillars which stopped traffic from carrying through the narrow lane which led under a railway bridge to the Glasgow road. He stopped under the bridge, resting the bike against the wall, and pushed Charlie's hair back between his ears. The horse whinnied and rubbed its lower nose against the oilskin.

"If I knew a spare field I'd put you in it, old hoss," he said. A man came towards the bridge, collar up, shoulders hunched. Dunky picked up the bike and started off again. People were very nosey. They'd wonder what he was doing.

They stopped at the main road, waiting for a break in the traffic. It was cobbled here, still inside the burgh boundary. Ayrshire County Council covered its roads with asphalt. Charlie might slip on the cobbles, he needed a good long break in the traffic to get across. A BRS lorry slowed up and the driver waved at him through the clear arc made by his windscreen wiper. He nodded his thanks and took a tighter hold on the rope, his fist against Charlie's mouth. He nodded again at the driver when he reached the other side. The real workers always took care of each other.

On that side there was a joinery behind a red-brick wall. It was darker now and he could hardly see the top of the braes for rain. The street lights were on, not the blue sodium of the scheme but orange lights on tall concrete pillars, a diseased orange which, in the dark, made people's faces seem all blotchy. Rain was getting down his back. Charlie kept snorting it out of his nostrils.

A girl called Mary Gibson lived up this road, a real smasher who'd been two classes higher than him in school. Her daddy was a policeman and she was a cracker, dark skin and jet black hair. The first time he'd really noticed her was at the school sports, she'd been in a relay race, big diddies bouncing up and down under her white shirt. He'd been too scared to ask her to any of the class parties, and he hadn't seen her since. She'd be working now, or at University or something. Pity she couldn't have seen him with Charlie, she'd have realised he was bigtime now, not just a stupid scholar. He'd have nodded to her, gruff like, big men with horses couldn't be wasting a lot of time with silly girls. Then they'd have met at the jigging at the Town Hall and she'd have asked him for a ladies' preference and said she'd seen him with the horse, wasn't it dangerous, and he'd have shrugged, all strong and silent. . . .

"More likely she'd sniff the aroma of dung and go off with some gallus cunt from an office," he said to Charlie.

The big notice, J. AND F. CAIRNEY LTD., yellow letters on green boards, stood above the main gateway of the knacker's.

He led Charlie through into a red tarmacadam yard surrounded by sheds. He walked across to the small office building and propped the bike under a lighted window. The rain was slacking, easing off to a downpour as Telfer said. He rapped on the glass. A hand rubbed off condensation on the inside and a woman's face appeared. She opened the window an inch or two.

"Who are you from?" she asked.

"Craig's farm." She looked like a married bit, weren't they supposed to be hellish experienced? Telfer said you could get it from practically any married woman.

"Oh aye, that's Mister Prentice you want, the last door on this side."

"Thanks." Thanks for nothing, you hee-haw office woman. He crossed railway lines sunk in the asphalt. It was a cutting off the same line that ran up to the hill from the Town through the farm. Once, during the war, there had been a big outbreak of anthrax or some cattle disease and they'd brought dead cows to Cairney's by the wagonload, so many Cairney's couldn't keep pace with them. The wagons had piled up on the siding for days, the stiff legs of dead cows sticking into the air, a hellish stink of rotting carcasses blowing for miles. There were men who made a living nicking stuff out of parked railway wagons but they'd kept well clear of those cattle wagons, he remembered his father saying that, as though it proved something. What the hell could they have nicked from diseased cows?

It was chilly inside the big slide doors. He led Charlie into the shed out of the rain.

"Hullo?" The floor was of bare cement, with a pile of empty sacks in one corner. "Hullo?"

A man appeared from the back of the shed, a hefty man in Wellington boots that came up to his hips and a black rubber apron over blue dungarees. His bare arms were thick with gingery hair.

"Aye, it's a great day for the ducks," he said.

"I'm looking for Mister Prentice."

"That's me."

"I'm from Craig's."

"Oh aye, he tellt me he had a horse. An' how's Willie this weather, he's a terrible man that Willie, terrible."

Prentice laughed. Terrible could mean all sorts of things. You could say a man was a terrible drinker or a terrible pic-

46

ture fiend or a terrible joker. You could even say a man was a terrible nonentity. Sometimes the word meant very and sometimes it meant terrible. From the way he laughed, Prentice seemed to be suggesting that Willie had done some terrible things in his time, which could mean anything from murder to letting down policemen's tyres.

Charlie stretched his neck, his mouth near the ground, and shook water off in a spray. Prentice put his hand on his shoulder and shook his head, eyeing the horse from head to tail.

"He's seen better days," he said. "Bring him through the back. Ye can leave the bike here, it's safe enough."

Dunky kept hold of the rope and the bike, Kilcaddie was full of fly boys who'd nick anything, a bike, lead from a church roof, anything, quicker'n you could say Wee Willie Winkie.

They went through another slide door into a smaller area cut off by inside walls which didn't go all the way up to the corrugated glass roof. Prentice looked up and shouted.

"Hey, Ally!"

Through another door appeared a younger man, dressed like Prentice. Dunky thought it was funny he'd never seen either of them in the town. Maybe knackers' men didn't go about in public much. The young man took a chain off a hook on the wall and pulled it towards Charlie, the chain leading up to a pulley which ran above their heads. Prentice went to a metal locker on the wall and brought out a contraption which looked something like a revolver (not that he had ever actually seen a revolver, only in pictures). The young man took the rope from Dunky's hand. Water dripped from the horse's belly. Poor old Charlie, he seemed too big to be inside a place like this.

"The painless killer," Prentice explained, holding the revolver contraption for Dunky's inspection. He nodded but didn't look at it properly. Prentice walked up to Charlie, the painless killer masked by his body. The young man put his hand on Charlie's nose. The horse swung his head in to the warmth of his body. Prentice put the killer against his head, near the ear. Charlie flicked water off his tail.

There was a noise like a hammer hitting a rotten post.

Charlie lurched once. Prentice stood back. Charlie lost his footing, then began to topple sideways, his rear legs buckling, his head drooping lifelessly even before his great body flopped on to the concrete floor. One of his hind legs straightened out

47

in a slow kick. The young man dragged the chain across the floor and while Prentice lifted the head by an ear to free the rope halter, he whipped the chain in a loop round Charlie's rear right hoof.

Dunky stood back, left hand gripping the handlebars. The two men began pulling on another chain. Slowly Charlie began to rise off the ground, hind leg first. His body now seemed to have become pliable, as though death had turned his bones to rubber. When his nose was an inch or two off the cement floor the two men shoved him towards the sliding doors. These led into a long, darkish shed, where two other men were waiting, pink faces against shadows. Dunky put his bike against the wall and followed the rattling chains and the slowly-swinging body of the horse. The other men had long knives. They were on to Charlie in seconds.

Dunky felt his stomach churning. Their knives worked so fast you couldn't follow the pattern of their cuts until the skin began to peel off. Under the skin was dark yellow fat, a slash of dark flesh where the knives had gone too deep. Then there was the slitting open of the great belly, the tumbling out of warm blood and steaming guts, the brown hide thrown to one side, the naked carcase looking like something that hadn't been born.

"He'll be gone in no time," Prentice said. "The blood's for artificial manure, the flesh for dog food, the rest boiled off in fat, nothing's wasted, the bones go for fertiliser. No, nothing's wasted here. Ye don't look well, son, is this the first ye've seen of knackers at work?"

"I'm all right," Dunky said. Indecent, that was it, something you were never meant to see. He'd been working that hanging lump of red and yellow meat this morning.

"Of course, a lot of folk'll tell ye Cairney's meat goes into sausages and pies," Prentice said, smiling. "We boil the carcases in these vats, they hang from the chains. Ye'll also hear that margarine comes out of here. Don't believe all ye hear, ha ha. In the war, maybe. Ha ha. See they pulley chains? The rats get along them at night when the carcases are hanging – we wait till the oil's boiling and then lower them in, it boils the skeletons clean as a whistle. The rats are that desperate they come down the chains on to the carcases, oh aye, a helluva lot of rats ye get in a place like this. The secret's to come up quiet like so's the rats don't hear ye, hundreds of them hotching about on the carcases. Then ye pull the switch and

48

shoot the carcass down into the oil, before they've time to get back up the chain. Man, I'll tell ye, the shriekin' would give ye nightmares. Ha ha. It's all put to good use, rats and all, I can tell ye."

"You'll be well used to it?" Dunky asked, knowing somehow that this was what Prentice wanted him to say.

"Oh aye," he laughed. "Ye couldn't afford not to be, not if ye work here. Ach, rats are dirty brutes anyway. They add a bit of taste to the margarine. Ha ha, that's a joke, son, don't be goin' round the town telling people Prentice says the rats go into the marge. It's for axle grease and train oil, all that sort of thing. Nothing's wasted."

Dunky felt cold and shivery. The smell was thick, like a cold, clammy cloth shoved in your face. He didn't look at what was left of Charlie.

Before he was halfway down the Jungle road the rain changed to hail, icy drops stinging in his face as he pedalled the heavy-frame bike. I bet McCann's never seen what goes on in the knacker's, he thought. That would be something to tell them. It was the speed of it all that amazed him. One minute old Charlie shaking his tail ... he felt curiously excited. It was only a horse, wasn't it, what did horses know, they were just dumb animals. He felt like laughing and telling jokes. This was the great thing about being away from school, when you started real work you got to know a lot of things they kept quiet from kids. Wait till the new housekeeper heard he'd been to the knacker's. She'd be impressed all right.

They mucked among the bullocks in the byre for the rest of the afternoon, Willie, McCann, Coll and Dunky, digging out the solid sharn with the big grapes, filling the rubber-wheeled barrow, which was heavy enough to give even Willie a bit of trouble as he pushed it across the yard and up the single plank to the centre of the midden. By four o'clock it was dark and the hail and rain had stopped.

"It'll freeze the night," McCann said. "I'm glad I'm no' a howker, they'll be frozen the morn's morn."

"You don't call this cold, do you?" said Coll. "It's chust a wee bit nippy, that's all. Wait till it's so cold your piss freezes back up to your cock and you have to be breaking an icicle to get free."

"Ach, it gets colder here'n anywhere up in the hielands," McCann retorted. "It's worse for us, anyway, we're no' a lot of savages."

49

"Savages, is it? There's more savages in that scheme than there is in the whole of Africa. You won't catch a highland-man fighting with boots and razors."

"No, ye cannae razor a man from the back."

Willie said that McFarlane the bobby had told him a gang of thieves had dug up forty feet of copper piping from one of the scheme roads – just drove up in a van and got out the picks and shovels and torn up the road in broad daylight. Willie thought this was a great laugh.

"There's people aboot here who'd steal your eyes," he said. If Telfer had been there he'd have defended the scheme people. Dunky pressed the grape into yielding straw and dung, the smooth handle burning on his palms. He could never get as much on his grape as the men, his body lacked the right rhythm, or something. The secret of farm work was to get into the right swing, to walk at a certain speed, to take a certain grip on a spade or a fork, to go at things in a steady fashion. His trouble was that he tried too hard to do as much work as the men, with the result that he was either staggering under too heavy a load, or tripping over his feet in his eagerness to get the grape up from the floor. Yet the work must be doing him good, he could feel his arms and shoulders and back, a dull aching that made him want to groan every time he straightened up.

At five they went across to the stable. He took the broom and went to work on Charlie's stall, stiff bristles on lumpy cobbles, a light, dry sharn, horses not being as skittery as cattle.

"No more Charlie then?" he said to McCann.

Blackie stopped, leaning against the end of the partition.

"It's like a wee bit of history," he said, "this stable's about a hundert year old and I'll bet you that's the last horse that'll ever be in this stall. I'll tell you the truth, if they could get machines for us *we'd* be at the knacker's, I'm no jokin'."

Wasn't that funny, McCann speaking to him in that sad, low voice, as though they were friends? And wasn't it even funnier, how he – and Willie – tended to speak almost proper English when they were on their own with you? No doubt there was some reason for it.

McCann shook his head and went into Big Dick's stall with the bucket of corn. He was in a good mood because tomorrow he'd have something to shake them up a bit. Tonight he was going over to the Brig to see a man there about buying his motor bike. Wait till Telfer saw him come charging into the yard with it the morn's morn, he'd do his nut with envy. He'd seen the bike once, a big powerful brute, do eighty or ninety no bother. He'd had a motor bike before, but this time he was getting one that wouldn't conk out every five miles. Great for taking women for rides into the country. If he played his cards right he might even get the limpy housekeeper interested, being a cripple she'd probably never travelled much, he'd say, like the bike? How about a wee spin, safe as houses? Next thing he'd have her away down to Troon, stop on the way, back of a hedge, riding the arse off her, that's what they all needed, easy as pie if you had a motor bike.

Yet the best part was thinking of Telfer when he saw the bike in the morning. It was time Telfer was shaken up a bit, he thought he was something great.

While McCann was in the stall, Dunky leaned down into the cornkist and shoved handfuls of grain into a paper bag. Willie let him take sacks of hay and straw home for his rabbits, but corn was different, it was safer just to knock it. He made a circular screw of the top of the bag and shoved it inside his jerkin.

Before they went home for the night the men always came into the stable. Coll and Telfer stood watching Blackie and the boy finish sweeping along the gutter, Telfer smoking, Coll looking on with what could have been a smile on his big, open face. Monday was his night for going to a pub in Kilcaddie with two other Oban men, getting a good bucket of whisky down him out of the proceeds of the five child allowances which his wife drew and he spent.

Willie came into the stable looking for his bicycle pump.

"What's for tea the night, Willie?" Telfer asked, winking at the other men. "Two boiled eggs and a sausage up the housekeeper?"

Willie bared his teeth at Telfer.

"Ye ravishing scoundrel, Telfer," he said. "Ye're a sexual rogue." He grinned at them all, as though they should be astonished that he knew such expressions.

In the farmhouse Mary O'Donnell limped across from the gas cooker to the big table, where Auld Craig sat staring at his hands, although she couldn't actually tell if his eyes were open or not.

"I hope you like black puddin' and fried potatoes," she said, putting the plate in front of him. The three collie-crosses lay at his feet, eyes wide, chins on the floor, trained by dint of many kicks to lie still until the old man threw them whatever was left on his plate.

"Hrrmmmph." He twisted his head to look at her. "Don't be givin' us any fancy cookin', plain food's the best."

She put down his blue-ring china mug of tea, watching the stiff movements of his arms. An old man like him would feel the cold, no wonder, in a house like this. When she'd arrived the first thing she'd noticed in the kitchen was the sink with dirty dishes piled almost as high as the taps. There was an old gas geyser for hot water, but it wasn't working. After taking her case into the ground-floor bedroom, she'd changed into her working clothes and got to work on the dishes. Willie Craig had promised her that a ton of coal would be delivered the next day, but until that there was nothing for fires. Already she'd sensed that the old man, ancient as he looked, was the real power in the house. It was him she had to pay attention to. Willie? He was a man and she knew what sort of attention he'd be after, no, the old fella was the one, too old to want to throw a leg over her, and a lot harder to get round because of it.

When he finished eating Auld Craig took his plate and swept the remains of his black pudding on to the bare stone floor. Mary O'Donnell's lips tightened; she had swept and washed the floor that afternoon, dragging the big table and the mahogany dresser and the heavy old chairs this way and that to get her broom into corners where crusts had gone green and dust gathered in thick rolls. Auld Craig stretched his hand to the centre of the table, to the white loaf. He tore several lumps of bread and crust, his ancient hands still wide and bony at the knuckles, the skin slack only round the purple veins on the back of his hand. As she watched him throw the fragments to the scrabbling dogs Mary O'Donnell controlled an impulse to shut her eyes and scream at him. Her chest was still heaving with rage as the old man pulled himself up out of the chair, his body jack-knifed over the table as he straightened his legs.

"Hrmmph." He looked at her for a second, cold blue flints peering at her from under the great eyebrows. "I'm awa' tae bed." He took a bad-tempered kick at a dog which moved in front of him, the stiffness of his knee giving the dog ample time to escape the hobnail boot.

"Righto," she said, watching him clump away to the lobby. She cleared his place, a familiar choking anger in her throat. Was the rest of her life to be spent watching men treat her like a servant, dropping their messes all over the house which she had to clean, the house in which she had all the duties of a wife with none of the rights of a wife? Sure as the fires of hell it was not. A house was a woman's place, to run as she thought fit, and she was a woman now, twenty-eight years of age, old enough to know many things about men, things that would have seemed dark and strange to a girl, things that would have stuck on her tongue in the shadows of the confessional, memories of words and faces frozen into her mind, a man's white back twisted away from her face, whisky-tainted air, not knowing what the unseen face was doing, not believing when she did know, not understanding – don't Andy, that's *dirty*!

Dirty? Of course, dirty, but the shock had gone by now, worn away by the years. There was power in the wasted leg and its ungainly apparatus. What she had learned was to see behind men's eyes, to see behind the first outward look of surprise and contempt. To see into the secret places where men had thoughts they themselves didn't know existed. And to use that power to gain her rights, to make her as good as any hard-eyed, nose-high, contemptuously sniffing *wife*.

Craig turned right on the upstairs landing, off which were two big bedrooms, one occupied by Willie and one by himself. Switching on the light he saw that his bed had been made, for the first time in a month or so.

"Damn and hell, it's cold," he said. There was a single-bar electric fire in the empty grate. The girl had switched it on, electricity burning away all afternoon, damn the girl, did she think he was an old woman to need money burned for heat? He wheezed as he bent down to switch it off. He took off his jacket, arms stiff behind his back as his fingers pulled at the sleeves. He put the jacket on the chair, the heavy old rocking-chair his father had brought when they moved south from Aberdeenshire, eighteen-ninety-one, his father's rocking-chair, they'd sawn off the rockers just before the great war – the right one had split at the front end; now it was a high-backed wooden chair with a ribbed back and arms honed shiny and yellow where paint and polish had been smoothed away by the elbows of the years.

He put his thumb against his nose and cleared one nostril
53

into the cupped palm of the same hand, repeating the heavy snort with the left nostril. He wiped his hands on his trousers and sat down on the edge of the high double bed, bought by him for him and Jessie in nineteen-seventeen at the auction rooms, two pounds six shillings, a good bed. He could feel the cold in his back, but these days his back was never quite right. He wheezed again as he bent down to unlace his boots.

"A dram's the best thing," he said, turning to a walnut stand which stood by the bed, on it a small wooden barrel with a brass tap. Opening the door of the bedstand he took out a china mug, his father was given that mug when they opened the railway siding in eighteen-ninety-four, the old Kilcaddie and District Railway and Traction Company, aye, the siding was to bring in cattle to the market, the big open mart, all football fields now, he could remember his father saying the mug was to be saved for special occasions as clearly as he could remember eating the new woman's black pudding. He held the mug under the brass tap, real malt whisky, a thin amber flow from the same barrel his father had kept by his bedside, must be near a hundred year old.

"Damn the lot of you," he said, raising a slightly shaking hand to his mouth. He drank the whisky, a third of a pint or so, in three good gulps, the warmth spreading out from his belly almost as soon as he had coughed his usual cough, the same whisky and the same cough for near on fifty years now, just as his father had done, drinking is a fool's ploy, his father had told him, hiv yer ain whusky by the bed an' content yersel wi' a guid dram afore ye ging tae sleep.

Groaning inwardly with the stiffness in his back he levered himself backwards on to the bed and pulled up his legs, panting slightly, dragging the blankets up over his trousers and his thick shirt and his braces. Willie would put out the light, Willie who'd turned out not such a bad boy, better'n Jessie and him had expected, never a good boy when he was young, not like George, George was the bright one of the pair of them, but George was never happy about the place, always wanting to be off, desperate to be away from the day he left the school. Sons, ach, they wouldn't be told. The one you wanted to stay was for away and the other hung about the place and never got married or anything at all. A hundred and ninety acres then and now it was houses and the factory and scum from the town ruining the good land, aye, maybe George was bright enough to see it all coming, that's why he'd gone away to Africa, a letter and pictures of his bairns at Christmas, the one letter a year. George took after himself, he knew what was what. Left to Willie they'd have nothing left at all. The old man smiled. A hundred and forty-eight acres left, not counting the four rented fields from the old Campbell place, not bad for an old man that everybody thought was in his dotage, aye, he knew now how to handle these town boys, he'd hung on to his fields, seen the price go up from fifty pound an acre to fifteen hundred an acre and still he wouldn't let them buy him out, no, let the damnt factory boys hold their horses, land was going up all the time, damn the corporation and their compulsory purchase orders, aye, Willie ye don't know the half of what your old father gets up to, you don't have the brains, didn't even have the wit to fake your own school report, signed my name like a hen scratching in a midden, had to leather you for that, always had to leather Willie for something, ten pounds wasn't a bad price for an old done horse, he remembered that land before Jackie Cairney started the knacker's, it was trees then, the cattle used to stand under the trees when it was raining, the old folk used to say the trees were in a round clump because that bit went back to the pagan people, he'd never had much time for that sort of history stuff and fairy tales, but at least he remembered what the old folk had said. Nowadays? Ach, the damnt people nowadays wouldn't spare the time of day, all they knew was their picture palaces and their chip shops, still, maybe the Logan loon would turn out all right – for a scheme boy. They'd finish the tatties this week, that meant he could give Coll his books, too many damnt men about the place for all the size it was, that's Willie on the stairs.

"WILLIE!"

Willie Craig came up the stairs in his stockinged feet. What did the old bugger want now? He'd never liked going in that room, not since his mother died.

"Ye're in bed then?" he said, standing in the doorway. The old man turned his head on the pillow.

"Put off the light," he said, "I'm for sleep. We'll give Coll the bag on pay-day. The boy's a fair worker."

"Aye," said Willie. "Righto."

He switched off the light and went across the landing to his own room, which looked less now like an old bothy than it had done since the last housekeeper, Mrs. McNidder, had left to go south and live with her widowed sister in Ipswich. They'd talked before about sacking Coll once the main tattie crop was in the pits. He put his boot on the rexine cover of the bedroom's only chair and untied the lace from round the ankle. He'd heard a good joke that day from Lapsley, the corn merchants' traveller. It was about Irish women, he'd decided to tell it to Mary O'Donnell once he'd changed out of his working gear. Tomorrow he'd get her to light a coal fire in his grate, he was over fifty, he was entitled to a fire in his bedroom. Rummaging in a drawer he pulled out a new flannel shirt, cream with blue stripes, he'd been saving it for a special occasion like Craig's funeral – his own would come first more likely.

He put on the shirt and fastened its collarless neck with a brass front-stud. Then he threw his wet socks into the fireplace, they were rotten and could be used for rags. He changed his trousers but not his long woollen combinations. The trousers were of the same rough, hodden grey material as his father's, both suits made out of the chest in his father's bedroom, the chest that contained yards and yards of hodden grey, put there by Grandfaither Craig before the First World War, to be taken out every ten or fifteen years when a new suit had to be made up, cloth that came out as stiff and as greasy as it was when Grandfaither Craig laid it down fifty years ago, cloth that never seemed to run out.

He went downstairs in his bare feet, carrying a new pair of wool socks and his number two boots.

She was at the sink, washing dishes. He ignored her, taking the chipped enamel basin from under the sink and running hot water from the geyser. She glanced at him, their elbows almost touching.

"I heard a good tale today about Irish people," he said, taking the basin over to the table, where he laid it on the floor. He spoke properly to her, not because she was Lady Muck or anything, but because it was better for people you didn't know too well. He knew he didn't look like a man who'd once taken his Scottish Higher Leaving Certificate in five subjects (Latin, English, Maths, History and French, the last two at lower level, not nearly as good as George had done) – he liked to suprise people occasionally, show them there was more to him than common dirt. Not that he needed to care what they thought, there wasn't many had as much cash in the bank as his father.

She went on washing dishes, although he could tell she was waiting for the story.

"This woman moves to a new house a few miles outside o' Dublin and she comes back to see her friend next door and she says, d'you know what's happened, the corner shop's been taken by a Jew, a fella called Cohen. What's a Jew? says the other wife. You don't know, sure they're the dirty bastards who took Jesus Christ and kicked him about and nailed him to a cross and reviled him. Is that a fact, says the other wife, it just shows you, you move away for two weeks and you don't know half of what's going on at all." He nodded, his big, staring eyes fixed, unblinking it seemed, on her face. Then his lips curled back and he shook with a soundless laugh.

"Very funny," said Mary O'Donnell, wiping her hands on the dish towel, eyebrows raised in a haughty manner.

"Ye like a good joke?" said Willie, putting his feet into the basin. "D'you know the one about the Glesca hoor who thought an endless belt was a weekend in bed wi' a black man?"

Again the searching eyes. Mary O'Donnell knew she was being sounded out. If she laughed she was fair game and he'd come clomping into her room that night. If she didn't he'd say she was high and mighty and he'd give her no peace until he'd rubbed her face in the dirt; she knew his type.

Reaching round to the table drawer, Willie took out a large pair of scissors and began cutting his toenails, parings sparking across the stone floor, grunting with the strain of the knee pressing into his chest.

"It's well seen ye haven't had a woman in the house for a long time," she said. Willie went on cutting. He'd had a good look at her, fine, big arms, a good pair of paps, not a bad-looking wench, considering.

"Throw's over the dishtowel till I dry my feet," he said, looking up.

"Ye'll do no such thing," she said, taking care not to sound too bossy "Here, use this old thing, I'll have to wash it anyway."

"Oh, I see, fancy notions," he said. But he took the old towel and she knew she'd won something. She cleared the table while he shaved at the sink, the cut-throat blade rasping clean, pink swatches on the grizzled grime of his broad chin and heavy cheeks. Now he was cleaned up and fresh and ready to throw the leg over anything that was warm and moving. But not her, not as soon as this.

57

"You're a Roman Catholic, a Pape?" he said, turning so that she could see he was using the dishtowel to wipe the remains of soap off his face.

"I used to be," she said. "Wouldn't ye like a better towel than that for your face?"

"Ach, I'm no' bothered," he said. "We'll be having the priests sniffing round, I suppose, trying to get you back among the Papes."

"Why should they?"

"Oh, they're hot on that, the Papish boys."

"They can keep it for all I care. I got my blessing a long time since."

He knew she meant the withered leg. For some reason he wasn't all that caring about her being a limpy dan. It made her easy to talk to, as though she had no right to be the equal of normal folk.

"I can aye give ye a hand wi' the milkin'," he said.

"Oh, that's all right. There's one thing ye could see to, get these dogs out of the house, they're just a mess."

"Aye," he said. "It's time they were out anyway, I'd shoot them if I had my way."

He went out then, not saying where he was going or when he'd be back. She made herself a cup of tea and sat at the big table. He'd wanted to see if she was game for dirty jokes, which meant was she game for him in her bed, and when he couldn't see that way clear he'd offered to help her with the milking, and then he'd admitted to her that his father had the say about the dogs. In time, she supposed, a wife could get him to have a bath . . . it was a hard thing to have to discuss in your own head, but she knew he'd be the best man she'd find to father her baby, the trouble being that these dour Scotsmen wouldn't marry a woman they thought was an easy ride, yet if she didn't do something quickly it would be too late and she'd never be able to make him believe he was the real father. She was a month gone by already. She might get away by saying it was two months premature, but not much more. And once she let him into her bed how did she know he'd ever consider marrying a crippled Irish Catholic? They were hard, the Scots, hard as granite. Him and his father might look and live like something out of a byre, but underneath they'd be as stiff and respectable in their ideas as only mean old Protestant bastards could be.

CHAPTER FOUR

To be quite honest, Telfer thought as he sat in the back row of the Granada cinema watching Burt Lancaster and Gary Cooper in *Vera Cruz,* he wasn't bothered if it was too cold or wet to get a quick shag with Agnes at the back of her house, he'd been up her three nights a week for four months, ever since he'd chatted her up at harvest-time, and he was getting a bit fed up with her. He had his right arm round her waist, the tips of his fingers gently prodding her breast.

"Mmmmm," she mouthed into his ear, blowing hot air and letting her tongue touch it, wet and tantalising. He should've known he'd only to get his hands on her tits and she'd be wanting to climb all over him, when he was more interested in Burt Lancaster.

"Watch the picture," he said, pulling her back to her seat with his right hand, his left arm on the back of the next seat. Agnes had been one of the dames he'd watched coming out of the office block at the factory, glamorous they looked then, him sitting on a tractor in working clothes, them in high heels, wearing make-up. Now she was just Agnes, familiar, you didn't buy the shop for a dab of sherbert.

They walked home through the Cross, Telfer keeping his hands in the pockets of his brown sports trousers, her hand on the inner elbow of his chocolate sports jacket, obviously well pleased to be seen about the town with a big handsome blond bloke. It was frosty and dry, ideal weather for a swift poke at the back of her parents' house in Barcraigie, a good-class area of detached bungalows where bankers and the like lived. He didn't even feel like making his usual joke, "They always did say the knobs hang out in Barcraigie." It was all too bastartin' obvious, start off looking for a new ride and end up being stopped at jewellers' windows "just for a wee look at the engagement rings, oh, that's awfully nice, my friend Beth got one just like that, isn't it a *lovely* wee stone?"

He was different, he knew that. He wasn't like the men who were rolling out of the pubs after a good bucket, he wasn't interested in talking about football, he was –

"You're very quiet tonight, Don, is something the matter?"

Don! At the farm he was Big Telfer – everybody was either

Big somebody or Wee somebody. He wasn't the same as the lads from the scheme, maybe because he was over six feet and curly blond, whereas they were all wee bauchly men with dark hair (one of Willie's favourite jokes – "Ye hear aboot Erchie McEachern the dwarfie, he's suing the corporation, says they built the pavement too near his arse"), maybe because his mother and father were both what they called a bit fast. Maybe. Maybe aye, maybe hooch aye, as McCann would say, poor ignorant clown that he was. But he didn't like Don. Don was a nancy boy's name. Typical of Agnes!

At first it had been enough to give him a hard-on walking down the street, just thinking of him, a scheme fella, a midden-scraper, riding Agnes from Barcraigie, the floor manager's daughter, enough just to get into their toffs' living room on a Sunday night, when the pan-loaf McFarlanes had gone to bed, to get him steaming, enough to know they thought he was a scruff. Now he didn't give a fuck, she was just another girl wanting a ring on her finger. He wanted something different, he was different himself, he wanted something out of the ordinary. And when he thought of that he thought of his hands going under the strong arms of the new housekeeper, and the haughty look on her face and the cold look in her green eyes. That would be something out of the ordinary. To bang the cripple. He started singing. They were walking up a Barcraigie road, alongside neat privet, a good-class area where a car could be parked outside all night without having its windows kicked in.

> "The village cripple he was there,
>   He wasnae up tae much,
>   He laid the virgins on the ground,
>   And banged them wi' his crutch."

"Shoosh, Don." He wanted to annoy her.

> "Singing, balls to your partner,
>   Arses tae the wall,
>   If ye've never been shagged on a Setterday nicht,
>   Ye've never been shagged at all."

"Shoosh, Don, people'll *hear* you."
"I don't care about people."
"You care about me, don't you?"
"Oh, yeah, sure."
"That doesn't sound very enthusiastic."

A squeeze on the elbow. A ring on the finger. A steady job. Kids to the Sunday School. Gran McFarlane's coming to tea tonight. Auntie Meg's asked us up for Sunday.

ALL THAT FOR A QUICK RATTLE?

"I'm thinking of emigrating to Canada, serious like."

No squeeze this time. Kilcaddie women! Sensible shoes and heavy tweed coats, just like their fatbag mothers, looking like wives the day after they left school.

"Oh! I thought we were, I mean, sort of –"

"You and me? Aw, look, Agnes, I'm just a common tractor driver, you're – different."

Wheedling face at his shoulder, looking up.

"You don't think I'm different when I'm letting you do *that*?"

Tell me the old, old story. For men it was a game, for women some kind of favour they did you. God help you if you weren't grateful! They'd let you sin – now take your punishment – get married. In other countries it was different, he'd read things that would make a Kilcaddie woman's hair stand on end. America, Canada – over there women thought no more of a poke than lighting a cigarette.

"You like it as much as I do."

She turned her head away. Embarrassed.

"Go on, admit it, you like it, don't you?"

"I do *not*."

"You do sot."

"I only did it because I loved you."

Reproachful now. Tears on the horizon. He didn't give a rat's fart. She was just another on the list. Ticked off. He had it in him to roger every bloody woman in Kilcaddie. Thirty-four was the current tally. Not bad in seven years, considering all the time you wasted with prick-teasers and professional virgins.

"Did I ever tell you about the first time I got into a woman," he said. He could feel she *hated* that. "It was a bint called Aitken who lived in the next close to us. I used to deliver papers to her – she was married, had a baby, her man was working on the hydro-electric somewhere up north." She pretended not to listen so he went on talking, knowing she'd blow up. "One time I'm round collecting her paper money and she asks me in for a cup of tea, I was about fourteen. She was a right mawkit piece, I'll tell you, never got out of her nightie one week to the next. She gave me a biscuit and put her hand

61

on my dick and says, 'How d'ye fancy ridin' me?' Just like that. You should've smelt her, never washed except when it was raining."

"That's *horrible,* I don't want to hear any more."

"Aye, but that wasn't the worst part, every time I went with her paper she used to be waiting for me behind the door and pull me inside by the balls, I'll tell you, she was that desperate she couldn't wait to get on the bed, she used to grab me in the lobby and make me do it up against the wall. It's a wonder I ever reached fifteen."

He felt her shudder. He laughed. People like Agnes were easy meat. All they had was their respectable front. As soon as you got through that you could walk all over them, they didn't have the guts of a jelly baby. It hadn't even been him that used to ride the Aitken piece, it was Sammy Campbell. What a laugh! Stupid Agnes, maybe she wasn't sickened properly yet. He began to sing again:

> "The village postman he was there,
>   He had a dose of pox,
>   He couldn't stuff the wimmin
>   So he stuffed the letterbox."

"Please stop that, do you want to disgrace me?"

When they reached her gate she was still in an icy mood, but he didn't try to bring her round.

"Right then," he said, "where'll it be the night, the coal bunker or the garden shed? I'm easy."

She stood at the gate. It was freezing now. Nice and quiet in Barcraigie, folks pulled their curtains here and put chains on their doors and sat round their big fires. Nobody kicking a wife through the wall, no nests of half-starved kids screaming into the night, no lurching boozers on the pavements. Agnes was the only one of them in the street, the only Barcraigie resident out in the night.

"I don't know what's got into you," she said. He'd heard that quiet, brave voice before. It was trying to tell you something. He didn't want to know.

"Into me? All I said was where are we going to perform the night?"

"Is that all you're —"

Then, interrupting herself, she turned and fumbled for the gate latch and was up the path. He stood for a moment, then shrugged and walked away. It was a great feeling to rub their noses in it and make *them* break it off. Rub her toffee nose in it. Ram it into them and then shove their own dirt into their faces. He walked down the windy avenue, looking over solid privet hedges at the drawn blinds and curtains of Barcraigie's well-to-do. They had to hide themselves away in their big houses, the creepy bastards. Stuck-up load of shite, trying to pretend they were something, once the knickers were down they were all the same.

Big gloomy gardens always made him think of slipping quietly among bushes, tip-toeing up to windows, looking in, seeing some toff woman sitting high and mighty, then smashing in the window and climbing in, a dirty grin on his face, she'd start all haughty and then he'd make her grovel in front of him and beg for it and then he'd slash her face with a knife, take that, you stuck-up cow, think you're Lady Muck do you, cut her, cut her face and her body ... he felt better when he reached the old tenements on the north side. He felt more at home in the real town, under proper lights. Anybody could have strange notions inside their heads, no need to worry, anybody could think what they liked, it didn't mean anything. ...

At the old slag heaps, ragged black dunce-hat shapes against the lights of the factory perimeter fence, Willie got off the bike and wheeled across rutted grass and slag, his path lit by the early moon, a frozen, green light that shimmered on the outlines of the old slag heaps and threw narrow shadows under big stones. He knew these black hills well, after nearly fifty years, their grass patches (one worn smooth as a bowling green from the feet of the Sunday morning pitch and toss school), their ridges and valleys, the stretch of water where he'd caught newts and tadpoles, forty-five years ago, where wee boys from the scheme still caught newts and tadpoles and sticklebacks. By day the black hills looked like a rubbish coup, a litter of broken McEwan's bottles and cans and flock-spewing mattresses and bits of bikes. By night the litter was hidden. Nobody had mined anything here since before the First World War. Turning round the base of one heap he saw the light from the fire, a brazier standing just inside the low opening of the Tink's wee house – half cave, half shale hut backing into a slag heap, its flat roof of railway sleepers and corrugated sheets long overgrown with grass and dokens.

"Aye aye there," Willie called into the opening, unable to

see past the white coals and the shimmering heat-rise of the brazier.

"Friend or foe?"

Willie put his bike against the wall of flat shale pieces.

"It's me," he said, edging into the hut between the brazier and the railway sleeper doorpost, the door being a quilt of old grainbags stitched together by the Tink, pulled across only in storms.

Inside Willie saw that the Tink had been reading, sitting in his wrecked armchair (legs sawn off) with his feet on his bed, an arrangements of bricks walling in a well-packed grounding of straw, with two old blankets.

"Aye, it's a cauld wan," he said.

"Have tea from glass, Willie my friend," said the Tink, pouring from a billy can into a jamjar. "Your well-to-do folk, aristocrats and the like, they all drink tea from glass, they know that china imparts an oil to tea, glass is what your true gentry use, especially abroad, I believe the society folk in Russia and Germany regarded china as dead common."

Willie felt the heat from the brazier on his legs and hands. He sat on the straw bed, legs straight out in front, size eight boots pointing roofwards. He never told any of them at the farm that he regularly dropped in on the Tink's wee house in the black hills, to them he was just the daft tink who lived like a rat in the slag heaps, a real looney who didn't even have a front door, just a hole. Willie knew everybody in the area, scheme folk, police, travellers, farmers and their men, the factory gate police, the ministers and even a priest or two, but the Tink was his friend. He wasn't really a tinker at all, his name was Archibald Stewart, he'd lived in the black hills for years, ever since Willie was a wee boy and terrified of him, running away from the hills when he appeared, running all the way home trying not to spill newts or tadpoles or stickeybacks, running away from the bogey man of the black hills.

Willie had first spoke to Archie Stewart during the war, when men were scarce and his father had said to ask the Tink if he'd turn out for the harvest.

"No, I won't work," the Tinker had said, surprising Willie with his well-spoken accent, Willie who even at forty-odd was still a bit scared of going near the Tink's cave. "Not that I wouldn't want to give you a hand, but I cannot break my rule, not after all these years."

And while Willie stood by, changing feet, half-expecting

the Tink to jiggle his eyes and scream bogey-man's lingo, Archie Stewart had told him why he lived in the black hills.

"I was training for the ministry when the great war boke out," he'd said. "They made me a lieutenant in the HLI, I thought it was our duty to fight for King and Country, I didn't want to be a padre. You know, I'd never mixed much with men before that. At first I thought they were terrible rough, the scum of the Glasgow slums, but I soon got to know them, not the way a minister knows people, no, not like that. And the more were killed the more I kept thinking, what has this English war got to do with us, English and Germans, I could hardly tell the difference, what had it to do with us, a lot of Scotsmen standing about in trenches full of water, our feet going gangrenous, rats as big as cats waiting to eat off your toes, a wee tot of rum before the whistle went? At first I kept praying to God to make me believe it was for civilisation, that's what they always tell you, no matter what war you're in or what side you're on. And I realised there was no God, we were only fighting for the rats, they were getting fatter and we were getting shot. Either the Bible was true and we were all God's people and the war was wrong, or the Bible was wrong and the English were right. But if we were shooting each other for the benefit for a shoal of French rats it didn't matter who was right, it was all wrong. The Jerries had ministers telling them the same things our ministers were telling us! I just lost the whole notion of God. I said to myself, if you ever get out of this, Archie Stewart, you're never going to have any more to do with them and their civilisation. I think it was all these wee men from Glasgow, men I wouldn't have hardly spoken to before, wee bowly legs from rickets and whatnot, hunger on their faces, even boys of eighteen. I kept asking in my prayers, what the hell has the King of England ever done for these wee men? Ship them out to France to feed a lot of rats? No, I came home and I left my family and I wandered the countryside till I found this place, the mines were spent by then, and I just built my wee house and here I'll stay."

Willie hadn't been in sympathy with this line at all, at that time.

"It wouldnae do if we all jaked it in and lived in a rubbish dump," he'd said. He was in a reserved occupation, nothing to be ashamed of it, just him and his father and mother and a mental defective to bring in the hearst, he was as much against Hitler as anyone else. Armies had to eat.

"It was Kaiser Bill in my day," the Tink had said. "He was a baby-eater as well. But I won't argue with you, I'm not interested. One day Scotland will wake up to itself, but I doubt it'll be after my time. You see that scheme over there, that's the civilisation the King gave all the wee men from Scotland. I'll tell you, I never go into the scheme, it makes me want to cry seeing the terrible old faces on the men and the children without shoes, I could cry in the street. A lot of wee men getting eaten by rats for that! I'll maybe believe in their civilisation the day I hear of God and the King of England sharing a two-apartment corporation house."

Willie had laughed then – and felt guilty at hearing such talk in wartime, he had heard tales of Scottish Nationalists being traitors who made secret broadcasts to Hitler and listened to Haw-Haw on the wireless. But over the years he'd come to accept Archie's views as just a part of him, like his curious cave. Although it would never do to tell the likes of Telfer or McCann that he came down here, he often wished he could come out in the open and tell them that Archie had a lot of brains. He never talked about football or told jokes about the Pope or even mentioned women, the most exciting thing in his life was the annual nesting of mavises under his roof, year after year the same thrushes coming back to the same place, living with Archie, only rising in a great chattering when strangers came near. These days Archie was more or less accepted and ignored, although there had been a time when the neds had come down to smash up him and his hut, just out of principle, the way they'd give a kicking to a man wearing a stiff collar, or a Celtic scarf. After they'd pulled the place apart Willie had expected Archie to be angry – or even scared – but there he'd been, calmly rebuilding his walls.

"No, no, it's my fault," he'd said. "They know I'm free and they aren't, it's only natural they resent me, I know how they feel. But someday, Willie, they'll wake up to the truth and then they can look out, they'll be kicking down the walls of Buckingham Palace."

Willie had never told Archie that he'd heard who these neds were from people he knew in the scheme and had given the wire to Big Watson, the bobby in those days, and that Big Watson had bided his time till he got them, one by one when there was nobody about, and that Big Watson had given all three of them a hammering, three hard neds walking into a big Aberdonian fist on dark nights, bang. Big Watson was dead now. He'd said the Tink was a looney, but harmless, like a child, needed protection. They didn't have bobbies like Big Watson nowadays.

"And how is the tea would you say, be honest now?" Archie asked him, as serious as if he was asking the price of corn.

"Fine," said Willie. It had neither milk nor sugar and didn't taste like tea at all, but he drank it.

"It's made out of dandelion leaves" Archie said, triumphantly, nodding across the fire-lit hut. "It's something the McGleishes told me about."

The McGleishes were real tinks, claimed to be descended from Charles Edward Stuart, a roving band who lived wild and mended pots. Since the scheme had grown they came less about the farm, preferring to stay over towards the Brig. The story about them was the day Sandy McNair, a farm-worker, had met Old Man McGleish on the road, the day after one of his daughters had married another tink. Old Man McGleish had said the couple were away on their honeymoon and Sandy, surprised, had asked where they'd gone. As far as the dam in Kilberrie Woods, McGleish had replied, quite serious. That was at least quarter of a mile away from the McGleish encampment in the Brig woods.

"We've got a new housekeeper," Willie said, knowing that Archie liked to hear about the farm's goings-on. "She's Irish, y'know, a gamey leg on her into the bargain."

"That's nice," said Archie. "And how's your father?"

"Oh, no bad, his back's hurtin' him."

"No wonder. It's amazing he still gets about, shows you the value of a good healthy life in the fresh air. I've watched him for forty years or more, a fine big man he was, too. Now he's like an old ghost walking the fields. I can imagine men like him on the moors when the Covenanters held their meetings, he's like the very granite. Wars will come and towns will spread and children will be brought up for slavery in the factories and kings will die and your father will go on, not giving a damn for any of it."

"Aye, maybe," Willie said. "He's a ghost that won't lie down."

They were both quiet, knowing that something had been said that should not have been said. Archie leaned back to throw some more anthracite on the fire, the glow shining through his fine grey hair, his head looking like a big egg covered in thin fuzz. There was something Willie wanted to talk about. Was Archie the man to discuss it with? Who else was there?

"Ehm, Archie, ye know how I've never got merriet?"

"Yes. A great pity, I always think – it's not for me, mind, but you'd like having a wife fine."

"Aye. Ye're mebbe right." He hesitated. Mother Craig had died when he was thirty-five, leaving him alone with Auld Craig; the old man had never been an easy man to talk to before but after that he'd kept himself very much to himself. It was difficult to come out in the open about things that affected yourself. "D'ye think I'm past the age for it?"

Archie Stewart knew, by the abruptness of the question, that Willie wanted serious words from a friend. He put his head to one side.

"How old are you, Willie, fifty-three is it?"

"And a year."

"Hmmm. Well, I would say it depended on what you wanted. Is it love, or children, or just a wife to keep your feet warm and darn your socks?"

Aye, Willie thought, what is it I want?

"I'm thinkin' mebbe I should get merriet."

"Well, at least you're a realist, Willie, just like your father. I remember saying to him when he sold those first thirty acres to the factory, what was it he got, twelve hundred an acre? I remember saying to him, you're a realist, Craig, it's a pity Scotland didn't have a few more dreamers and a few less realists."

Suddenly embarrassed, Willie decided to make a move.

"Aye, well, I don't know about that, I think I'm for away."

"I'd advise you to follow your heart and not your head, Willie. Life isn't all saving up cash to pay for a decent funeral."

"So ye say. Well, I'm off. So long."

"Bring your scissors next time, I'm needing a haircut now that we're into the New Year."

His face flushed with the direct heat of the brazier, Willie went off round the shale heaps, frosty air nipping hot razor-raw skin. He rode slowly round the back of the factory, seeing lights and machinery working through a gap in the big slide doors. Plenty of overtime, nightshifts and such capers, that suited them fine at the factory. They were welcome to it. Having the woman in the house had put him in the notion.

He hadn't intended to visit her, not after the old man saying he was going to give Coll the bag, but having the woman in the house had started him off and the heat of the brazier had done its work. He cycled about a mile round the back road.

The old miners' cottages stood in a single row, three or them empty and boarded up to keep out kids and tramps, old Mrs. Graham living in the fourth and the Colls in the fifth. When they left the cottages were to be demolished. Ayrshire County Health said they were unsuitable for habitation.

He got off the bike on the grass at the rear and wheeled it towards the back door of the end house. He laid the bike against the wall and had a peek through the curtained window. He listened, then he knocked on the back door. It opened, showing a small kitchen lit by a paraffin lamp.

"Come on in then," Morag Coll said, speaking her precise Highland tongue, "are you wanting the whole world to see you?"

She bolted the door behind him, a small, bustling woman of about forty, with brown hair going grey. She took off her apron as Willie sat in the high-legged wooden chair by the black range.

"Do you want a cup of tea?" she asked. "The bairns are all sound asleep."

"I hud one wi' the Tink," he said. "By God it's a chill one. Coll'll need his dram the nicht."

"Aye, but he hasn't got a lot of cash on him, he may be home early."

"We'd better no' waste ony time then."

She stood up and turned down the paraffin lamp, which stood on the mantelpiece above the range. She took a step towards him. He rose and began unbuttoning his flies. She got down on the smooth-worn carpet in front of the fire. He got down on one knee beside her, pulling at his long underpants. She pulled up her skirt and he came down on her, his full weight resting on her chest. He pushed himself up on his elbows to give his hand room to pull down her woollen knickers. Then he was into her, no bother, not after four years, he should know the road by now.

"You're desperate tonight," she murmured, her plump face warm against his shaven cheeks, her arms around his back.

"Hmmmph."

Had Archie never had a single woman all these years? Love or children? Mary O'Donnell, would she be a good ride, iron leg and whatnot? He came and immediately felt better. He let his fourteen stocky stones flop down on her, crushing her against the floor.

"I'm finished, ye auld hoor," he said, panting.

"You're flattening me," she said.

"I'm a ravishing scoundrel." His heavy body shook with laughter. He felt like rolling on his back and laughing out loud.

Then she was getting out from under him and he was on his knees, buttoning up his coms and his trouser flies.

"I'll away then," he said, giving her backside a heavy pinch. "Ye're an auld hoor, Morag Coll."

She slapped at his hand, then let him out of the back door, not turning up the lamp till it was closed. She put the black kettle on the range fire and sat down in the big chair to read the *Women's Pictorial*. What a pity Willie had never found himself a wife, poor man, for all their money she felt sorry for him and his father, not that Willie saw a lot of the money. What she let him do was wrong, sinful, but she always thought of him living in that dirty old house, all alone, a man of his age, poor Willie, it was the least a woman could do.

Outside Willie got on his bike and headed back along the road he'd come, making for the factory gatehouse where he'd have a cup of cocoa and a gab with the nightman. When Coll moved away he wouldn't have his Monday rides with Morag. Maybe Archie had lost the notion of it altogether. *He* hadn't, he knew that. And now there was a young hole under his own roof he might not need to stravaig about the countryside on dark nights looking for an old hag who'd lift her skirt on the kitchen floor.

CHAPTER FIVE

It was dark when Dunky pushed his bike through the gas-lit tunnel of the close, dark and frosty with stars so bright they seemed nearer than the lights of the town. The Logans lived in a smallish, three-storey tenement building which stood isolated on a stretch of rubble-strewn ground, Shuttle Place, gradually demolished as folk were moved into the new Darroch scheme. Already one of the ground-floor flats was empty, its windows boarded up by Corporation workmen to keep out tramps and drunks and kids. There was some big row going on about delays in extending the scheme and finally clearing Shuttle Place, something about government grants and rates. In the meantime fifteen families lived on in the last tenement, living in two rooms with shared landing lavatories.

His mother would be putting out the tea upstairs but he'd work to do first. He padlocked the chain through the back wheel and put the bike in the wash-house at the back of the tenement, taking the front lamp off the handlebar bracket. His rabbit hut stood across the broken concrete yard against the railway sleeper fence of the coal-yard at the back of the railway. It had been old Mister McAllister's pigeon loft. When he died his wife said Dunky could have it for rabbits. As he knelt to feel for the key on a cross-beam under the hut he glanced up at the rear windows of the block. If only he never had to go up there again. Lights behind curtains, coal fires, windows closed, cramped and hot, no room to move, no place you could hide away on your own, away from *him*. His father and mother and Senga in the bedroom, Senga's bed behind the curtain, his bed in the kitchen, no room to move. Maybe that's why he remembered having such a good time in the air-raid shelter during the war.

They didn't know he kept the key under the floor of the hut, in case it fell out of his pocket at the farm. He didn't want them poking about the rabbits when he was at work. For one thing his mother didn't know how many he now had. She was against him having rabbits at all – "just wasting your time when you should be at your homework" was what she'd always said. Against everything, she was. If she told his father the hut was fair packed he'd go wild and say they'd attract

71

rats. Funny, even Alec, his best pal, was against the rabbits, said they were only silly pets for wee boys. Sometimes he thought Alec was right, but once the door was locked nobody knew the silly things he said to the rabbits.

He climbed up inside and slipped the bolt behind him. He put the bicycle lamp on the tea-chest so that it shone along the netting fronts of the hutches. The light made the rabbits thump and scurry. The buck's eye shone red as it stared at him, head to one side.

"It's only me, me bonny beasties," he said. This was his place, his and his only. He'd built the hutches from old boxes and crates, some knocked from a joiner's yard, some from Laidlaw's vegetable shop. The door was shut behind him and he was the boss. Only he knew what went on in here. First he fed the nursing doe, a three-year-old bought from Findlay the big Chinchilla expert at Bridge of Kilmorchan, Findlay o' the Brig. He'd been three or four when a man called Murdoch or Murtagh or something like that had kept a few black and white rabbits at the back of the tenement. One day his daddy had taken him down to Murdoch or Murtagh's hutches and showed him a pair of young rabbits in an orange-box hutch.

"They're for you," his daddy had said. "Mister Murdoch says you can keep them here, but you've got to feed them and clean them out or he'll take them back."

Of course he'd been too young. And then one day, he went down to feed them and he saw what looked like wee mice lying about on the straw, one of them was bleeding. He'd run to tell his father, and then had to stand by and watch while Murdoch or Murtagh and his father pulled out the babies and put them in the bin, Murdoch saying the father rabbit always killed the wee ones if you didn't get him out quick enough. Imagine keeping a buck in with a litter! They'd said he couldn't have them after that, they were too much bother, he remembered crying.

He'd almost forgotten those rabbits (Murdock fed his on dandelion leaves, silly bastard, anybody knew dandelion was an emetic!) until one Saturday he'd gone with Alec on the train from Ayr to Glasgow, to see the Dairy Show and then Rangers and Hibs in the semi-final of the League Cup. They'd gone to Kelvinhall in the morning, sitting in the upstairs front compartment of a tramcar, out past the Art Galleries. They had proper rabbits at the Dairy Show and as soon as he saw them he thought of Murdoch and the dead babies. He'd hung about until a man started speaking to him and told him the different breeds. Chinchillas were the best, a sort of bluey-grey with thick fur, solid, sensible somehow. This man gave him a book with breeders' names and addresses and it was there he'd found out about Findlay, whose rabbits won championships. About that time old McAllister died and next thing he was building hutches (using the old man's tools) and going out, rather nervously, to Findlay's. Fifteen bob for a mated doe! He'd brought the money (eleven and six in his biscuit tin and the rest from selling his football pictures to boys in the class) the next Saturday and Findlay gave him the big doe in a cardboard box. By the time he'd walked over the braes from Findlay's small-holding, which was at the back of beyond, to the Brig bus stop the doe had wet the bottom of the box and fallen out on the grass. He'd carried her under his arm, the people staring at him in the bus, the scheme kids following him as he walked down from the High Street.

Now he had that doe and three other full-grown does kept from her first litter, plus the buck (also bought from Findlay, for eleven and sixpence) and two half-grown does kept from Doe One's last summer litter. He'd only been at it a couple of years, Findlay said he wasn't producing show standards yet, but he could take all the young ones he produced to Ayr (in his mother's leather shopping bag) to sell to the pet stores for half a crown each. Findlay (a funny sort of man who liked to make a bit of mystery about rabbits) said that if he bred one with the correct fur density and markings he would help him to show it. Proper feeding, that was it, hay for bulk, corn for nourishment, a pinch of wheat for fur-gloss, just enough cauliflower leaves for liquid, water only for nursing does. Dandelion leaves!

He fed them corn from National Dried Milk tins and hay from the tea-chest. On Sunday he'd clean them out, good dry manure (if you fed them right the droppings were like soft, dry marbles) which Laidlaw the vegetable man dug into his allotments. At least it gave him something to do on Sundays, when you weren't allowed to play football on the Corporation pitches, or even listen to the Light Programme on the wireless. Imagine not being allowed to listen to comedies because your mother thought they were sinful on the Sabbath. Stupid old Dickens's serials were all right though!

When they were all fed he opened the door of the old doe's

nesting compartment, while she munched corn from her thick clay Woolworth's dish, husks dribbling from her mouth. Placing his hand gently on the warm mound of downy white hair torn from her belly, he parted the nest and shone the lamp on the litter. They were the colour of a Gillette razor blade, blind little piggies with tiny furled ears and blunt snouts, fat little bodies already tinged with whitish hair. He moved them with his fingers, counting eleven. One was white-skinned, a throwback to the beginning of the Chinchilla breed when Angoras were crossed in to give the grey rabbits a thick coat. The whitey could go for a start. Four was plenty for a winter litter – Findlay didn't believe in winter litters at all, but the mating and counting the thirty-one days' gestation and watching the wee ones develop was the best part of it. It didn't do any harm, as long as she was fed right.

Two runts. They could go. The bucks were supposed to have square, blunt heads. He decided to keep one buck and three does. The other seven went into the cleaning-out pail. Before he'd left school he'd knocked two thick science books to use for breeding records, weight graphs and income and expenditure. You had to do it scientifically, grandfather and granddaughter but never brother and sister, grandmother and grandson, interbreeding the way they did with racehorses, to develop your own strain. It was something, Findlay said, you could only learn by years of experience, books were no good.

He shut the nesting compartment and took the pail to the far end of the hut. Once he had two or three does littering together he could kill all the poor ones and foster the remainder equally among the mothers, a delicate operation but nothing to a bright laddie with the right knack (and the knowledge that it's the smell that they notice, the secret being to rub your hands in the foster-mother's dirt pile before giving her the new babies).

"You see, you're all thinking this is cruelty," he said, out loud, thinking of his mother and the cripple woman and the girl friend he didn't have, "but it's just sensible stockmanship. Farmers can't afford all this sentimental blether, animals are only animals, these wee brutes don't even know they're alive yet. Women just don't understand what it's all about."

He knocked their heads on the rim of the pail, one at a time, their warm, delicate bodies giving one long last pull against his palm, then going limp as the life went out of them. When they were all growing cold he shoved them down among the dirty straw in the pail. Laidlaw might get a shock – if he found he was digging in a heap of wee corpses! By now old Charlie would be lubricating trains, no doubt.

Only once in his life had he killed something for the hell of it, he'd never forget it, a dirty brute of a tomcat that kept hanging about their landing, yowling for their she-cat to come out, he'd got sick of that tom, especially one day he was in the house himself, in the afternoon, doing homework, they must have been let out early from school, anyway, the bastarding tomcat was up on their landing, yowling like a demented creature, he'd been about twelve at the time, his father had a hammer which he used to cobble their shoes, he'd stood behind the door with the hammer and let the tomcat into the lobby, slamming the door behind it, grabbing it by the tail and thumping its nut with the hammer, it'd gone out after two hits, but it wasn't dead, so he'd taken it downstairs to the lavvy on the landing and locked himself in and shoved the dirty great brute down the seat, head first, holding its head under the water by the scruff of its neck, it'd come round and tried to scrabble backwards up the seat, he'd had to belt it again with the hammer and hold it under, Christ it'd taken *hours*. He must have been dead callous then, he couldn't do anything like that now. You had to have a good reason to kill – even wee blind rabbits.

Before he left he gave them all a small hunk of turnip, something to chew on, to stop the ever-growing teeth from coming out and round in a circle, back into their own brains.

"Right then, now for the happy home."

One day he'd have a big shed and keep enough Chinchillas to live off them, some for fur coats and gloves, some for showing, some for eating, some for selling to the young breeders who'd come around his place, aye, ye cannae dae better'n buy frae Logan, finest strain o' Chinchillas in Scotland. . . .

He had already taken the worst of the mud off his boots in the stable but at the door on the first-floor landing he dragged the studded soles across the scraper, metal rasping on metal, twisting his ankles to make sure the heels were free of dubs. He then took off his boots and stood in his stocking soles, perspiration-soaked feet leaving wet marks on the clean stone, until his mother answered his knock. He placed his boots at the bottom of the small cupboard inside the door. He could smell kippers. Much and all as his mother didn't like Papes she certainly stuck to fish on Fridays. He hung his jerkin on the hallstand, lifting off the cloth cap his father would probably never wear again.

"You've been messing about with those rabbits, haven't you?" his mother said, accusingly, as he went into the kitchen, a brightly-lit room with pale blue wallpaper and shiny linoleum, with a brown rug in front of the black-range fireplace. She was at the kitchen sink, her stout back towards him, her aprong strings tied tight into her green woollen cardigan, her brown skirt pulled up to show the backs of her knees, the way he always thought of her, bent over the sink, the back of a wet, red hand pushing away a loose strand of brown hair.

"Only for a wee while," he said, "we were late getting away."

They'd get a bigger house in the scheme but for some reason his mother thought Shuttle Place was decent and Darroch wasn't. They needed a bigger house. As it was you could hardly turn round in the kitchen for furniture, his bed in the alcove, his chest of drawers, the heavy, dark sideboard, the sewing machine, another chest of drawers, the sink, the sink drying-board, the gas cooker, the big armchair where his father used to sit with his feet on the range fender, the small armchair with square wooden arms and slots for magazines and papers (the *Kilcaddie Advertiser,* the *Daily Record*, the Church of Scotland *Life and Work,* the *Women's Pictorial,* Senga's *Girls' Crystal,* the couch, brown rexine with antimacassar squares. He sat on the couch and turned to the *Record* football pages. For all he knew that there wasn't much she could do to him (just let her *try* to belt him!) and *nothing* that his father could do, he was still a bit scared of her. When they were alone, which was as seldom as he could help, his voice became hoarse and reluctant, short, gruff half-sentences dragging themselves out through awkward lips.

"Put on your slippers and don't sit about the house in your socks," she said. "It isn't nice." Moving as slowly as he dared he pulled the worn cloth slippers from under the heavy sewing-machine pedal and pulled them over his thick, damp socks.

"Where's Senga?" he asked.

"She's away to Aunt Bessie's, she had to have her tea because you were messing about out there," his mother replied, always the threat of irritable anger – or even tears – in her voice. In the kitchen press they had a cardboard shoe box full of old family pictures and in some of them she was young (hair short and bobbed, wearing a leather coat) and smiling.

He'd hardly ever known her smile like that. Long ago he'd decided his father was a brute and that was why his mother was always snapping at him, but even now, when the old man was shut up in the bedroom, she was still the same. Not so much with Senga, though, just him. He didn't know why they hated him so much. Bobby Evans was back for Celtic, he read. He didn't care, either, they could hang themselves for all he cared, soon as he was over eighteen he was off out of it, away to England or even Canada, maybe go with Donald Telfer, two of them working on big wheat farms, moving about the country, doing what they wanted without being told off, picking up big women –

"Give me over the matches," she said, always the same, do this, don't do that, never give you a moment's peace in your own house, hated to see you sitting still for two seconds in case you were doing something *you* wanted to do, run about like a wee boy going for the messages. Blackie would have spat in the fire and said get the bastards yourself. He got up slowly and looked along the mantelpiece, the china dog bought in Oban on *their* honeymoon, a chiming clock always kept half an hour fast because *she* said it gave her extra time in the morning, a brass tea-caddy embossed with a stag, never used for tea but kept on the mantelpiece as an ornament, holding matches and Kirbigrips and elastic bands and a spare hairnet and a thimble and needles and three French coins brought home from the First War by Grandpa Aitchison. He took out the matches and held them towards her, careful not to go close enough for them to touch each other.

"I wish you'd come in for your tea at the proper time," she said, taking the matches, trying to fix him in the eyes. He looked at his feet and turned away.

"Any proper farmer feeds his beasts before he feeds himself," he said, his voice falling away, knowing that nothing he said would make any impression on her. One day he would just tell her to shut her gob and get the bloody tea on the table.

"Farmer, farmer," she hissed. "it's a disgrace, you and your schooling, we worked hard to get you into the Academy, now look at you, wasting your whole life in that dead-end job."

He stared at the picture of Bobby Evans, a burly guy, he wished he'd a chest like that.

"No more dead-end than getting your back broke in a stinking engineering shop," he said. That would shake her up a bit.

"You're selfish through and through," she said, eyes glaring, hands clenched at the side of her apron. He shrugged. "Wash your face and hands, your tea's ready."

About fuck'n time. Ignoring her closeness, her waiting face, he scrubbed his hands under the thin geyser flow, careful not to let dirty water splash onto the dishes drying on the zinc draining board, well-worn bristles not making much impression on the solid black dirt under his fingernails. Yet, he wanted to try to show her *he* didn't want to bicker all the time.

"I took the old horse to Cairney's the day," he said, sitting down to his kipper and fried potato slices and greasy rings of black pudding. "You shoulda seen the way they hacked him open, one minute he was standing there, the next his guts were all over the floor, fantastic to see it."

"That's horrible," she said, watching him begin to eat, then starting to dry the dishes. "You're not going out tonight I hope?"

"Aye, I'm meeting Alec at the Cross at seven."

Kippers, enough to give you dry boke. Telfer said his mother usually got in fish and chips from the mobile caravan that went round the scheme at nights, but his mother said bought fish and chips was only scruffs' food.

"Tsk, tsk, you've got no thought for anyone but yourself. You've been out this week already. Don't you ever think of your poor father lying in there day in day out?"

"Ach, all he wants to do is give me rows," he said, eating fast so that he could get out as soon as possible.

"Duncan, you've not to speak about your father like that," she snapped. Sometimes he found he had the courage to stare back at her, silently defying her to try and give him a belting. "You're not a man yet, you'll show proper respect. And another thing, you've started speaking very coarse, it's that farm, you should never have left the school to work there, it's that Donald Telfer or whatever he calls himself, you shouldn't be mixing with people like that, they're *common*."

This time he pretended to be very casual.

"Donald'n me are thinking of emigrating to Canada," he said, washing down the last of the kipper with a noisy swallow of tea.

"You'll do no such thing!"

Aye, hare away into the old man, see if he can do anything. It'd taken him a couple of years to realise that his father was a permanent invalid, completely helpless, no fear of a thrashing. And being out at work was giving him the right idea of how to talk to her.

"You've to go in and see your father," she announced, triumphantly, when she came back from the bedroom. Once that would have given him a dose of skitters in his pants, but now he felt the time was right to let her know things had changed.

"Why, is he going to give me my Saturday penny?" He looked at her coldly, trying not to let his face go red.

Beth Logan sensed that the boy might do something wild if she went on. She felt helpless. . . .

Beth Logan's father, Robert Aitchison, had been a grocer, well set up for himself in the north end of Kilcaddie, lucky to have the kind of business that didn't suffer too much from the slump, owner of his own three-apartment house in the sort of good-class tenement where even the ground-floor close was always spotless and no wee boys chalked filth and no drunks wet the walls. Beth, his second girl, had gone to the Academy, Kilcaddie's best school, where parents had to pay fees of a guinea a quarter. The Aitchisons were furious when Beth started walking out with Duncan Logan, a boilermaker's apprentice, one of the black gang, they wanted her to marry somebody decent, like Norrie Spence who was in the Burgh Factor's office and who was sure of getting on in life.

They agreed to the wedding in the end only because Mrs. Aitchison thought her daughter's continual state of depression must be due to pregnancy (they could never have spoken of such things out loud so Mrs. Aitchison never found out that, far from being pregnant, Beth's depression was caused by Duncan's continual attempts to get her to let him go too far). After the wedding, at which Duncan's Uncle Archie had got drunk and sung dirty songs, thus ensuring that the two families never met again, she'd found herself living in a single-end, one room with a shared outside lavatory, in Garrashiel Road, the very *lowest* part of Kilcaddie. And Duncan had turned out for the worst, especially after wee Duncan was born and the doctor said she shouldn't have another child for at least three years, even knowing that he was still *incessant* in his demands and she'd found she hated *that* part of it, it was so horrible and disgusting, and after Senga was born, in nineteen-forty, she'd told him she wasn't going to do it, not ever again, and he'd tried to *force* her, in her own bed, it made her sick.

After a while he'd realised she wasn't ever going to let him do it to her again and he'd left her alone, but somehow he'd taken a dislike to wee Duncan, she loved the boy like a proper mother, of course, but as he grew up she'd seen his father coming out in him all over again, the same coarseness, the same nastiness (when he was only three and a half he'd come into the kitchen and smiled and said to her, "Thepopesacunt, mammy", just as the workmen building the Darroch scheme had coached him to say).

And now, with Duncan stuck to his bed, with only the insurance and the interest on the compensation coming in, she was as poor as ever again and wee Duncan sounded more and more like his father, so much that at times she had to make herself remember it was her son and not her husband sitting across the kitchen table. Once, in her whole life, she'd been at a posh hotel, in Girvan, for the Fair Week. All her life she'd remembered that hotel, the clean tablecloths, the big bedrooms, cotton sheets that were stiff and white and cool, the waitresses taking away the dirty dishes, the soft carpets. For years she'd hoped that one day, when the children were older, they'd all go to a hotel for a holiday. Now they never would. . . .

"You're not natural," she sobbed. He shrugged, not knowing what to do. He felt helpless.

Standing with his back to her, Dunky changed into his clean socks (white, like Telfer's), black shoes, grey flannels (pegtopped, like the Ayr ice-hockey players'), brown shirt, no tie, light grey sports jacket (no pocket flaps, wide shoulder pads), throwing his farm clothes under the bed, careful not to let her see his prick, feeling guilty at having one at all when she was in the same room. At the sink he rubbed Brylcreem and water into his dark hair and combed it straight back, making a little wave at the front by pressing it with the palm of his right hand. He wished Senga hadn't gone out so early, it was always easier when she was there, her and her mother chattered away and he could pretend he didn't exist.

"All least you can say cheerio to your father," she said, now the hard-done-by mother.

"All right," he said. Funny how in the pictures you often saw kids give their mothers a kiss or a hug. He could no more have done that than shagged a horse.

Through the closed bedroom door he heard Jimmy Shand

and his band on the Scottish country dancing programme. Too bad they couldn't have the wireless in the kitchen so that everybody could hear it. Hands stuck down in his trouser pockets he went into the bedroom. It, too, was crammed with old, dark furniture. He could hardly bear to look at his father, whose head was propped up on two pillows, arms resting on the quilt, his face pale and slack after three years in bed. The room, to him, meant the smell of his father, a big man's smell, hot pyjamas and sweatiness, the gruesome thought of his father and mother doing it in bed together.

"Hullo," he said. He'd never called him Father or Daddy, not since he was too young to know they hated each other. He stood by the door, ready to escape. "How're you feeling?"

He couldn't bear it, the smell, the look, the bed-clothes, the unnaturally clean hands, the eyes that seemed to be saying he was doing something wrong – as usual.

"Oh, jist marvellous," his father replied. "Ah've got the wireless and the *Advertiser*, whut more does a man want?"

IT'S NOT MY FUCK'N FAULT, IS IT?

"Whut's this aboot Canada?"

Dunky looked at his shoes, fists clenched in his pockets. Other people had bad things happen to them, didn't they, without making a profession out of it, like the limpy dan housekeeper? If *she'd* been his mother she'd have known that working men shouldn't be nagged at all the time like wee boys.

"Ach, I was just joking," he said.

"Hmph. Funny kind o' jokes. Your mother's got enough to put up wi'. An' I suppose you're away oot, eh, away enjoyin' yersel? God almighty, ye don't know the meanin' o' anythin'."

Jimmy Shand in strict tempo, the best of the Scottish country bands, playing away regardless of what they were saying, somebody said the Y.M.C.A. had tried to book him for a big dance at the Town Hall and his asking price for the one night was four hundred pounds!

"Aye well, I've got to meet Alec at the Cross at seven. I'm late already, I'd better be going."

His father raised his head an inch or two from his pillows, one of the few movements he could make.

"Jist because ye're playin' aboot at bein' a workin' man disnae mean ye can dae whut ye like," he said, his voice raised as though he wanted to let her in on the act,

"Cheerio."

81

It didn't matter if the old man did bawl after him, there was nothing he could do.

Did everybody hate their own father?

The first two scheme buses roared past the stop, packed to the door with Monday-night jiggers and boozers and winchers from the scheme desperate to enjoy themselves after a grim Sunday shut in their houses. He decided to walk, although he was ten minutes late already. Alec would wait. Although it was the long way round he usually went up Brediland Street partly because it had more people, partly so that he could pass the school, now dark and quiet, thinking of it as an actual person who would see him pass by, a gallus lad, hello Patsy Fagin, a dacent working boy, a working man, stick your rotten old school, I'm free of you now. He walked on the outside of his heels, toes turned inwards to give him a shorter, faster stride, like the professionals. Once when he'd been only eight or nine they'd gone to Kilmarnock to see Dundee and after the match they'd waited outside the stand to see the players leave. Dundee had just bought Billy Steel back from Derby County in England, the blond and dynamic Steel who'd formed one of Scotland's greatest inside-forward partnerships with wee Jimmy Mason of Third Lanark. Steel had walked like that. Although he actually modelled himself on Bobby Evans, the Celtic right-half, he often imagined he was Billy Steel, jinking up the pavement, dodging imaginary defenders, carving in on the English goal, hard as nails, beating tackle after tackle, small and blond and deadly ... when he reached the brighter pavements of the High Street he quickened his walk and put his hands back in his pockets, guilty at having such secret notions. ...

Duncan Logan lay back, panting, staring at the wall. In the name of God what was wrong with the boy? God? Would a proper God let a man rot his life away in bed, helpless, finished at forty-one? He'd be better off dead, but there was no way he could even kill himself. Why did it have to be *him*?

At times he would wake up from a dream – nearly always a dream in which he and Beth were running to catch the boat at Millport Pier, in the sunshine – and for a moment or two he wouldn't remember what had happened to him. It was worst then, suddenly realising that his body was a half-dead thing lying between the blankets. He'd lie in the dark, while she slept beside him, happy no doubt that he was incapable of anything towards her, and think back to that day at Millport, they sat on the Crocodile Rock and took a pony-cart round the island, and bought ice-cream and watched the boys fishing off the pier and followed the black backs of the porpoises and paddled, with his trousers rolled up.

Other people still did that. But he didn't kid himself, they'd only gone to Millport once and then there never was time or money, always the baby to look after, the illnesses after the babies, the – oh Christ, his life had been a right ruination from the start.

No, there was nothing left for him here, a son who treated him like dirt, a wife who was just as happy to have him helpless on his back, a daughter who'd soon be wanting to be out every night. He was just a burden to them and to himself.

That's what Doctor Barr had said to him, a month or two before.

"Really you'd be much better off in Killearn, Mister Logan," Barr had said. "You'd be in a big ward with other men, lots of company, and your wife would have things a lot easier, think about it, they're doing marvels at Killearn these days, they wouldn't take you if they didn't think they could do something for you, it's a hospital not a home. . . ."

These walls were driving him mad. Just suppose they did find a way of treating his spinal cord, oh God Almighty, take pity on me, for the love of Jesus Christ . . . when the sobbing started he was unable to control it and he turned his face into the pillow so that she wouldn't see the tears when she came in with his cocoa. . . .

Up the town, that's what you said, I'm going up the town, up the town, see the people, eye the talent. Poor bastard, *he* would never get up the town again. Did *he* ever eye the talent, when *he* was a young bloke? Maybe his mother had been talent? No, never, not her, it must have been different with them, parents were different, everything they did was – *official,* sort of. In all his life he could remember only one time when his father had really seemed to like him, one Ne'erday, Uncle Roddy was alive then and the three of them had gone to Ibrox to see Rangers and Celtic, the two men laughing when his mother said it was too dangerous for a boy, Uncle Roddy saying the bottle-throwing was only newspaper exaggeration. Uncle Roddy had a flat bottle of whisky, it smelled awful on their breaths, they'd stood at the Copeland Road end, the two of them lifting him onto the crush barrier, Uncle Roddy shouting back at two Celtic supporters, very nasty Glasgow scruffs they were, they seemed to suit what he saw of Glasgow above the shoulders of the crowd, the big shipyard cranes standing high above the docks, the bottles that were thrown onto the pitch, flying out from the packed terracings like black crows coming down on a field, him terrified in case they'd be hit.

At night they played *Monopoly* (which Uncle Roddy had brought for the big family gathering) on the kitchen table, he'd been too young to know what it was all about but Uncle Roddy had shown him what to do and when he'd bankrupted Aunt Jennie with his two hotels on Park Lane, Uncle Roddy had shouted out, "The boy's got the makings of a capitalist."

His father had smiled at him.

But his eyes were funny from drinking whisky, he remembered that all right. Pity the bastard hadn't got drunk more often. Jesus Christ, why in the name of hell did *he* have to have a father who lay on his back, paralysed, and looked at *him* and made him feel *he'd* done something wrong?

Alec was standing at the War Memorial, skinny and daft-looking in his big padded overcoat. His father had never liked Alec. He said he was a typical young spineless idiot, because he wore casual shoes with brass chains across the uppers.

"Hey," said Alec, hands in his coat pockets (one thing about working on a farm, you got hardened to the cold), "fancy going to a big Communist Party meeting in the Co-op Hall?"

The Cross always seemed exciting, plenty of talent about, always the chance of getting chatting to a big piece of stuff and making dates, but for some reason Alec was always wanting to go to political meetings and things instead of getting into the cafés and dances where there was a chance of a decent lumber.

"You thinking of becoming a Communist, eh?" he said.

"I would if I knew what it really meant," said Alec. "My father says they're the only party with guts."

Alec had been in his class in the first and second senior years before he was kept back for being dead slow. Now he was an apprentice quantity surveyor, his father had made him go into that although Alec wanted to be a printer ("You can easily get a bigtime job on one of the Glasgow papers"). He shaved every day, to make his hairless chin develop a thick stubble, he said, although Dunky thought it was really because of his spots. He was a good enough guy for a pal, even if he was a bit naïve and stupid.

"Ach, come on," he pleaded, "it's only for an hour, then we can go to the Eldorado and chat up some bigtime wimmin."

They went over the Cross and up Fergus Street. Dunky saw a big gallus-looking guy with his arm round a girl's waist. That's what he wanted to be, bigtime, gallus, a hard case. He wished he was older. Funny, he could still remember the very first Americans coming to Kilcaddie, soldiers, they walked about holding girls' hands openly, never seen in the town before, a disgrace, his mother said, the way scruff girls made an exhibition of themselves in public chasing Americans. When he got a steady he'd maybe just hold her hand in the street, but none of this smooching nonsense. Alec was going on about the men who worked on building sites.

"Ignorance isn't in it," he said. "All they want is a fag and the sports pages, they don't even read the real news. I thought they'd all be red-hot socialists and commies and bigtime political guys, but all they're interested in's the football and the racing. They don't even care if it's Labour or the Tories, imagine that!"

To Alec things were either bigtime or dead rotten. Lumbers were bigtime but girls who wouldn't let you see them home were dead rotten. Going to the pictures in Ayr was bigtime, much more bigtime than Kilcaddie's three cinemas. Owning a car was real bigtime.

They climbed two flights of stairs. There was a table at the entrance to the hall. The man behind it said it was sixpence to go in. Dunky wanted to turn away – sixpence got you a coffee in the Eldorado and for that you could sit for an hour – but Alec gave the man the money.

"The Communists have got to charge," he whispered as they eased onto a bench at the back of the hall. "They're all poor people, everybody's against them."

Alec thought it was exciting and dangerous to be there, but it seemed more like school, with men instead of kids. Fancy grown men sitting through a boring meeting when they could be out enjoying themselves! His mother would have a fit if she knew. Communists – they looked more like a round-up of all the saddest men in Kilcaddie, sitting dreary-like in a draughty hall on a Monday night when anybody with any sense was giving the patter to some big piece of stuff. Alec was rattling on about what his father had told him about Karl Marx. He

85

always called himself a true Communist, nothing to do with Russia. It was just another silly notion he'd picked up from his father and his two brothers, who were Communist daft.

"Hey, don't look now but d'you see who's sitting over there," Dunky said, surprise in his voice at seeing Nicol, the English and History master, sitting by himself, four rows in front of them at the other side of the hall. Alec looked the way he always did when you told him not to look, straining round, gawking with his mouth open.

"It's Nicky," Alec said, "I bet nobody at the school knows he's a bigtime Communist."

"He doesn't look very bigtime to me," Dunky sneered. Nicol was an untidy man in a dark blue suit, his hair parted in the middle, too long at the back. He'd been in the Tank Corps in the army, an officer or something, he never talked about it much. Dunky had thought he was quite a decent guy for a teacher until one day in Free Discussion (Nicol had started them on Current Affairs and other subjects the older masters never bothered with) they'd had a debate on the Welfare State. Billy Aird had stood up and said the unemployed men who went to the burroo were just lazy. Dunky had already been working at Craig's farm in the holidays, he thought that Billy Aird was against working guys, his father being a cop.

"It's all right for a schoolboy who's never done a day's work to lay down the law about the unemployed," he'd said, catching Nicol's eye when Billy Aird sat down. "Especially when your father's been in the fortunate position of never being out of work in his life. If Fatty Aird had to live in the Darroch scheme he'd soon change his tune, he's got no business criticising people he doesn't know anything about."

Nicol had stopped the discussion to use his speech as an illustration of the *ad hominem* argument, which they knew from Latin. Dunky resented being the object of the lecture and he'd never said another word in Nicol's Free Discussion period. It was typical of school, a lot of baloney.

A man stood up behind the trestle table on the platform and welcomed them to the meeting and then read out a list of future meetings. Dunky kept looking along at Nicol, but there was no particular expression on the teacher's face.

"... and now here is our speaker for this evening. Comrade MacLean, whose long career in the socialist movement is well known to us all. ..."

MacLean was *the* local Communist. His name was always

in the *Kilcaddie Advertiser* in connection with some row or another. His father always called him a dirty red traitor who should be sent packing to Russia if he liked the place so much. He was an old man with red cheeks and white hair. He turned out to be quite funny at first, which surprised Dunky, who'd always thought of Communists as being nasty men, all bitter and anti-British. MacLean made jokes about the Labour Party and about Attlee, calling him Major Attlee, which Dunky didn't understand.

"... and so we had the ludicrous position that a so-called working-class party gave the boss class cheap coal, cheap rail-ways and cheap steel and put their welfare responsibilities onto the state – in fact they made British capitalism work, something the Tories have never been able to do. Believe me, comrades, capitalism could have been sunk without trace in 1945. That's what the people voted for, wasn't it? And what did we get? Major Attlee and Ernest Bevin! Were they any better than what we've got now – Crofter Macmillan and Mister Butler? Would you rather be told to eat snoek or over-ripe pheasant?"

Everybody laughed. Dunky noted, however, that Nicol kept a straight face.

"We have no quarrel with the rank and file of the Labour Party," MacLean went on. "But we have to understand that the socialist movement cannot be allowed to remain in the hands of quislings and traitors. . . ."

The main part of his speech followed. MacLean had just come back from a tour of Australia. He told the audience that the emigration scheme was not much better than the German slave-labour system. He said he'd seen with his own eyes the forced work camps ("No, they don't actually have dogs but they do have wire fences") into which the ten-pound emigrants were driven when they reached Australia. He said there was no housing and few good jobs. Dunky thought it was a lot of rubbish. Alec whispered that this was the benefit of coming to Communist meetings, you heard things the capitalist press wouldn't let you know about. Dunky wished he knew more about politics. They'd only reached the Char-tists when he left school. MacLean mentioned Ramsay Mac-Donald, saying he was the man who taught Attlee how to betray the working class. This got a big handclap. Funny enough, his father had also once said that Ramsay McDonald was a traitor, but his father had said all politicians were crooks. History was interesting – as long as it didn't have anything to do with school.

Then there was a question period. To their surprise Nicol was first on his feet, his hands in his pockets, his scruffy head slightly to one side, the way it used to be in class.

"I would like to ask the speaker for his views on the preservation of Scottish culture," he began, his voice dry and sarcastic, like all schoolteachers. "If the Communist Party were to get into power what would their policy be towards the disappearing language and history and literature of Scotland?"

MacLean said that was a very good question. As everybody knew he was a staunch Scotsman and on his many trips to Moscow he'd always been more than welcome as a fellow-countryman of Rabbie Burns. Rabbie was favourite in Russia. In a socialistic society the preservation of folk cultures was of prime importance. This didn't mean the feudalistic, nationalistic and Catholic-fascist attempts by the Irish government to force a dead language on its people – that was a cold-blooded manoeuvre by Catholic land-owning interests to keep the working class of Ireland in ignorance and economic slavery. No, it wasn't to be like that, but whatever it was it would be good for Scotland. The audience murmured "Hear hear."

Nicol got to his feet again.

"Mister MacLean has made a great deal out of his belief that Scotland always has and still is being milked dry by English capitalists," he said, as sarcastic as ever. "To my mind this Scottish patriotism of his is a particularly hypocritical form of chauvinism, for all we know how much independence Scotland would have under a Communist central dictatorship based on London – less, I imagine, than Mister MacLean's puppet-masters in Moscow allowed independent Hungary –"

Nicol went on trying to speak above a growing noise from the men in the hall. The chairman rose to his feet and said he couldn't allow provocateurs to disrupt the meeting with attacks on the speaker. Nicol kept on.

"You're using patriotism to kid these people into being Communists and when you get power you'll shoot them for wanting to be Scots," he shouted. Then, as the uproar grew again, he walked down the gangway and out of the hall. MacLean said something to the chairman, who waved his arms for order. The meeting ended. As Dunky and Alec came to the head of the stairs they saw Nicol face to face with a man who was shouting at him. Dunky thought there was going to be a fight. As long as they weren't involved he couldn't care less, Nicol was old enough to know better. He managed to get Alec past the two men without Nicol seeing them, Alec, of course, wanting to get into the act. Bigtime. They were on the first floor landing when Nicol overtook them.

"Ah, Mathie and Logan, the two working men," he said, his stubby face slightly red but otherwise sounding just as if he was in the classroom. "Without actually seeming to run I should advise you to make haste, the mob seems thirsty for blood."

They followed him down the stairs. He always spoke like that, Dunky thought, you could never tell what he really meant, even when he told you education was necessary for getting on in life you had the feeling he was being sarcastic about people who did get on in life. Schoolteachers were all namby pamby. Alec winked at him. Bigtime, escaping with a real teacher from a commie riot! Dunky looked down at Nicol's untidy hair and stooped shoulders. Shovel shite for a day and he'd break his back.

Alec fell into step with the teacher as they went down Fergus Street to the Cross. It was five to nine on the Town Hall clock. There was a cold breeze. The street was almost empty. Most people would be in the pictures or at the dancing or in cafés.

"Well, I trust you enjoyed the free flow of debate in a Communist ambience," Nicol said, looking sideways at the two boys. For a man who'd shouted so much about Scotland he had a very English-sounding accent, Dunky thought. That was another thing, all teachers were snobs. "Are you two interested in Communism?"

Dunky wouldn't have replied at all, but Alec couldn't hold his water.

"Eh, we just go to meetings, sir," he said. "It's very interesting to hear different speakers and so forth."

"Aye, an' it's cheaper'n the pictures," growled Dunky, looking straight ahead. Alec trying to suck up to a teacher was enough to make you sick.

"That's my Logan," said Nicol, "always the realist. And how are you enjoying your career in agriculture, eh?"

Nicol had given him a talk about staying on at school. Dunky was, at first, sneakingly pleased the man remembered him at all, but then he felt annoyed at even caring what a teacher thought.

"You don't get the belt from a lot of silly old women," he said. Half of him was still frightened, he hadn't been out of school all that long and Nicol was still a figure of authority. But he was determined not to suck up to him. What did he care about schoolteachers any more?

"Spoken like a man with a thousand chips on his shoulder," Nicol said. He allowed himself a thin laugh. Bitter and twisted, that's what he sounded like. No wonder, if you had to wear an attached collar and a stiff suit all the time.

"Are you a Scottish Nationalist, sir?" Alec asked. Dunky could have kicked him on the ankle. Sir!

"I believe we're being swamped by cheap commercialism and public ignorance," Nicol replied. "Scotland was the first nation in Europe to have a proper system of mass education, never forget that. This used to be one of the leading countries in European culture. But here we are at Kilcaddie Cross, gateway to the new darkness. Don't look so browned-off, Logan, it's not a complete social disgrace to be seen with a schoolteacher, not yet anyway."

Christ, how did he know that's what he'd been thinking? Maybe his face wouldn't show red under the street lights. Nicol smiled briefly and went on his way, one shoulder slightly higher than the other, unworkmanlike shoulders. Thin and sarcastic, dry skin and dry hair.

"Come on to the Eldorado," he said to Alec. "Thank Christ we're out of school."

"He's not a bad bloke when you get to know him, isn't he?" said Alec.

"Hrrmmph." Real men didn't suck up to schoolteachers. Was Nicol always like that, even when he was a wee boy? All right, so he had brains and compared to him guys like Telfer and McCann and Coll were ignorant morons – but what good did his brains do him? Fine for lording over kids in the school, but outside he looked frightened, as though he knew he wasn't a real man. Still, he'd nerve, to get up like that at the commie meeting. Maybe it was because a meeting wasn't all that much different from the classroom, it was *safe* to speak your mind. Education was something you went in for if you weren't good at anything else – guys who played football well never bothered with school much, guys who could get off with women easily never came top of the class. Who did? The swots – and everybody knew that swots were always hopeless with women or football, or anything but their lessons. It wasn't

90

quite the same with girls, in his class the four or five smashers all got good marks at exams. But it was different for girls – education suited them, they'd nothing else to do with themselves anyway.

In the *Wizard* and the *Adventure* and the *Rover* comics he'd never liked school stories – they were all about English boarding schools where they played cricket and went to tuckshops. In the best film he'd ever seen, *The Naked City*, the detective walked about the New York slums looking for a killer and he'd decided then he wanted a job where he worked outside. In fact, for a while he and Alec were going to be either plain-clothes detectives or film directors after seeing *The Naked City*!

The Eldorado was crowded and they had to stand by the counter until they got two seats. On the jukebox it was mostly Johnnie Ray (girls), Nat King Cole (boys) and Tennessee Ernie's *Shotgun Boogie* (hard cases).

"Not much talent about," said Alec.

"How about that piece with the red coat?"

"Nah, rotten body."

"How d'you know?"

"You can tell. Hey get a load of the new waitress, hubba hubba."

She reminded him of the very first time he remembered noticing a woman's legs. It was on a scheme bus during the war. At that time nylons were scarce and some women used to dye their legs orange to look like stockings. The conductress had thick legs and he'd suddenly found himself wanting to lick the dye off.

Ian Nicol let himself into his four-apartment flat in the row of three-storey buildings (tenements in all but name, this part of the town being for respectable folk) in Polson Street, on the east side of the town.

"Is that you, Ian?" his wife called from the living room. He hung up his coat and jacket and went in, waistcoat over striped shirt. "You look frozen," she said, getting up from the armchair. "Sit there by the fire while I make some tea."

"Thanks, Bobs," he said, kissing the side of her head as she passed. He had a nervous habit of rubbing his hands together, only he didn't quite understand why he should be nervous now. Logan had upset something inside him, Logan in a dark shirt and sports jacket, hard-faced and tough, only out of school a matter of weeks and already changed. He looked at the open book on the fireside stool. Poor Roberta, she was becoming addicted to Francis Brett Young. He looked at himself in the concave mirror above the fire. The thin, contracted face, the lifeless hair, the stiff collar, the narrow shoulders, no, it was no wonder the Logans didn't find their hero figures in the classroom. He sat opposite Roberta while she poured tea.

"I met two of my former pupils at the meeting," he said, the tip of his tongue slightly stiff, as though a dentist's injection was just wearing off. "Remember I told you about Logan, the one who went to work on the farm? God, when I think of that boy I want to kick something."

"Was he the one who was awfully good at English?" she said.

"Yes, remember I brought home his composition on Kilcaddie? You should've seen him, like a Hollywood gangster, hard as nails, I didn't know whether to laugh or cry, you know, brown shirt and lots of Brylcreem."

"Don't let it upset you," she said. "You can't work miracles for them all."

When he'd met Roberta – at a summer course in the big house at Abington in Lanarkshire – she'd been what he always thought of as the typical Edinburgh girl student, bright eyes and short hair and a conscious determination not to sound like the narrow-minded little Edinburgh *Hausfrau* that she was so obviously destined to become, taking a teacher's course because even a *Hausfrau*-to-be had to go through a respectable interim of outside activity until Mister Right came along and gave her the keys to her own kingdom.

"I wish I'd never seen a blackboard," he said. It was true. Chalky hands, bleary eyes, beginning of a stoop, the studied sneer and, if that failed, the belt; parents who drove their children on *not* for the sake of educating them, oh no, that was the very last thing they cared about, no, to be able to show off their children's exam marks to other parents, like a new fur coat, the parental rat-race. Boys who thought of school as a punishment. A whole system of education designed to cater for the parental pride league.

"Oh, Ian, don't let it depress you so much," Roberta said. "You're already a senior master, it won't be long before you're made a head, then you can bring in some of your own ideas."

Well, *was* he a man? Were the boys right, were you just

92

the same as the spinster teachers who drank tea through pursed lips and complained about parents who didn't know how to bring up well-behaved children? He wanted to talk to Roberta, honestly for once. She understood him, or so she always said, she encouraged him to go to meetings, to read as much as he wanted, never complaining when he brought home a case full of exercise books to be corrected ... yet he was discontented, that part was only a small bit of him. She'd decided, however, it was all of him. She never seemed to realise that there might be more, a part of him that wanted to wear dark shirts and get out among the other kind of people. God, it was as well she didn't know all of him, least of all about the thoughts he often had about some of the older girls. That would test her powers of understanding. He half-listened to her description of Francis Brett Young's description of the Black Country.

"Bobs, there's something I –" he looked down at the thin china cup (tea-set wedding present from her Uncle Trevor, cold-nosed Edinburgh solicitor), "I want to ask you something." Better to get it out all at once. Learn to take the twist out of your sentences. "Would you say I really satisfy you, *sexually*?"

I mean, how can I? Once a week, if that, generally on a Saturday evening? Be honest with yourself, man, what you're trying to say is – she doesn't satisfy you, sexually.

"Oh, you *are* in a bad way." She smiled. He knew damn well she was putting on what, in her terminology, was a "roguish" look. Still a bit naughty, to talk about sex with a man, out loud, even if he was your own husband. White breasts, long rather than full, fuzz of black hairs on her forearms. Oh yes, he knew everything about her, everything that was decent for a mere husband to know. Yet, maybe deep down, there might be something different. Some deeply-concealed desire to let *something* loose.

"No, I'm serious, I mean, you could hardly describe my lust as insatiable, could you?"

Still the same defensive sneer at himself. Too much time spent with children.

"Oh, Ian, you're being silly, you're a perfect husband, you ought to know that."

"No children, though."

"They'll come. You let the school worry you too much, that's all. That's why I fell in love with you, you were so angry

93

about things and so serious, all the girls at that course were bonkers about you, the way you stood up and told that old gasbag from the Education Department that he was turning Scottish education into an apprenticeship for mindless robots."

"Ah yes, my moment of heroism."

In bed, her arms pulling his head close to her cotton-covered breasts, he made a conscious effort not to pursue a line of thought which led to the conclusion that he despised a woman who could be so fixated on a shrivelled apology for man like himself. He started telling her what was wrong with everything about his work, he wasn't a teacher, he was stage one in the disciplinary process, knocking them into shape, a sergeant-major, belting them into memorising mere facts, into behaving themselves, above all into keeping quiet. Facts they didn't understand and would forget immediately exams were over, closing their minds instead of opening them.

"I pity Logan and envy him at the same time," he said. "I know his life's being wasted but he doesn't, he'll just sail along, sex, booze and football, thinking he's having a great time. Next year or the year after it'll be the pub. If they thought the teacher was a real man, like a footballer or an ice-hockey player, they might listen, that's the whole rotten thing about it, they *despise* us. And in ten years time I'll be just like our beloved headmaster, dry as dust, not caring a damn about them as long as they keep quiet and pass their exams. The swots plough on towards their decent little jobs, and the dead-heads fall by the wayside and the one or two who might have a spark of something different see the whole thing is a fraud."

"You're an idealist," she said, pressing her mouth on his forehead. God, make her do *something* she couldn't tell her mother about. He made love with his eyes closed, knowing that he was only using her body as a masturbatory substitute for heavy-chested girls in white blouses, ripe girls with bottoms that strained against pleated hockey skirts and full, bare calves.

"There, darling, that was lovely, wasn't it?"

He held her tightly, as though to make up for everything. At least it was a lie that made *her* happy. . . .

Dunky left Alec at the Cross, after standing there for twenty minutes or so, when it became obvious that it was another night when they weren't going to get a lumber. Two girls they

94

knew had come into the Eldorado, but they'd sat at another table. What the hell, only four days to Saturday, pay-day, the game against Glenryan Juveniles and at night a dance in the canteen at the Blackinch chemical factory. Football was the best. Not having to play in the mornings for the school team was a help, work didn't take it out of him as much as a match. He'd a secret idea that Baldy Campbell, the big boss of Cartneuk's four teams, might give him a trial in the first eleven, most of whom were seventeen. That would be fantastic. Cartneuk was famous in the West of Scotland, lots of their players had trials with big clubs, scouts watched them all the time. They said Baldy got so much money from English clubs he didn't have to work at all, just collect his divvy for every boy who signed professional. Who needed women if that happened?

At the top of Brediland Street there was a small gang being turfed out of the fish and chippers, a right load of scheme neds and hairies. He crossed the street lower down, it was easy to get mixed up with drunken blokes. In a dark close entrance two men tottered together, one pulling a bottle from the other, knees ready to buckle at any minute. Drunks were insane, anybody knew that. Yet ... well, everything else his mother was dead against seemed to be enjoyable, so maybe drink was the same. The old man had only been really nice to him once — and that was because of drink. But drinking was poison if you played football.

Ahead, on the straight stretch of road past McCracken's coal yard he saw three girls walking arm in arm. He always felt embarrassed, passing girls at night. Kilcaddie people had a habit of turning round to see who was coming up behind them — with good reason at this time of night when gangs of neds roved the streets looking for fights. And girls from the scheme could have very coarse tongues, especially if they knew you weren't one of their mob. He walked as quickly as he could, whistling to let them know he was harmless. Be a hard man. Ignore them. Pretend you're deep in thought about serious matters. They were only girls who didn't have their own blokes.

"Well, hell-o there," said one as he came abreast. He went on whistling, looking straight ahead, pretending not to hear. They giggled.

"All alone then, handsome?" More giggling. He kept on, hands sweaty in his pockets. They were just hairies. Ignore them.

"Here, it's that fella from Craig's farm," he heard another one say. "All high and mighty then, pal?"

"Get lost," he said, half-turning his head.

"Ach, come on, pal, how don't you give us a bit o' your patter well?"

He walked on, trying not to make it obvious that he was quickening his step.

Then, what you always dreaded, the sound of someone running towards you from the back. If it had been blokes he would have run, straight away. He looked over his shoulder. A dark-haired girl, her pink coat flying out at her sides, was almost beside him. Brazen, that's what his mother called scheme girls. Watch your step with they hairies, McCann always said, they've all got big coal-heavers for brothers, they'll turn vicious as quick as look at you.

The girl was laughing. She got hold of his right arm with both hands, looking at him with a silly grin on her face, slightly breathless. So was he!

"Don't kid on you don't know me," she said. "I saw you looking at me when we were howking."

Play it tough, don't let her know you're shaking. Maybe it was just a kid's game. She didn't look young enough for kid's games.

"I didn't recognise you with your face washed," he said, hoping the sarcasm would put her off. She was close beside him, hands gripping his jacket sleeve. He felt terrified. What kind of girl would do this sort of thing?

"Oh," she said, raising her eyebrows, "coming the old vinegar, eh? Your own wasn't so hot either, y'know. Where d'you live when you're at home?"

"Shuttle Place," he said. He did remember her, now that he could think again. Telfer had pointed her out at the beginning of the howking. "I'll bet she rattles like a tin can tied to a tomcat's tail," was what he had said. He said it about almost anything in skirts.

"That's being demolished," she said. "I bet you wish you had a decent house in the scheme?"

"No thanks."

"Too common for you, I suppose you think you're the bee's knees just because you've got a horse to play with."

"Hmph. Play with?" He looked round. The other two were following about twenty yards behind, arm in arm, heads together in a big giggle.

96

"What's your name?"

"Dunky Logan. What's yours?"

"Elsa Noble. You went to the Academy, didn't you, my pal Betty saw you at a dance, she thought you were smashing."

He looked at her, ready to sneer like a hard man. He'd taken girls out before, from the school. Prickteasers told lies and buggered you about. The others were too shy to talk to you at all. She was grinning.

"You've got a brass neck," he said.

"My pal Betty dared me. Are you a pal of Donald Telfer's?"

"Yeah. We're thinking of emigrating to Canada together. How you know him, do you?"

"Everybody knows Donald Telfer, he's a dreamboat."

Wouldn't it be fantastic, walk into the stable in the morning and drop the word to Telfer, all casual like, see yon black-haired piece, yeah the Noble woman, well I lumbered her last night, not bad at all. FANTASTIC.

"Where d'you live?"

"Down the sceheme."

"I'll see you home then?"

No, he shouldn't have asked her, he should just have kept on walking. Whenever you tried to get things straight with a dame she got all funny. It would all end now. Too good to be true.

"Just to the corner," she said. "My father's very strict. Here, I hope you don't think I was picking you up or anything, it was just a dare."

She'd think he was another bigtime guy, like Telfer, because he worked on the farm. Because it had all happened in such a daft way he didn't feel nearly as shy as he would have if he'd tried to chat her up at a dance. Her hands began to take a less firm grip of his sleeve, her pals were out of sight now, the big dare was beginning to wear off.

"Telfer said he fancied you at the howking," he said, making it sound as though he and Donald were big buddies when it came to eyeing the talent.

"Pull my other leg it's got bells on," she said. Funny, sometimes she talked "nice" and then the real scheme edge would come into her voice.

"It's true, cut my throat and hope to die."

"Did you think I was er, ehm, like bold, coming up to you in the street and that?"

"It happens to me all the time. How old are you?"

"Seventeen. D'you go to the Town Hall dancing? Me and Betty go every Saturday, it's smashing."

"D'you ever see Cut the Lugs Reilly?"

"Who's that in the name of God?"

It was because Alec was scared of guys like Cut the Lugs Reilly that he wouldn't be coaxed to go to the Town Hall. One night they'd been passing when the dancing was coming out and they'd gone up to a crowd at the main entrance. It made it easier to talk to her, having a story to tell.

"The blood was all over them, one of them had his shirt torn half off him," he told her. "It's this bloke from the Brig, he's always miroculous on V P wine and wants to cut people's ears off with his scissors. I'm not joking, he carries scissors about in his pocket, that's what he's called Cut the Lugs Reilly for. You shoulda seen this other fella, he was hammering him, like a madman he was, no wonder if you were going to get your lugs cut off, and then, you know what, this woman got out among them trying to separate them and she got a whack on the jaw, you shoulda seen her, flying she was."

He felt breathless at having spoken so much. He wished she'd take hold of his arm again. It made it feel as though they knew each other. Maybe she was getting fed up with him already. Just his luck. Same at school, the good-looking ones wouldn't go steady with you, too much competition.

"I don't like men who fight," she said. "It's just crazy."

Bet Nicol never got a seventeen-year-old lumber from the scheme. *Him*, he'd be scared to walk down it in daylight. Nicol always said that crowds came down to the lowest common denominator. He'd have to kid her he was seventeen as well.

Going down the main Darroch road, deserted except for two blokes trying to drag their drunk pal out of a hedge, watched by an old woman at an upstairs balcony, she told him she worked as a folder in a printing works, and that her father had once caught her with a boy at the back of their house and sworn at him something awful and given her a belting.

He told her he was only working at the farm until he saved the fare to Canada. He told her his father was permanently paralysed through an accident, she said she was awfully sorry. Maybe when you were older you got to know what to say to women the first time you lumbered them.

"This is far enough," she said. They were at the corner of Barskiven Road. She was getting all shy now.

"Hey, you don't live here, do you?" he blurted.

She stared at him, cheeky dark eyes no longer smiling.

"What about it? We're not all scum, it doesn't matter what folk say."

Barskiven Road was The Undesirables. Bad corporation tenants (didn't pay their rents, didn't dig their gardens, let their kids smash up windows) were transferred to The Undesirables until they showed they'd improved. His mother called them scum. Barskiven Road houses had all-metal fittings. Only the window panes could be broken, unless you had a blow-torch. McCann said they'd have them, soon. At the dancing blokes always made jokes if they knew a dame was from The Undesirables. It was supposed to be the worst street in the whole of Kilcaddie.

"I don't think you're scum," he said, smiling at her nervously. "You think we're all toffs in Shuttle Place?"

He stood with his back to the battered privet hedge, still holding her hand. Her hair was very black. She was a smasher. If he tried to kiss her now she might not like it. If he didn't she might think he was dead slow. Girls made him panicky.

"I'd better go then," she said, not taking her hand away. She seemed shy, too, even if she *had* run up to him in the street. But that was only a dare.

"Eh, I'm supposed to be going to this dance at Blackinch on Saturday night," he said. "You wouldn't . . . ?"

"I've promised Betty to go to the Town Hall," she said. For a moment he thought of suggesting Alec should pair up with Betty, but Alec wouldn't go near an Undesirable.

"You've got to go with her, I suppose?"

"I promised. She's my pal."

"Eh, you wouldn't like to go to the pictures, would you?" His tongue felt as though it wanted to stick to his teeth. Please let her. . . .

She looked at her feet. Funny, he knew she was thinking it had only been a dare and now it was more serious than she'd bargained for.

"Okay," she said, quietly. "But I can't manage it till next Monday, my father only lets me out once during the week."

"Great." He moved nearer her, looking at her face for any sign of what she felt. He put his hands round her waist. Her body felt soft through the pink coat. He started to pull her

99

close. She let her face come up to his. He didn't connect properly with her lips, but he could taste her skin. There was a sort of shock through his whole body. Then she was pulling away.

"See you at the Cross then, next Monday, seven o'clock?"

"I'll try. Ta ta."

She ran down into the gloom of Barskiven Road, where half the street-lights had been smashed. He waited until she was out of sight. He turned away. He started to run, weaving past defenders, sprinting, wanting to throw his arms up in the air. A big date. A smasher! FANTASTIC. . . .

When he'd crawled into bed, relieved that for once his mother hadn't shouted through how late it was, he kept thinking of her name. Elsa Noble. Dear God, please let her love me, please. . . .

CHAPTER SIX

It was just after half-past five on the following Saturday morning when Willie came down the stairs into the kitchen. As soon as he switched on the light he could see the evidence of Mary O'Donnell's first week's work, the shining window panes, the swept floor, the breakfast things already laid, their big blue-ringed mugs upside down on a clean white tablecloth, not a dirty dish in sight.

It made him feel cheery – the way holidays used to, or days when they dressed up to take cattle or pigs to the market. His heavy flannel shirt rolled up past his elbows, he ran hot water into the enamel basin and splashed his face with cold water, feeling it wash into the sleep in his eyes. Looking out through the shiny panes, he saw that it was cold and dry, the yellow sliver of moon still high above the cartshed. Normally he couldn't be bothered shaving one week to the next, but with the kitchen looking so clean he felt he should. It was Saturday anyway.

Mary O'Donnell came into the kitchen as he was drawing the open razor down his cheek, left hand holding his jaw to one side. He saw her briefly in the cracked mirror. Her hair was down but she was dressed.

"Aye aye," he said, taking a fresh grip on his chin, hard fingers biting into slippy skin. "Ye're up then?"

"I'll have your breakfast ready by the time you're back from the byre," she said. Milking was supposed to be the housekeeper's job. Willie had said he'd keep on doing it her first week, to give her a chance to get settled in. It made no odds, he never slept well after five o'clock, he'd have risen anyway. He'd never been in bed later than seven o'clock in the morning in his whole life and that was when he was a schoolboy.

Splashing away soap traces with cold water he dried himself on the clean face-towel she'd hung by the sink. A woman's touch, he thought to himself, supposed to make you feel better.

She'd started frying when he put on his cap and went out into the yard, fastening the collar stud at his neck against the still, cold morning. Before he went to the byre he had a walk

101

round the steading, checking that nobody had broken into the hen-house or set fire to the hay-ricks or stolen anything. The black dog came out of its kennel but one guttural grunt was enough to send it back inside. Was she just playing up, because she was new, trying to make a good impression? Bobby Kerr of Barrhill had married his housekeeper, thinking she was a good worker, and no sooner was she back in the house from the kirk than she announced she wasn't going to break her back about the place, he'd have to get *her* a housekeeper. You could throw a leg over any woman alive but you didn't marry them for that.

Switching on the light in the byre he took the three-legged stool from its hook on the whitewashed wall and the big galvanised bucket from under the wall tap. His feet trapping the base of the pail, he put his head against the first cow's flank and felt for her teats, massaging them downwards with his fingers before taking them in the palm and thumb grip for milking. The white jets spurted with a tinny noise on the bottom of the pail. Soon the squirts hissed into creamy milk. He'd have to know a bit more about her, too, the kind of woman who went about housekeeping from farm to farm might be any kind of rogue, might even have a couple of wee bastards hidden away somewhere. He'd only once before thought seriously about getting married, that was when Big Watson the bobby died. He'd been visiting them for years and was well used to the woman's ways. When she was a widow she'd occasionally come down past the farm for a walk on a Sunday afternoon, not a bad-looking figure of a woman for her age. He'd got into the habit of hanging about at the entrance to the yard when she might be passing – it wouldn't have done for him to keep on visiting her when she was a widow living on her own, that would have started the neighbours gossiping, sure as anything, but it was respectable enough for her to come into the farmhouse for a cup of tea, his father being there.

Once or twice he'd been on the point of telling her they should get wed, but something had stopped him. Although she came from Aberdeen herself, and had been a farmer's daughter before she married Watson (who'd been at school with her and had married her on leave from Kilcaddie police), there was too much of the town about her. She wore hats and silk stockings and her hands didn't look right for the kind of toil the farm needed. It was a different life from what she was used to in her corporation house – no rugs or nice carpets, not even a wireless in those days; Auld Craig wouldn't have a wireless in the place, said it would just addle their brains and put them off the notion of work. They had one now, but that was mainly for the weather forecasts.

He took the other two teats and soon the big bucket was heavy with milk. When he'd emptied her udder he poured the milk into the urn and sat beside the other milker. He'd tried to tell his father that they'd be better off going onto dairy farming altogether, get a milking herd and a milking machine and forget all the tatties and whatnot, save on wages, but his father couldn't be bothered with all the business of getting a Tuberculin Tested herd. He'd always been a mixed farmer, dairy farming was a lazy man's idea, it wasn't real farming at all unless you had to work at it. Today McCann and the boy would be muck-spreading and Telfer ploughing with the tractor. Coll and himself would start putting up a new fence on the field by the factory, Coll due for a shock when it came to paying time. Mind you, a cripple woman wouldn't be wanting to be running away to the town all the time, she'd count herself lucky to get a place of her own.

The oats had been soaking in the big pot all night. When she had them on the boil, the big bubbles popping up through the thickening porridge, she put a dab of lard in the frying pan. When it was sizzling she cracked in two eggs. Beside them she laid two big beef sausages. It wasn't her place to take her breakfast with the Craigs, not yet. There hadn't been any sign from Willie Craig that he was thinking about her, but that wasn't surprising. Stephenson at Beith hadn't said a word to her for about six months and then one night, when she was darning his socks and he'd been reading the paper, he'd just stood up and said: "Come awa' to bed, woman."

Willie was as likely to come out with it just as sudden, but unless it happened in a day or two he'd never believe the baby was his. Yet if she made the first move and later on the baby came a lot earlier than was normal, he'd get to thinking back. Suspicious wasn't the word for them. She wished she could be as hard as they were, instead of being weak and sinful. Even now, when she knew what she had to do for her own good, she was still not able to stop thinking about the big blond fella. Why was there always somebody like him about, confusing her, never giving her a chance to concentrate on what was sensible? God had cursed her, sure enough. Even her own

103

mother had said that and it was true and not all the priests in the world could change it.

Willie's boots scraped on the porch cobbles. She was tasting the porridge when he came in, leaning to one side against the weight of the narrow-necked urn.

"There's a few of them need extra milk at the weekend," he said, putting the urn by the sink. Most mornings they sold about a gallon and a half to people from the scheme, but at the weekends, with the men all sitting about their houses swilling down tea, extra customers came for fresh milk from the farm. It was hardly worth the bother taking the money, but they'd always sold it and no doubt they always would. Just as they sold a few dozen eggs to people they knew, even during the war when all the eggs were supposed to be accounted for to the government.

"Do you let them all have it?" she asked.

"Oh aye, jist keep eneuch for oor tea and oor parritch."

"Your porridge is ready," she said.

"Aye, where wud we be withoot oor parritch, eh?"

She ladled it into the brown chipped bowl and put it in front of him. Her hands had seen a wheen of work, he thought. Her fingers looked as though they'd been scraped with wire wool. The Watson widow had very nice nails, too nice by far for a farm. Looking down at the dirty pores on the back of his neck she felt like taking a scrubbing brush to him. He'd be a smelly brute of a man to lie beside in a bed. She thought of the other man's yellow hair and slim, red neck. But good looks wouldn't keep a woman and child in the house and home. . . .

Willie had already tended the beasts in the byre, turnips and hay, by the time the men were in the stable at half-past seven. Telfer was smoking, McCann was brushing behind the horses and the boy was carrying their water. Coll arrived just behind Willie, pushing his bike, his gas-mask case strap across his chest, his cloth cap on the back of his head. Coll wore his cap with the skip slightly off centre and the rest of it pulled back. He and Willie were the only ones to wear nicky tams, strings tied round their trousers below the knees to stop dirt rising up their legs. Telfer watched Coll shove his bike against the stable wall. What a galoot he was, a real highland hayseed.

"How's Bonny Prince Charlie this morning then?" he said.

Coll grinned.

"How's yourself, you perfumed ponce-boy?"

If you went too far with Coll he could get really annoyed and then he'd throw his cap on the ground and stick up his fists like a bare-knuckle expert and ask you if you were wanting your ugly features altered. Telfer decided he couldn't be bothered.

"Aye, well I don't smell like something the cat dragged off the midden," he said, nodding at Willie. The boy began brushing the mare. "How's you and Mary getting on, Willie?" Telfer asked, winking at McCann. "Is it true what I hear, she's fair daft about your father?"

"Ach you shut your big mouth, Telfer," said Willie. "If ye'd a decent pair of balls on ye mibbe ye'd get yersel' a grown woman instead o' all the wee hairies ye smell round."

McCann swept the last horse sharn into the pile at the end of the gutter and threw the broom against the wall. When he'd gone to the Brig to buy the motor bike it wouldn't start and now he wouldn't be able to collect it till Monday night. It hadn't made him any cheerier, having to go back to his mother's house and hear his stepfather's cracks about people who wasted their money on second-hand trash. Nothing ever went right for him, he reckoned. Nobody liked him. They all knew he was a bastarding failure from start to finish. Here it was, Saturday, with no fancy piece to take out, no pals to go to the dancing with, nothing.

Dunky knew he and Blackie were to be carting dung from the midden all morning, on their own.

"Fancy coming to a big dance at Blackinch canteen?" he asked McCann, standing behind him with the empty water pail. "Me and my pal are going, plenty of talent."

Blackie McCann looked at him, sleepy blue eyes staring out of dark stubbled face.

"Nah, whut dae I want wi' a lot of kids?"

Dunky shrugged. He hadn't really wanted McCann to come. He'd asked him more out of cheek, just to show him he was bigtime enough to go to the dancing. What did he care about McCann? Let the bastard rot.

Telfer went to start up the tractor. Willie and Coll started off down the track road, Coll carrying the bale of wire. Willie with the mell hammer over his shoulder. McCann and Dunky yoked Big Dick into the four-wheeler and backed it against the midden. The hills were still dark, a deep purple. Overhead the first light of the hidden sun sprayed out through high clouds like fingers of water moving jerkily across a greasy surface.

Telfer whistled *Oh What a Beautiful Morning* as he yoked the tractor to the plough. A nice steady morning's work on his own, nothing to think about except keeping the drills straight, just him and the tractor, time to think about things. Like Agnes. He was well out of that. For a while it had been enough just to know he was banging the arse off a toff's daughter – he laughed to himself, banging was the right word for it, first time in she'd squealed like a stuck rat. Most Kilcaddie women were the same, anything more than a quick necking session was some kind of big sin – until you got married and then you didn't want to anyway. Something unusual was the best. The trouble in Kilcaddie was they were all small-minded – unless they were like Agnes, falling over themselves to do anything that would make you marry them. You couldn't put up with a woman like that, it wasn't the same once you knew she'd let you do anything. Forcing them into it the first time was the only good part of it.

As he turned round at the end of the first drill he looked across the field at the factory. He'd been in it once, terrible dump, no wind or sun, the noise fit to split your skull, nothing to look at but iron walls and assembly belts and bits of aeroplanes hanging from chains, starved of fresh air. No wonder they had to pay them fourteen and fifteen pounds a week, cooped up in that joint.

He knew that would be different, now. A woman with an iron on her leg! What would it look like, up at the top where it joined on? What would she do with it when you were riding her? Had any other guys ever poked her? Christ, it was hellish interesting just thinking about it. But how the hell could he do anything about her? She'd been stuck in the house all week and he could hardly bowl over to the kitchen door and ask her if she fancied a wee walk on a dark night down the black hills. He'd have to be very fly to get in sniffing distance. Still, if anybody could, he could. Tits on her like turnips! Imagine getting her down in the hay and ripping the clothes off her!

Not many guys had interesting ideas like he had, he was sure of that. Most of them couldn't think further than a quick knee-trembler at the back of a close. . . .

Willie decided to say nothing to Coll about his sacking. They talked about a farmer on the other side of the Brig whose two-year-old son died in a milk urn being scalded with boiling water. Only two weeks later his Ayrshire bull had got his wife against a henhouse and battered her unconscious, doing serious damage to her pelvis. Things like that happened in threes, said Coll. They tried to think of the worst things that could happen to the man himself. Willie said he'd once seen a collie bitch getting its back broke by an Ayrshire bull, chucked in the air and headed against a wall. Coll had a nephew who'd been ploughing on a slope and the tractor had fallen backwards and whipped off his head. They hammered in posts and stapled wire and racked their brains for other stories to pass the time.

Jabbing the four tines of his fork into the solidly packed dung, Dunky hoped he wasn't going to be dead tired for the game that afternoon. As it was he'd have a hell of a rush to get back home and changed and up to the Cross to meet the team at quarter past one. He'd still not been able to tell anybody about Elsa Noble, and he was gasping to hear what Telfer would say. His boots ploughed down into the yielding surface of the midden as he turned to throw each forkful onto the back of the flat cart. The further down they got into the layers of byre and stable dung the heavier it got, until, at the bottom, it was like peat. There was a rest during the short trip to the field, but then he and McCann had to get up on the top of the load and fork it out over last year's stubble, for Telfer to plough into the ground on Monday. McCann didn't say much. He could have taken out his temper on the boy, but being asked to go to the dance left him no excuse. It was aggravating having nobody to lead the horse up and down the field, that would have speeded them up a lot. It would be better on Monday, when Willie and Coll would have finished fencing and the boy could lead the cart in the field and one of them could stay behind at the midden loading the second cart. The job had to be done, so the quicker the better.

Mary O'Donnell was peeling potatoes for their dinner when the old man came out of the front room, where he'd been making up the wages into envelopes, the money having been locked in there since Friday dinnertime when, as usual, Farquharson the lawyer had called for Auld Craig in his car and taken him up to the bank.

"Peel away, woman," the old man said, then made a noise that could have been a laugh and stamped out of the kitchen, his bowed head narrowly passing under the door lintel. She followed him to the porch, standing back in case he looked

107

round and saw her idling. Willie and Coll were the first back in the yard, Coll walking splay-footed, his back straight and the skip of his cap twisted round so that it was almost over his ear, Willie ploughing along on bowly legs, the pair of them looking like Mutt and Jeff. Then the boy and the other man came in leading the big horse, unyoking the flat cart beside the midden, ready for the first load on Monday. She didn't fancy the looks of the man McCann, he was a dour-looking creature. The boy meant nothing to her at all, he was just the boy, there was always one about a farm, either full of cheek or else so quiet you'd think he was wrong in the head.

A hen tried to peck its way past her into the kitchen. When they'd had no housekeeper the Craigs hadn't bothered to keep hens out of the kitchen. They cleaned up what the dogs didn't eat, Willie said.

"Whoosh." She blew out her lips and waved her arms and it squawked away across the yard. The others were turning the stable corner when she heard the tractor. Telfer brought it past the midden at top speed, standing up behind the seat, bending over to put in the throttle and turn her in a spectacular curve towards the opening between the stable and the barn.

But he had a look towards the house before he passed the stable and she drew back from the door in case he saw her. He was like a film star, not like the others at all. Clean. Handsome. A fella like that would never look at a cripple, he'd have all the girls he wanted. Not that she would have anything to do with him anyway, he was just a common farm servant and she needed more than that.

As usual Auld Craig took his time about paying them. First he had a bit of a stand and a stare at the hills. Then he watched Telfer backing the tractor into the narrow cartshed. Then he had a bit of a peek at his boots, in case they were thinking of making a dash for it on their own.

"Look at him, the old goat," said McCann, standing at the dusty stable window. "He's shiting himsel' about givin' away his money."

"You'll be doing well, boy, if you're half the man he is when you're that age," said Coll.

"They can tak' me to the knacker's afore I get to that state," said McCann.

Dunky gave Big Dick his hay and then stood by the corn-kist waiting for the old man to decide it was time to part with his precious cash. They were finished work, there wasn't another bloody stroke that could be done about the place, but the old bugger would hang on till the factory hooter went at half-past twelve. That was lowsing time, pay time, not a minute before. Willie nodded to his father as he came into the stable and took the hammer through to the harness room. The hooter went as Telfer went into the empty stall – Charlie's stall – for a slash, a fag already hanging from his lips.

"McCann!" shouted the old man.

Blackie went out and took his envelope. He counted it as he walked to his bicycle, which was propped against the trough outside the stable. He shoved it into his hip pocket, got on the bike and pedalled out of the yard.

"Telfer!"

Donald sauntered out and they heard him speak to the old man as he took the envelope:

"It's all there, I hope, you wouldn't try to swindle me, Craig, I hope?"

Craig looked at Telfer, and made a short braying noise. The fair-haired man went across to the cartshed and leaned with his back against the wall, one foot drawn up under him. Coll should have come next but Dunky heard Craig shout, "Logan."

As he walked the couple of yards from the stable door to where Auld Craig stood beside a melting puddle, he tried hard to look as casual as Telfer had done. It was time he stopped being afraid of the old man – not everybody was the way his father had been, ready to thump you one as quick as look at you.

"Here's your siller, boy," said Craig, putting a fold of notes and some silver in Dunky's hand. Only the men got it in envelopes. Inhumanly pale blue eyes squinted at him from under heavy eyebrows. "You'll be throwing it away in your picture palaces I suppose?"

"No, I'm saving up for a motor car," said Dunky, grinning cheekily at the farmer.

"Hrrmph. Get away tae hell out of it."

Dunky grinned at Telfer as he walked over to the cartshed, where he counted his five pounds twelve and sixpence, his back to Craig in case the old man saw him and thought he didn't trust him. That wouldn't do.

"One thing about Craig, he doesn't pay you much but it's regular," said Telfer. He spat, not the way the others spat, wet and noisy, but in the American way, a smooth jet. Dunky wondered if Telfer did all these things naturally, or was he deliberately copying the films?

"Coll," cried the old man.

The moon-faced highlander walked with his hand out, palm open, like a big schoolboy. Was he pretending, too, just acting the idiot to give everybody a laugh?

"I'll no' be needing you after next week, Coll. There's your money. Too damnt many men about the place. You can pick up your books on Friday. Plenty of jobs about."

The old man looked at his boots for a moment, then turned and walked away round the stable. Coll stared after him, mouth open.

"Are you giving me the bag?" he shouted after Craig. The old man stopped, half-turning.

"Aye. So don't be throwing the siller over the bar counter, you'll be needin' it."

And he was gone. Dunky felt frightened.

"He's joking," Coll said to Willie, surprise giving his voice a squeaky tone. Willie stood in the stable door and shook his head.

"Craig never jokes," he said. "Ach, what're ye worryin' aboot, Coll, ye're a lazy bugger anyway, ye'll suit them fine in the factory."

"Factory? I've been here eight year!"

Dunky wished he'd gone straight home. Coll looked ready to cry.

"You're well out of it," Telfer said, putting his foot on the ground. "You'll easy get another job."

Not looking at the slack-jawed Coll, Dunky fetched his bike from the stable, hoping they'd have gone when he came out. Craig had given Coll the bag because *he'd* come to work there – at less wages. He waited as long as he could but when he wheeled the bike outside Coll was still there. Telfer and Willie were walking into the yard.

"Eight year," Coll said to Dunky, looking at him with a frown. "Eight years working for that man and now I'm bagged, just like that?"

Oh Christ, Dunky thought, Coll was going to cry. The first big tear ran down his red face. He didn't even try to hide it. Dunky put his leg over the bike, balancing himself on one foot. It was the worst thing in the world, to see another man crying. There was something daft and soft and silly about

Coll, the stupid way he wore his cap ("More like a barrage balloon than a bunnet," McCann said), his splayed feet, his idiotic back straighter than a fence post.

"You'll get another job in no time," he said. Hmph, fancy a boy trying to mother a grown man!

"Oh aye," said Coll, bitterly. "Get a new job, just like that! And a new house! They treat you just like dirt." He had stopped crying now that he'd got over the shock. "You be as cheery as you like, sonny, someday it'll happen to you and you'll know what it's like."

"I must go, I'm playing football," said Dunky. "Cheerio."

Pedalling furiously, he rode away from the farm towards the scheme houses. He'd be late for the team meeting. Imagine a grown man crying in public just because he'd got the sack from an old goat like Craig! Some people were too soft.

Late as he was, he still decided to go home via Barskiven Road, but there was no sign of Elsa Noble. A gang of wee boys threw a stone at him. He stood up on the pedals to get up speed, not caring if they thought he was frightened. Coll had got the bullet because Craig thought he could do a man's work. Maybe he'd get a rise! That would show his bloody father!

From the way Telfer dawdled about in the yard, not in his usual hurry to be away home, Willie guessed that Mary O'Donnell was the attraction. When the black dog looked out at them Telfer bent and chucked a stone at its kennel. The dog shot back inside.

"Black bastard, it could've torn the throat out of her," Telfer said. Willie stared at him, eyes wide open, the slightly insane face he put on when he was going to make one of his dafter pronouncements.

"There's more than the dog wants to get his teeth into the O'Donnell woman," he said.

"You fancy her, do you?" Telfer asked, glancing towards the kitchen door. "I suppose you think she's easy meat for you, living in the same house?"

Willie's eyes didn't blink as he spoke.

"You mind your own business, Telfer, none of your monkey tricks with her."

Telfer grinned. Imagine smelly Willie thinking he could do better with a woman than him!

"You'll be short of a bit now, I suppose – with Morag moving?"

Willie's eyes were still wide open, but any suggestion of humour left his face.

"What's that supposed to mean?"

Telfer made a knowing face, lower jaw pulled down but mouth closed, right eye closing in a big, slow wink.

"Certain parties have seen certain goings on," he said.

"Certain parties might get their faces massaged wi' my boots if I catch them spreading their dirty lies."

Telfer laughed. No sign yet of Mary O'Donnell at the kitchen door. He hadn't quite made up his mind whether sacking Coll had been Willie's idea, to get Morag Coll well out of it so that he'd have elbow room to work the oracle on the housekeeper. Willie wasn't as green as he was cabbage-looking.

"Maybe I'll drop by for a cup of tea this afternoon," Telfer suggested, eyes slightly narrowed. "Saturday afternoon's often the best time about a farm, I sometimes think."

This time there was no mistaking Willie's seriousness.

"You keep out of it, Telfer," he said. "She doesn't want anything to do with a common tyke like you. Stick to your wee hairies from the scheme, they're more your level."

With that he went away into the house.

"You big-headed bastard," Telfer muttered. "Just you bloody wait."

As he walked up the road to the scheme he thought of various ways in which he could get Mary O'Donnell on her own. If there was one thing calculated to make him deadly serious about the woman it was Willie laying down the law. What the hell was Willie anyway, a man of fifty still bossed around by his father? I'll fuck'n show you bastards, he thought, think you're the be all and end all, eh? Common tyke!

"Well, hallo there, if it isn't the queen of the howkers," he said, overtaking the dark-haired girl who'd got off the bus at the stop in the main scheme road. She turned and as she didn't have a scowl on her face he took it she was willing for a bit of patter. "Fine day for a walk up the Braes!"

Elsa Noble hoped her father didn't see her walking beside Donald Telfer. He had a bad reputation, supposed to be very fast.

"I've got a date with a friend of yours," she said.

"Who's that, McPhail the knee-padder?"

"None of your business. I hope you enjoyed the walk."

She crossed the road away from him. Not bad legs. His mother would know her name, she knew almost every family at this end of the scheme, she'd certainly know which Undesirable family had a girl like that, hot little eyes and all. Who did she mean she was dating? Somebody at the farm? No, Blackie was the only remote possibility and he messed his breeks whenever he got within two yards of a woman. He'd note that girl for future use, his main aim was to get at the housekeeper. Apart from fancying her anyway, it would be as good as rubbing Willie's nose in the midden, to rattle the Craigs' own housekeeper! On his way up Dalmelly Drive, where half of one large block was still a ruin from the bombing, the open end now a tatty mess of peeling wallpaper and rusty fireplaces, he overtook old Mrs. Docherty.

"Carry your bags for you, sweetheart," he said, giving the fat wee woman the eye. She had fourteen of a family, most of them lazy great brutes who wouldn't work, but she still had to do her own shopping.

"Oh, that's awfy nice of ye, Donal', right enough but," she said, sighing as she let his hands slip through the leather handles. "Ma varicose veins is fair killin' me, so an' they are."

"Good job bread's off the ration," he said, looking at the eight or nine big unwrapped loaves packed on top of the other messages in her two bags.

"Ye're no' kiddin', Donal'," she said, wheezing a bit, her voice like gravel. "If we didnae hiv bread tae full them up whut wud we dae, that's whut Ah aye say, right enough but."

He had always had nerves before a game, worse if there were people watching. Glenryan was a village halfway between Kilcaddie and the smaller town of Bridge of Kilmorchan – the Brig. Twenty or so men and boys were on the touchline of Glenryan's cinder and grass pitch. They'd been known to attack visiting teams.

Baldy Campbell made him even more nervous. The great fat man in the belted gaberdine raincoat and flat checked cap was watching the second eleven for only one reason – to see if any of them were fit to move up into the big team. One silly mistake could ruin his chance. He put the rest of the chewing gum packet in his jacket pocket. The new chiclet slipped about between his teeth and tongue until he'd bitten through to the gum. He always felt the same way before a

113

game, nervous, half-thinking he wasn't good enough for the team, wondering if he'd play a stinker. He'd been playing almost every Saturday, morning and afternoon, since he was about twelve or thirteen and he was still nervous. Nobody else knew just how seriously you took it, how much you hoped that one day you'd play a blinder and a strange man would come up to you after the game and write your name down in a wee book and ask you if you wanted a trial with Rangers or Aston Villa or Leicester City. Or even Ayr United – he wasn't fussy. Nobody else knew that you thought of each game as a tightrope along which you walked hoping you wouldn't fall off. You had a feeling that the rest of the guys in the team didn't think you were good enough to be playing, so you couldn't really think of them as pals.

You ran out onto the pitch wondering whether your studs were hammered in properly, would a nail come up through your sole, were your laces tied tight enough. Your thighs seemed darker and hairier than usual against white shorts. During the kickabout you didn't exert yourself, you took the odd shot at goal, you jumped up and down feet together, you rubbed your hands against the cold, you sneaked a look at the other team – who always seemed bigger and stronger and more sure of themselves. You wondered which one you were marking, was he a hard case or a fantastic sprinter or a tremendous dribbler? Did you really need to go to the lavvy again, or was it just nerves?

The first ball you got was the vital one, if you bungled it you'd probably have a stinker. You saw the houses and the trees and the people but you didn't think about them. After ten minutes you'd know what kind of a game it was, hard and fast, a kicking match, a walkover, a hopeless defeat? Once you knew that you could fit yourself into it, play as well as possible. But the beginning was the worst, waiting for your first ball.

As they lined up for the kick-off he saw Baldy talking to his crony, Joe Overend. Were they talking about him? All Joe had said was that Baldy would be coming to their game, he never told you who Baldy was supposed to be interested in.

His first kick came after a few minutes running up and down behind the forwards. He saw it hit somebody's shin and run loose. He was able to trap it and look up before Glenryan blokes came at him. At this stage in the game everybody was full of wind, there was no time to hang about.

He hit it up the left-wing, wishing there had been time to make sure it went to one of their forwards. It landed near enough to Sammy Muir to make it look intentional, so maybe he was going to have a good game. As he ran about there seemed to be two parts of his brain. One followed the ball, deciding when to tackle and when to fall back. The other seemed to talk back to him, as though he was really two people, one making a speech to the other.

Go in hard. No time for fancy-work in juvenile football. Go in hard and don't waste time. One day play like Bobby Evans. Not really fond of playing wing-half. Centre-forward best position. Be Billy Houliston. Rummle 'em up.

One thing you've got – iron determination. Hard as nails. Don't care about being hurt. Only get hurt if you go in half-hearted. Do or die.

After half an hour the pattern was there. Glenryan's inside right, the man he was marking, did most of the dribbling in their team. He was a nifty dribbler, fancy with it, too. Hands splayed out at his sides, palms towards the ground, copying Willie Woodburn of the Rangers, the spread-out hands.

Just before half-time Glenryan got the first goal. A long ball came up from their defence and by the time Dunky saw that he was nearest to it he was caught in two minds whether to go for it in the air or wait to collect it after the first bounce. On the greasy, melting surface, his feet slipped as he first went forward and then decided to run back. The ball bounced over his head. Big Colin Thompson, their right-back, tried a sliding tackle on the fancy inside-right, but he flicked the ball forward and did a neat little hurdling jump over Colin's scything legs. Swaying his head from side to side to confuse the goalkeeper he ran forward into the penalty area and shot it into the net just as Bobby Black, Cartneuk's centre-half, crashed him to the ground.

Cartneuk's goalie, Billy Forsyth, sat on one leg, the other stuck out in the mud, looking accusingly at his defenders.

Dunky spat. It was his fault. He made a tight mouth and shook his head.

"What was the fuck'n matter wi' you?" demanded Bobby Black, glowering at Dunky.

"Piss off."

Bobby Black was fond of shouting the odds about other players' mistakes. Dunky thought Bobby didn't like him
115

because he was the only one in the team who'd gone to the Academy, which a lot of the guys called a toffs' school.

The whistle went and they walked over to the dressing-room hut, where Baldy Campbell stood with Overend. Dunky went inside for a new bit of gum. The sun was shining, although it was cold. Overend had oranges for those who felt thirsty. Dunky didn't bother. What did Baldy have to say? Men who ran football teams were funny buggers. They never saw the game the same way as you did. Some of the guys always made a point of buttering up Baldy, getting in their versions of what'd gone wrong, trying to put the blame on somebody else. He didn't. He was lucky to be in the team at all, he supposed, yet he wasn't going to smarm up to anybody. If Baldy didn't like the way he played too bloody bad.

'You're not covering each other enough," was Baldy's pronouncement. He spoke quietly, not annoyed that they'd lost the first goal. Although he was big he had very small eyes. Funny eyes. Different from the rest of him. His mouth said one thing, but his eyes seemed to be watching you listening to him, as though his eyes were separate from the rest of him. Dunky blew his nose, thumb against one nostril, snort, head bent forward so that it would miss his legs, middle finger against the other nostril, snort. Spit. It could be a bad sign, Baldy not being annoyed. Hundreds of guys wanted to play for Cartneuk. He didn't have to persevere with players. If he didn't think you were any good he just let you go. You had to fight to get a game, let alone become a regular.

"That inside-right's the danger man," said Joe Overend. Normally he was in charge of the second team, a scruffy wee man who was very friendly towards everyone – and who told tales to Baldy all the time. You had to be careful what you said to Overend.

"I want the full-backs to play closer together," Baldy said. "Concentrate on the middle, their wingers is nothing hot."

Dunky bent down and touched the dried blood on his knee, thinking that it would nip later on when he had to scrub the embedded cinders out of the skin.

"And Logan," went on Baldy, "don't be scared to take your man, if he thinks you're scared of him he'll do what he wants."

Dunky nodded. Who the hell was *scared*?

A slight stiffness after the half-time rest. Get stuck in, that's what Baldy wanted. All right, I'll show you who can get stuck in.

At school it was all sportsmanship. You didn't play to win, oh no, you were told off for fouling. The referees were all schoolteachers, you couldn't play it hard or they'd give you a dressing-down, as though you'd been caught wanking in class. But once you were out in real football it was different. The ref could only give fouls against you, not treat you like a wee boy. And Baldy was only interested in playing to win. As long as you didn't give away penalties or get sent off Baldy didn't care what you did. He didn't care what the other team said, either. He said there was only one way to play the game. Hard – to win. He believed in real football, not a lot of namby-pamby schools stuff. If you got in trouble he was on your side. As long as you were one of his players he would stick up for you.

The hand-waver trapped the ball near the touchline. Go in – hard as nails. Dunky leaned back as his left leg swept round from behind, knocking the inside-right to the ground, forcing the ball over the line. He shot up his hands and shouted "Our ball" but the referee gave the throw-in to Glenryan. It was a short one to the outside-right. Dunky took a kick at it through the outside-right's legs.

"Hey watch it," shouted a man on the touchline. The outside-right looked over his shoulder at Dunky. The ref gave another throw-in to Glenryan. This time it went into the middle. Dunky moved forward, taking up position to cover any breakaway attacks, aligning himself with Bobby Black and the full-backs. Another ball to the inside-right, who'd taken up position at the touchline, near halfway, giving him room to trap and move forward. Run out to block him. Body jack-knifed, eyes on the ball, never take your eyes off the ball. Go in – hard as nails. The inside-right put his foot on the ball and dragged it back out of range of Dunky's jabbing boot. Then he pushed it forward, past Dunky.

Up and after him. The wing-half must never stop running. Keep harassing him, don't give him a moment to get control. Thought so, like all fancy guys he wanted to hold on to the ball, work it a bit, show off. Dunky came up, cold air rasping on his throat. As the inside-right swung back his right leg to cross he went in, left foot first, knees together, throwing himself at the ball, seeing only the ball.

The swinging boot caught him on the knee. The ball skidded a yard. Bobby Black cleared it. Dunky drew in a gasping breath and bit his lower lip. His knee was in agony. Teeth clenched, he went on swearing until the pain faded. Limp a couple of steps, nothing wrong with it, bite your lip, all right. That was deliberate, pretending he couldn't stop his kick. Well, he'd asked for it now, the dirty rat.

The next time the inside-right came running up with the ball Dunky went in from the side, right hip thumping into the guy's side. At that speed he had no chance. Up you go, fancy pants.

"You dirty bastard!" roared a man on the touchline, his face red with anger, shaking his right fist. Dunky ignored him. Spectators meant nothing. Fancy pants made a great show of standing up in pain, rubbing his back, stretching, agony on his face.

They fell back for the free-kick. The ball was scrambled away. Overend was shouting them on. Glenryan didn't look so hot now. Like all village teams they were stronger than they were skilful. You had to have years of playing in the streets, a tennis ball on cobbles with twenty a side, sometimes under the streetlights, a tin can if there wasn't a ball – that's what you needed. Village boys were never nippy enough.

Go in hard. Their outside-right with the ball, dribbling up the wing, Glenryan's supporters stepping back to give him room. Sammy Muir was out there with him, but Sammy wasn't so hot at tackling. Go out to the wing, cover Sammy. The outside-right coming past Sammy on the outside, pushing the ball forward with the outside of his right foot. Choose your moment, then go in hard. Get the ball or man, both if possible, either will do, a free-kick out here won't do any damage.

He took the outside-right and the ball and himself over the line, crashing through the spectators, putting up his hands to protect his face, falling. Men shouting at him, a face looking down, an angry face.

As he got up a bare-headed man kicked his leg.

"Take that ye wee pig!"

Dunky spat at the man's feet and trotted, not too quickly, back on to the pitch. The outside right knelt to replace his shin-pad. No foul! The ref must be blind. Still, you took what you could get. From the throw-in he muscled in on their right-half and came away with the ball. You had to try and *feel* them coming at you from behind, keep running forward, make ground. About now.

He jumped as he ran and the boot that came from behind only scraped his ankles, not enough force to trip him. Pretending to make for the wing he pushed it inside to Sammy Muir, stroking it with the inside of his right foot.

Sammy to Joe McNenemy. Joe going across the field, small and left-footed, he'll have to turn back again to cross it, his right foot's only for standing on. Move up for the cross. Light not so good, difficult to see the ball against the mud and cinders. Watch Joe's body, that'll tell when it's coming. Joe's cross. Coming from the right, kicked with the left foot, ball curling in towards the goal. Don't chase in after it, enough forwards in there already. Hover on the edge of the box, move this way and that following the scramble. Here it comes, high ball. One of their guys going to jump. Go up with him, push yourself up, elbow out in his chest, go in hard. Full strength header, back into the goalmouth.

Glenryan's centre-half took a mighty swing at the dropping ball, trying to volley it a mile. He misconnected. The ball hit the outside of his ankle. Before their goalkeeper could move across to cover the deflection the ball had spun, quite gently, in a series of bounces, into their net, a full-back entangling himself in the rigging as he tried to rush back and hook it clear.

After that they seemed to play for only a few more minutes and then the whistle went. Ah well, a draw wasn't bad, Glenryan were a strong bunch on their own ground.

As they ran towards the dressing-hut the Glenryan supporters were waiting for them, in a small bunch, directly between him and the door of the hut. He kept up with the rest. They ran through the men, ignoring their shouts.

There was a bucket of cold water in the dressing room. He wiped the worst of the mud off his torn knee, dipping one of his socks in the bucket. Baldy didn't say much till they were dressed and out of the hut again, having shaken hands with the Glenryan team, fouls seemingly forgotten.

Carrying his boots and socks, dirty strip and pants, shin-guards and spare laces in his small brown case, Dunky walked with the team to the bus stop, listening to what Baldy was saying. Funny how much some guys talked about a game once it was over.

"You'll get your postcards about next Saturday during the week," Baldy said as some of them left to get the bus to the Brig. It was almost dark now. Upstairs on the bus, Sammy Muir dragging on a fag like a grown man, Baldy sat next to Overend, the guys in the seat in front twisting round to speak

119

to him, the same guys who always smarmed up to the big man. Dunky sat with wee Joe McNenemy. His knee was getting stiff. He'd have to scrub it with hot water and iodine or it might go septic. At Kilcaddie Cross Baldy at last spoke to him, just before he left to catch the scheme bus.

"No' a bad second half, Logan," he said. "We'll mibbe see about trying you out in the first team."

"Oh, great."

Baldy looked at him, big face under the flat cap.

"Aye, just a bit more weight and you'd do fine."

On the way down in the scheme bus he thought of all the balls he'd had during the match and how he could have done better. Christ, wouldn't it be great if Elsa Noble could come and see him playing for Cartneuk first eleven! That would impress her, dead right it would. Or maybe Baldy would mention him in the report he put into the paper. His father would have to read that. Then he might admit that he *could* play football. . . .

Tonight would do for a start, Willie thought. He felt like it tonight. Nearly a week since he'd rammed it into Morag Coll and he felt like it again. As Mary dished out their tea he felt like shoving his hand up her skirt and getting hold of her arse and giving it a good twist. He got a hard-on just looking at her move about the kitchen. Once the old man had gone to bed he'd have a chat with her. He hadn't waited all week on account of her maybe not wanting to let him into bed, he'd never even thought that she might not be willing. He'd waited out of commonsense, to see what she was like about the house. He had a feeling she'd have to be married – if he started at all. Something else had been keeping him back. Other men might laugh at him, for wedding a cripple, an Irish Pape at that. But the moment he'd realised that Telfer was after her as well he knew he wanted her, married if it had to be that. He knew that Archie Stewart would say to marry her regardless of what she was. Archie always said to pay no heed to other people's small minds.

"Hrrmmph, I'm away to my bed," said Auld Craig, dragging his tackety boots across the stone floor.

"I'm putting they dogs out in the old pighouse," Willie said, elbows on the table, not looking at his father. "They're no good in here."

She'd wondered if he'd do anything about that. She carried

dirty dishes to the sink, running her teeth over her bottom lip. He hadn't forgotten, so he must have been thinking about it all week. It being Saturday he'd be thinking he wanted a bit of fun and games tonight. All right, you smelly brute, I'm ready for you. Once you've enjoyed yourself you're as good as its father. She would do it, because it was the best way to get what she needed.

"Aye," said Craig. "They're better off out of it."

So that was that, the dogs would go out. Willie kept his elbows on the table as she finished clearing up.

"Another cup of tea?" she asked.

"Oh aye," he said.

She poured the tea. He poked his nose with his thumb, howking into it as though he was delving for tatties.

"I'll be feeding the hens then," she said.

"Aye, right."

She limped across the yard, shining the torch on the ground. Inside the door of the hay-barn she found the bucket by the door, already filled with corn. Willie had done that, she knew. Oh, he was keen enough, sure enough. She smiled to herself. It wasn't much to have to do for a home of your own, give yourself to a smelly brute a couple of times. She limped round the corner, by the stable and the cartshed. The henhouse was just beyond the haystacks. She put down the bucket and shone the torch at the padlock. She'd never been on a place so near a town they had to lock henhouses against thieves. She turned the key and took out the padlock, opening the door, bending down for the bucket.

"Fancy meeting you here."

She jerked round, swinging the torch. A man's hand caught her wrist and forced the torch down.

"Who's that?" she said, fear catching in her throat.

"Don't panic, it's only me."

He took the torch from her and she found herself being pushed into the low-roofed henhouse. All she could see were a pair of trousers and light brown casual shoes. Then he shone the torch towards the roof, lighting the inside of the hut. He was grinning.

"Do you come here often?" he asked. "The band's not bad but the floor's very sticky."

When she saw it was Telfer she tried not to look frightened. If she pretended she wasn't frightened it might pass over as a joke. She knew it wasn't a joke.

121

"What're you doin' here?"

"Just out for a walk, you know. It's nice and quiet at night, don't you think?"

He was grinning, his back slumped against the dusty wall, his head low.

"You gave me an awful fright."

It'd been risky but as soon as she didn't start yelling and screaming he knew he'd be all right. Hens perched on rows on the sharny poles. They were used to night-feeding.

"Sorry."

When a man grinned at you in that way you tried to tell yourself he was only guessing, but you knew all the time that he knew what you were really like. She noticed his flat, hard chest under his shirt. She tried to put on a severe face.

"If you'll let me move I've got to feed these hens," she said, hearing the crack in her own voice.

"If it was up to me I wouldn't let you do all this dirty work," he said. But he moved back and made no attempt to touch her as she tipped the bucket into the v-shaped trough. They bent down to leave through the low door, behind them two rows of hens picking away at shiny corn. She waited for it, her whole body seeming to jolt with each thumping heartbeat.

He walked slowly, keeping pace with her dragging walk. Past the haystacks. Make a joke, see how she feels. He touched her elbow.

"Nice night for a wee walk," he said.

She knew what to say. She knew what would send him away like a scared rabbit, *wait till I tell Willie you were hanging about the henhouse, he'll die laughing.*

"Sure so it is."

"Fancy it?"

Go on, tell him, make out you don't understand why he's here.

"What?"

"Oh sure, I know what kind of walk that would be." She tried to laugh out loud, as though she was far too fly to fall for that old bit of blarney, as though it was harmless.

Once they made a joke of it you were half way there. It meant you could go on with it the next time you met her, a safe wee joke. The main thing was, she hadn't squawked. She knew what he was after but she hadn't squawked. His fingers felt for a grip on her arm, a good strong arm it was, too.

"Ach, come on," he said. "You don't want to sit in there

on a Saturday night. You should be out enjoying yourself, a fine-looking wench like you."

"Oh I enjoy myself, don't worry. There's better things to do than tramping about in the dark on a cold night like this."

Don't rush it. Pretend you're just having a bit of nonsense. Nothing put them off quicker than letting them see you were desperate. As they turned the corner into the yard, stepping into the light from the kitchen window, he put his arm round her waist and gave it a pat:

"Maybe I'll take you out on the town some night, you never know your luck. Don't let Willie inveigle you into any wild orgies."

She hadn't expected him to leave so easily. At the very least she'd been waiting for him to grab hold of her for a kiss.

She spoke before she thought:

"Is that all you wanted?"

Telfer turned back. It was like tickling trout, your fingertips waited for a touch, you never rushed it – and when you got very good at it you showed them who was boss by playing them along for a bit – as though you were sure you could land them any time you chose.

"Who me? What did you think I wanted?"

"I'm sure I've no idea," she said, trying to cover her confusion with a sort of uppity indifference. "You tell me why a grown man hangs about a henhouse late at night."

"I'm a good employee, I don't want anybody knocking Craig's property."

She knew he was grinning, although she couldn't see his face. Damn him, she shouldn't have stopped him leaving.

"I'm glad that's all you had in mind."

"Oh yeah, what did you think I had in mind?"

"I've no idea, I'm sure."

"I'll bet."

He was pretty sure he could get a hold of her now and she'd let him take her over the haybarn, but there was still a chance she'd squawk. No, he'd wait till she came to him. She was keen enough, all right. It would help her to get her steamed up if he left now.

"Ta ta," he said. "If you need any more help let me know."

As she limped across the yard she felt flushed and confused. She wouldn't have let him do anything, it was too near the house even if she'd been of a mind. Yet she'd expected him to try a bit harder. Was he having a joke with her? Didn't he think she was worth the effort? Cheeky devil, who did he think he was? Donald Telfer! Just a common-as-muck farm servant.

She'd been ready to fight him off and now she'd been left, just like that! Somehow she felt insulted. When she came into the kitchen Willie was sitting beside the fire, head bent over the Kilcaddie paper.

"There's mibbe something on the wireless," he said, not looking up. Yes, Saturday night, sitting with a smelly brute of a man listening to daft rubbish on the wireless. She breathed in between clenched teeth as she turned the knobs of the set, a tall old Bush with a round canvas front. She tuned the band to the Light Programme. It was an old set and unless you concentrated it was hard to tell what the voices said. She sat opposite Willie and picked up her darning.

"D'ye ever wish ye could go dancing at all?" Willie asked, looking over the paper. "It'll be kinda dull for ye, no' bein' able to jink about so much."

She could see he was trying to be friendly.

"You never miss what you never had," she said, fingers picking at his sock. "There's other things to do with yourself."

"Aye, there's aye something to be getting up to."

She let the mushroom-shaped darning stool rest on her lap.

"Just because I've got a bad leg doesn't mean I'm some kind of freak," she said. He liked her accent. Compared to the way everybody else spoke it had a sort of a fancy touch to it. She watched his face.

"I never said ye were."

"No, you were thinking it."

"Ach, don't be silly, woman." He spat into the fire, a solid gobbet of yellow-green catarrh and saliva which hissed on red coals. "Ye're as good-looking as any of them. How come ye've never merriet?"

She shrugged, at the same time raising her brow and blinking slowly.

"Maybe I've never met a man I liked well enough."

"Ye've been beddet, I suppose?"

She blushed. His face was hard. He still hadn't made up his mind. It depended on what she said, how she reacted to his chat.

"It's none of anybody's business," she replied, but there was a kind of weakness in her voice.

"Mibbe no'. How would ye fancy bein' beddet by me?"

She could tell he wasn't asking her out of desperate need. He was trying to find out about her, testing her.

"Just like that?" She snorted. "Scotsmen are all the same, you think everyone else is cheap whores. Me being a housekeeper makes me just a bed mat, does it, something for you to pass the time on?"

Willie shook his head, eyes not leaving hers.

"I never said that." His voice was quiet. "Ye're a fine-looking woman, it's natural, isn't it, bedding a woman? Ye'd bed the Queen o' England if she gave you the chance, wouldn't ye? Ye think I'm some kinda nancy-boy homo?"

"I'm sure I've no idea –"

"Oh!" Willie grinned. "Ye want me to prove it? Ye think I wear corsets and things? Ye talk a lot o' havers, woman. I'll tell ye one thing, it's high time I got merriet mysel'."

"I daresay it is. In the meantime I suppose you think I'll do you fine for the odd night or two?"

"Ach, I could do worse than you," he said. He kept the grin on his face as he watched her. It was more than he'd meant to say. If she'd said yes straight off he'd have gone to bed with her and left it at that, handy to have a good steady ride under your own roof. If she wanted to hear wedding bells first – it made no odds, at his age he wasn't likely to find anybody better. Craig would have a fit, that was dead certain. Craig had never liked the idea of him marrying at all. To him any wife would be an outsider and the thought of somebody bar himself, the old bastard, getting a hand on the money made him mad. Craig had once told him to go up to Abderdeenshire and find himself a proper wife, a farm woman who knew how to work and look after money, not some fancy bag from the town who'd throw it all away on lipstick and nylon stockings and enjoying herself.

She didn't think he'd said enough in that direction.

"That's a nice way of putting it, you could do worse than me. You sound as though you're hiring a skivvy."

He spat into the fire. He stropped his nose on his knuckle.

"Ach, I'm not a great one for fancy talk," he said. "If we were to get on all right, you know, we could easily get married. It's not all that different from housekeeping anyway. I've been thinking about it, I'm game if you are."

She looked at the darning stool. This was important, serious. Why was she still thinking about the other man?

"I don't know whether to laugh or cry," she said. "Is that

supposed to be a proposal? We hardly know each other. You're just having me on."

"No I'm not." Talking out loud had made up his mind. "I'm serious, woman. I'm game if you are. Will you have me?"

"Your father wouldn't agree for a start, it's ridiculous, you don't know anything about me."

"There's only one way to find out." He grinned. "Craig can do what he damn well likes, he can't run the place without me. What d'ye say?"

She had him now. It was too easy. She had what she wanted. It was her moment of triumph. She wanted to enjoy it. She'd show that big-headed Donald Telfer!

"It's ridiculous," she said, shaking her head, smiling weakly. "I've only been here a week. It's not me you want, it's just a wife, any woman would do, you'd have married whoever was the housekeeper. Anyway, I'm only twenty-eight, you're twice as old as me, I mean, I'm sure you're a good man but you're just saying you want to marry me, you'll change your tune as soon as you get what you want."

He snorted. Once a woman started talking like that you knew you had her.

"Wheesht your havers, wumman, an' come tae bed. If we're getting merriet the sooner the better."

They looked at each other for a moment.

"I hope you're not having me on," she said. He laughed.

She made him wait while she went to her room and undressed. He went out into the yard and had a run-off against the byre wall. You've done it now, he said to himself. When he went into her room he was disappointed to find the light off. Still, it didn't matter, he'd get a look at her stump soon enough. He was curious about it. Maybe it would scunner him of the notion altogether, maybe not.

"You're a heavy brute," she said as he came down on her.

"Ach, don't worry, I'll only flatten you a wee bit."

Dunky stood on his own at the men's side of the hall, watching for Alec and his woman in the eerie light thrown on to the dancers by the revolving globe in the middle of the canteen, reds and greens and purples and blues, the kind of light they had in a lot of dance-halls, moving rays of light flickering across the walls and the people. It was supposed to make the joint glamorous. Diseased, more like it. He had to keep thinking of his date with Elsa Noble to stop himself becoming depressed. Dances were all the same, no matter how much you looked forward to them thinking *this* time it would be different. You shaved and your collar burned against your raw neck. You wiped Brylcreem and water into your hair and combed it and combed again in the lavatory mirror. You tried not to let your hands get dirty or sweaty in your trouser pockets. Your shoes were shining and your best trousers creased.

You didn't come too early, when there were only a few guys there and the lights were still up and everybody could see you. But you came before the pubs closed and the boozers had fights with the men at the door. About half-past eight was a good time. You paid your six shillings (at private dances there was a ticket, stiff cardboard with curly edging and a pink border) to the two men sitting at the trestle table in the entrance and then you went to the lavatory and had a run-off and a last comb at your hair.

Then you went inside, trying to look as casual as possible, hands in your trouser pockets. Private dances were better because there weren't so many hard men as there were at the Town Hall jigging and also because there were a lot of olde-tyme dances, Pride of Erin, St. Bernard's Waltz, Gay Gordons, Military Two Step – they were easy to do, easier than quicksteps. The band always looked the same, three or four men in red jackets and evening-dress trousers and bow-ties, a pianist, a drummer, an accordion player and a saxophone player. They always sounded the same, not like a real band on the wireless, thinner and more harsh, loud and a bit squeaky.

You stood with all the other blokes at one side of the hall, looking across the empty floor at the dames. You looked for girls you knew, because you weren't so embarrassed at the start if you got a dance with a girl you knew from school or from some other dance. You discussed the talent with your mate, trying to make it sound as though you were a couple of bigtime guys who'd been to bigtime places and thought this was smalltime jigging for kids. You felt you'd never have the nerve to walk across the floor, all the way across, and ask a girl to dance with you.

There was always an M.C. – "Ladies and gentlemen, take your partners for a slow tango" – and you decided you'd wait this one out, saying to your mate that you wanted to eye up the talent a bit more. Maybe a guy you knew from school or the football would come up and have a chat with you. You'd tell him about your game that afternoon, he'd interrupt you to tell you about his game. He'd say he was winching steady, a smashing piece who'd had to stay at home that night with her sick mother. You'd say you'd been winching steady but you'd chucked her in, going steady was a mug's game. You knew you were lying so you took it for granted he was lying.

The first dance was the worst. As soon as the M.C. said what it was all the blokes started across the slippy floor, walking fast in case some other guy got in first, not so fast so that you actually broke into a run. She always looked away when the rush started, pretending not to notice, chatting desperately casual to her pal. You touched her elbow and said "May I have the next dance, please?" or just "May I?" If you knew the girl or if you were a hard case, you might say something else, a joke, like "Lend us your body for the next struggle" or maybe just nod your head towards the floor.

If the girl you headed for was grabbed by some other guy you kept on walking hoping to see something good-looking. You might be unlucky and be left with only the horrors, the wallflowers, and then you had to turn away and move round the hall, back to the men's side. She might even say "No thank you" and everybody would see you getting the brush-off, that was the worst thing of all.

You felt tense, most of the time, except when your mate and you were standing together between dances. Twice or three times at every dance the M.C. would announce a ladies' preference. That could be worse than ever. You'd no idea what girls thought of you but this was when you found out. You might not be asked at all – quite a lot of girls didn't get up for ladies' preference. Or you might find your elbow being touched by a tremendous horror. You couldn't refuse, that would be too difficult. You had to go round and round the floor with her, all the other guys knowing she was the best you could manage. You could take the easy way out at a ladies' preference and nip out to the lavvy – but you could get tired of going to the lavatory.

Older guys had it easy, they knew what to say to dames and some really bigtime guys would actually stand *at the ladies' side*, chatting up the dames they were going to dance with.

Once you'd danced a few times you had to start thinking about getting a lumber, the only reason you went to a dance, a girl who'd let you take her home. By about ten o'clock you had to have some idea, maybe danced with her twice. You asked her where she lived. Sometimes it might be the first thing you actually said to her. Maybe on a good night you'd have two possible lumbers lined up. You had to make up your mind which was the best looking, which would let you go farther, which lived at the end of a long bus journey (meaning a seven- or eight-mile walk back home, probably for ten minutes' necking and a quick hand down her diddies), which was known (if you could believe what other guys told you about how far they'd got) to be game for as much as a grope.

You generally asked her during the last two or three dances.

"Eh, can I see you home?"

If she said "all right" you thought you were bigtime and in the crowded lavatory you made sure the other blokes heard you telling your mate that you were lumbering Big Moira or whatever her name was.

But if she shook her head ("I'm sorry, I go home with my friend Betty", or "No, I couldn't, I've got a boy friend") you'd had it – unless for the very odd occasion in which you and your pal bumped into two dames at the exit and were able to work the oracle with a quick bit of patter.

Dunky kept thinking to himself that the greatest thing in the world would be for him and Elsa Noble to go steady, so that he'd never have to go to a single dance again in his whole life.

When Alec came back from his dance with Katie Semple, a girl who, Dunky thought, looked like a camel, he shook his head.

"She's a waste of time," Alec said, "no use."

"You could do worse."

That was true enough. Alec had no idea at all about getting off with women. Once Dunky had asked him what he actually said to them during a dance.

"Just the usual things."

"What, exactly?"

"Well, I start off saying it's not a bad dance, the band's all right, the floor's a bit slippy, then I say, 'It's your turn to talk, my patter's finished'."

"You mean you actually tell them that, 'my patter's finished'?"

"Yeah, sure. Why not? What the hell do you talk to wimmin about anyway? They're a waste of time."

He saw a girl called Magda Gemmell from the school. He went across and asked her for a slow foxtrot. She was a dark-haired girl who wore glasses, shortish but she had a good pair on her. At school they always said she had everything – except a good face. Close-up it wasn't all that bad. It was the glasses that put guys off. One thing about her, she was easy to talk to.

"What's it like to be working?" she asked him.

"Not bad. Better'n school."

A slow foxtrot was easy, you just slipped round and round, right hand on the small of her back, left holding her hand somewhere near your left ear.

He could smell her perfume or shampoo or something. At school he'd never fancied her much, she talked all the time, even to boys – as though you were her pals. You didn't fancy a dame like that. Especially with specs. It wasn't so much what you thought of her that mattered but what the other guys would think of you for going out with her.

"Why didn't you like the school, Dunky?"

That was typical of her, calling him by his name. Not many girls would have done that.

"I dunno, I just didn't like it. They think you're a wee boy. Working's better."

Actually she wasn't bad-looking, not close-up. Guys didn't fancy her because she was sort of – *pally*. The dames you fancied were the good-looking ones who kept their noses in the air. What was it McCann said – who cares what they look like when their legs are round your neck? He couldn't imagine why you'd want a woman's legs round your *neck*. What would Telfer think of Magda Gemmell?

"What class are you in now?"

"Four B. I'm taking domestic science instead of Latin, that's why I went into the B class."

Then the foxtrot was over. He walked her to the edge of the crowd of girls.

"Thanks very much," he said. He walked back towards Alec. Another thing he hated – being looked at by a crowd.

"You should try her," he told him, "she's got enough patter for both of you."

At the other side of the hall Magda's friend, Joyce, waited to hear Magda's verdict on Dunky Logan.

"He hasn't half changed an *awful* lot," Magda said. "I don't think he likes me but."

"How not?" asked Joyce.

"Oh, I just know."

Magda Gemmell knew that boys didn't like you if you weren't afraid of them. Sometimes she wished she didn't like boys so much. They were lots better company than girls. Duncan Logan had never paid much attention to her at school. He was one of the wilder boys in the class, always fighting and playing football, scruffy, his school tie never in place, his hair all tousled, dirt marks on his face, his socks round his ankles. Now he was all grown up. It made him even more interesting.

At the interval there was a barney in the gents. Behind him and Alec as they stood on the ledge facing the wall was a guy called Hunter Rennie, a bloke who thought he was really bigtime because his old man was a coal merchant. He was half-drunk – or pretending to be half-drunk, to impress the blokes crowding into the small lavatory. He had a quarter-bottle of whisky in his hand. Once he'd told his mother that Rennie the coalman's son got drunk at dances and she'd said it was a disgrace that a family with that amount of money should let their boy go round the town making an exhibition of himself. He was about twenty. He wasn't in the army because he was still at Glasgow University.

The fight started when Rennie began singing.

"Shut your fuck'n row," said a guy standing along the ledge.

Rennie went on singing, waving his free arm in the air. He always wore a dark suit, something that Dunky associated with having a well-off father.

The other guy – who looked as though he might work at the chemical factory – turned his head and spoke out of the side of his mouth.

"Shut up, yah big-mouthed cunt."

Rennie smiled, eyelids droopy, swaying slightly. He reached out his free hand and patted him on the head.

"Do I bother you, little man?" he said.

The other guy jumped round, left hand pushing away the hand on his head. Alec backed away quickly, bumping into Dunky. The other guy hit Rennie on the face. Close-up it made a soft, pulpy noise. Rennie staggered back. The other guy jumped at him, right elbow pulled back. Dunky and Alec fought to get out of the narrow doorway, pushing against other blokes queuing to get inside, Dunky trying to button his flies.

"He'll murder him," Alec said on the stairs.

"Too bad. He thinks he's something special."

"I hate violence," said Alec.

"Ah shut up, you always try to make things sound dramatic. Why didn't you go to his rescue?"

They were schoolboys on the edge of a man's world. He wished he was eighteen.

Magda Gemmell asked Dunky for the next ladies' preference.

"You know Rennie, the coalman's son? He was getting his face smashed in downstairs."

She was impressed, as though his having seen the fight made him part of a bigtime man's world. When she asked him if he ever got into fights he shrugged and didn't say much, making her think he did it all the time. He liked that. Alec said Magda was a no-gooder. Your mates always said things like that if they didn't have a lumber of their own. Another good thing about going steady with Elsa Noble would be seeing less of Alec. At the age of sixteen (almost sixteen) you were too old to be playing silly boys. By half-past ten the hall was packed. Alec went off to try his luck with a black-haired girl called Ethel Carruthers, who was almost six feet tall and wore flat-heeled shoes so that she wouldn't tower too much above the heads of her dancing partners.

"You can always put a bucket over her head and swing on the handle," Dunky said.

Dunky went downstairs to the gents. By now there were several guys drinking from bottles. There was no sign of Hunter Rennie or the guy who'd bashed him. Stepping on to the ledge in front of the stalls Dunky bumped the raised elbow of a bloke swigging from a bottle of V P wine.

"Who d'you think you're pushing?" the guy said. His two mates looked hard at Dunky.

"Sorry, pal," he said, deciding he didn't really need the lavatory.

"Don't say fuck'n sorry to me."

He turned his back on them and squeezed through the door.

"He thinks he's a hard case, I'll show the bastard," shouted the guy.

Dunky ran up the stairs, trying not to panic. Guys like that would give you a kicking just for looking at them the wrong way. And Alec wouldn't be a great help if they came after him to put the leather in. He moved through the crowd of blokes. Christ, he'd get a real hammering if they caught him.

132

He saw Magda Gemmell standing with her mate. He asked for a dance. What he should have done was make a bolt for it, to hell with worrying if you were a coward. As they danced he watched the entrance over her shoulder. They didn't appear. They'd stay in the lavvy drinking till the last dance. They'd wait for him at the door. He'd seen enough of it to know that's just what they'd like, they couldn't get women so they'd make up for it by bashing him.

"Would you like me to see you home?" he asked Magda.

"It's too far, all the way to Barskeddie," she said. Unlike a lot of girls she took a good firm grip when she was dancing.

"That's not far," he said. "D'you think we could go now, there's some guys wanting a fight, it'd be better if we left before the end."

"I'll get my coat and handbag," she said. Dunky stood on the edge of the floor until Alec and Ethel came round. He nodded for Alec to come over.

"I'm pushing off," he said. "There's three guys in the lavvy want to bash me."

Big Ethel was impressed. A lot of girls liked to hear blokes talking about having a rammy.

"You should just have thumped him one," Alec said.

"What, with three of them? I detest violence, especially against me."

He and Magda had to run to catch the eleven o'clock Barskeddie bus at the Cross. They sat upstairs, Magda doing most of the talking.

"You were very good at English and history," she said. "You could get a better job than just working on a farm."

"Oh aye, like working in a stuffy office all day?"

Halfway to Barskeddie, at a scheme stop on the south side of the town, the driver had to get out of his cabin and come round to help the conductress chuck a drunk on to the pavement. He leaned across Magda to see what was happening down below on the pavement. The drunk fell backwards into a hedge, shouting and cursing. Dunky laughed.

"I think it's terrible the way those men get drunk so much," said Magda. She was wearing an Academy scarf. Dunky felt rough and hard, like one of his heroes, the sailor in *USA* by John Dos Passos, the one who kept coming back to see his respectable sister. Magda was his sister, refined. He was a working bum. Nice people stayed on at school and went to university or got jobs with a future in offices. They wore col-

lars and ties and spoke with pan-loaf, Kelvinside accents, the
kind of stumers who went to school reunions and lived in
bungalows outside the town, like Magda Gemmell, who lived
in a semi-detached bungalow in a dead-end road just before
the small town of Barskeddie.

Nothing was said as they walked round the back of the
house. He'd lumbered her and she knew he hadn't come all
this way for a handshake. Magda turned round at the coal-
bunker, stepping back against the wall. He stood in front of
her, left leg forward so that it touched her knee. He put his
hands round her waist. She started wriggling as soon as he
kissed her. When he put his tongue in her mouth she pressed
her tongue against it, her arms holding him tight. Gradually
he let his hand drop till it was touching her bottom. She didn't
push it away. Their mouths were wide open. She played with
the back of his neck, making his scalp tingle. He put his right
hand on her shoulder and worked it down. She kept wriggling.
He pressed the palm of his hand on her breast. She didn't push
it away. He pressed again and then let his fingers pull at the
top button of her coat. Her tongue ran round his teeth. He
undid three buttons and slowly slipped his hand down until
it was under her dancing frock, touching the taut brassiére.
You nearly always got this far with most girls you lumbered.

Her hand moved across his stomach. He'd never imagined
she was as fast as this. It just showed you! She let her hand
drop quickly over his flies, touching his hard-on. He forced
the tips of his fingers under the brassiére. Her breast felt warm
and fragile. She took off her spectacles with her left hand and
put them on the coal-bunker, their mouths still locked. She
breathed hot air into his ear.

"You don't think I'm fast, do you?" she murmured.

He thought of Elsa Noble. She'd made him feel – well, good.
Excited. Nervous. Just holding her hand. It was different
with her. He was nervous in his stomach just thinking about
his date on Monday. He didn't feel nervous with Magda.
Funny, his mother would never believe – not that he'd tell her,
not in a month of Sundays – that a girl from The Undesirables
was not nearly as fast as an Academy girl.

"You're not fast," he said, now leaning his whole weight on
her, his knee jammed between her thighs. His right hand was
aching from twisting round to feel her breast. Slowly she began to massage him through his trousers. Oh Christ, don't
stop, don't let her stop. He had her coat unbuttoned the whole

134

way down. He pressed her thighs, feeling the hard suspender. She kept rubbing his front. He began lifting her skirt. She shook her head but he pressed harder with his mouth and she didn't stop him when he ran his hand up her stocking and felt the bare skin. Girls were warm and soft and perfumed. They drove you mad.

Then his finger was into her wet fud and she was wriggling more and more. He didn't even like touching her wet part, it felt all sweaty and slimy, yet he didn't want to stop. Her fingers took hold of him through his trousers. He made to unfasten his flies but she pulled his hand away. He didn't risk it again. Don't let her stop now.

Then he was shooting his load into his pants.

"Oh Magda, Magda," he moaned. She let him jerk his body against her.

He felt wet and dirty. He wanted to get away. He couldn't bear to kiss her, let alone go on groping.

"I love doing that," she breathed in his ear. "It's awful of me, isn't it?"

He'd never do anything like this with Elsa Noble. Never! They'd love each other and be real sweethearts. This business was all sweaty and hot and clammy. He wanted away.

"Will you be going to the cricket club dance next Saturday?" she asked. He stood back now, his hands round her back, looking down at her, wanting to make jokes.

"Maybe," he said. "Alec'll have to get the tickets."

"I hope so. I'd better go in now, my father might come out looking for me, he's very narrow-minded."

So that was that. He set off on the six miles back to Kilcaddie, his legs stiff from football, the wetness in his pants cold and nasty against his skin. Frost shone on the road. Occasionally he was dazzled by oncoming headlights. Six mile for a grope and a wank! Still, he was away from it all now. What would it be like if you were actually in a bed with a big woman, like Mary O'Donnell? Would you feel the same once you'd ridden her, sort of disgusted? Women looked great in the pictures, all lovely and cool like Rhonda Fleming and Virginia Mayo. But when you actually got near them they were hot and smelly. In a dirty book Alec had nicked from his big brother there was something about learning the art of making love so that the woman came to a climax at the same time as you did. What the hell did that mean?

He whistled *Leezie Lindsay* and walked on in the moonlight, imagining the marvellous things he and Elsa Noble would do, nice things, when they were really courting. It would never be dirty and sweaty with her. Never....

CHAPTER SEVEN

For February the weather wasn't bad, a dry wind and high cloud, and that Sunday Dunky rushed through cleaning out the hutches, wanting to be away in good time to meet Elsa at the Cross. The winter litter should have been weaned at eight weeks old, but he'd never seemed to have the time to knock up the new hutch. They were good youngsters, a buck and three does, good coats and upright ears, very lively. He'd definitely spend two or three nights during the week to build the extra hutch. Then he'd have to think about taking them out to Findlay for his inspection. Maybe he and Elsa could go together next Sunday. She'd come to see him playing for Cartneuk, the Saturday he got his first team trial, they were winching seriously enough now to do things like that, even if she had come with her pal Betty and had been too shy to wait around for him after the game but had gone on back to Kilcaddie with Betty. Luckily she didn't know anything about football, she'd said he was very good. Baldy had said he'd need a bit more weight before he was ready for the first team. Be honest, he'd had a stinking game, too nervous to do anything brilliant with the ball when he did get it and too slow to make many good tackles.

He rushed away after Sunday lunch, telling his mother he was meeting Alec.

When he'd gone, Duncan Logan shouted through to his wife. She came into the bedroom, untying her apron.

"Have you finished with the *Sunday Post*?" she asked. For Duncan they also took the *News of the World*, but it embarrassed her to have it in the house.

"Aye," he said. "Eh, Beth, I've been thinking. . . ."

"What about?" She sat on the edge of the bed.

"What Doctor Barr was saying I should dae, go to Killearn." He looked at her, his face expressionless, his eyes heavy, as though he was trying to say something else. "I've decidet it's the best thing. I want ye to get him ower here and tell him."

She shook her head. Poor Duncan, he didn't know what he was saying, his mind was wandering, being cooped up in the bedroom.

"Don't shake your head at me!" he said. "I've decidet. It's

137

the only thing to dae. I'm no good to you here, jist a lot of extra work. Beth, I'm goin' out of my mind lyin' here all the time. Doctor Barr says they're good company at Killearn, they might even find a way that I can walk again. It's no use arguin', I've decidet."

"Don't talk daft," she said. "You think I'd let you go into a *home*! You'll stay here where I can look after you, with your own family."

"Family! Don't make me laugh. The boy hates me and Senga's too young tae care and you – well, it's killin' ye, woman, runnin' back and forth for me."

"I don't want to hear any more about it," she said, rising to go back to the kitchen. There were set times when she sat with Duncan, talking to him. This wasn't one of them. She wanted to sit by the fire and read the *Post* and put her feet up on the stool.

"Aye, well ye've got to hear about it, because I've decidet and I'm the man and I make the decisions."

He must have guessed that she'd been secretly wondering what it would be like if he was off her hands! She felt angry at having had such evil notions.

"You may be the man but I'm the one that does the work," she said. "You just lie back and rest yourself. I'll bring in a cup of tea in a wee while. I'll take Senga to church tonight. Isn't there anything good on the wireless?"

"To hell wi' the wireless! I've made up my mind, woman!"

She walked out of the room. His clenched fists thumped the bedclothes. Jesus Christ, if he could just get on his feet for two minutes he'd bash some sense into her. He was the man in the house and he'd decide what happened. His mind was made up.

"Aye," he said, "an' before I go I'll tell that young bugger a thing or two."

He could imagine them once he'd gone away, they'd start to realise the truth. Their own father – in a home, permanently. They'd realise then how little attention they'd paid to him. He could even see Beth sitting beside his bed in the ward, her lips trembling the way they always did when she was going to cry. And one day he'd be dead and they'd feel even worse. Thinking about his decision made him feel good. Running round the back of his mind was a thought that he knew he shouldn't have: *What if they did find a way of getting him on his feet again?*

138

No, don't even think about it – or it won't happen.

But what would you do – if . . .?

Be a man in my house again. Show that boy who's boss. Walk up the town and go into a pub and have eight halfs and eight pints and come back home and when she started moaning about him drinking, belt her one. Right across the chops. BANG! There, you bitch, I should've done that twenty years ago. Now shut up your whining, you know what I want. Don't talk back to me. BANG!

Try to remember what it actually *felt* like. Tight, he could remember it being tight. Up and down. Tight . . .

WHY IN THE NAME OF GOD DID IT HAVE TO BE ME!

When Willie heard the old man coming down the stairs, tackety boots banging on bare boards even though it was a Sunday, he picked up a paper and pretended to read. Aye well, he thought, here it comes, don't be scared, he's only a done old man, he can't touch you.

"Hrrmmph," grunted Craig as he looked at the kitchen table where the woman had put a small bunch of dried flowers in a little blue jug. "Floeers now, is it?" he growled.

"Aye, ye're up then," said Willie, glancing up from the paper. Of late the old man had taken to staying in his bed till after noon on a Sunday. It was the first sign he'd given of feeling his age.

Craig looked round for the housekeeper.

"Nae tea, is there?" he asked, not looking at Willie.

"She's got somebody wants milk," said Willie. He could hear her moving about in the dairy. "Her and me's goin' to get merriet."

"What's that ye say?" Craig turned to look at him, eyebrows raised, his voice an old man's squeak. Willie thumbed into his nostril, eyes on the paper.

"Her an' me's goin' to get merriet," he said.

"Ye are, are ye?"

"Aye."

"Can ye afford it?"

"I'll need mair wages from ye."

"Oh, ye will, will ye?"

The farm and the money was all going to be his anyway, when the old man died, that was why he'd never bothered about money, ten pounds a week in his pocket had always been more than enough for him, it wasn't as if he was a drinker or a smoker, he'd never even had a single day's holiday in his life, not since he'd left school. And out of the ten pound a week he'd saved near enough a thousand pound, something the old man didn't know about.

"We can sleep in her room," he said. "It'll make no odds to you."

"It won't, will it?"

By Jove, it was just like Willie, never found a wife all these years and now her, a useless cripple bugger and an Irish Pape into the bargain! Just after the money, that was all there was to it.

"An' will the bairns be Papes or what?"

Willie delved at the other nostril. He'd expected Craig to take it like this, not saying much at first, giving himself time to make up his mind.

"She's a lapsed Pape," he said. "It'll be at oor kirk."

"Them, they never lapse."

Mary O'Donnell came back into the kitchen. Craig's bowed head turned to stare at her. No wonder she'd stuck flowers on the table, she thought it was her house already.

"I've just telt my faither we're gettin' merriet," Willie said.

"And does he approve?"

"Hrrmph, I've to *approve,* have I?"

"Oh yes, it wouldn't be proper unless you gave us your blessing." She went across to the sink and ran hot water into the basin. Willie had said his father wouldn't like it, not with her being an Irish Catholic, but Willie had never had a woman to sleep with every night before and he'd stand up to his father to make sure of keeping it that way. She smiled to herself as she bent over the basin, rinsing out the two cups.

"I'll have a cup of tea," Craig said. He pulled a chair from under the table and sat down stiffly. He looked down at the tablecloth. She looked over his head at Willie, who bared his teeth at her in one of his mad grins.

Back home men didn't marry till late and she was used to grown men who behaved like boys until they were old, when they started behaving like tyrants. Willie would be no trouble to handle at all. Craig said nothing.

Willie looked at her backside, solid under the dark tweed skirt. I'm riding a young woman, he said to himself, feeling like laughing in Craig's face. I may be daft but I'm not stupid. A fine young piece that Telfer would've liked to get his leg over. Hard lines, Donald Telfer!"

"Go outside, woman," Craig said, "I want to talk to Willie."

It was on the tip of her tongue to tell him she wasn't the housekeeper any more to be ordered out of the house like that, but Willie nodded at the door. She limped out into the yard. It was a clear, sunny day, quite warm for February. She rubbed her bare forearms. If she got this she would be happy. She'd always felt like an intruder in the more important lives of other people, a useless cripple who had nothing of her own, a single woman who was lucky to get a bed in somebody else's house.

She walked down the length of the emptied midden, now a drying bed of tarry-looking mud. The black dog knew her step and didn't come out. She'd get Willie to do something about its kennel, poor brute, nobody cared if it was wet or cold the whole winter through. It had taken less than two weeks to make sure she had Willie where she wanted him. She hoped her luck would hold.

As she stood at the end of the yard she saw a column of boys coming up the outside road. On Sundays they took them for a walk in the country, the boys from the James Lyle Approved School. They marched in threes, led by a master, a long column of boys who wore boots and long grey stockings, grey suits with short trousers and navy blue school caps. The oldest ones didn't look much more than sixteen or seventeen. They had pale faces, or so they always seemed to her, as though they could do with a good while in the open air and some proper nourishment. Whenever there was any noise from the column the master at the front would look over his shoulder. When she'd first seen the James Lyle boys on their Sunday walk she'd said to Willie she didn't think it was fair, making them march around the countryside in full view of everybody, as though they were criminals.

"Whut d'ye mean?" Willie had said, surprised. "That's whut they are, criminals, a lot o' hooligans from the town. They don't get sent to the James Lyle for nothin', ye ken."

To Willie and his father they were just scum, the dregs of Glasgow and all the other towns round about. She'd even heard Craig say that shooting was too good for them, the criminals, but Willie had afterwards said that Craig's remedy for practically everything was to shoot folk, it was just an expression.

"Ye'll have got her in the family way no doubt," said the old man.

141

"More'n likely," Willie replied.

"Damn and hell. Ach, you've got no more sense than a dementit heifer," growled the old man. He hawked and coughed and spat into the fire, retching and wheezing for a bit before he got his breath back. "Marry her then and be damnt to ye."

"I'll be needin' mair money," Willie said.

"Aye, I don't doubt it. Ye can have twenty pound a week, I'll tell Farquharson to see the bank. I suppose ye'll be askin' me next for a cheque for the wedding present?"

"Oh aye," said Willie, "I've worked a few year for it."

"Ye got your wages. I made the siller with my brains. When I'm gone ye can do what the hell ye like wi' it but I'm no' gone yet, tell her that, I'm no' gone yet. An' don't let her get any fancy notions she's too grand to do the housework. There's no room for idlers on this place."

"Oh aye, she'll do the work all right."

Nothing was said about the will. Craig had that much power over them. When he announced just after tea that he was away to his bed they both knew what he meant. He couldn't bear the sight of her, not now that he knew she was getting her hands in amongst *his* money. To him she was just common Irish trash, no more and no less, no better than a tink, just fly enough to have inveigled Willie into marrying her.

"Well?" she said, looking over her shoulder from the sink.

"I tellt ye he'd be all right."

"He didn't seem very sociable."

"It's jist his way."

"How much is he going to pay you?"

"Twenty pound the week. An' a cheque for the wedding present."

"And how about the will?"

"Don't you bother yer heid aboot the will, jist treat the auld man proper an' he'll see us a' right."

She'd known there would be a snag and the wiil was it. Even Willie didn't know how much money the old man had tucked away in the bank and in shares. His own son! Never mind, if she had to keep in the old man's good books she would, no matter what he thought of her. In any case, it wouldn't be for very long, and while he lasted she'd be a match for the old devil. He wasn't just dealing with Willie now.

Upstairs, sitting in his armchair, Craig stared at the unlit coal and sticks and paper in the grate. He could see through that woman as clear as glass. The money, that's what she was

after. Well, she didn't have it yet. He'd just see how she behaved and then he'd decide what to do. She might be able to
trick Willie but not him. The money would go to somebody
who appreciated it, he hadn't worked his whole life to hand
it over to some fly-by-night. He snorted with amusement.
Maybe it would do Willie the world of good having to hold
the reins on a wife who was only after him for what she could
get. It might be the making of the boy. He'd just bide his time
and see how things turned out and if it was all for the worst
there was always George out in Rhodesia, *he'd* know the proper value of the money. George was like himself, hard-headed
and canny. And he hadn't been content to hang about all his
life waiting to be handed siller on his lap. George had said be
damn to you, I'll make my own way. That was a real man for
you. . . .

It had always been Dunky's ambition to have a steady girl
and here he was, sitting with her on the coarse grass near the
top of the Braes, sitting on his jacket with his arm round her
waist, looking out over the flat land that ran to the sea, Kilcaddie stretched out below them, the new schemes in reds
and browns, the old town black and grey.

"It looks all right from up here, doesn't it?" he said. "If you
fancy scenery that is. I'd rather gaze deep into your mysterious eyes." He tried to make her laugh, but there was something wrong. She'd been in a funny mood since they'd met at
the Cross and walked the four or five miles to near the top of
the hills.

She turned her face away from him with an irritable sort of
movement.

"You must think I came up the Clyde on a bicycle," she said.

"What's wrong, come on, tell us or I'll bite your ear off."

Under her black coat Elsa wore a blue blouse and a navy
blue cardigan. He was in his best clothes, dark shirt, sports
jacket and flannels. Her nylons were the kind that didn't let
you see the skin. He guessed she wore that kind because the
skin was a wee bit reddish above her ankles. The only thing
he didn't like about her were her shoes, black with fairly high
heels, all right for the dancing but a bit daft for climbing hills.
He'd once seen a film in which the girl went out with her bloke
wearing a cardigan and skirt and bare legs with brown
brogues. Dressing like that meant she was really *friendly* with
her bloke, not just going out on a date.

143

"It's nothing," she said.

He couldn't think what he'd done wrong. In the time they'd been going steady he hadn't tried anything fast with her, they hadn't had one row, today he'd been on time and managed to be cheery enough, even if it was bloody Sunday. Sunday! Even up here, miles away from the town, it was impossible to get away from Sunday. It was something you felt in your brain and your stomach. Dull and hellish. Dead. You've not to listen to the wireless on a Sunday. It's time for Sunday School. Dressing up, getting your ears washed, sitting on dark wooden benches, listening to Mister Lockhart, the Sunday School superintendent, talk about rotten dull things from the Bible, always the big picture of Jesus with the children round his feet, then splitting up into classes with the Sunday School teachers, Miss Robb, who also sang in the church choir, reading to them from some kids' magazine, different from school yet just as bad in some ways, dry as dust, your legs itching from the elastic garters which held up your long stockings, your new shoes cutting into your ankles. No football on a Sunday, no playing in the street, no wireless, nothing but being dressed in your best and thinking of school in the morning and the homework you'd been putting off till the last moment, mummy sitting reading the papers, all dull and stuffy, no fun on a Sunday at all, the shops all closed. He *hated* being a wee boy, and Sundays were the worst of all.

"Did you hear about the big negro who gave a woman a cross-bar on his bike for ten miles and when she got off she saw it was a ladies' bike?" he said. Going steady meant you could tell your girl dirty jokes.

"Tell us another," she said, bitterly.

He felt sick. She was working up her courage to tell him she didn't want to see him any more!

He took her hand and squeezed it.

"Can't you tell me?" he said, his voice quiet and anxious.

"I've got my periods," she said, suddenly, staring at him.

"What's that?"

"Don't give us that, you know what they are."

He shook his head.

"No, I don't."

He did and he didn't. He'd heard the word before, blokes made jokes about girls' periods – "having the rags up" – but he didn't really know what they were. Something to do with girls' troubles.

"Didn't any of your other girl friends tell you?"

He made a daft, vacant face.

"No. Ma mammy said Ah wasnae tae talk tae girls."

"Don't make jokes about it."

"Sorry. You're the first girl I ever really talked to at all, you know that?"

She made a little unbelieving face. He leaned against her, his nose into her black hair.

"It's menstruation. Girls get it every month. It means you bleed between your legs. My mammy says it's a curse for being bad."

"What d'you mean, *bad*?"

"It's to do with having babies. It makes you feel sick."

"Oh."

"If you don't have it every month it means you're pregnant."

Most of all he loved her face. It was better than other girls' faces. Her eyes were light blue, no, more like very light-coloured slate. Her hair was smooth, parted in the middle and combed smooth to a page-boy sort of business below her ears. Her mouth wasn't like other girls' mouths either, she had very thin lips and smooth teeth, unusual teeth, they had almost no gaps between them at all, not like most people's teeth, they were all the same length. He had two long milk teeth in front, too long they were, he hated them, silly boy's teeth he had.

Best of all she was all warm and she smelled nice. Not sickly perfume-smelling, no, just nice. When she kissed him he liked the taste from her mouth, it wasn't like some girls whose lipstick came off on your face in greasy dollops, it was like the taste you'd imagine you'd get if you chewed a rose. He'd always wanted to chew a rose, which just proved he was a bit soft in the head, if only folk knew.

"If everybody gets it it can't have anything to do with being bad."

"My mammy says it's God's punishment."

"Oh shut up. People's mothers are all the same, a lot of old henwives."

It was her father who'd got them transferred to The Undesirables. He had an awful temper and he drank heavily and when he came home drunk he generally smashed up the house and threw things out of the window and two or three times he'd put her mother out on the landing in her nightdress and she'd had to knock up neighbours because she was freezing to

145

death, people called him Noble the Wife-beater. Elsa was always ashamed in case people in the street recognised her.

"Oh Dunky, I'm that miserable, I don't know what to do, it's awful, you don't know what it's like."

She turned towards him and hung on to him, beginning to cry. He stroked her hair and held her tightly. I'll soon be sixteen. I'll make her happy. I love her.

"Oh Dunky," she went on, sobbing away into his chest, making him feel all manly and protective, "you don't know what it's like, I don't want to get pregnant and be married like that, you get old and fat, they're always fighting and shouting at each other, I don't want to be like that, will I be like that, Dunky, tell me I won't."

"No, of course you won't get like that," he said. He was supporting them on his left elbow. He eased it free and they lay facing each other, her face against his chest, his arms round her, her nose sniffing as she tried to stop crying. "When we get married we'll be different, we'll save as much as we can and get a house of our own and we won't have any babies till we've enjoyed ourselves a bit and I'll give you all my pay –"

"And we won't *ever* start calling each other Mum and Dad, will we?"

"No, never. And we'll go to dances just like now and you'll be a right smasher –"

"And I won't get my legs burned from sitting in front of the fire, will I?"

"No, if I catch you sitting in front of the fire with your legs splayed out I'll smack your bum for you."

"And you won't go out and get drunk and leave me in the house and let me become just a fat wife, will you?"

"No, we'll go places on the bus, like Girvan and Edinburgh. It'll be different from them, don't worry."

"Oh Dunky, I hate it at home, I wish we could run away, just the two of us."

"Elsa, there's something I lied to you about."

She looked up, her eyes wet and her face red with wiping away her tears. He looked at the sky.

"I'm not seventeen yet, I just told you that in case you thought I was too young for you."

"How old *are* you?"

"Eh, sixteen – just about. My birthday's in May. I left the school early."

"Gosh, you're old for your age," she said. She still loved

him. He hugged her and kissed her hair. With Elsa he'd never once felt like doing anything *dirty*.

"You don't think I'm too young for you?"

"No," she said. He knew she got embarrassed when she wanted to say anything affectionate. Even girls weren't supposed to say soppy things, not in Kilcaddie. Never mind, he was daft enough for both of them.

"We could emigrate to Canada," he said. "It's different there, you get a lot better wages and there's lots of things to do. Not like dead-end Kilcaddie!"

When it became too cold to go on kissing and talking they stood up and brushed the grass and burrs from their clothes.

"You're the best-looking girl I've ever seen," he said, kissing her once more before they set off down to the hill. "Being married to you would be fantastic."

She smiled shyly and wiped her cheeks with the back of her hand.

"Do I look awful?" she asked.

"Lovely."

It was getting darker and colder by the time they were back in the town. They went for a coffee in the Eldorado, which was almost empty at that time in the late afternoon.

That was about all you could do on a Sunday in Kilcaddie. There was a tea-room halfway up the hill called The Croft. When he was still with the gang at school they'd often gone up there on Sunday afternoons, eyeing up the talent, sitting with their Coca-Colas, talking about women and football and other guys, finding out how to cause a riot by pouring a teaspoon of sugar into a Coke and letting it spray up to the ceiling, watching for certain girls to leave so that you could pay your bill and follow them down the road, trying to chat them up by shouting things after them. Or you could do what a lot of them did, spend most of Sunday evening parading up and down the High Street, just walking from one end to the other and back again, eyeing up the talent, pretending you were having a great time with your gang, all the time wishing you were winching instead. Telfer had been winching a big piece from the factory office and her parents had always gone out visiting on a Sunday afternoon so that Donald and his bit could have a necking session on the living-room couch, but that was more like something out of the pictures. Imagine his mother going out so that he could neck Elsa in the kitchen! Imagine going up to Noble the Wife-beater and asking him, dead gallus like, "Hey, Mister Noble, you mind pissing off for a couple of hours so's me and your Elsa can get snogging in peace?" Imagine!

No, you could sit in the café and drink coffee or you could walk up and down. Elsa had to be in by ten o'clock on a Sunday, her father might be fond of wrecking the house and administering the leather to his wife but he was dead strict about Elsa being home in time. They'd walked far enough for one day, his legs were quite stiff, especially the left one where he'd been kicked during Saturday's game. It was ten past five. Also, he was hungry.

"What d'you fancy doing now?" he asked her. "I'm starving. All you can get here is biscuits. If we had our own house you could be getting the tea ready, I love mutton pies and fried tomatoes and chips."

"When I've got a house of my own I'm never going to have a single thing out of a tin," she said. "My mammy's tin daft."

"And your father's canned all the time."

It was all right to make jokes like that now they were both looking forward to being married and being totally different from their own parents. She wasn't annoyed.

"Maybe I should come down to your house and ask for your hand," he said. She liked him making daft jokes about things, like pretending that her father would clap him on the back and send the butler for the whisky and ask him what were his prospects. Imagine Noble the Wife-beater's reaction to the arrival of Dunky Logan, boy farmer and general hard case!

"No, I'll go and see your mother and tell her I'm marrying you so's I can feed you properly."

"She'd think that was hilarity unbounded," he said. His mother would go wild if she knew he was going out with any girl. He couldn't imagine himself ever having the guts to take a girl back to the house and telling his mother they were getting married, but if the girl was an Undesirable. . . .

The only thing he wanted to tell *her* was goodbye the day he got on the boat for Canada. He asked Elsa if she thought it was evil to have thoughts like that about your own family.

"It's no wonder," she said. "Parents just think you're there to be bossed about."

Ian Nicol and his wife were walking along the High Street on their way home after Sunday tea with Ian's cousin when he saw the boy with the dark shirt walking towards them,

148

holding a girl's hand, not a bad-looking girl, either, heels a bit high for that age, trust Logan.

"That's my *bête noire* Duncan Logan coming towards us now," he murmured to Roberta. "The brown shirt. He'll hate this."

Dunky saw Nicol and thought for a second about trying to cross the road before they met, but decided not to lower himself. Anyway, he didn't care about schoolteachers any more, not now that he and Elsa were in love.

"There's one of my old teachers coming along," he said out of the side of his mouth. "The one with the suit. I wonder if that's his wife or his Girl Guide captain."

Then the enquiring looks, turning to nervous smiles as they decided to recognise each other. Dunky wouldn't have embarrassed Elsa by introducing her, but Nicol made a point of saying this was his wife, and Dunky felt cheeky enough to describe Elsa as his fiancée. She made a little face. She'd only been to King Street junior secondary, she thought Academy boys were snooty enough never mind actually talking to an Academy school teacher in the middle of the High Street! Dunky knew he was blushing and felt more determined than ever to show Nicol he wasn't just a silly scholar any more.

"I don't suppose there's a lot to do around here on a Sunday, is there?" Nicol asked. His wife kept her hand through his arm as they talked, but Dunky had let go of Elsa's hand. Nicol's wife wasn't a bad piece – for a teacher's wife. Her skin wasn't as smooth as Elsa's.

"No," Dunky said, looking at Elsa, beginning to grin. "We just go up the Braes and admire the view, don't we?"

Elsa grinned and said nothing.

Nicol felt something daring stir in his mind. He'd felt something unusual would happen, right from the moment he'd woken up in the morning. *Make* it happen, he told himself.

"I know you think teachers are on a social level with pariah dogs," he began, "but how would you and your fiancée like to come home and have a coffee with us?" He looked to see how Roberta reacted. She seemed a bit surprised. It was certainly not the done thing – to have social intercourse with pupils. People might talk!

"Yes, would you like to?" she said to Elsa, who went a little red and looked at Dunky. He looked back at her, clearing his throat. He'd never heard of such a thing.

"Eh, well, we were sort of . . ."

149

Nicol knew the agonies that Kilcaddie adolescents went through, he always told himself. At that moment he felt he represented the new force in education, teachers who'd been in the army, seen real life, not one of the superannuated prunes of the blackboard.

"Don't worry about us, we're quite normal really," he said, smiling encouragingly at the girl. There was something very delicate about her, the black hair against the pale forehead and the red cheeks. Not an Academy girl, though.

"Well, if it's all right . . ." Dunky said, hesitatingly.

"Fine."

There were several awkward moments as they walked the High Street, Mrs. Nicol on the inside, then Nicol, then Elsa and himself on the outside. At the front of the Playhouse cinema a gang of blokes were horsing about on the pavement and they had to move outside to pass them, Mrs. Nicol almost getting bumped. A policeman passed them, his face hard set. Dunky looked back and saw him stop before the small mob, who moved off, reluctantly. What was it like to be a bobby? Willie was always telling them of the time when Big Watson was taking in a ned from the King Street gang when a mob tried to rescue their mate. Big Watson, whom Dunky remembered vaguely, had drawn his baton and stood with his back to the wall, one arm round the throat of the guy he was running in, the other bashing at the gang with the baton. By the time other bobbies arrived he'd laid out three of them and still had his prisoner. One guy had tried a knife on him and Big Watson had broken his wrist with the truncheon. What Willie liked best about the story was how the three guys couldn't be taken to court for weeks because they were too badly bashed up. And when Sheriff Long saw them in the dock, with bandages over their skulls, he'd made some crack about the need to protect Kilcaddie policemen from violent mobs!

Kilcaddie bobbies were a hard lot. They needed to be. They lived in the real world, something a guy like Nicol knew nothing about. What did a guy like Nicol know anything about? You'd think with all his brains he'd know all sorts of interesting things, yet on their way to his house at the East End of the town, a better-class area which Dunky associated with women in fur coats and dentists' brass plates, he didn't say much at all. Dunky felt embarrassed on behalf of the four of them.

"You know that meeting you were at, Mister Nicol?" he began, looking across Elsa at the teacher. "Er, I was wondering why you went to it?"

Nicol let out a nervous sort of self-conscious laugh.

"You could hardly call it a love of free debate," he said. Elsa didn't understand. Dunky winked at her. They were holdings hands again. The hell if anyone saw them. "No, I occasionally stir out of my lethargy to try and find out what's happening in our beloved Kilcaddie. I suppose I was a trifle foolish attacking the great Comrade MacLean. Almost as dangerous as Free Discussion with the third year at the Academy!"

Logan would probably be uncomfortable with too many school references. He could hear the false note in his own voice. Many older teachers suffered from insecurity outside the classroom, now it was happening to him. Already he'd given up the habit of changing into a wool shirt when he got home in the late afternoon, finding it less trouble to sit in his school attire, striped shirt, attached white collar, waistcoat and suit trousers. There was a sort of ready, functional *voluptuousness* about Logan's tieless brown shirt. Had he ever belted Logan? No – perhaps in the first year, when the new twelve- and thirteen-year-olds were still anonymous faces. The boys laughed at the belt, he knew that. But was the laughter real – or a necessary sign of bravado? How deep did the strap reach? How deep did he *want* it to reach?

"Sit wherever you like," he said as they entered, in their varying degrees of shyness, the living room. Dunky associated bookcases with public libraries. He'd been in houses like this before, more space than he was used to, a carpet that wasn't worn smooth to the cord fibres. Nicol switched on a standard lamp while his wife knelt at the fireplace, removing a painted screen to turn on the two bars of an imitation coal fire. It had a warm red light which waltzed slowly through the translucent mould of simulated coal.

"I'm sorry we don't have the fire set," Mrs. Nicol said, smiling at Elsa. "We didn't bother today."

"It's a lovely fire," said Elsa. Mrs. Nicol took her coat and left them with her husband. Ian Nicol had often thought of moments like this and to that end he'd collected various items, curios, a ram's-horn snuff-mill dating back to the eighteenth century, old maps of Ayrshire with Kilcaddie spelled Kilcawdey, an ostrich-egg, early photographs of the old town, showing men in leather aprons standing by low-roofed cottage-type buildings, bits and pieces that visitors might be interested in. They rarely were, not their usual visitors.

"You might be interested in this," he said to Dunky, handing him a newspaper cutting which he kept between the pages of Lewis Grassic Gibbon's *A Scots Quair*. "My mother sent it to me, she still lives in Aberdeen, one of the old generation, y'know."

An awkward moment, Dunky half-rising from the armchair to save Nicol the bother of coming right across the room to hand him the cutting, Nicol hurrying his step to save Dunky the trouble of getting up.

"I thought you might like to compare agricultural *mores*," Nicol said, standing back, smiling self-consciously at Elsa. Dunky took the delicately-folded cutting, reading the headline:

SO BOTHY LIFE IS

STILL LIKE THIS!

Enforcement of hygiene has been the battle-cry of sanitary inspectors for years, but the lads who live in the bothy make a mockery of their plea.

Bothies have changed little over the years, but perhaps a few of the smells have changed, diesel oil and paraffin prevailing over the pungent horsy odour that made the townsman's nostril twitch and curl.

A look at one of these farmyard hostels the other day made me wonder how civilization even managed to get a foothold in this world, writes a *Journal* man. And yet these bothy lads have survived and they must be one of the hardiest races.

This particular bothy, which one it was I cannot divulge lest the society for prevention of cruelty to oneself should catch up with the characters, was perhaps a more de luxe version than some.

The lads were fortunate that one of the cottar women took a motherly interest in them.

They had real soup, none of these tinned varieties that other farm loons thrive on, a varied meat course, a drop of pudding, and tea.

But here the difference ended.

Each of the men ate every course out of the one white clay bowl – including tea!

"It gangs the same wey onywey," was one of the tractormen's earthy comment. "You should'a' seen this afore the wifie cam' in every day. Man, the dishes were never washed, and I jist washed my bowl wance in a six-month."

One who had been spreading manure sat down at the table without washing his hands. Another was like a snowman. He had been spreading lime and was covered in the dust.

Both assured me they had never had a serious illness in their lives, and their rosy cheeks and clear eyes convinced me.

"Pit the tatties on then, Wull," shouted the senior. The tatties were for the evening meal, which is not prepared by the cottar woman.

Wull got up from the table, his boots leaving a muddy trail to the door. He picked up a pot with custard sticking to its side, filled it with water, and threw in a few potatoes from a bag.

"They taste better when they're done in their jaickets," he said.

Shaving brushes and razors adorned the window sill and single beds crammed one corner.

"We're better aff than some," said Wull. "The last farm I was at they had double beds and ye jist jumped intae the first ane that wis empty.

"The sheets are changed here aince a fortnight, but in some places they're jist changed when they wear oot. Bothy life's changin' richt enough."

Mrs. Nicol brought in a tray with china coffee cups and saucers and a plate of sultana cake and another plate of assorted biscuits.

"I don't suppose you'd like farming so much if you lived like that," Nicol said.

Dunky gave the cutting to Elsa, who looked at it and then laid it carefully beside her on the couch while Mrs. Nicol gave her a cup and saucer.

"The farmer's son at our place says he never changes his shirt till it starts falling off his back," he said. "Did you come from a farm, Mister Nicol?"

"Oh no, my father was a minister. He had a church up near

153

Fraserburgh and then he moved down to Largs. My mother went back when he died. I consider myself true West of Scotland. But my wife's from Edinburgh, aren't you dear?"

Look dutifully at Mrs. Nicol. Hope Elsa isn't fed up. Doesn't look very comfortable, perched on the edge of the couch. Don't look at her legs. How about telling Nicol her father's Noble the Wife-beater!

"I'm not ashamed of it," Mrs. Nicol said. She had cold hands, nice nails. Women like her always had tea and coffee on trays round a wee low table. Lot of fuss and bother. Why not just sit up at the table and get it down you and cut out all this perching cups on your knees?

"I went to Edinburgh once with my auntie," Elsa said. "We went to the Zoo. All I can remember's a big golden eagle and a tiger."

"You've left school, I take it?" Nicol asked her. Elsa was uncomfortable at being asked a direct question. It had taken her a bit of nerve to tell them about the Zoo! Dunky must have been awfully clever to be asked to a school-teacher's house.

"Yes, I'm a folder at McKechnie's printing works," she said.

"And how long have you been engaged?" asked Mrs. Nicol. Elsa looked at Dunky, making a funny mouth. He didn't smile in case she got a fit of the giggles.

"Not long," he said. "We've not actually bought a ring or anything."

He wanted to giggle himself. It reminded him of a joke Telfer had told them in the stable. A young bloke and his girl get on a Glasgow tramcar. There's no seats. The bloke says to a grown man, "Hey, Chief, how's about givin' your seat to a lady?" "A lady?" says the man. "She's only a girl." "Aye, but she's pregnant." "Pregnant! She doesnae look very pregnant to me. How long's she been pregnant?" "Forty-five minutes, but her knees are still trembling."

Nicol wanted to say something to Dunky without offending him – or sounding like the man at the blackboard.

"And tell me, Duncan, is there much future in farming as a career today, would you say?"

Future? What was he going to get, a Careers' Council lecture?

"I think there's courses you can take for farm managers' jobs," he said. Aye, imagine telling Auld Craig you'd a dip-

154

loma in farm management. "I don't know much about it." Craig would tell you to go and manage the midden.

There was a bit of chat, but Dunky could see that Nicol was working up to some serious gab. When it came he put on his classroom face, eyes on the teacher, mouth neither yawning nor smiling, head shaking slightly to let him know you were still listening, mind wandering through football matches, rabbit hutches, necking sessions, looking up his wife's legs, grown-ups talking at, at, at you, from a different life, boring, going on and on and on....

"... it may suit you now but d'you think you'll still be happy when you're over twenty? The money seems good enough now when you haven't any responsibilities, it's the curse of our society, big wages for school-leavers in dead-end jobs, you grow up but the money stays the same...."

Dunky didn't feel any need to put his side of the case. Nicol wasn't really asking him questions, not really interested in *him*, just giving him a lecture in class.

Before they left Nicol made a last attempt to get through to the boy.

"Duncan," he said, and they both recognised the strained attempt to knock down barriers with the use of his Christian name, "would you tell me one thing, as honestly as you can? Forget I'm a schoolmaster, I'm asking you man to man. Why did you really want to leave school so much? Really."

Because I felt silly. Because I hated it. Because I got the belt from Miss Colquhoun and Miss Peacock and Mister Sinclair and Mister Everybastard. Because I hated exams. Exams and more exams. Because I hated being treated like a wee boy. Because you got an hour's homework every night and two hours after the third year. Because it was *official*.

He coughed. He knew Elsa was fed up, too. He didn't know what to say to Nicol.

"Er, well, I didn't want to work in an office and staying on another two years would just have been a waste of time, I dunno, I just wanted to leave."

I didn't want to get like you, I mean, snobbish, peely-wally, pan-loaf, stiff-collar, useless hands.

"Well, if you ever change your mind you can always come and see me," Nicol said. "You can do a lot in night-classes these days."

"Thanks very much. Eh, I think actually we should be going now." He didn't know what made him come out with the

155

next bit, but suddenly he was saying it, straight to Nicol's face. "Elsa lives in The Undesirables, her daddy doesn't like her out too late in case something happens to her."

"What did you have to tell him that for?" she asked, angrily, in the street. "That was a dirty trick."

"I didn't mean to," he said. She wouldn't let him take her hand. "You don't care about people like them, do you?"

"You'd no right to tell them. People say you're scruffs if you come from Barskiven Road. I didn't know where to put my face, so I didn't."

"You're as bad as they are," he said. "Ach, forget it, we never died o' winter yet. Hey, didn't they have *wee* cups?"

There was a scheme for getting your passage paid to Canada if you were a farm-worker. In Canada all the guys would live in a bunkhouse, not a sharny old bothy. Now that they were engaged Elsa and he could probably start doing *it*. Engaged? Telfer always said that you'd only to walk by a church with a Kilcaddie woman and she had the rope round your neck. Telfer was just a big-mouth and a smart aleck. He didn't know anything about real love.

Still, they'd had something to eat now, they could go to the Thomson Park and sit on a bench till it was time for Elsa to go home. Their necking sessions always left him shaken. It must be a great relief to be a man and not be frightened of sex.

CHAPTER EIGHT

It was April now. When the trailer lorry came into the yard there was only him and the boy about the place. Willie knew the straw bales would be a bit heavy for the boy, but McCann and Telfer were sowing and that job couldn't wait. Logan would just have to do as best as he could, the trailer had to be loaded and turned round before night. The driver said he'd help once he'd been to the phone box at the end of the scheme road to phone his boss, but Willie knew how long that errand would be spun out. Drivers didn't go much on toil.

"You get up on top, Logan," he said. He climbed on the back of the trailer, which was backed against the open-side barn. Dunky climbed the square bales of straw to the top, high enough to be able to touch the rounded corrugated roof with his hay-fork. Willie looked up at him. He dug the hay-fork into a bale, the tines taking it in the middle, under the tight string. It was a helluva weight. He had to hold it out from the side and then lower it so that Willie could catch the bottom end and pull it off the fork. The bales were about two foot high and three foot long, solid packed. On the end of the fork they seemed to weigh about a hundredweight.

"Chuck them down," Willie sang out. Back and forward he went under the big iron roof, jerking bales out of their close-packed layers, stumbling across other bales, knees bent to give him balance under the weight, arms and hands and wrists threatening to give out on him as he stood at the edge, keeping the bale on the fork until Willie had a hold of it, slipping out the tines at the right moment so that Willie could swing into position as it was dropping, clambering back for another while Willie heaved it into position, Willie always ready for another, waiting, his stomach taking most of the strain, the shiny hay-fork handle burning into his palms.

When the driver came back he got on the trailer with Willie. Building the load so that it would stay on the trailer was skilled men's work – *anybody* could do the heavy lifting. On and on they went, bale after bale going down to the two men, the level on the back of the long trailer hardly rising at all. Once he stumbled and a bale almost fell over on to them.

"Don't kill us, Jimmy," shouted the driver. He hated that,

showing he wasn't as strong as a man. He went faster, the lead creeping down from his shoulders into his forearms. Muscle, that's what you needed. There wasn't time to stop and take off his shirt and pullover, whenever he was slow in appearing above them with another bale they'd shout up "Don't go to sleep" or "only five ton more". One layer from the great block of bales in the barn made two layers on the trailer. It would have been easier to load them all from the front of the barn, but Willie wanted the bales taken off evenly. He had to walk to the far wall, delve into a bale, pull it away from the others, lever the hayfork handle across his thigh, stagger back to the open edge, swing it out, careful, keep a grip on the fork so that it didn't fly away still stuck in the bale, perhaps belting one of them on the face. Between bales there was just time to stretch back your shoulders and arch the small of your back and blow out air in a silent groan.

Then the full ten tons was loaded and the two men lifted the great canvas hap and they threw it up and over the load, lashing its ropes to hooks under the trailer. They threw the big ropes over the canvas-wrapped load, the driver in charge now, working quickly, pushing him out of the way, snatching a loose rope-end, breathing so hard you'd think *he'd* been working, Willie getting loose ends of rope and pulling them tight, his own hands too raw with opened blisters to exert much pull on the thick rough rope, his back feeling as though somebody had tied a knot in it.

In the stable at five o'clock he moved stiffly as he fed the two horses. Telfer and McCann filled a bucket of water from the horse trough and splashed the white dust off their faces. Dunky had told them about the bothy in Nicol's cutting and "decent table manners" had become a joke, with Telfer and McCann trying to catch each other out with dirty nails at tea-break. Willie getting married to Mary O'Donnell was still too much of a surprise to be joked about. When Dunky had quietly asked Telfer if he thought she was up the stick Donald had turned quite sharply on him and told him to watch his tongue. He'd given up bothering about McCann. Now that Coll was gone he was getting a lot more heavy work about the place. As he swept behind the horses, holding the brush as gingerly as possible in his raw palms, he told himself McCann wouldn't have forked ten tons of straw bales in that time without making a song and dance about it.

That night he went home and had his tea and then went out to the rabbit hut, to clean them out for the first time in two weeks. The evenings were becoming lighter now that it was into April, but he had to switch on the bicycle lamp before he'd finished. By half-past eight he had mucked out the hutches and given them new bedding. The rabbits were going to pot. There never seemed to be enough time, what with seeing Elsa two and three nights a week, her pretending to her father she was at her pal's house, and playing football on Saturday and going up the town with Alec on midweek nights when he wasn't seeing Elsa. Jesus Christ, he still hadn't made the new hutch for the four half-grown ones. The buck would be serving his sisters in a month or two if they weren't separated. Rabbits were a lot of work. It would be much easier if he got rid of them. His back was still sore as he walked across the yard. There was a slight taste of fog in the air. He felt heavy, all over, good job it wasn't a Friday or he'd be ruined for playing football. They were only three points behind the leaders of the Ayr and District Juvenile "B" League and they had to win every game if they were going to catch up.

He closed his eyes as he leaned against the landing wall to take off his boots. On Saturday, on the way home from the game, he'd call in at McKillop the butcher's and ask him if he'd buy two or three rabbits. His mother wouldn't take them for eating in the house. Or maybe he'd bike out to the Brig and see if Findlay would buy the whole lot back. They were getting too much for him.

"You look exhausted," his mother said. "Wash your hands and face, your father wants to see you."

For once Senga wasn't out at the Girl Guides. He'd tried to interest her in the rabbits so that she could do some of the work, but she was always going out to her pals' houses or the Brownies or some bloody thing. Girls had it easy. Senga was in the "C" class at school and she didn't even get much homework. As he dried his hands and wrists he looked at her and wondered if other guys thought she was good-looking. You couldn't tell with your own sister. At home all she did was sit in the corner and read her stupid girls' magazines and grunt when you spoke to her. His mother said it was "just a stage she was going through". He couldn't remember her ever giving him the benefit of "a stage". It must be great being a girl. No bloody worries at all.

159

"What's my father want?" he asked his mother, putting as much tired complaint into his voice as possible. "I'm tired out. I wish I had a bedroom to myself!'"

Imagine having to go to bed in the kitchen, with your mother and wee sister still sitting by the fire! And she wondered why he stayed out late every night!

"Go in and see him," she said.

He went into the bedroom, rolling down his shirt sleeves. Once you'd washed yourself the tiredness seemed to go, normally, but tonight was different.

"Tell your mother I want her as well," his father said. It sounded serious. He'd even put off the wireless, that was pretty drastic.

"He wants you, too," he said to his mother. Senga looked up. "Not you, hen, you sit and read your wee girl's comics."

She made a face at him, sticking out her tongue. Once she'd been quite good fun but now she seemed to be in huffs all the time. She had light brown hair, like her father. On the odd nights she did stay at home she was always playing at it, putting in rollers and washing it and whatnot. He wondered if she was winching. At thirteen? You could never imagine another bloke fancying your sister.

"I've got something to tell ye," his father said when they were both in the bedroom, his mother sitting at the foot of the bed, Dunky standing by the window, hands in his pockets, glancing out at the lights of the coalyard. "Doctor Barr's arranged for me to go to Killearn."

His mother obviously knew all about it from the way she looked at him.

"What for?" Dunky asked. He supposed he had to say something.

"For proper treatment," his father said. He seemed well pleased with himself. "I'm jist a burden on ye all here so I've decidet I'll be better off in a hospital."

He didn't know what to say.

"I think it's terrible you going away from your own home," his mother said. She seemed to be talking to *him*.

"What, can they do anything about your back?" Dunky asked. That would mean more room in the house, God strike you down for thinking evil thoughts.

"Ach, I don't suppose so," his father said. "I don't care, I'm fed up lying here bein' treatet like some useless *thing*.

160

I maybe wouldnae be goin' if I'd ever had a single civil word out of you."

The room seemed very small. Tense.

"Speak for yourself," he said.

"Dunky!"

"Oh aye, the big man can cheek his father, I'm only a helpless invalid."

"At least you're no' able to kick my arse now, are you?" He glowered at his father, thinking of the heavy bales and the ache in his back.

"I niver kicked ye near offen enough." His father raised his head, trying to get up on one elbow. It was the most energetic he'd looked since he'd been laid out. "There's bad blood in you, sonny."

"Mibbe but I'm workin' like a cunt an' you're lying there, ye're happy enough with the money."

Deep down you weren't really sorry for cripples at all. Not really. They'd got out of it somehow. People were *supposed* to feel sorry for them. They could be the most evil bastards in the world but if they lost a leg people would immediately feel sorry for them.

Duncan Logan shook his head. His own son, speaking to him like *that*. Unnatural. In front of his own mother. Not an ounce of respect in him.

Her face was white and empty. To hear your own son use a word like that, in his own home. Wasn't there anybody who could do anything with him? She started crying.

"There's whut ye've done to your mother," Duncan Logan said. "I hope ye feel proud of yourself."

They were crowded together in the small room, too close together. Christ, he'd often imagined leading Big Dick up the stairs and into this stinking wee house and let him kick at it, smash it to pieces, pound the stinking furniture to bits, bash down the walls, great horse hooves wrecking *everything*.

"I'm sorry, mum," he said, hanging his head. He wanted to cry, too. "I'm sorry."

She went on weeping.

"Stop your greetin', woman," said his father. "Things is bad enough without you bawlin' your eyes out."

"I can't help it," she sobbed, lifting the end of her apron to her eyes, dabbing at them, her chin quivering out of control as each new burst of sobbing made her shoulders shake. "I don't want you to go away."

Did that mean his mother really *loved* his father?

"Come on now, Beth," Duncan Logan reached a hand towards her shoulder. "They don't take incurable cases at Killearn. The only reason Barr's gettin' me in there's to see if they can sort my back. They're doing wonders up there."

Was his father just pretending to be nice? Why couldn't they have been nicer to each other before? In some way all this crying and sadness was *his* fault. He'd been enjoying himself playing football and breeding rabbits and going to dances and courting Elsa, and they'd been suffering. But why couldn't they have been nicer to *him*? Maybe he didn't deserve it, maybe it was true what his father said, he had bad blood. Other people didn't like him much, either, did they? It was a fluke that he was going out with Elsa. His only pal was a bit of a half-wit. It *was* unnatural, for a bloke his age to be mad about rabbits. He didn't like people and people didn't like him, that's what Jim Querns had said about him one day in the Croft tearoom. It was true. Even when he was a wee boy Grandpa Logan had called him a thrawn wee devil, the time he'd hit Neilly Graham from the next close with a half brick during a row about a marbles game in the gutter. If only he could say something nice to them. His own father was going away, maybe for good, and he was such a thrawn, unnatural person he couldn't think of anything nice to say. God had given him bad blood. He felt like being sick, anything to get out of the bedroom.

His mother dried her eyes. His father patted her arm. When he looked up his eyes were wet, too. His voice was squeaky.

"Ye're goin' to have to act like a man now," he said. He didn't sound angry. "It's your responsibility. I'm jist a useless wreck. If there's any heart in ye at all ye'll no' let your mother down."

Instinctively Dunky glanced in the rusty-edged wardrobe mirror, wondering what he looked like at that moment. He'd always been too fond of looking at himself in mirrors, he knew that.

"Don't worry, we'll be all right," he said. For some reason he felt he should shake his father's hand, but he couldn't. There was something unnatural about him. God was punishing him all the time for that dream, the one where he'd been in bed with his mother, the one that made him sweat just to think about. Jesus Christ, why didn't you make me just like other people?

162

"Right then, I'm away for a wee donner," said Willie.

"Off to see your pal the Tink?" laughed Mrs. Mary Craig, née O'Donnell. "Don't pick up any fleas."

"He's cleaner nor me," said Willie.

"That wouldn't take much, you smelly old billy-goat."

As he passed the sink he gave her buttock a hard pinch. She jumped forward, twisting round to push his hand away.

She watched him out of the window until she saw his dark shape in the light at the end of the yard. She felt like clapping her hands and letting out little squeals. She had her own husband now and her own home, set up as well as any woman in the land. Sure and a lot better than most, for how many women had managed to get what she'd got – *and* a bit of fun as well?

She was waiting at the kitchen door when she heard the quiet footsteps and the gentle knock. She opened it just wide enough for Donald Telfer to slip through, sideways.

"He's away down the back road," Donald said.

"You're sure?"

"Sure I'm sure. There's no flies on me, Missus."

Holy Mary forgive her for a mortal sin but Donald was a lovely man. The very sight of him made her itch to get her hands on him. Nodding for him to follow she limped slowly to the door to the rest of the house. She cocked an ear at the foot of the stairs. There was no sound from Craig's room. He'd be dead to the world, the old brute. Putting her fingers to her lips she beckoned him to follow her into the bedroom.

"Are you sure the back door's snibbed?" he whispered, his long, clean hands already at his shirt buttons.

She nodded, closing the bedroom door. It was as safe as houses. Willie would be away for a couple of hours and Craig could sleep through an earthquake. The only light in the room came from the window, its curtains drawn back, the April moon and stars throwing a misty glow over the buildings outside. Even in the half-darkness Telfer's hair was bright, the brightest thing in the room. She ran strong fingers through the yellow hair as he knelt before her, pulling down her skirt, kissing the hard front of her, smoothing his hands up her nylon slip, then rising to press his tall, hard body against her while he felt round her back to unloosen the row of brassière hooks. She pulled at his trouser buttons while he ran his hands down her back and pressed the palms against her buttocks.

He was so hard and slim and long. When he lay on top of

her there was no weight to him at all, just the long body hard in her arms, his rockhard thing going into her, deeper and deeper, filling her up, never ending, her hands kneading at the hardness of his ribs. It couldn't be wrong to want a man who could make you feel like this! Even his bum was hard, smooth and hard. There was a smell of soap off him, everything was hard and smooth and warm.

"Into you, into you," he hissed, now lifting himself on his palms, looking down at her, his body like a length of smooth steel.

Then he lay on her, one hand flat under her buttocks, the other feeling the outlines of her breasts, his face pressed against the muscle of her upper arm. Only the cold touch of the metal supports on his knees reminded him that she was a cripple, the rest of her was strong and warm and muscly.

"Is that better than Willie?" he asked her, his voice a murmur that she could feel vibrating from his chest.

"Wouldn't you like to know," she said.

It was the one thing he wanted to hear her say, but she never would. Some daft idea about being loyal, he supposed. It was all right to let another guy ride you, in your husband's bed, but not to tell you what *he* was like.

"You're a devil, making me do this," she whispered.

He snorted. It'd been as much her doing as his. He ran his hand down her belly.

"Crivvens, you're putting on weight," he said. "Anybody would think you'd a bun in the oven."

"Would they now? And whose doing would that be, I wonder?"

She was a sonsy bitch all right, she knew what she wanted and she didn't care how she got it.

"Come on," she said, digging her fingers into it, "we haven't got all night." She knew how to get him going again, too, pinching the tight skin over his ribs, biting his ears, jabbing her good heel down the back of his leg, squirming under him like an itchy pig.

"I'll tear you in two," he said, his hands pinning her arms back on the pillows. "I'll gie you a baby all right, see what they say when it's a wee yellow bastard like me!"

She laughed up at him.

"You think you're man enough?"

He hissed at her and then he was forcing the smile off her face, making her shut her eyes and roll her head from side to side, her master, her real thing, knowing what she needed and giving it to her, hot and strong ... look at me now, Willie Craig, who's the man and who's the common tyke?

"Well, it sounds as if you've done all right for yourself," said Archie Stewart. "You're lucky it's all worked out so well, Willie. Have some tea. Isn't it grand when the nights get lighter and you know summer's coming? Summer's the time I enjoy best. The rain's even enjoyable in the summer."

It made Willie feel better to hear Archie say he'd done the right thing getting married. He had a notion other people – the men, some of the scheme folk, his father to be sure – were laughing at him behind his back for marrying the cripple woman. He guessed they'd say things like "Nae fool like an auld fool" or "She got her hooks intae him quick enough" ... or even "Is that the best he could dae for hisself?" Of course Archie didn't get about the place much, he wouldn't know what folk were saying.

"What would ye dae if ye had to leave here?" he asked, the hand holding the jam jar resting on his thigh, his back against the wall, his legs stretched out towards the glowing brazier, his feet crossed.

"Leave here!" Archie the Tink put his head to one side. At times he acted like a wee boy. "I wouldn't fancy that, Willie, not at my age. No, I want to die here, in my wee cave. Where would I go anyway? The McGleishes tell me it's getting harder for them every year to find a place to put their tents. If it's not the councils it's the farmers. I hear they're talking of building a whole new scheme at the back of the Brig, right up to the Kilberrie Woods, acres and acres of council houses! Have you heard anything about that?"

"Aye, I believe there wis something in the papers aboot it. Don't worry your head aboot the McGleishes, they'll aye find some neuk to nest down in."

"Oh aye, they're canny folk for all they're supposed to be ignorant tinks."

"But what aboot yerself, Archie, ye're a fair age, would ye no' be better aff somewheres they'd take care o' ye?"

"What, a home you mean, an institution for old folk? No, no, Willie, you'll never find me in one of those places. I'm my own man down here in the Black Hills. Can you see me in a bed in an institution, a toothless old haverer getting fed on pap and having my bum wiped for me?" He laughed at the

165

very idea. "I'll go to a place like that the day your father does."

"Aye, that would be the day all right."

He only half-listened while Archie talked away about the countryside and how it was gradually being swamped by the towns. The day before his father had told him Kilcaddie Burgh Corporation were talking about using the Black Hills as a site for an industrial estate. Ayrshire County Council owned the land. Kilcaddie Corporation wanted the new factories because of the jobs they'd bring to the town, but they'd need more than just the Black Hills. They also wanted the two low fields between the Black Hills and the road.

"We'd have less nor a hundert acres," Willie had said to Craig. The rented fields didn't count. You didn't depend on land you didn't own, that was Craig's motto.

"Aye," his father had replied. "Hardly worth the bother farming at all. An' they say they'll want more land once they've levellet it up."

Willie had seen them preparing a factory site before. First they carted away the topsoil. For a year or so they'd drive in lorry-loads of rubbish from the corporation destructor, tipping it on to the fields, bulldozing it flat, the dirty rubbish from the town, ash and cans and muck. They'd bulldoze the hedges. While the coup was being laid the sky would be dark with crows and seagulls. Packs of rats would swam over the rubbish. The fields round about would be covered in dust and the roads littered with papers and cans and cardboard boxes off the lorries. Combustible waste would smoulder under the surface, its dirty, stinking smoke reeking the whole countryside. The whole place would become an eyesore. Then one day they'd have levelled it up to their requirements and they'd begin to lay the foundations for the factories.

And in two or three years you'd never even know that land had once been a farm.

He knew his father was as much against this as anybody, but he was a funny old bugger, Craig. Maybe he'd rather let the land go to hell in factories than die knowing Mary and him had taken his place. A lot of old farmers were like that. They'd rather see a thing destroyed than lose it to somebody else. He decided not to say anything to Archie. His father might decide not to sell them the two low fields and without access the Black Hills site wasn't much good to them. They'd probably go for a compulsory purchase order, but

166

that took a fair while to go through. Maybe Archie would be dead by then.

He left the hut with Archie walking him to the dirt road.

"Aren't the stars just glorious?" said the Tink.

"If ye keep lookin' up ye'll fall down a hole."

Mary was already in bed when he went into the house, after a walk round the buildings and a look in at the horses. He put his clothes on the chair and sat on the bed to take off his socks. His body was white, his neck burned red, his forearms hairy and dark with engrained dirt. She didn't look up from the pillow as he went across to switch off the light. She didn't want to look at his waist-less body and his thickening gut. Not after the slim hardness of the other man.

"I'm tired," she said, irritably, when he climbed between the sheets and put a hard hand on her backside. It was like feeling a sack of coal sliding over you. As soon as was safe she'd tell him she was pregnant and couldn't be bothered with sex.

"Ye'll be mair tiret when I'm through," he said, panting as he laid his chest on hers and got his knees between her legs.

One thing at least, he didn't seem to care if she moved about or just lay back and let him get on with it. When Willie got going he snorted away like a horse pulling uphill. He wouldn't have cared then if she was his wife or a bag of chaff with a hole cut in the middle. . . .

Of course it wasn't serious, only a bit of an ache from moving all those bales. Or could it be something more? Whatever, Dunky couldn't get to sleep. The fire was a dull glow of red coals under a thickening spread of soft ash. He got out of bed and opened the bottom of the window. Fresh air, that's what the house needed. Windows open, cold draughts blowing out the heat and the staleness. He made water into the sink, standing on tiptoe so that it would flow down the side and not make a splashing noise. His mother expected him to go down to the landing lavvy, in his bare feet in the middle of the night!

He tried thinking about women, Mrs. Nicol letting him undress her on their soft carpet, Mary the cripple crawling into a pile of hay, Miss Peacock the maths teacher keeping him in late after school and telling him to run his hands up her nylons, then taking him home and ordering him to take off her clothes with his teeth . . . he couldn't concentrate on any of his usual bed-pictures. What he needed to do was to *think,* about real things, about Elsa and the rabbits and Canada. About the future. There was bound to be even less money coming into the house when his father went to Killearn. He was already giving his mother four pounds ten shillings a week, only keeping eighteen shillings for himself. He'd have to ask Willie if the old man would give him a rise. He could always chuck in his job at Craig's farm and go into the factory – at his age he might get eight or nine pounds there. But as long as he worked on the farm he was exempt from National Service. Having to go into the army was about the worst thing he could imagine, just as bad as two years in prison. What was it like to work in a factory anyway? Shut in all day, the noise of screaming machines, having to work with *metal* – hellish.

Telfer said there was an assisted passage scheme to Canada for farm workers, but Telfer didn't think it applied if you were under eighteen, or if it did you have to have your parents' written consent, they'd never give it, they'd say he was leaving them in the lurch. Bad blood. Where did it start? He remembered sleeping in this bed with his father when Senga was being born in the bedroom. Hated that, sleeping close to *him*, still felt funny thinking of that, remember the time you saw his cock and felt ill, terrifying, horrible. Getting belted for throwing his brand new Sunday School cap over a wall on the way home, hated that stupid thing, *must* have been a thrawn wee devil to be chucking away a good cap ... never really *liked* the other blokes at school, they always seemed to be laughing behind your back, most of their fathers were better off, not common boilermakers! He'd much rather have gone to King Street than the Academy, the only boy from Shuttle Place among a nest of smalltime toffs' kids. He'd never fitted in at the Academy with its silly school tie and its mammy's boy football teams, frightened to get their knees dirty, scared to death of teams from "scruff" schools....

Wee Ernie Lavelle's father had given him a new rubber ball a half-size imitation of a real leather football. It was the best ball they'd ever had for football on the lower school playground, where the surface was fine gravel on hard earth. Billy Aird, the bobby's son, kicked the ball over the high wall at one end of the playground. He said he wouldn't go round to the tenements to fetch it because playtime was almost over. He said he didn't care about Wee Ernie's ball. Ernie was a hopeless wee gnaff who wore specs and cried if the teacher

168

was nasty to him. He was crying at the thought of having to go home and tell his father the ball was lost. I'll go, he'd said, and he ran all the way out of the other end of the playground, along Clark Lane and up Brediland Street and through the tenement close, panting, running about in the backyard of the high black tenements until he found it wedged between some dustbins and a wash-house wall, running all the way back, seeing the empty playground, trying to walk to his desk before Miss Walker saw him, where do you think you're going, Duncan Logan? Three of the best, hands crossed, palms upwards, her face twisted as she shook her right elbow clear of her black gown, shutting your eyes as the thick leather belt whammed on your outstretched hand. He waited for Billy Aird at dinnertime, he could remember every bit of that fight, he'd rushed at Billy Aird as he came down the steps, walloping him on the nose before he knew what was happening, hitting at Billy Aird the big fat policeman's son, funny you didn't feel any pain when you were actually in a fight. Billy Aird ran away and he'd chased him to the lavvy, Billy Aird trying to hide his face and kick him at the same time, the crowd followed them, then somebody shouting that Miss Bell, the head primary teacher, had seen them out of the staff room window, running to the main gate, thumping Billy Aird on the back of his neck, Billy Aird's fingers poking in his eyes, wanting to murder him, grabbing his blazer lapels and hitting him on the face with his forehead. An eleven-year-old Academy using his noddle to butt somebody! Putting the head in was a scheme scruffs' trick, even if the other guy was a rat and a cheat and bigger than you.

Being dragged into the school by Mister Mason, the only man teacher in primary, Miss Bell sending him to see the headmaster in the big school, walking on his own up the hill while everybody else was at school, waiting outside the head's office, senior scholars staring at his bleeding lip and torn button, frightened out of his wits, Zorro Sinclair the headmaster, called Zorro because he was supposed to have a Z carved on his belt and it left Z cut in your hands after he'd belted you, the Mark of Zorro, a thin creep of a man with glasses and flat grey hair, a terror, the man who never smiled, six of the best from Zorro Sinclair, stingers, being embarrassed more than hurt, that should have been it but Zorro made him wait outside and then gave him an envelope addressed to his father and sent him home early. The sneaky rat! Telling his

169

mother the truth, her not even listening when he said it wasn't his fault, waiting hours for his old man to come home from the works, praying to Jesus and God, lot of good that was, wanting to be sick, red sweat line where the cap had pressed on his father's forehead, face grim as he opened the white envelope, then rolling up his sleeves and taking down the shiny black razor strop which hung beside the fire, the real belting then, round his legs, across his hands when he tried to push it away, embarrassed, *them being nearly as big as each other, two of them alone in the kitchen, the strap cutting into the back of his legs, trying to move away without running, that would make it worse, his father growling, not actual words, all he could think was of being* ashamed, *getting a leathering in your own house, his father not interested in his side of the story, then the last and worst, his father lifting his boot to him, kicking him on the bottom of the spine, right on the bone, bawling like a big baby, his mother coming in to stop it, having to undress in front of them in the same room, nobody speaking, pulling the covers over his head, lying there in the dark with them sitting beside the fire, one day I'll be bigger and stronger and harder than* him *and I'll come in the house and grab him by the throat and ram him up against the wall and hammer him in the guts, holding him up by the adam's apple, battering into his belly, I'll kill you, don't worry, I'll never forgive you, you'll be sorry, dead sorry....*

Even thinking about that had made him breathe faster. Naturally his old man had forgotten all about it, now he needed to be loved by his family. He'd never forgotten, though. Never would. Nor the guys at school. That still puzzled him. Next day when he'd gone back they'd taken Billy Aird's side. They wouldn't speak to him, none of them. Even Norrie Cochrane, whose gang he'd been in, wouldn't speak to him or let him play football with them. God, when he thought of all those days he spent hanging about at playtime, pretending he didn't want to play football anyway, hearing Billy Aird's sneaky laughing behind his back, desperately wanting them to ask him to play again, being pathetically happy and smarmy when one day they didn't ignore him any more....

Was it silly to remember things like that? When Nicol asked him why he didn't like the school he would have felt like a big gawkit schoolgirl telling him *that*. But it was the start, no doubt about it. He'd never forgiven them, not even when they reached the second and third year in the senior school, Billy

Aird, Norrie Cochrane, Ian McInnes, Bobby Young, Dovat Shand, Tom Cadenhead, Peter Fleming, Hugh Gilchrist, Hammy Alston, Ian Barclay, Jimmy Barr, Jimmy McDonald, Rhonach Kennedy ... that was why he'd made big pals with Alec, he'd come to the Academy in the first year in the senior school and hadn't been one of them.

If he lived till he was ninety and he met any of them in Kilcaddie High Street he'd still want to kick the ballocks off them. And if ever Cartneuk were against a team in which one of them was playing that's exactly what he would do. Bad blood, maybe they were right. Too bad. Better to have bad blood than be a big mummy's boy and have to suck to keep in the gang. ...

CHAPTER NINE

"So ah says tae him, listen here, mister, ah says, if ye think ye kin talk tae me like that ye've got anuther think comin', so ye huv. I wis fair livid, so I wis, richt enough. A big strappin' fella like *him* tellin' me whut fur! I felt like cloutin' him ower the heid wi' ma message bag."

Telfer had intended to stay in the house that night, read the paper or *Wide World* magazine, listen to the radio or play some gramophone records, but Mrs. Sneddon had come across the landing to borrow a shilling for her meter and now her daughter Bertha had come in as well and they looked set for the night, gassing away to his mother like houses on fire. His mother was too soft with them. He tried to make it obvious he wanted them out by swinging his feet up on to the arm-rest of the shiny rexine couch, lying back with his hands under his head. The very sight of Bertha's newly-washed hair, combed flat back and still wet, and her pale pink lips with their chapped edges, and her bare feet in tatty slippers and the leg veins burned brown from sitting too near the fire, made him want to boke. Years ago, when he was a wee boy about ten or eleven, he'd stuffed her among the Black Hills. Even though she was now married to a bloke serving with the army in Germany she often tried to give him the eye. Boooogh!

"Don't mind our Donald," said his mother. "He always puts his feet up when there's folk in."

"I'll leave you in peace in a minute," he said. "I can tell when I'm not wanted."

"Och, don't be gaun' oot jist because of us, Donal'," said Mrs. Sneddon. "Me'n Bertha's gaun' tae the flicks, she's peyin' me in."

"Ah am not," said the girl.

"Ye are sot," said her mother. "Here, Donal', ye couldnae lend us a fag, could ye, Bertha's been smokin' like a linty a' day and I've run out so I huv."

He watched his mother rising to get her packet from the sideboard. How she put up with an old bauchle like Mrs. Sneddon and her mawkit daughter he didn't understand. His mother had class, blonde hair in a fancy style, a tight white pullover, fuzzy, black slacks and high-heeled shoes, long red nails – not cracked and chipped like Bertha's.

The Sneddons took the hint and left, or maybe they'd just been hanging on to borrow the fags.

"I'd lock the door to that lot," he said.

His mother shrugged. Only when you saw her face, close-up, the hard lines not quite hidden by make-up, would you have known she was forty-six. From the back she looked like a thirty-year-old. "You stayin' in the night then?"

He scratched his hair.

"Suppose so, nothin' better to do."

"Your fancy womans' got pregnant on ye, I hear."

"Oh aye. You hear a lot, don't you."

"Word gets round."

Just once, that was all, one time and never again. Ne'er-day, the first after his father ran away, even his straitlaced brother Davie got drunk, Davie was just demobbed from Korea, people dropping in, bottles of whisky, bottles of VP wine, screwtops by the dozen, drinking and dancing, wild "hoochs" and the floorboards jumping, the front door open, records on full blast, windows rattling, Bobby McCaffery and his three mates wanting a fight, him and Davie throwing them down the stairs, drinking and dancing and shouting, then about four or five in the morning the people going away, Davie flat on his back behind the couch, dead to the world, just him and his mother, her wanting to go on dancing, his own mother, just the once, an accident, too drunk to know what they were doing, his mother crying and holding on to him, big brother Davie unconscious on the floor behind the couch, thinking he was a big man helping his own mother to bed, her too drunk to stand properly, just the once, her fault, she was his mother, she was old enough to have known better, could never forget it, neither of them ever forgot it, never daring to talk about it, remembering all right, see it in her eyes when they looked at you, try never to look at her too much, just like other women, not how you were supposed to look at your own mother, not like other women, try never to be alone with her too much, not to let her touch you, once was bad enough, happen again you might want to cut your throat, like a disease, Davie never even guessed, Davie very cold and straitlaced, big noise in the Boys' Brigade, Davie would be shocked out of his mind, not even like somebody

173

from the same family, never got drunk again after that Ne'er-day, him and her not like Davie, too much alike, knew what each other thought before they spoke, never forgetting that once, remembering it every time he had a woman, nobody could say you were abnormal if you had other women, lots of them, prove it, normal, just the once and too drunk to know what they were doing. . . .

"George not coming round the night?"

"No, it's his wife's birthday."

George was his mother's fancy man, unhappily married to a real shrew, not a bad bloke for a fancy man, at least with him hanging around her he knew she was getting her ration. As long as there were other people about, his women and her fancy man, they weren't sitting around looking at each other.

"I think I'll away out for a ride round on the bike," he said.

"I thought you were going to stay in."

"No, I think I'll away out for a bit. Get some fresh air."

Other people had families that meant something to them. Not us Telfers! A father who'd run away. Two brothers who might have been strangers. Him, always having to remind himself that she wasn't just another woman, but his mother. What was it all supposed to be about, anyway? From the moment you knew anything you knew it was supposed to be wrong. Yet it happened all the time. Joyner the coal-heaver got seven years for fathering bairns on both his daughters. Reid the farmer at Cauldrum was fined fifty pounds for letting his own kids sleep together until they were fourteen or more – one of the girls getting up the stick by her own brother. You knew it was wrong all right – but nobody ever told you *why*.

He cycled down their road and round the corner into Crags Avenue. No point in going near the farm, not that he minded Mary being pregnant but she said it was too risky, if Willie caught them he'd say the baby wasn't his and kick her out. Of course it wasn't Willie's baby! It stood to reason it must be his. As men there was no comparison between them. It was just his rotten luck, most women gave him the screaming hab-jabs as soon as he'd won the battle to get the knickers off them, the only one who could keep him on the boil was married to somebody else. Just his rotten luck, to have to think of her and Willie, himself and his mother. Was that why it was wrong? Did it affect you with other women? Spoil you? What,

174

just that once, all that time ago? Never. Yet why the attraction for the kind of women he went with? For a cripple? Was it like a *disease*?

It made you think of yourself as some kind of stranger, a man alone, cycling about the dark scheme streets, looking in other folks' windows. . . .

"Och well, it's just that nothing ever seems to happen about us," Elsa said. "It'll be years before we get married."

"Stop your moaning," Dunky said, bear-hugging her head into his chest. He'd felt sick after getting out of his father's bedroom, but being with Elsa made him all right again. They couldn't get married quick enough. She was marvellous! Now that it was April and the nights were warmer they'd got into a habit of spending their midweek nights on a wooden bench seat on the edge of the Corporation football pitches, holding hands, necking, talking and thinking about the great days ahead. Only on Saturday nights did they spend any money, five and sixpence on back stalls seats at the pictures.

"I'm fed up never enjoying ourselves," she said.

"Don't you enjoy yourself with me?"

"Oh yes, but it's always the same, a wee walk down here and then home again." For some reason she *wanted* to make trouble, no, that wasn't it, she didn't *want* to fight, it was something inside her, a wee devil voice egging her on. Her mother kept telling her she was far too young to be running about with a serious boy friend but her mother was against all men because she thought they were all like her father. Something her pal Betty had said was in her mind as she lay against his chest, his arm round her shoulder, his right hand on her lap.

"When I get engaged it's goin' to be with some fella who's got bags of money, I want to enjoy mysel' while I can," was what Betty had said. At first Betty had thought it was "awfy romantic" for Elsa to be courting seriously, but it didn't look as though they could even afford a ring for *years* and there was no fun in being unofficially engaged, you were supposed to save your money and you didn't even have a ring to show to the girls at work. That was the exciting part, first showing them the engagement ring, then planning the wedding, people regarding you as *important* . . . other people had fathers who gave them the money to get married. Her father put all his money over the pub counter and Dunky's father was permanently paralysed and even if they did have any money they'd never let them get married, not at their age.

"We agreed we wouldn't waste our money on daft things," Dunky said. "Didn't we?"

"Yes but it'll be *ages* before we can get married."

It came over him in a rush, as though he'd jumped into water and was kicking to get to the surface, then gasping in air and shaking his head.

"All we ever seem to do is argue," he said. He could hear the change in his voice, hard and abrupt. "If you want to enjoy yourself go ahead." He had a sudden picture of his rabbits being killed, all the work he'd put into them going to waste. It made him want to cry. He'd been prepared to kill them all for her. He'd really loved her, never even asked her to go farther than kissing! The hell with it.

"One of the girls at our work was engaged and she and her boy friend had a trial separation, to see if they still loved each other after two months."

"All right, if that's what you want. I'll tell you now but, I'm not going to go out with other girls."

"Me neither."

He could go home and start work on the hutch straightaway! It felt great. And he wouldn't have to go on worrying in case his mother found out about Elsa.

"What, you're not going out with other girls?"

"No, silly. I won't go out with other boys. Just dance with them."

There was no reason to go on necking so they got up from the bench and walked, hand in hand, across the football pitches towards the street-lights.

"Don't bother coming all the way down to my place, I'll be all right on my own," she said as they reached the top of the street.

"Okay."

They both knew it was probably over. Their last kiss was against the roll-down door of the Co-operative butcher's shop in Balloch Road.

"We'll know if we're really serious," she said, as if it was a promise of good things to come. When they parted he waited behind the corner for a second and then looked round after her. It was a funny thing about girls, when they were strangers you thought it would be the greatest thing in the world to get to know them, and when you'd been going out with them for a while you didn't even notice that they were good-looking. He could never tell guys like Alec or Telfer that he'd never stuffed her, they'd say he must be a homo or something. They didn't understand real love. What do you know about real love, you coldblooded bastard, you're not even sorry it's over.

As she walked along the pavement in Dalmount Drive, which ran from the shops and two-storey houses at one end into the Darroch Scheme at the other, Elsa thought of all the things she would do in the next two months. Betty had started going to the dancing in Ayr, she said it was fantastic compared to Kilcaddie Town Hall, the fellas were dead fast and experienced, you had to watch yourself in Ayr all right. And even if she met a really smashing bloke, rich, with a *car,* she'd never forget Dunky.

At first she ignored the man on the bike, pedalling slowly to keep pace with her, hoping he'd go away.

"Getting too high and mighty to recognise your old friends then?" said Telfer. Recognising the voice she looked at him for the first time.

"Oh hallo, it's you," she said. "I thought it was a strange man."

"I'm a very strange man," he said, sitting back on the saddle, steering with one hand. "Where's lover boy tonight?"

"I've just left him. We've decided to have a trial separation."

"Just like film stars, eh? What's wrong, would he no' give ye half of his dolly mixtures?"

It made you feel *very* important, to tell people you were having a trial separation.

"Very funny I don't think. If we still love each other after two months we're going to get married."

"Where, in your cradles?"

"You think you're awfully smart, don't you? I never see you with a girl friend, how's that?"

"It depends where you go. I don't fancy kids' dances in Kilcaddie. What're you doing on Saturday?"

"Wouldn't you like to know."

"Fancy going to the pictures in Ayr?"

"We've promised not to go out with other people."

"He'll no' know. How about it, eh?"

Betty would be dead jealous. She thought Donald Telfer was better looking than Dirk Bogarde – and he was her dream-boat film star!

"You're very fast, aren't you?"

"Who, me? I'm very shy if you want to know the truth."

"Pull the other leg, it's got bells on."

"I'll meet you at the bus stop in Ayr, all right. Nobody'll know."

"But I have to get home on time or my father'll melt me."

"Do I look like the kind of bloke who'd lead young girls astray?"

"Definitely, I wouldn't trust you with boxing gloves on."

"Tuts tuts, you've got a very suspicious mind for your age, what kind of fellas have you been going out with?"

"I don't go out with fellas."

"What's young Logan then, bit of a nancy boy is he?"

"That's different."

"Come on, what d'you say?"

"Oh all right if it means that much to you. I hope you haven't got any funny ideas but. You'll be disappointed."

"Funny ideas! I'm only asking you to the *pictures*, kid. I'll wear handcuffs if it makes you any happier."

"Ta ta then."

"See you at six o'clock at the bus station?"

"If I can."

"You'd better."

She ran across the road and round the corner into The Undesirables. Funny how you could see a bint knocking around and not even begin to fancy her until some other bloke was taking her out. Now that he thought about it, she looked just like one of those film star women, what was her name, the dark-haired piece. Whistling *High Noon,* he cycled along the main scheme road. For once they'd had two whole days without a drop of rain. Hard lines on young Logan, ha ha, wee boys shouldn't get big ideas before their time. . . .

CHAPTER TEN

"Here, Logan, away an' get the big horse from the school field," said Willie. "Hey, Blackie, whaur's a rope for the boy?"

"I'll better go wi' him," said Blackie, giving Dunky a cocky look, one cheek twisted in a sneering grin. "We want tae get startet the day."

"I can manage fine," Dunky growled, but McCann took the rope halter off the hook and didn't offer to hand it over. Telfer was filling water and paraffin into the tractor. He ignored them.

"Doesn't the year go by quick?" he said to McCann as they walked across the yard and out into the road. "It's hardly like yesterday we were at the hay last year."

He liked to think that nowadays he was above McCann's sarcastic remarks. On the three or four occasions Blackie had looked like having a real go at him something had always happened before they got to fighting and now it was only now and then that Blackie would drop the odd insult.

"Last year!" said McCann as they walked under the railway bridge and up the metalled road in the early July sunshine. "That's nothin', I can remember this field stretchin' all the way tae the scheme."

High red metal fencing separated the asphalt playground from Craig's grass. Big Dick was grazed in this part, he was enough of a menace to keep the scheme kids off Craig's land. It was too near the houses for anything but grazing a bad-tempered horse. Craig liked his crops and his cattle on the other side of the railway line, protected to some extent from gangs of marauding brats and rubbish-dumpers and neds who thought nothing of a game of football on spring corn. They went into the field and shut the rusty iron gate behind them. The mare was already in the stable, brought in by Telfer on his way down to work. It was as well McCann had come, Dunky thought, for Big Dick was a fly devil who knew very well what the rope halter meant – back to work after two or three months' loose grazing.

As they approached the big horse, Dunky scuffed the toes of his boots into the darker circles of long grass which still grew thicker than the rest although no cows had dropped

179

pancakes there for two or three year. There was no dew on his boots. Summer was here and the grass was dry by half-past eight. For almost a month they'd been at turnips, hoeing and thinning, monotonous, earthy work, day after day in the long drills, your neck muscles feeling it most of all. Starting among the hay was the sign that the summer was really here.

"Hullo, Dickie, Dickie," said McCann, gently, walking steady towards the horse, the halter in his right hand behind his back. The horse took a final bite at the grass and then raised his head, cocking it just enough to see them come up from his rear. Dunky stopped. McCann had to get the rope over him first go, before he realised he was being yoked.

The horse took a sideways step as McCann lifted his hand. McCann murmured something, patting at the great neck. He worked himself nearer its head, one hand among its black mane, the other slowly bringing up the halter. Then the rope was being lifted up round its mouth. Dick shook his head in the air and walked away from McCann, stopping with his back to him. McCann moved forward. He had on creased blue dungaree trousers whereas Dick's legs were brown and hard and smooth. There was more power to one of his towering hind-legs than there was to McCann's whole body. He knew, he didn't want to work, to have the rope round his neck. Why the hell should he?

Maybe he knew what had happened to old Charlie. If he was bright enough to know what a rope meant why shouldn't he wonder where the old, done horse had gone?

On McCann's second attempt Dick reared more energetically, front hooves leaving the ground, dropping down, a casual gesture as though he was trying to show them what he might do if he took them seriously. Then he trotted away, four legs moving evenly, head up, mane flying, an easy disciplined canter like practice for trotting in a circus.

"Come on," said McCann. "He's jist playin' up."

Laughing to himself, he followed McCann across the grass. Perhaps people were watching them from the windows of the scheme houses. Two men chasing a big horse, silly men in silly trousers and jackets, fragile wee bodies. Pursuing the noble beast. Man came down from the trees and only his superior brain kept him alive among the predatory creatures of far greater strength. What superior brain?

At that side the field was fenced with wire, three strands

through thin metal shafts. This time he made a wider circle and stood about ten yards in front of the horse, McCann again approaching it from the rear, talking to it in the quiet voice that was supposed to keep him calm. This time Big Dick kicked up in earnest. McCann ran a yard to the side and then tried to throw the halter noose over its head. The rope flicked Big Dick's neck. McCann half-fell. The horse trotted towards Dunky. He raised his arms, meaning to turn its head back to the fence. It came straight at him. He jumped for the wire. The horse went trotting past him, the earth vibrating under its drumming hooves.

McCann's face was flushed under his stubble,

"Get a hold o' him, for God's sake," he said.

They walked twenty yards.

In *The Dog Crusoe* the man caught his wild mount by creasing its neck with a bullet, great marksman that fella! Or maybe, if it wasn't okay to try shooting it unconscious, they could try tiring it out! Your cinema cowboys went right up under their front feet and threw the rope over their heads. He wasn't going in for any fancy tricks like that and by the looks of him neither was McCann. A fine pair of Neanderthal men we'd make!

This time Dick was waiting for them. As soon as McCann slowed his walk, the halter rope across his chest, right hand holding the loop at the running-knot, it turned on them. They saw its ears up and its teeth bared. They sprinted for the fence, scrambling over the three wire strands.

Dunky floundered on the grass verge of the track road, laughing as soon as he saw the horse wasn't coming over after them but had veered away, hair flying, towards the middle of the field.

"Whut's so funny?"

"Nothing."

McCann would get the blame. Ha ha.

"You take the rope then if ye think it's that funny."

"I'm too young to die."

"Come on, Craig's no' goin' to be laughin'."

All right, we've got the brains, what do we do now? Kids in the school playground, they'd have a great laugh. They climbed the wire fence and set off on a pincer movement. It wasn't so funny, not really, not when you came nearer the brute. Here's your domesticated work-horse, gentlemen, bred to work and obey. But something's wrong. It wants to be free and we've forgotten how we tamed it in the first place. All right, Big Dick, you've had your fun, how's about getting on with the hay?

"That way!" roared McCann as the horse jerked to life, pointing to the corner near the gate. Dunky raised his hands in a wave, shouting. Big Dick came round in a heavy semi-circle, straight for him. He was too far from the fence. For a split second he watched its high-flying head, its great rolling shoulder joints, the hooves flat-pounding the grass. He ran to the left, looking over his shoulder, studded boot soles slipping on grass, McCann shouting.

Dick chased him all the way to the tall school fence. In jokes men chased by wild bulls were able to vault hedges in their stride, but he could see no grip on the smooth red fencing. He was going to be kicked, would it be painful? He slipped, one knee touching the ground, floundering to get up, glancing wildly over his shoulder at the horse, still coming at him, run along the fence, kids on the other side, only a joke to them, no joke to me, horse isn't giving up, don't worry about looking scared, get moving, just run now, don't look back.

Between the scheme and the field, the boundary of the farm, was another wire fence and a continuous hump of clay soil overgrown by hawthorns and wild roses. He ran at the fence, one sliding boot on the slack bottom wire, hands pulling on thin metal, right boot catching on the top wire, sprawling into a mess of grass and tin cans and bottles. He looked round. The horse had given up the chase and had turned on McCann, who was running like a madman from a silent film, knees going up and down like pistons, stiff elbows, his cap flying off.

Behind the fence the kids were yelling at them.

Dunky climbed back into the field and walked round its edge to the gate, always ready to leap to safety if Dick turned towards him. McCann reached the big gate.

The horse, hair streaming dramatically, careered back to the centre of the field, where it halted and began to graze.

Willie was there, on the road, with Telfer.

"Whut's wrang wi' ye, McCann?" Willie was roaring. Dunky climbed the metal gate.

"The brute's gone mad," said McCann.

"Ach, ye stupit eejit, can ye no' even fetch a bloody horse when ye're asked?"

Willie climbed the gate and held out his hand for the rope. He walked straight for the horse. They leaned on the gate,

Telfer smirking like a schoolgirl. Dunky saw it in a flash, smoking cigarettes, liking tractors better than horses, wearing ordinary shoes – Telfer was a *town* man, through and through, and town men were no good. Yellow bellies. Safety first. Clean hands.

"We'd better give Willie a hand," he said to McCann.

"Suit yourself," said Blackie. Dunky climbed the gate and walked out towards Willie and the horse. He could hear McCann's voice behind him, the very sound of it suggesting a man covering sneaky fear behind a know-all sneer.

Then the horse was chasing Willie and when he saw him making for the gate Dunky turned and climbed, not too quickly, out of the field.

With three men beaten it was suddenly a matter for a big joke. Willie was just saying they'd have to coax him over to the gate with a pail of corn when Auld Craig came stumping across the road towards them, in a fine state judging by the unusually high angle of his head.

"Get out of it ye lazy hoors," he shouted at them, snatching the rope from Willie. Dunky stood back. Craig pushed the heavy gate open, nobody giving him a hand. Should he follow the old man, prove he wasn't yellow, get in Craig's good books? Why not, he could out-run the horse.

"This'll be worth watching," said Telfer.

Craig was bawling at the horse as he stumped over the grass, right hand holding up the rope. Big Dick waited, ears cocked. Craig walked straight for his head. Dick stamped one forefoot. Craig roared at him. He reached the horse just as it began to draw back into the air. Dunky followed behind, already thinking of the advantage this would give him over McCann. The old man drew back his right arm and slashed the halter rope across the horse's face. Still bawling. For a moment it looked as though Dick would rear up and pound him into the grass. Craig kept slashing at its face. Then it was on four feet, only its head raised. The old man, neck now inclined at its usual position, grabbed a handful of its forelock, then its ear.

"Here, pit the halter on him," he said to Dunky.

It took an effort to go that close, but he wasn't a cheap townee hiding behind a gate.

"Take him in," said the old man. "Call yerselves men?" he roared at the other three. If the horse should buck now he'd let the rope go and the hell with caring what it looked like,

183

but Dick walked quietly out of the gate and across the road and down into the yard. . . .

Later, in the afternoon, he was walking behind the hay-mower, pulling the greenish hay over the churning teeth with the wooden hay rake, McCann sitting on the cantilever bucket seat with the reins loose in his hand. Telfer and Willie were cutting with the tractor in the low field. McCann was still in a temper with the big horse and when the dragging rein ends – which a good horseman should have kept off the ground – caught in the mower axle he lost his head completely. The saw stopped chattering between the iron teeth, which skated across uncut hay, scarring into black earth.

"Jesus Christ," shouted McCann, hauling the reins tight. As he came round the back of the mower he gave Dunky a push in the chest. Always the same moment – did you go in? Was he bigger than you? Were you keyed up to beat his brains out – for once you went in that's what you had to do.

Dunky let himself sit down heavily on the swathe of mown hay.

"Temper, temper," he grinned.

McCann growled, head into the machinery. The rope was twisted tight, dragged into the cog wheel that drove the saw. They backed the horse but the rein would not come free. McCann had to cut it out with his pocket-knife. Dunky thought of the bothy men he'd read about at Nicol's house. They sounded like real farmers, even though they lived in an Abberdonian midden. The idea was coming to him that Craig's men weren't real farming people at all. Too near the town. Who was he like? Who did he want to be like? Telfer? Mc-Cann? No, they were nothing. Didn't amount to anything. Auld Craig was a real man, maybe the only one he knew.

They started mowing again, round and round the ever-decreasing area of hay, McCann holding the reins, turning Big Dick, working the mower-lever at the corners, swathe after swathe lying behind them, the sweet, natural smell of bruised grass strong in his nose, almost able to taste it. He kept his eyes on the mower blade, watching the dancing stalks stiffen as the blade took them, then fall like millions of minia-ture tree-trunks, his rake making sure they fell the right way, over the mower arm. A mouse ran under the swathe, his eye catching the dark movement, his heel on it almost without breaking stride, a second downward hack crushing it. Dark blood mixed with earth.

184

Why did I do that?

Because you always killed mice, or rats, or rabbits. Wee sleekit cowrin timrous vermin.

It wasn't a bad life, out in the open air, the sun on your face, dodging along behind the rattling mower, free to think of anything that came into your head, watching the field being laid low, your bare arms and chest going red, the muscles toughening, whistle a bit of this and a bit of that, imagine daft things, have a laugh to yourself at the thought of Dick chasing them over the field, wonder if *next time* you'd be ready to open McCann's skull for him, a great life if you didn't weaken.

On days when it was going to be hot the mornings were cool and slightly misty, the men's clothes dark against the pink and grey smear of medium-height cloud, their voices taking on a suggestion of echo through the damp air. Real farmers knew all about the weather and he was beginning to pick it up.

It stayed dry for a week and by that time the cut hay had been turned and dried and built into bowl-shaped coles a couple of feet higher than a man. Raising the great pole for the horse-fork in the yard was, to Dunky, another signal that summer had really come. The year before, in the school holidays, he'd been taken on the day the pole was raised. Then he'd led the mare, pulling the rope which lifted the grab-fork up to the men who built the haystacks. That was a boy's job, nothing to do all day but stand at the horse's head, take him forward again, back and forward, ten yards worn into a dark earth scar on the patchy grass of the stack-yard.

This year he was one of the men and when they went to the stack-yard, in the small field adjoining the steading, Craig put him at the end of one of the pole's four ropes. The pole looked as thick and long as a ship's mast. Willie and McCann had the other holding ropes, and the fourth was tied to the tractor's tow-bar.

First Willie and McCann lifted the far end of the pole off the ground, bending with knees splayed out like men picking up a caber at the Highland Games, straightening up like Samson bracing against the pillars, hands above their heads, then walking, stiff-legged, under the pole, lifting its head farther from the ground. As soon as it reached the right height Telfer opened the tractor throttle, taking the weight on the tractor

185

rope. The pole started to rise. McCann ran to his rope end and slipped it round the spike. Willie took the rope on the opposite side to the tractor. Craig stood to one side, waving and shouting instructions.

He never liked this bit. He put his left boot on the spike, his back to the pole, the rope hard against his left side, running round the shiny spike and held by his right hand. If the pole began to fall to McCann's side he was supposed to take its full weight, heels dug in, hands holding on no matter how the hard, rasping rope burned his palms, trying to make out what Craig was shouting – too much pull on his rope and the pole would swing towards him and McCann would have to hold it from falling, too much slack and it might fall towards McCann.

Daftie Coll had once misheard Craig's shouting and let his rope go when he should have pulled. The pole had fallen and split and the hay had been held up for a day and a half until a new one was delivered. He looked over his shoulder. Craig was waving at Telfer, Willie was jack-knifed over his spike, heels into the ground like a one-man tug-of-war team.

Then it was up and all he had to do was put a double loop round the spike and hold the rope until Willie came over and tied the proper knot. This year Telfer and McCann were bringing the coles from the fields, on low, rubber-wheeled trolleys, Telfer on the tractor, McCann driving Big Dick. Willie and McPhail the knee-padder were to build the stacks. He was to work the hay-fork.

There was a boy to work the horse, a thin-faced scheme boy wearing the shiny, back-pleated jacket of an old chalk-stripe suit and narrow-legged light blue trousers and crêpe-soled shoes. In the stable in the morning he hadn't said much and Willie hadn't told them his name, although Telfer seemed to know him.

When Telfer and McCann went off to the field Willie and McPhail and the boy and himself sat on the first stack's straw foundation to eat their pieces and drink their vacuum-flask tea. The boy had nothing to eat.

"Your mither doesnae believe in spoilin' you then?" Willie remarked. Boys were fair game to take the rise out of. Dunky chewed on white bread and Cheddar cheese. McPhail brought an unwrapped sandwich of white bread and jam out of his jacket pocket, blowing off hairs and bits of pocket-grit before munching into it with the kind of thin, deliberate bites of a man adrift on a raft eking out his day's share of hardtack.

"I don't need it," said the boy, sniffing a slow balloon of catarrh back up into his nostrils.

"What do they call you then?" Dunky asked him.

"That's a Rafferty frae Kilmairns Avenue," said Willie. "He's a car-wrecker, aren't ye, Rafferty?"

The boy sniffed. Dunky knew who he was now. The summer before a gang of scheme boys had taken big stones up on the railway bridge and dropped them on the roofs of passing cars. Willie had helped the bobbies catch them and they'd been taken to the Juvenile Court and given probation.

"Ye've got three sisters a' brides o' Christ, haven't ye, Rafferty," Willie went on.

"Yeah, so whut?"

"What's that, brides of Christ?" Dunky asked.

"They marry Jesus when they get to be nuns," said McPhail.

Rafferty wiped at his nose with the sleeve of his jacket. He didn't seem to care what they said. Dunky had never heard of brides of Christ. Apart from the fact that the Pope kidded them on he was better than Jesus and they weren't allowed to read the Bible in English, he didn't know much about Catholics. They had their own school in Kilcaddie and apart from playing football against them there was hardly any contact. It interested him, to think that in a small town like Kilcaddie, where in the street everybody looked the same, different religions meant that some kids went to one school and some to another. He'd once asked about this in class and Mister Mason had said it was the Catholics who wouldn't come to the Academy, not the other way round. All the people he knew were Protestants – bar his mother none of them gave a fart for God, although most of them, even Alec, went to church fairly regularly. Why did Catholics, wee scheme rats like this Rafferty, take their religion so seriously? Didn't that mean it must be better than Protestantism? Even his mother said that Catholics were much more sincere in their worship, going to mass early on Sunday mornings while they were still in bed. They could go to chapel in working-clothes, too, whereas their church was the height of respectability – his mother had once given him a belting for going to Sunday School without garters.

He knew the usual things about Catholics: they supported Glasgow Celtic, the priests told them what to do and took away their money, they confessed their sins in a wee box, they had beads, they preferred Eire to the Union Jack, they worshipped Holy Mary instead of Jesus, they bred like rabbits, their priests weren't allowed to marry but had fancy women and children, they would let you marry a Catholic girl only if you promised the kids would be brought up as Papes. From the day you were born people told you Catholics were the enemy – they'd take away your freedom if they got the chance. Every year there was a big Orange Walk with banners and men in fancy clothes singing songs from Ulster about King Billy slaying the Papish crew at the battle of Boyne Water and hanging the Pope with a northern rope. Was it just another of his daft ideas, secretly thinking that Catholics couldn't be all that bad? In the school debating society he'd argued against the idea of the masons – lot of nonsense, grown men dressing up in aprons and gabbling on about Solomon's Temple and giving each other the best jobs. Billy Aird had said his father was a freemason, it was the only way to get promotion in Kilcaddie police. The teacher had interrupted Billy and told him he shouldn't say things like that. If Billy Aird said it it must be nonsense, yet even his mother always said her father got on well at business because he was a mason. In Eire, they said, books were banned and priests ordered the folk how to vote. McCann was fond of telling everybody that. Some day he'd tell McCann that shouldn't bother him, he'd never voted or read a book in his life. Folk were funny about it – you'd hear them shouting the odds about Mary, Queen of Scots, how John Knox terrorised her and how Queen Elizabeth murdered her, but when you asked them if Mary, Queen of Scots, wasn't a Catholic anyway, they didn't know what to say. Same with Bonnie Prince Charlie – they all thought he was the greatest yet if he'd beaten the English they would have had a Catholic king. Very strange, folk, most of the time they didn't know if they were coming or going.

He had to show Rafferty how to work the horse. Looking at the sniffing wee gnaff he wondered if *he* believed in God, he didn't look as though he knew the difference between God and a poke of chips. He tried to be friendly.

"D'you hear the joke about the Two Proddestants who went to Parkhead and saw a priest and one says, 'Hey, Alex, I'm going to take a rise out of that priest' and he goes down and says, 'Hullo, Father, is it true what they're saying, your new Pope's a big drunkard and a homo and on the drugs and

188

steals all the Vatican cash and fancies wee boys and behaves like a big animal?' The priest says, all polite like, 'Is that so, my son, my my,' and the man goes back to his pal and says he can't get a rise out of the priest at all, so his mate says he'll have a go, so he goes down and says, 'Hullo, Father, is this true what they're saying, your new Pope's a freemason?' and the priest says, 'Aye, so your friend was just telling me.' "

Rafferty shrugged and sniffed.

"I don't know nuthin' about the Pope," he said.

"It's a joke. It's supposed to be against the masons."

"You can fuck off any day."

"Oh, coming the big hard man, eh?"

"Fit for you anyway."

"Ach, don't be daft."

Telfer backed the trolley into place beside the big pole. He helped Telfer push the cole towards the back, then heave up the front of the trolley, holding the rope round the cole while Telfer started the tractor and dragged the trolley from under the hay. He whipped off the ropes which held the cole together.

"Right, take her forward till I shout," he said to Rafferty. The boy obviously knew nothing about horses. He walked beside him, hand on the bit ring, until the fork was dangling just above the rounded top of the cole.

"That's all you've got to do," he said. "Don't jerk it about, just take it up steady and down fast."

He clambered up the smooth side of hay and guided the four fork prongs down until they had a good grip. Then he stood back, the thin release-rope in his hand.

"Go forward, slowly but," he said. Rafferty pulled on the mare's bit-rope. She'd done this so often she probably didn't need anybody at her head, but you could never rely on a horse not to take the notion to do something daft. The fork lifted a foot into the air.

"That's enough," he shouted. As it swung out over their heads he pulled the release rope and the hay fell between Willie and McPhail. Moving about like men in a snowdrift they forked the hay evenly over the straw. "Back now," he shouted at Rafferty. The boy was too slow and the fork swung back again, making Willie and McPhail dive to avoid it.

"Start her back's soon as she's dropped her load," Willie shouted at the boy. Dunky felt sorry for him. It had taken him days and days to get the right rhythm at the horse's head

189

– when you were new to it you were half-scared all the time in case you did something wrong.

He guided the fork into the top of the cole.

"I'll show you," he said, going to the horse's head. The boy sniffed.

"As soon as I've got the teeth into the hay and raise my hand you take her forward, steady like," he told Rafferty. "Then as soon as I pull my rope and the hay falls start her back, fast as you can. I can pull her clear of the stack on the way down. I can't guide her on the way up or I'll pull the catch. You get me?"

"If you're so smart you work the fuck'n thing," said the boy. Dunky sucked air through clenched teeth.

"Just do what I tell you," he said.

Rafferty started the horse too early the next time and the fork sailed up into the air clutching only a few whisps of hay, knocking Dunky off the top of the cole.

"For fuck's sake wait till I tell ye," he shouted. The boy shrugged and spat a thin gobbet out of his curved tongue. The next thing he did wrong was to start backing the horse before the trip-rope was pulled. The forkful of hay landed on McPhail's shoulder, knocking him onto his knees.

They were only halfway down the first cole when McCann led Big Dick into the yard with the second.

"Never let boys dae man's work," he shouted up to Willie.

"Ah ballocks," Dunky shouted back. "Come on, Rafferty, get a bloody move on."

For the rest of that day they were behind, either Telfer or McCann having to stand about waiting for the previous cole to be lifted up on the stack. Dunky found he could only keep Rafferty working properly if he ran back and forth from the horse's head to the coles, snatching the halter-rope out of the boy's hands, pulling the trip-wire then starting the horse back, running to meet the fork and shove its teeth into the hay.

In the afternoon when they had their break, he tried to explain the whole business again to the boy. Rafferty didn't seem to give a bugger either way.

"Look, I'm no' going to run myself to death doing your work as well," he said. "If ye don't brighten yourself up they'll sack ye. Aren't ye wanting the money?"

"I can get plenny money," the boy said. "I can make more'n this nickin' stuff. This kinna work's for mugs,"

"Aye, but it's better'n goin' to jail."

"Who goes to jail?"

Dunky didn't know what to say. All he'd ever stolen was small stuff from Woolworths, pencils and notebooks and packets of envelopes, just for dares during school dinnertime – and even then they were so scared of being caught they used to drop everything they'd knocked off into letterboxes.

"What's your father do?" he asked.

Rafferty sniffed and spat and turned his head away. Where his dirty, fair hair met his neck there were blackheads and small pimples.

"Casual labourin'," said the boy.

Willie must have been listening, above them on the top of the stack.

"Aye, casual labourin' in Barlinnie gaol," he shouted.

"Fuck you," the boy shouted back.

Dunky expected Willie to slide down and give the boy a hammering, but instead he laughed his mad laugh and repeated what he had said:

"Casual labourin' in Barlinnie gaol, Rafferty. Nae wonder yer sisters got merriet to Christ, naebody else would huv them."

Thanks to the boy they had to work till after six to get the first stack finished and the canvas hap put over its top and the hap's brown ropes weighted down with bricks. As he brushed hayseeds out of the horses' coats Dunky waited to hear if Craig had paid the boy off – casuals got their cash at the end of each day. As he cycled home he wondered why on earth Craig had kept him on. It was hard to get boys to do the work, everybody knew that, but it wasn't that hard, surely? Rafferty wasn't right for a farm. What kind of people were his kind, to talk about mugs working and nicking stuff for a living? People in Shuttle Place were no better off than people in the scheme, yet he felt completely different from them. As though your family was older and more respectable – *decent*. At school it had been easy to think about things like that – feudalism had given way to the industrial revolution and eventually the working classes had fought for votes and rights and whatnot. By working class you thought of men in overalls in factories, tending machines, big, grown-up men with families to keep – honest working guys as Alec called them.

"What class would you say we were?" he asked his mother at tea. It was easier to talk to her now that the old man was

191

out of the house. *He* felt like the man of the house now, all tough and hard after a day's toil.

"We're middle-class," his mother said. "D'you want some more mince?"

"Aye, but how can we be middle-class, I mean my father only worked in a foundry, didn't he?"

"Your father's job has got nothing to do with it. We're middle-class."

"I'm working-class," he said. "I work for a wage, don't I, and get my hands dirty? What's middle-class about that?"

His mother tut-tutted as she ladled more mince onto his plate.

"It's not what you work at, it's what you are," she said, "Your grandfather had his own business, don't forget that."

"Aye, but we don't have any business."

"It doesn't matter. It's just something you *know*."

"What class are you, wee Senga?" His sister was fiddling with her hair in front of the mantelpiece mirror.

"I'm not wee Senga," she replied.

"Big Senga then. What class would you say you were, Big Senga – cookery class?"

"Very funny I don't think."

Out in the hut he gave the rabbits new hay and, while the light lasted, cut wire-netting with pincers for the front of the next new hutch. It was a pity they didn't get more sunshine. Soon he'd be seeing Elsa again, the rabbits were thriving on good summer feeding, he'd built two new hutches and sold a couple of duds to the butcher, he was dead lucky not to have been born a Rafferty, on Saturday they had a good chance of winning their semi-final against Darroch Youth Club, even the house didn't seem so bad – now.

Back inside he decided to clean out his shelf of books and rubbish. His mother was listening to the *McFlannel* family on the wireless. She always said they were very, very common and shouldn't be allowed on the wireless, not that coarse Glasgow talk, but she always listened to the programme. She knitted, occasionally shaking her head and making little tsk-tsk noises as Paw McFlannel came out with his real Glesca sayings. He carried an armful of old exercise books from the kitchen press to the couch.

"You don't go out so much these days," she said,

"No?"

No, I'm saving up to get married!

"Senga goes out more than you do."

"Why don't you stop her?"

"It's only to the Guides or her pals' houses." On the wireless Paw McFlannel was saying, "Crivvens, wumman, ah always cuts ma coarns oan the livin'-room cairpit" and his mother shook her head in agreement with Mrs. McFlannel, who said, "I don't care, you clear up this mess, I'm not having you disgrace us in front of Mrs. Cotton."

If his mother thought Paw McFlannel cutting his corns on the living-room carpet was "common" what would she think of the way they talked at the farm? Funny, how you could speak one way at work and another way at home, without too much effort. Did you put in the swear words artificially at the farm or take them out artificially at home? That reminded him of Gillespie the science teacher – or Wee Sammy as he was known – saying there was no such thing as cold, just absence of heat. And ice broke natural laws by floating instead of sinking with its denser gravity. If ice did the normal thing whole oceans would freeze up. What good did it do you knowing stuff like that?

He decided to throw out his books of pasted-in football pictures. Kids' stuff. He tore out each page in turn and put it on the range fire. The flour-and-water paste had gone green with age, giving some of the pictures a funny tint ... then the best pictures, England 1, Scotland 3, 1949 at Wembley ... first Jimmy Cowan of Morton put up a fantastic display in goal, saving point-blank, time after time, from Mortensen ... then Reilly crossed to Jimmy Mason, there he was, stabbing the ball with his right foot, past big Frank Swift, the ball going in off the post ... number two for Scotland, Billy Houliston of Queen of the South going into Swift and Aston, hard man Billy Houliston, toughest guy in the game, the ball hitting Swift and running to Billy Steel, head down, blond, picture number three from the *Sunday Express* showing him left-footing it into the net and turning already, hands going up, the great Billy Steel ... and number three, Willie Waddell crossing from the right, the great Deedle-Doddle, Lawrie Reilly, Hibs, body parallel to the ground, heading it past the falling Swift ... that was *the* team, Jimmy Cowan, Morton; George Young, Rangers; Sammy Cox, Rangers; Bobby Evans, Celtic; Willie Woodburn, Rangers; George Aitken, East Fife; Willie Waddell, Rangers; Jimmy Mason, Third Lanark; Billy Houliston, Queen of the South; Billy Steel, Derby County;

Lawrie Reilly, Hibernian. He'd only been a wee boy then, but ever since almost every man he knew had gone on talking about that game. Christ, what would it be like to play for Scotland? Must be fantastic. He decided to keep the pictures. One day he'd have a wee boy of his own and he'd show them to him and say, "That's what I call a great Scottish team, son." Ha ha. Everybody thought the teams they saw when they were young were the world's best. The hell with keeping a lot of silly pictures. They went into the fire. The last one he burned was of Jock Tiger Shaw with the Scottish Cup, being carried on the shoulders of Willie Thornton and Sammy Cox. Jock Shaw had no teeth in front, his hair was shorn up the sides of his head – Tiger right enough. He threw the covers of the exercise book into the fire. There was a knock at the front door.

"I wonder who that can be?" said his mother, looking worried, gripping the arms of her chair.

"I'll see." He shoved the other books into the press, not wanting visitors to think he was still a wee boy playing with football pictures.

Alec was on the landing, the gas-light reflected on the shiny red skin of his cheeks, which had been shaved clean of spots and rubbed with Valderma.

"Hullo there," he said. "How's the lad?"

"Come in," said Dunky. "It's Alec," he told his mother as he led the way into the kitchen.

"Hullo Mrs. Logan," said Alec, who could be awfully polite to grown-ups. Little did they know. For some reason his mother always seemed to be apologising to visitors. She stood up and moved a cushion and looked embarrassed, as though Alec was the minister!

"I'll just make a cup of tea," she said.

"Don't bother for me, Mrs. Logan," said Alec.

"Oh, it's no bother."

"No, don't bother, mum. I'm going to show Alec the rabbits."

"Will you be out long?"

"No, not very long."

He put on his shoes in the lobby. Alec watched him. He'd never come much to the house when his father was there. It was an awful thing to say, even to yourself, but everything was a lot freer and easier nowadays.

"I've got something to tell you," Alec said as they went

194

down the stairs and into the close. "Guess who I saw up the town last night?"

"Who?"

"Guess."

"Charlie Tully?"

"No, guess, go on, somebody you know."

He unlocked the hut door and they climbed inside. Like most people Alec glanced at the rabbits without real interest.

"Come on, tell us."

"Guess."

"Come on, cut the cackle."

"Elsa!"

"Oh yeah? So what? She's allowed to go up the town, isn't she?"

"Ah yea, but who with?"

"Whaddye mean, who with?"

There were moments when your brain seemed to leap about inside your head, thinking all sorts of thoughts, working so fast you touched on hundreds of things in a second. He felt a shock coming, even before Alec said it:

"That big blond guy from your farm."

"What, Donald Telfer?"

"That's the one."

"Maybe she was just walking up the road with him."

"Oh aye, sure, at half-past ten at night with his arm round her? They were winchin', definite."

Alec was pleased, he knew that. Telfer knew she was his woman, so he'd done the dirt on him deliberately. She'd done the dirt on him, too. Telfer was older than him. He'd treat her just like another stray shag. Why did she want that? He'd been in love with her. Saved seventeen pounds fifteen shillings up till last pay day, to get married on.

"Oh," he said. Alec was waiting to hear him go wild. He wouldn't. She'd betrayed him. Bugger her. He was finished with women, permanently. "Just as well I wasn't serious."

"Tell us another, you were dead serious."

"Was I hell! She was just a good shag, that's all."

"You were actually – ehm – poking her then?"

"What do you think? What else d'you go with women *for*?"

He forced Alec to look in all the hutches, explaining how old they were and which was the buck and pulling the nest apart to show him the latest litter, six babies about nine days

195

old, eyes open, ears just unfurling, all the time thinking about his so-called pal Donald Telfer. For some reason he decided it had been a shame to burn his football pictures.

CHAPTER ELEVEN

Dunky didn't speak to Telfer all day, ignoring him when he drove into the stackyard with each new load, walking away when he tried to talk. He didn't want to speak to any of them. Maybe it isn't true, he kept saying to himself. Telfer eventually realised that he was sulking.

"What's wrong with Smallcock then?" he shouted up to Willie and McPhail.

"You call me that once again an' I'll bloody do you," he shouted to Telfer.

"What's wrong with you for God's sake? Getting one of Blackie's moods are you?"

"Never you bloody mind."

He knew he'd made a mistake letting them know he was in a temper when Telfer started singing *Ghost Riders in the Sky*, substituting Smallcock for Ghost Riders. He kept his teeth clenched. Telfer must have said something to McCann as they passed on the road for when he came into the yard he, too, made a point of calling him Smallcock. It was like telling somebody you hated the sound of two knife edges being rubbed together, soon as you told them they got out two knives and kept rubbing them until you went mad.

"A lone Smallcock went riding out one dark and windy day," sang Telfer. Just you wait, you dirty rat, I'll fix you.

They put the hap on the new stack just before six. In the stable Telfer again tried to speak to him .

"What's got your goat then, kid?" he asked.

Dunky spat on the stable floor. He wanted to fight Telfer, he wasn't afraid, he knew he might get a battering, he could take it. To *start* it was the worst thing. His stomach churned, just the way it did when he was necking with Elsa and they were getting more and more excited. He wanted Telfer to start it. Just as he wanted Elsa to tell him when she decided he could go the whole way with her.

But Telfer wasn't interested enough to make it into a fight. Dunky felt cheated. Telfer should have started it.

He fed and watered the horse and then got his bike and left them without saying cheerio. He cycled up to the scheme and along to Barskiven Road. On summer nights The Undesirables was like a nest of tinks. Wirelesses blared out of open windows. Children threw stones at each other, chased up and down in howling packs, climbed into living-room windows. He sat on his bike, left foot on the pavement kerb, hands in his jerkin pockets, lips tightening whenever he thought of her. If it was true she was just a dirty wee Undesirable hoor.

Eventually she came out of her house, walking down the path to the open gate. He stared at her, face as grim as he could make it.

"Hullo," she said. He glanced at the ground floor kitchen window. Maybe Noble the Wife-beater was watching. So what? He couldn't care less.

"I want to speak to you," he said. She came across the pavement. She had bare legs in fluffy slippers. She looked guilty.

"My tea's ready," she said.

"Are you goin' out wi' Donald Telfer?"

"What?"

"You heard."

Somebody hammered at the kitchen window.

"That's my daddy, I've to go in for my tea."

"Just tell us, yes or no. Are you goin' out wi' Donald Telfer?"

He saw two boys rolling about the pavement, one bigger than the other, the smaller one crying in agony as his arm was twisted up his back. She wouldn't look at him properly.

"Are you?"

There was a face at the kitchen window. Big Noble doing his nut because she was out on the pavement, talking to a lad. Disgracing the decent family!

"I just went out with him, that was all, it wasn't serious."

"No' much."

He looked at her.

"I've got to go in," she said, looking back at the house.

"So that's it then?"

"We're too young to be serious," she said. Maybe she did still love him. If she didn't she'd probably have sent her father out to him.

"I would've waited."

"I've got to go in."

"On ye go."

"Cheerio then. . . . ."

"Cheerio."

He cycled off down Barskiven Road thinking of all the
198

things he could do to Telfer. He'd get that rat, one way or another. Maybe he couldn't smash his face in but he'd do something. At tea his mother said he was to go and visit his father in Killearn the following Sunday. He didn't care, he'd nothing else to do, now. After tea he biked through the town to Alec's house in the Meiklepark scheme. With Alec's big brothers both married and out of the house Alec had a bedroom to himself. They sat and listened to Alec's records on his wind-up gramophone.

"I went to see Elsa the night," he said. Alec's best record was *Down the Road Apiece* by the Will Bradley Trio, Ray MacKinlay's Orchestra playing *Chicken Gumboogie* on the other side. "I've chucked her in."

"Good riddance if you ask me," said Alec. "Wimmin just give you a pain in the neck. Hey, it's our Y.M.'s bus outing to Portpatrick on Saturday, you fancy coming, your friend the big Magda woman's going?"

"I'm playing football."

"Can't you skip it for once?"

"Are you kidding? I've a good chance of getting into the first team. Give up football for a stupid bus run? What'll they do at Portpatrick anyway, play rounders and have a picnic, just like the Sunday School?"

"Not on your nelly. Big Shanky's going. He goes in pubs, y'know that?"

"Bigtime eh? You wouldn't go in a pub, would you?"

"Try anything once, that's my motto. Anyway, who's going to see you in Portpatrick?"

"You won't get me in pubs, it's a mug's game."

Who would he go out with on Saturday night? Being on your own was hellish. He didn't want Alec to go on the bus run. Alec was supposed to be his pal – okay, so he'd ditched him when he was winching Elsa but that was different, you expected your pals to ditch you when they had a steady woman. He could always go to the Y.M.C.A. and see if there were any guys he knew in the snooker room. Yeah, a right lot of bigtime bastards they were. Why didn't he have more pals? He looked down at Alec as he wound the gramophone. The playing-arm was held in place by one rusty screw and the mainspring was broken. Alec had bought it for five bob in a junk shop. When he played a record he had to keep the arm in place with his left hand, fingers pressing down on its base, and keep winding it with the right hand. Alec had soft hair without a proper parting. It was a nondescript brown colour, combed straight back. He never used Brylcreem or water. He had clean, *office* hands. When he was with Alec he felt hard and grown-up – was that why he liked him as a pal? In the snooker room he always felt young and shy compared to the bigtime characters who went there on Saturday nights. Tomorrow he'd walk into the stable in the morning and be faced with Telfer! Everything was lousy.

Alec went through his own records – Glenn Miller, Woody Herman's *Hail Caledonia* ("What makes your big head so HARD?"), Tennessee Ernie's *Shotgun Boogie*, Spike Jones and the City Slickers ("Leave the dishes in the sink, Ma"), Jimmy Shand's *The Laird of Cockpen*. It was still light outside. Through the gauze over the bottom half of the window he could see wooden palings, green clothes' poles, the tops of concrete coal bunkers, high stakes for Alec's father's sweet peas, a garden hut. Jumbled, that's what it looked like. Small gardens, tidy lawns – cramped and jumbled. Compared to the farm it was all too small – unnatural, somehow. The only time you'd feel you weren't being watched from the windows of the houses opposite was in the dark. Meiklepark was one of the older schemes. Instead of big blocks it had grey roughcast houses, two families upstairs and two on the ground floor. Paths were gravelled and front doorsteps were always newly step-stoned. They even had greenhouses!

"D'you want to hear my old man's records?" Alec asked.

"Yeah, sure."

They were in a black box with a hinged lid. Thick old records marked with grey scratches, edges chipped with little half-moon shapes ... Count John MacCormack singing *The Kerry Dancing*, Harry Gordon's monologue about the sweetshop, accordions playing *The Blackthorn Stick Quadrille*, *The Punishment fit the Crime* from *The Mikado*, an orchestral selection from *The Maid of the Mountains*. Alec had a little tin box of steel needles, his clean office fingers fiddling with the tiny screw as he changed the needles after every six records.

Dunky felt daft, sitting there in the gloomy bedroom listening to the scratchy old nonsense, thinking about the terrible things that were happening to him, watching Alec on his knees beside the mawkit old gramophone, wondering what the hell was going to happen to him.

"You're dead cheery I must say," said Alec, stretching over

200

the gramophone to put records back in the black box. "It's all this love rubbish. You're lucky you're finished with that Elsa piece. I'm going to have nothing to do with wimmin till I've seen some real life. Know what I'd like to do?"

"What?" Dunky asked, knowing he'd heard all this a thousand times.

"Join the merchant navy and see the world."

"You could get a job on the McBrayne boats."

"Ha ha very funny I don't think. I mean the real navy, bigtime, bags of spending money, big nights out in foreign ports, what a life, eh?"

"Big nights out in Rothesay you mean. Nobody ever does the things they say they'll do."

Elsa was the only person in his whole life he'd really *talked* to. Imagine that, a dirty little traitor knowing all your secrets! She'd tell Telfer all the daft things he'd said! It made him sweat, just to think about that. Telfer was a big gallus smart-aleck rat, he'd tell everybody else. They'd all laugh at him.

"Will we go to the Eldorado tomorrow night?" he asked Alec when they went round the back of the house to his bike. He was actually nervous in case Alec said no!

"I've got my evening classes," Alec said. "I'll be out by nine o'clock but."

"See you at the Cross then, about nine?"

"Okay. Pity you can't come on the bus outing."

"Ta ta."

Why the hell couldn't they have had their bus outing after the football season was finished? The Y.M.C.A. league finished in June but the Juveniles went on into July. Another two weeks and he'd have been able to go with them. Football was great but once the game was over you still had the rest of Saturday to get through. And on Sunday he was going to see the old man in Killearn!

He cycled through the town, looking for people he might know, pedalling slowly in case he might see Elsa – or somebody. At Shuttle Place he locked the bike in the wash-house. He didn't feel like bothering with the rabbits again. They were just a stupid hobby. People would be laughing and saying, "Look at that geek, he's unsuccessful with wimmin, all he's got is his stupid rabbits." He even talked to them!

When he got into the lobby, a key now kept for him on the end of a string which hung through the letterbox, his mother came out of the bedroom in her cotton nightdress, her hair in curlers, her face white and smeary with cream.

"You should've been here," she said, "there was a man looking for you about the football, I didn't know where you were."

"I was at Alec's house. What did he want?"

"It was Mister Overend, at least that's what he said. You've to go to his house tomorrow night, it's important."

"Didn't he say what it was about?"

Trust her to let Overend go away without even asking.

"Just that it's to do with Saturday. You shouldn't have been out so late, he waited till ten o'clock. I had to sit with him in the kitchen, I didn't know what to say to him."

"Oh all right. Night night."

In bed he wondered what it could be. Maybe the game was off. Maybe he was dropped. He was just a failure. God was punishing him for everything he'd done. God knew every single thing that happened. Maybe Jesus would forgive him if he prayed for forgiveness ... *Dear Jesus I didn't really mean it when I said God didn't exist it was just talk I'm sorry. As I lie down to sleep tonight I pray the Lord my soul to keep. If I should die before I wake I pray the Lord my soul to take, I'm sorry I don't pray every night, Jesus, I do believe in you, honest, it was just smart-aleck talk, you understand, please help me to be happy and I'll never let you down again make Elsa love me, I'm sorry I don't know any real prayers I'm so lonely and miserable, if you'd just make Elsa give me another chance I promise I'll never do it to myself again and I'll never swear again and I'll love my mummy and daddy and I'll go to church on Sundays and say my prayers, please Jesus help me I'm sorry, really I am. . . .*

"Ah come on, what's wrong with you?"

"Nothin's wrong with me, I just don't believe in doing that. You think I'm one of your fast pieces, don't you, a right doxy? Well I'm not."

"Ah come on, what's the harm in it?"

Telfer and Elsa Noble were in the bottom field at the back of the factory, hidden from the back road behind a cole of hay, sitting on his jacket with their backs against the hay. It had been hard enough getting her to come for the walk and even harder coaxing her into the field, but he'd thought once she'd agreed to that she'd be game for anything.

"What's the *harm* in it? You think I came up the Clyde on a bicycle or something? You're just like all the others, Donald Telfer, you're just out for what you can get."

The trouble was he really fancied her like mad. Since he'd been going out with her the most he'd managed was the hand in her blouse yet here he was, after more than a month, still steamed up if not foaming at the mouth. It wasn't like him — to let a stupid wee virgin keep him on the hook. Christ, he'd banged some really class dames after one night at the pictures!

"Well what are you going out with me for then?" he asked, pulling a length of hay from the cole and chewing it between his front teeth, chin sunk on the chest. He could see her knees and about an inch of thigh. Young and firm and smooth. That was part of the trouble, she *was* young and he wanted her more than he'd ever wanted any of the others. There was a big difference with a young thing like Elsa, she wasn't only attractive on the surface, he knew she'd be sweet and juicy under her clothes. With older pieces you got steamed up looking at them dressed and then, when it was all over, you noticed they were a bit flabby or had a touch of varicose veins or smelled or some bloody thing.

"Oh you're all right to go out with," she said, "but if you think I'm the kind that'll let you go too far you've got another think coming."

"Too far! Jesus Christ, you're like an iceberg."

"Why d'you want to go out with me then?"

"Because I want to, that's all."

"Aye but it's no' me you want, it's what you can get. I don't believe in that."

"What d'you believe in then, if you don't mind me asking?"

She'd told him she'd been fed up because Dunky Logan had got too serious and they'd never had any fun. He'd thought the way to get round her was to keep her laughing. Make jokes all the time. That was fine while it lasted, she was good enough company which you couldn't say for a lot of women, not like Big Agnes, for instance, *her* brains were all in her knickers. But now he was serious, he wanted a bit.

"I believe in lots of things," she said. She seemed quite cheery about it all. "You wouldn't understand."

"Oh no? I suppose I'm just a big thick tractor-driver, eh?"

"Don't kid us on, you think you're real smart, don't you? Can I test your brains?"

She rapped his head with her knuckles,

203

"Ow." He put up his arms as a shield. She dug her fingers into his ribs, pinching and poking, raising herself onto her knees, tickling him and chapping on his head. He rolled about trying to dodge her hands. Then she stood up.

"Christ, you're *vicious*," he complained, looking up at her.

She smiled.

"Only dirty old men look up girls' skirts," she said. "Come on, I've got to go home."

He sat up and pulled hay off his neck.

"What's your hurry? The night's young yet."

"Come on," she said, buttoning her pink, three-quarter length coat. He took as long about getting to his feet as he could, hoping she might change her mind. Once again she'd got him steaming and once again she'd made up *her* mind to push off. She had a bloody nerve. Maybe he'd just grab her and –

"Crivvens, there's a man watching us," she said.

His first thought was that it would be McPhail. The dirty wee bastard, spying on *him*. But when he got up and looked round the side of the cole he saw that it was Willie, standing by the gate, the bike at his side. He'd seen them all right, Willie had eyes like a hawk, nothing could move within five miles of the farm but Willie spotted it.

"It's Willie Craig," he said. "Give him a wave."

"I will not. You said there wouldn't be anybody about down here."

"Willie doesn't matter. We might as well go and talk to him, he'll wait all night if we don't."

They walked across the field.

"I hope my father doesnae get to know I was here," she said.

As they approached the gate she wished there was some way she could prove nothing had happened. From a distance Willie Craig had looked very stern, staring at them from under his cap, but close up she saw that he was grinning.

"On overtime then, Telfer?" he said. She sneaked a look at Donald. He was trying to hide the fact that he was blushing!

"Nice night for a wee walk," he replied. "How come you're no' at home, the wife drives you out, does she?"

When Willie looked at her he had very big, round eyes. They made her want to laugh. Donald would never live it down, being caught with her in the field. He opened the gate and they stood on the grass verge.

Telfer knew that anything he said would come out first thing in the morning. Young Logan wouldn't like it.

"Looks like being a clear day the morn's morn," he said, looking up at the sky.

"Red at night's a shepherd's delight," said Willie, big eyes peering at her as though he was about to jump in the air and scream. She knew what he was thinking, yet for some reason she didn't really care. It was a funny sort of feeling, to be with grown men who joked with each other. Her father made her feel like a wee schoolgirl, yet here she was a real grown-up, old enough to suit herself whether she went into a hayfield with a man.

"Willie's wife's expecting," Donald said. She nodded. Willie nodded.

"Aye, she's like a prostitute in an institute wi' a belly like a parachute," he said. "I hope ye werenae smokin' in among they coles, Telfer, there's enough fires a'ready aboot this place."

"Do I look that daft?"

"He's a very heavy smoker," Willie said to Elsa, nodding, as though telling her a big secret. "He smokes like a wee lum."

"I know," she said.

"There's no smoke without fire," Willie said, winking. She knew he was getting at something else. She looked at Donald.

"Willie's father doesnae let him smoke yet," Telfer said to her, making a sly face. "Isn't that right, Willie?"

"Craig says if we'd been meant tae smoke we'd huv chimneys in our heads." Willie gave her his daft stare again. "It's good money puffed away up the sky."

"You must get some pleasure out of life."

"He's a pleasure fanatic, Donal' Telfer, that's what he is. Pictures and smokin' an' what else, eh?"

"It wouldnae do if we were all like you Craigs – he thinks a wee run round on his bike's a great event, don't you, Willie?"

They were both talking to her. She liked it. She knew a lot about Willie Craig from Dunky and Donald. She suspected from things they'd both hinted at that Donald had fancied the farm housekeeper before she got married to Willie Craig. She liked the idea of that, it must make you important, more than just a wee girl, to be going out with a bloke who'd fancied a grown woman. Donald had had lots of girl friends, she'd
205

have known that anyway, he was so *experienced* when he tried to do things to you.

"Tell the missus I was asking after her," Telfer said as they began to move away. "Tell her she wants to keep you in the house at night, dirty old man knee-padding down the back fields."

"I'll tell her all right," said Willie, getting on his bike. "I'll tell her what she's missin'."

"He's halfways round the bend," Telfer told her as they walked up the back road.

"He'll tell people he saw us but," she said.

"There's nothing to tell, more's the pity."

"Hard cheese. You'd better get yourself another girl friend who doesn't mind what you do to her."

It was still quite light when they reached the corner of Barskiven Road. He decided to walk her to her gate, the hell with Noble the Wife-beater, he might be a big man when it came to bashing his wife but he'd take him on any day.

"When'll I see you again?"

"I didn't think you'd be bothered."

"Don't talk daft. Wednesday night, eh, we could go to the pictures?"

"Does that mean you still fancy me a wee bit?"

"Don't ask silly questions. If I didn't I wouldn't ask you, would I?"

"How do I know?"

"Oh, you want me to tell you a lot of guff, like 'I love you, my darling' and all that?"

"Suit yourself."

"You're very sure of yourself, aren't you?"

"Just careful. I've got to go in now."

"I'll see you on Wednesday at the Cross, seven o'clock?"

"Okay, I'll tell my Dad I'm going out with Betty. You'd better wipe the grass off your back, folk might think *you've* been lying in a field."

She went up the path. He looked at her kitchen window but there was no light on and he couldn't see if Noble was watching.

When he got home Mrs. Sneddon and her Bertha and his mother were all at the entrance to the close, with Mrs. Docherty leaning out of her front-room window.

"Oh hallo, Donald," said Mrs. Sneddon, "isn't it a right pity aboot Eileen Graham's wee baby, did ye no' hear whut happened tae it, oh, you tell him, Mrs. Telfer, Ah'm fair wobbly jist thinkin' aboot it."

"What happened?" he asked, thinking to himself that they were a right load of old tea-wives, standing there with the latest gossip and scandal, just dying to tell anybody who came along.

"A cat got in the pram and suffocated the baby," his mother said. "She was only up in the house for a wee while and when she went to get the baby in for its tea it was dead."

"Christ. She should've had a net on the pram."

"Aye, that's jist whut Ah tellt her," said Mrs. Docherty, voice loud enough to let the whole of Darroch scheme know her views.

"It's they cats, they're a right scunner," said Mrs. Sneddon. "Somewan should destroy them, so'n they should."

"Come on up the house," he said to his mother. The other three women went on discussing the baby's death. Halfway up the stairs he told his mother she ought to think more of herself than stand at the close-mouth with a lot of old bauchles.

"It helps to pass the time," she said.

When they went into the living room his brother Davie was sitting at the table, writing his Boys' Brigade reports, wearing his spectacles. He was going to get married and out of it, the sight of Davie in his spectacles had made up his mind. When a bint had class enough to hold out on you like Elsa you knew you were meant to marry her. Willie had been impressed with her, that made a lot of difference. If she'd been just another hairy Willie would jeer at him for even thinking of marrying her. He'd do it, too. Better than wakening up one morning and find you'd nothing better to do than put on spectacles and write reports.

There were times now when he'd suddenly look up and see the walls of the bedroom or the kitchen and he'd be unsure what year it was, then or now, or whether he'd been dreaming. It was important to keep a grip on your wits, all about you were the scavengers and the rascals and the smooth lads, smiling to your face and ready to rook you to the last bawbee.

He found himself looking at the woman. He must have drowsed off. She was well kindled now, her belly sticking out like a cow with milk fever. Willie's wife. But no' Willie's bairn inside her, she might have kidded Willie on but she couldn't fool him, a man of Willie's age didn't take in a woman's belly the first time he mounted her.

"An' ye say that's Willie's bairn ye're carrying?" he said.

He spoke so seldom your ears weren't used to picking up his gruff old voice, and he usually spoke so fast you couldn't make out what he was saying. She put her knitting in her lap, fingers pressing on the half-finished stitch.

"What's that?"

"Willie's never the faither," he said. "It was too damnt quick."

"Sure'n that's a nasty sort of thing to be saying."

"Hrrmmph."

"Would you like a wee cup of tea if I get you one?"

Oh aye, they could be gey smarmy when they wanted to butter you up. He knew what she was after, dam' right he did.

"No. I'm no' wanting tea."

"What makes you say awful things like that?"

She'd found the best way to deal with Craig was to speak to him the way you would a wild wee boy. He detested the idea of her being married to Willie, but his brain was going, half the time he couldn't remember what he'd started saying. As long as she kept humouring the old devil he'd go to his grave without giving them any bother – provided he could remember to go to his own funeral.

Why bother wasting breath on her? He could hear his father speaking to him in the byre in Aberdeenshire, the time he'd taken his breeks down and given him laldy with his walking stick on the bum for fathering a bairn on the dairy-maid from the laird's farm:

"If he hiv tae mount a damnt servint ye'll tak' guid care na tae gie her yer bastarts."

His father met the laird's factor at the door of the house and he'd sat in the kitchen, eating his brose, with his mother, and driven the idea of marrying an Irish tink out of his head. You were never too old to learn a lesson from your father.

"Ye can tell Willie what ye want but ye're no deceivin' me," he said. "Who's the faither?"

She shook her head. His jacket hung in folds from his shoulders. He was shrinking away every day.

"You should know better than to say things like that at your age," she said. "You've a dirty tongue on you, Craig."

"It wasnae always like this," he said. She didn't understand him. Was he trying to say sorry?

His father met the laird's factor at the door of the house and he'd sat in the kitchen, eating his brose, with his mother, while the two men went out into the yard. His father came back into the house and told him to go out into the byre and wait for him. He was listening in the wee porch when his father was saying to his mother: "He's given wan o' the maids at the big hoose a bastart. Ah've tellt the factor Ah'll hanle him."

"Ye're no' tae tak' the stick to him, he's a grown loon o' siventeen." His mother aye stuck up for him.

"Ah dinna care if he's forty-siven, he'll learn better'n get queans in trouble."

Put your hands on the kist and bend down. He never cried once. Twenty times, the walking stick across his bare backside, just the noise of his father's breathing and the swish of the stick and the whack and the grunts of pain in his own throat.

"I learnt my lesson," he said. Mary O'Donnell made a face to herself and went across to put on the kettle. The old man was havering now, in his dotage. It must have come on him very quick. There was one thing Willie had to do, see Farquharson the lawyer about the will. The old devil might try and change it, put them out of it altogether. She'd *make* Willie see Farquharson, whether he wanted to or not. Willie was weak, through and through. He didn't even know how much money there was, imagine that, a grown man treated like a baby. He was lucky he had married her, left on his own he'd have been hopeless. Craig dragged his boots across the hearth and went to the stairs, grunting heavily.

"Night night," she said after him.

"Hrrmmph."

He went upstairs to where she couldn't follow. Jessie wasn't there, no, she'd been gone a long time. He still talked to her at times. He puffed and wheezed as he unlaced his boots, a terrible business getting old. You remember when we first came here, not a house for miles, they said father was daft buying a wasted old place like this, three fields near enough bogs and the land all sour. By Jove we worked to make this place right, worked, my father and my mother and then you and me, just one orra loon to help, folk laughing at us and saying we were soft they said, soil's gone bad. They'd never seen folk working like us, not about here, not round about the town. It wasn't so much of a town in those days, was it, a horse-bus once a day to Ayr. Two farms where they built that Darroch scheme. Remember on market days we'd put on our Sunday best and walk the beasts down the hill to the old mert, right up the High Street? The great war was a help, oh aye, they all like the farmers when there's one of their wars on, nothing's too good for you then, soon as it's over you can rot, we don't need the farmers now, not enough money to buy decent clothes for wee George, they didn't care, not them in the towns, we were good enough for them in the war, they don't like the farmer because he knows how to work and he doesn't want dole money and charity, oh aye, but when that other war came, oh aye, we're great folks again, remember that, Labour in, subsidies for this and subsidies for that, George aye made jokes about the subsidies cheques, he said we got subsidies for ploughing land and subsidies for planting this and that, and all the time we'd have done it anyway, Labour had no idea, they didn't have the brains, why did George really want to get away to Africa, eh, can you tell me that, Jessie? Och I know what you say, I'm too hard on Willie, maybe I am, he was never much good at the school, you remember that, if I'd ever had half his chance of schooling nobody knows what I might have been today, I never wanted to work on a farm, there was nothing else for me, my father had me out of school when I was eleven, two horse of my own to work, remember how we tied our boots round our necks to save them from wearing out when we walked to the school, winter and summer, och your feet soon got used to it, they had to, travelling five miles there and five back, now they've got wirelesses and gramophones and fancy clothes and picture houses, never been in a picture house in my life, nor to the dentist, remember the dances we had up north, just the fiddle and the squeeze-box, my they were *real* dances, Jessie. That was how I got the laird's maid in trouble, after a dance, walked her home from Mains of Dalgety, eleven mile, and mounted her at the end of it, just the one serving and she took. It could never be Willie's bairn that woman's carrying. Willie wouldn't take in one go, it's some damnt tink's bastart she's carrying. No, Jessie, I'm no' being ower hard on the boy, I'm jist damnt if some tink's bastart is going to get the money we worked for all these years. I'll see Farquharson first thing the morn's morn, he'll tell me how to do it. It'll do Willie the world of good, he can't depend on his father all his life. No, I winna be too hard on him, it's for his own good. She's only a common Irish tink,

Jessie, she doesn't deserve anything from us. I'll see Farquharson in the morning. . . .

Willie tried to tell Archie Stewart what he thought about Telfer, but Archie was in a funny sort of mood, as though he wanted to disagree on principle.

"You can't go round calling people rubbish, Willie," he said. "We're all human beings, it's just a lucky dip that some have land and money and some haven't. The rank is but the guinea stamp – remember? Poor old Rabbie, the same folk that hounded him all his life are now the very ones that get up Burns' suppers in his honour. Can you imagine what would happen, Willie, if Rabbie came to live near some of they masons and whatnot that make such a song and dance about him? They'd go off their heads. We Scots are that warped we can only admire our great men when they're safely dead and buried."

He didn't stay long in the Tink's house in the Black Hills. He felt annoyed. There was something wrong with the fact that a scheme tyke like Telfer should be having all the women he wanted and he was stuck with a wife who was too pregnant to let him on her. He'd thought he'd got the better of Telfer by marrying her – now he didn't even have her *or* Morag Coll, while Telfer went on regardless. The hell with her, he'd get it the night whether she liked it or not. It wasn't a good feeling, to know another man was doing better than you.

Mary was still in the kitchen when he got back to the steading. At first he thought she was just having another moaning session about the old man and he didn't pay much attention, but she kept on and on at him.

"You'll have to see Farquharson," she said, "the old devil hates me for some reason, are you going to let him say things like that to me in my own house?"

"It's his house," he growled. "Come on tae bed."

"I'm telling you, he's old enough and dottled enough to do the dirty on us just out of spite. He could make a will and leave you out altogether, d'you know that?"

"Ach don't talk daft. Come on tae bed, I'm feelin' like ye know what."

"You know you can't, will you –"

"I know nothin' o' the sort. There's nothin' stoppin' ye, it doesnae dae any harm tae the baby."

"Will you listen to me? You've a duty to me and your child."

"AN' YOU'VE A DUTY TO ME!"

So violent was the anger that flooded his head he hit her before he knew what he was doing, the back of his hand smacking her on the ear. She stood her ground, glaring at him.

"You're scared of him, aren't you, scared of him? You're not a real man –"

He hit her again, a real thump. Tears came into her eyes but still she was in at him.

"Go on, hit me, does it make you feel big? Go on."

As he went for her he could hear shouting in his brain about his father and Telfer and her all laughing at him, all taking him for a mug. She cowered her head, scrabbling round the table to escape. She found a china-handled knife near her hand and lifted it to him. He punched her arm and grabbed her wrist and held it between his big hard fingers until she thought it was breaking. The knife fell on the floor. He grabbed her by the hair and forced her towards the bedroom, thwacking her ear, her scalp in agony.

"Get your clothes off an' get intae bed, go on, hurry up, I'll kill ye if ye don't."

She was still crying when he came on top of her, the weight of him pushing down on the baby, his fingers digging into her shoulders. When he finished she lay with her eyes closed, moaning and sobbing.

"Shut your whinin'," he said, lying on his back beside her. He felt sorry for having lost his temper. She shouldn't have gone on at him like that. It was her fault. But he shouldn't have battered her. "Come on," he said, "it'll no' do the bairn any harm."

She said nothing.

"Ach, come on, I'm sorry. I'll go and see Farquharson the morn's morn if it'll make ye happy."

He thought he could get round her that easily. He'd bruised her whole body, her head was ringing with his blows, he'd just about torn her hair out by the roots – and he thought it was that easy, just say sorry and make a few promises? She was just a useless cripple woman, something he could thrash like a dog. She'd show him! And his father! She'd show them both.

After he'd got up and put on his pyjamas he tried to get

her to say something, but she lay so still and quiet he began to think he might have done her an injury. It worried him so much he couldn't sleep. He kept saying he was sorry but she wouldn't answer. He began to feel panicky, if he'd hurt the baby he'd never live it down. At last she decided to speak to him.

"Will you promise me you'll see Farquharson?"

"I tellt ye I would."

"Then you'll have it out with your father once and for all, you'll *make* him leave all the money to us?"

"Aye, I will, I promise."

"You swear you will?"

"Don't be daft, I said I would."

"All right then."

"Ye don't think I –"

"I don't know. We'll just have to wait and see, won't we?"

"I'm sorry."

"All right, you're sorry. It's time you faced up to the fact you've got a wife and a baby on the way. You're a man, act like one, your father's kept you down all your life."

"Aye, I know."

"All right then. Don't lean on me so hard, I'm sore all over."

CHAPTER TWELVE

Telfer came into the stable while Dunky was watering the horse. He'd felt scared before but never like this. His hands shook. His chin quivered. His breath seemed to go down only as far as his throat. His heart thumped. Blackie was feeding Big Dick, McPhail was at the stable door, Rafferty hadn't arrived.

He came out of the stall, the empty bucket in his hand. This was it. Telfer looked about seven feet tall. Run at him and sink the boot in his balls. Bang the bucket into his skull. Get your hands round his throat and choke him to death.

"Hullo, Dunky," said Telfer.

He could *feel* himself killing the big blond bastard yet —

Admit it, you're scared to death.

"Don't talk tae me," he said, pushing past Telfer to the corn-kist.

"Oh don't say we're goin' to get all that again?" said Telfer. "You're getting as bad as Blackie. What's the matter with you, for Christ's sake?"

"Ye know bloody well what's the matter."

He hung the bucket up on the nail. You could call it self-control or common sense or whatever you liked. You were a coward and you knew it.

"Look, I'm sick of all this," Telfer said. Dunky tried to push past him, but Telfer grabbed his upper arm. He tried to pull himself free but Telfer's hand was like iron. Grinning at him, big and strong, too big and too strong. "Tell us what's eating you or I'll dump you in the horse trough."

"Leggoa me! I'm no' frighten o' you, Telfer."

Telfer had white teeth. He was still smiling, but there was a sign of bad temper in his eyes. Close to he could feel the size and the strength of him. He tried to wrestle clear. Telfer held on, easily.

"Look, kid, nobody buggers me about. If you've got something on your mind get out with it. Come on, I'm no' jokin' about the trough."

He spat in Telfer's face.

"*I* was goin' out wi' Elsa Noble, yah rat!"

He half-closed his eyes, waiting for the first blow.

Telfer looked at him sideways on, his eyes half-closed, his face beginning to open into a wide smile. Then he shoved him away.

"So that's it. I stole your woman, eh? Christ Almighty, act your age. *I stole your woman?*"

Blackie and McPhail were watching. He stood back, hands clenched. Telfer was just laughing while he made up his mind what to do to him. All right, so he'd get a battering but he'd fight till he dropped.

Telfer shook his head, pityingly. The boy looked wild enough for anything. Poor young cunt, he didn't know what it was all about.

"I met her in the street and asked her if she'd go to the pictures with me," he said. "I didn't even know you were winchin' her. Then she told me you used to go out with her but you'd chucked it in. That's all there is to it."

It didn't sound so bad, put that way.

Dunky wanted to scream at him. Dirty big rat, he'd do the dirty on her and then leave her. He'd loved her, Telfer was just out for another ride. *His* Elsa.

But he knew how that would sound.

"Pinched your woman, did he?" McCann said, winking at Telfer behind Dunky's back. "Ah'd slaughter any bastart that pinched *ma* woman."

"You keep out of it," Dunky snapped. McCann shook his head and picked up the brush.

"All's fair in love an' war," he said, "that's whut they say."

Dunky stood, fists clenched, waiting for one of the men to come at him. Telfer looked amused, McCann went on brushing. They thought he was too young to bother with. He wanted to scream at them. He felt stupid. He wanted to run away.

They yoked Big Dick into the hay trolley and he took the mare to the stack-yard. Now they'd all be laughing at him. Cowardy cowardy Logan, all wind and water, big mouth and no guts. When McPhail tried to speak to him in a friendly sort of way he walked away. He didn't need to be friends with a dirty knee-padder. Or with anyone else.

By the time the hooter went at half-past nine he thought he could hear them talking behind his back. Every time he looked up at the two men on the stack they seemed to be wiping smiles off their faces. He took his piece and his vacuum flask and sat on the half-lifted cole, his back to the others. One day he'd get his revenge. He could hear what they were

215

saying all right, behind his back, pretending to talk about Daftie Coll and his new job on a farm at Kilberrie, winking and grinning at each other about him, whispering about him.

He worked with his teeth clenched, ramming the hay fork into the cole, nodding sullenly at Rafferty to take the horse forward, pulling the trip-rope as hard as he could, hoping it would hit Willie or McPhail, not even looking at Telfer and McCann when they brought in each new load.

"Come on, ya Papish bastard," he shouted when Rafferty was slow in backing the horse.

The scheme boy stood still.

"Whadye call me?" he shouted back, his eyebrows lowered, his mouth open. The hard man's expression. So Rafferty wanted a fight?

"Ah called ye a Papish bastard, d'ye want tae make something of it?"

He could feel satisfaction come over him as he saw Rafferty leave the horse and come towards him. He waited. Fighting was easy – if you knew in advance you could beat the other guy.

"You don't call me that," said Rafferty. Then he started running.

As they punched and kicked and kneed each other he kept thinking of something Willie had said: Townees think they're tough guys but they don't have the belly for it. They're fast enough lads till they get a fist in their guts.

Rafferty was slippery and vicious. They rolled in the hay. He tried to get his thumbs into Rafferty's eyes. Rafferty kept jabbing his knee up, biting as well. He grabbed Rafferty's ears and tried to pull Rafferty's face onto his forehead. Then he had him, knees across Rafferty's chest, hands pinning down his wrists. Rafferty jerked and wriggled. He lifted his left knee off the ground and rammed it into Rafferty's chest. If he could get Rafferty's wrists together in one hand he could smash his dirty face in for him.

Rafferty spat up into his face. He'd spat in Telfer's face. Telfer hadn't battered him. He was bigger than Rafferty. He didn't need to show off by hammering the wee rat.

He stood up quickly.

"Had enough?" he said.

Rafferty scrambled to his feet. They faced each other, panting, Rafferty's face swollen under the right eye.

"Shake?"

He put out his hand.

Rafferty tried to kick him. He jumped to avoid the shoe and then caught the boy in a bear-hug.

"Come on, chuck it in," he said. "I didn't mean to call you that. If I say I'm sorry will ye chuck it in?"

"Don't call me names again."

"Awright."

Willie and McPhail had been watching over the edge of the stack. They'd seen what he'd done. They would let everybody know. You didn't have to prove you were a hard man. Hammering guys was what animals did. He'd handled Rafferty the way Telfer had handled him. That made him equals with Telfer. The next time Willie made a joke he joined in the laughing. Telfer seemed quite keen to be pals again. By dinnertime it was all forgotten.

At least they'd forgotten. Oh yea, all big pals, now.

But he knew he was a coward, a *real* coward. Rafferty wasn't a coward. He was a coward. When Telfer had got hold of him he'd known he was a coward. Why else had he wanted to run home to his mummy?

By Friday the hay was in and stacked and the canvas hap put over the last stack. In the afternoon, with the sun quite warm and only a few small, white clouds in the sky, the four of them, Willie, Telfer, McCann and himself, went with two scythes to open roads round the corn in the field beside the road.

Willie and McCann worked the scythes, swinging from right to left, the big, chipped blades cutting down thin swathes of the shorter, not-quite-ripe stalks growing beside the ditch at the side of the field. He and Telfer came behind, bending to gather up the stalks until they had enough in an armful to make a sheaf, tying it in the middle with a twist of longer stalks.

"Lot of thistles this year," said Telfer, shaking his head.

"Hey, Willie, are we supposed to be working tomorrow afternoon?" he asked. "I'm playing for Cartneuk first team, it'll be awright, will it?"

"You're a football fanatic, Logan," said Willie in his B.B.C. voice. "You've got football on the brain."

"Aye, but can I get off to play if we're workin'?"

"Seen as how ye're no' everybody."

"What's the game?" asked Telfer.

"It's the final of the East Ayrshire Cup," he said. "I've got to play because two of the first team are too old, they're ineligible."

"Good for you," said Telfer.

Were they all really friends? Even McCann? It seemed like it as they worked their way round the first field, just the four of them, Willie and McCann scything, him and Telfer gathering, joking away to each and telling daft stories.

He wanted to be friends with them. Why was it that things always happened to muck you up?

When they'd scythed roads in the five fields of corn and wheat it was time to get the binder out and start cutting. Telfer drove the tractor with Willie on the binder seat, his hand on the lever that raised the mowing arm when they turned round on the corners, his eyes on the teeth that whipped twine round the sheaves, on the lookout for a break in the string. Corn fell forwards over the mower teeth on to an endless canvas belt that carried it to the middle of the binder. It was carried up one side of the triangle-shaped machinery and down the other, tied sheaves dropping out every yard or so.

It took a while to get into the way of stooking again. Dunky remembered how stiff he'd been the summer before. The weather forecast said it would be fine for most of August, not that you could rely on the forecast, but if it was they wouldn't have to rush the whole harvest through in a panic in case it rained. The year before had been wet and when there was a couple of fine days Craig had them working in the fields till it was dark.

Stooking was a plodding job. You picked up a sheaf by grabbing the corn just above the string round its middle. The sheaf didn't weigh much. You walked forward to the next one and picked it up with your right hand. One of you would start the stook by propping the heads of two sheaves together, like a Red Indian wigwam, short stalks on the inside so that it would stand in the wind. You bunged your two sheaves down in line with the first two, the ears at the top of each sheaf pushed together, the base close to the first two. When there were five pairs of sheaves leaning against each other the stook was finished. You walked on and picked up more sheaves and began another stook. The new stubble cracked under your boots. In some places there was thick green grass and clover shoving up among the stubble, in others, where it was drier, you walked on earth. Sometimes you came on a sheaf the binder had dropped without twine, then you had to take a handful of stalks and knot them round the sheaf, a job that needed a strong hand.

McCann and McPhail and Rafferty and himself stooked until Telfer and Willie had cut the whole field. Then they'd join in till all the sheaves were up, you didn't want to cut another field ahead of the stookers in case it turned to rain and sheaves went rotten lying on their sides. Corn was easier than wheat, it was soft and you could stook with your bare arms, even stripped to the waist, the sweat running off your brow, the sun on your back. They started about eight, having to walk or bike to the field. They had their break at half-nine, then the dew had gone and Willie and Telfer could start cutting again. He biked home for his dinner at half-twelve and was back again by half-one, his afternoon piece in the gas-mask case. It was harder bending down after dinner, with your belly full and your eyes wanting to go to sleep. By afternoon break you were starving again. They'd sit against a stook and grunt with stiffness as they ate their pieces. Then it would be up again, going round and round the field, never-ending rows of lying sheaves, your back so sore you couldn't think of anything but the next sheaf, the tips of your fingers beginning to smart from the hard straws. Around five o'clock Craig would come down to the field – God knew where he spent the rest of his time – and have a look at the sky and a look at his boots and a squint at his workers and then tell Willie whether you were doing overtime or not. If you were you went on at it till eight or nine o'clock, still going round the field, the six of you bending and picking up, banging sheaves together, walking forward, bending and picking up, another stook finished, another to start, each man with a different style of working, some always doing a wee bit more than others, Willie liking to place the first two sheaves, keeping his hands buried in the ears of corn till the next two were placed at their side, making sure the stook was steady, eye on the sky when there was a moment to look up, would it rain by morning, were they well ahead, had they fallen behind?

On the second morning you were so stiff you swore you wouldn't be able to bend to lift a sheaf to save your life. Your back was raw with sunburn. You felt giddy and sick and ruptured but nobody told you to have a rest, you started with the others and panted with the stiffness in your back and your shoulders and your legs and soon you didn't notice the stiffness any more.

People came up the road to watch the harvest, it always attracted them, women with prams, men on the panel, men on the burroo. That made it more enjoyable, somehow, as though you had an audience. By the second day you were used to it again.

"One time me and Coll and the man we had then, McAndrew, were stooking on the field where the factory office is now," Willie told them at morning break on the second day. "There wus two wifeys lived in a house across the road, it's demolisht now. Everytime ye lookt up ye could see the two o' them peerin' at ye through the curtains, McAndrew says, 'I'll gie ye somethin' tae luk at, ye auld hoors,' and he whips his breeks down and bends over and points his arse at them, the three of us did it, great muckle arses winkin at them, I'll bet they got the fright o' their lives."

"D'ye want to hear a good joke?" said McCann. "Well, there's this wee girl and this wee boy coming home from school and she says, 'Hey John, I'm bleedin' in my knickers' and the boy says, 'Come ahint this hedge an' let's see' and he gets down and has a look and then he says, 'By jings, Mary, nae wonder ye're bleedin', somebody's cut the knackers off ye.'"

Then they were up on their feet, hands on their backs as they stretched and groaned. He tried to remember a joke to tell at the afternoon break. The great thing about this kind of work was being able to think. About anything that came into your head. It was something he'd never been able to do, think, not if it meant sitting down and concentrating. Too impatient, he supposed. Once his mother had taken him and Senga to Troon for a week in the summer, Aunt Bessie had looked after his father. There was nothing to read in their room, nothing at all, not even an old newspaper lining one of the drawers, nothing, not even a piece of paper and a pencil to see how many words he could make out of a big word, like perambulate or metamorphosis. His mother and Senga were in their big bed by nine o'clock and there he was, stuck with nothing to read – the only time in his life he'd been in a bed with a small light of his own above the headboard. He'd decided he would have to *think*, something interesting. Huh, he couldn't even think of anything to think about! Thinking like that was dead boring. How could a person be interested in something they thought up in their own heads? You needed something to do, or something to read, your own life was boring because you knew all about it already. Alec said he often liked to go for walks on his own and think about the real meaning of things. He could never tell you what it was he'd been thinking about, or what he'd decided, maybe he knew but was too shy to tell somebody else. People like them, all the people he knew in Kilcaddie, never talked to each other about what they *really* thought. Football, the pictures, gossip, the weather, he'd heard all they had to say. Voices he'd been hearing all his life. All saying the same things ... I think it'll rain the day. Where ye workin' noo then? How d'ya like ma new boots? Rangers is the greatest. Rangers is a lot of gorillas. Rangers bribes the refs. Rangers doesnae need tae bribe the refs. Celtic's a lot of Fenian bastards. Celtic's more fair-mindet than Rangers, Celtic'll play a Proddestant, Rangers'll no' even huv a Catholic on the turnstiles. Big Frank Brennan's miles better'n Willie Woodburn. Don't talk soft, Woodburn's the greatest. Is it true what I hear aboot your Nellie, she's winchin' one of they Yanks? Our Bob's back's fair killin' him, so'n it is. Ma certes! The priest came to the McGrory's and took away their last ten bob, an' no' a bit of bread in the house. That McCandless fella, drinks like a fish and his wife's got awfy bad asthma, so she has. Jings aye, oor Jeanie in America's got a car and a refrigerator, imagine that! They GI war brides should be ashamet o' thersels, so they should. Ma John says Churchill was only good in wars. Ma daddy's bigger'n your daddy, so there. How come Meiklepark gets more buses than Darroch, that's what I want to know. Oor Nessie's been on the housin' list for eight years and the factor says they've got no hope, is that no' scandalous? Oor minister takes a good drop, you can't deny it.

When you were young and didn't know any better, you asked people idiotic questions, like "How does the wireless work, daddy?" or "Is the king a good man, mammy?" or "How can God listen to everybody praying at once, Miss?"

You grew up and learned not to talk daft. People laughed at you if you told them what you really thought, so you kept it in your own head. People laughed at you for almost everything. Like Uncle Charlie laughing at his diary, that time he found it under a cushion on the couch. Oh aye, big laugh, reading out all the things he made lists of ... Books I have Read ... Opera Seen ("*Carmen* and *La Bohème* at the Picture House, oh you're an opera hand, are you?") ... Places I have Visited ("Listen to this, King George V Playing Fields, bus, twopence, to Porterfield Road, Ayr – my, you've travelled widely, Dunky") ... Scottish Country Dance Bands Heard ... Films I have seen ... International Teams ... Modern Dance Bands Heard ... Catches I have Made ("Oh, Bessie, listen to this, Species, sticklebacks, number, twenty-one, result, put into bowls, the ones in the glass bowl lived but the rest conked out, oh Dunky, you're a scream so you are") ... Plays Heard ... Neutral Matches I have Seen ... Classmates ... Pals ... Film Star Favourites ("Who's this Broderick Crawford, Dunky, I've never heard of the man, you've got him down here as *excellent*, have you heard of him, Bessie?") ... Dances I have Attended ... Cafés Visited ("Oh Beth, your boy's a rerr terr so he is, listen to this, The Rainbow, Ayr, food no bad, service grim, dames rotten, oh Dunky, my sides'll burst from laughing") ... and worst of all he could have *died*, when Uncle Charlie came to the last page where he kept a list of all the girls he'd dated or lumbered, with comments on them in French! And his mother wondered why he never went near Aunt Bessie or Uncle Charlie! How would anybody like to hear their uncle reading out what was written on the front of the book, "This is the chronicle of the life of Duncan Aitchison Logan, plus some information appertaining to his interests"?

They made a song and dance about sending you to school and then they laughed their heads off because you learned words like appertaining! His mother should think of *that* next time she complained about him working at the farm. They *wanted* you to be as thick and dim as they were, so he'd show them he could win the Scottish Cup for ignorance. He'd grow up into a real moronic working-man and balls to them. What did Uncle Charlie know about anything, a bloody clerk, that's all he was.

At dinnertime he was surprised to see Willie Craig standing at the scheme bus stop, obviously heading up the town. Willie didn't see him pass on the bike and he didn't shout out. That was one of the things you learned on a farm, keep quiet and watch and learn wee things you weren't supposed to know. Keep it in your head, everything was safer if you kept it secret. Willie hardly ever went down into Kilcaddie, he couldn't tolerate the town. What would he be going now for, in the middle of a harvest day?

Farquharson the lawyer was more than surprised when Willie Craig came into his office above the bank in Fergus Street. Auld Craig had left only an hour or two before, wanting to change his will. He was just going to say "My my, two Craigs in one morning" when he stopped himself. The old man wouldn't be wanting Willie to know he'd been in, especially if he knew what the old man had come to see him about.

"This is a bit off your usual track," he said to Willie, noting that the man's only concession to the town was that he'd put on clean boots. He hoped too many folk hadn't seen him come into the office dressed like that, not even a collar or a tie.

Willie sat in front of Farquharson's desk, his cap in his hands, his knees splayed wide, holding on to his cap with both hands so that he wouldn't absent-mindedly start picking his nose, which Mary told him was one of his worst habits. He didn't like coming into the town and he didn't like being in the office, not with Farquharson looking like Lord Muck in his fancy clothes and the silly bits of girls giving him queer looks in the front office. Still, he was worth more than Farquharson and his fancy kind put together, or at least his father was.

"My father's gone a bit funny," he said, not really knowing how to start, speaking carefully to let Farquharson know he might look a bit rough but he'd had as good an education as anybody. "I'm thinking he's taken a scunner to the wife and eh, well, it's difficult like, but how do I stand? That's what I want to know. I mean, he's no' got all that long to go, what happens to me and the wife when he dies?"

Farquharson put the tips of his fingers together. This was a tricky one. He'd just been looking forward to his lunch in Semple's Tea Rooms, too.

"Haven't you spoken to him about it?"

They must have had some kind of row. Otherwise why would the old man come in at one moment, demanding to change his will so that his other son, George, the one in Rhodesia, got all the money and then Willie come in the next moment asking about the will?

"Och, you can't get through to him these days, he just humphs and jumphs and pretends he doesn't hear you. I'm worried he's thinking of doing something daft with his money, I mean, I've worked for him all these years, I should know what's what, shouldn't I? Has he *made* a will, for instance?"

"Aye well, Willie, it's not just as simple as that, you see, I'm actually his solicitor, not yours, d'you follow me? It puts me in a wee bit of an awkward situation, doesn't it? I wouldn't really be acting properly if I told anybody else a client's business, would I?"

"Aye but he's my father, I'm entitled to know."

It was really a bit much, people like the Craigs with more money than they had the brains to know what to do with. Farmers were all the same, peculiar folk.

"I can tell you the law, that's easy enough," he said. "Your father's entitled to leave everything he has to anybody he likes. He could leave the farm and the land to *anybody,* it doesn't matter if they're family or not, you couldn't do anything about that. However, under the law you can claim a quarter of the residue of the estate, that means all moneys and stocks and shares. That's as his son. Of course, if you felt you were being treated unjustly you could bring an action to have the will altered, you might even try and show he was of unsound mind when he made it, or that you were entitled to a large share by reason of the years you worked for him. Mind you, that's just hypothetical, you understand."

Try as he could Willie wasn't able to get anything but hums and havers out of Farquharson. He saw by the clock on the wall it was ten after one, time to be getting back for yoking again.

"Will you just tell me one thing?" he said, getting up. "*Is* there a will?"

"I think I can tell you that, yes, there is a will, and legal."

"And you can't tell me what's in it?"

"No, I'm terribly sorry, you must see my position."

"Aye. So if he's turned against me all I'll get is a quarter of what's in the bank, not the land?"

"*If* he's turned against you. Why don't you have a quiet word with him, Willie? I mean, he is your father, surely you can ask him outright? Old people can be a bit peculiar about wills, you know, one day they think one thing and one day the next."

Willie felt like picking Farquharson up by his scrawny neck and choking it out of him.

"Aye, I'll ask him," he said. "Do I pay you for this talk?"

Farquharson smiled.

"Oh no, no charge for a friendly wee chat with an old

friend. You're thinking of that story of the man who left his umbrella in a lawyer's office and when he went back inside for it the lawyer told him the second visit would be another six and eightpence. Ha ha, folk think the worst of lawyers, don't they?"

With good reason. He was glad to get back on the scheme bus and watch the town sail by. Farquharson was a real townee, shifty and devious. They were all the same, look at them, daft creatures in daft clothes fancying themselves as something important. Too much money and not enough work, that was their trouble. All he knew was that there was a will. He'd always expected the old man would leave the farm and the land to him and give George a half of the money, that was fair enough. Suppose he left the lot to George, what would George do? All these years in Rhodesia and not so much as a letter, just the usual wee scribble at Christmas. Not much of a brother even when he was here, either. His father's favourite, nothing was ever too good for George, George this and George that, no thanks to him for having stayed at home all these years, oh no.

"On ye go, McCann can sit on the binder," he said to the men. He went into the house.

"Where is he?" he asked Mary.

"Out in the garden, I don't know what he's doing," she said. "What happened with Farquharson?"

"Ach him, he wouldnae tell me anything. I'm goin' tae have it out wi' him."

She went through into their bedroom and stood behind the curtain, her hands clasped on her belly. She could see the old man jinking about in the long grass. He had three crab-apple trees out there, he was so mean he thought everybody was always trying to steal them.

Willie swung his leg over the low wire fence and walked between the trees towards his father.

"Settin' traps are ye?" he shouted.

The old man looked up, jerked his head in a sniffing sort of way and bent down again. Willie watched where he put his feet, the old bastard might easily have put down gin traps to catch wee boys.

"There's somethin' I want tae talk tae ye about," he said.

"I'm busy."

"Aye, busy wi' a lot of sour wee apples that's nae good tae

anybody ye mean?" Craig was stringing wire between the trunks of the three trees, about a foot off the ground.

"This'll stop their thieving," he said. "They'll mibbe trip and break their ankles."

Willie shook his head. It was a pity Craig hadn't kicked the bucket before his brains went. It wasn't very nice to see a strong man turned into an old dotard.

"I've been tae see Farquharson," he said. "He tells me ye've made a will, is that right?"

Craig's big claw hands fiddled with the wire. That woman had been putting Willie up to this.

"Is that all he tellt ye?" he said.

Willie remembered being in this garden with his father forty-odd year ago when he was about twelve. They'd caught a boy from the town stealing apples. His father had grabbed the boy's collar and told him to run and fetch the police. Get the polis for a pickle of crab-apples, even at that age he knew it wasn't right. The boy had squirmed and cried and then shouted out, in desperation, "I've kieched in ma breeks." He had, too. There had been a terrible guff off the boy. He'd pretended to be too frightened to go for the police and his father had let the boy go after giving him a good cuffing round the lugs. Then he'd got a few on his own ears for not doing what he was told.

"Aye, he says he's your lawyer, no' mine. I want to know what's in the will."

"I've no doubt," said the old man. "She'll be putting you up to this, I suppose?"

"Never mind her, it's me that wants to know."

"Aye, no doubt. Well, you'll just have to want, won't you?"

"I've a right to know."

"Have you now?"

"Aye."

"I wouldnae count on it."

He'd made his own choice, he'd sided with her against his own father, now he could rot in hell for all he cared. He'd go back to Farquharson tomorrow morning and *make* him change the will. He should never have let the lawyer get away with his impudence, telling *him* to think it over for a few days!

"Are ye goin' tae tell me?"

He stood up, the wire at last knotted round the foot of the tree. Man, it was a rare day for the hearst. One year it rained that much the corn was flat and they'd lost it all. When was that now? He saw Willie standing beside him. What was he wanting?

"Ye should be yoked," he said. "It's by dinnertime."

"I want to know about the will."

"The will? My will ye mean? Is George been putting ye up to this? Aye well, ye can tell him he gets nothing, nothing at all. An' tell his mother, it's no use arguin', if he wants to be away let him go but he's no' gettin' any of it. Tell them that."

"Ye're haverin'," Willie said. "Come awa' in the house, ye need to rest."

"Aye, I'm tiret right eneuch. It's a' this business wi' George."

No, it was with Willie, not George. He tried to remember what had been happening. As Willie helped him into the house he saw the woman staring at him from the kitchen door. It was her that was the cause of it all. Dam' the woman, Jessie should never have let her in the house.

"Damn ye," he roared at her. Willie tried to hold his arm, but the old man got away. His fist was up, clenched, as he tried to run at her. Willie knew he was only waving it at her, he knew it then. He let Craig go on. He wasn't as daft as everybody thought. Let him go for her. They'd all know he was mad then. He thought his mother was still alive! Unsound mind, Farquharson had called it.

The old man slipped and half-fell, his legs scrabbling stiffly for support. His mouth hung open, but his breath came in urgent, rasping pants through his nose.

Willie watched. He felt nothing for his father. All his life he'd done what the old man had told him. Now Craig was flopping about like a hen in its death dance. To the end, just before he fell on his chest, Auld Craig kept staring at Mary, saliva slopping between his lips. Only when he was still did Wille move. Nobody but Mary would ever know how he'd stood back and watched his father thresh about.

"We'll need the doctor," he said to Mary as he carried him, moaning and raving and muttering, up the stairs. "Go over tae the phone box and get him down here."

He waited by his father's bed till the doctor arrived and then he left him, the old man lying on his back, eyes closed, the doctor poking about with the stethoscope round his neck. Telfer stopped the tractor so that he could take McCann's place on the binder seat. It was a fine day for the hearst. Too good a day to waste sitting in the house. He'd know soon enough what the doctor said. No, he wouldn't have the old man put away in a home, there was no real harm in him. Poor old bugger, he'd just lived too long, that was his trouble. Well, maybe his time had come now so there was no point in thinking about any of it.

As they cut into the middle of the field a hare sprung from the small square of standing corn. The two dogs were after it in a flash. Telfer stopped the tractor. They chased it, waving and shouting, their caps in their hands. The hare darted up and down among the stooks, doubling back, the dogs barking like the clappers of hell. It was a big one. If it didn't see a way through the hedges it would run about in the stooks till its lungs burst. They always did.

"Keep it runnin'," he shouted.

Eventually it gave up and the boy Rafferty jumped on it, trapping it in his shirt which he'd pulled off as he ran. Not that it needed trapping, it was fair done.

He wrung its neck across his knee and carried it by the hind legs to the tractor, where he wrapped it in his jacket and laid it in the tool box.

"It's a buck, make a good bite or two," he said to Telfer.

"Bags I the next one," said Telfer.

"Fun's over you lot," Willie shouted to the stookers.

It made a nice wee break in the monotony, he thought.

"Get tore into these Victoria people," said Baldy. He patted each player on the shoulder as they passed him and clattered down the tunnel. "Don't let us down," he shouted after them.

Bigtime! Running out of a proper dressing-room and down a wee tunnel and out into the sunshine. A real football stadium – only a junior ground, of course, but it looked bigtime, with the wee wall round the pitch and the folk standing on the little terracing. The first team strip was the same as Hearts, maroon shirts with white collars and white pants, black stockings with white bands. All sorts of people were watching, Baldy had said. Scouts from big clubs. He'd told them how he'd been given this strip by Hearts when they took one of last year's first team on to the groundstaff. That was to make them feel bigtime. Baldy knew what he was doing, all right. It was guff but you wanted to believe it.

He and Sammy Muir were the only two from the second team. Sammy was a wee terror, smoked like a demon and yet could run like wildfire. He hardly knew the rest of the first team. Bigtime guys. He didn't run about too much in the kickabout, it was a hot day and they'd need all their wind for later on. This was his big chance. Keep the heid, that's what Joe Overend had said. Keep the heid. There was nobody in the crowd he knew. He trapped the ball and set it up for a cross. Have to impress them, show I'm good enough. Right foot. Not bad. Norrie Picken, their goalie, caught it and rolled it out to the forwards. He ran round to the corner of the penalty box, chewing hard, sleeves still rolled down to his wrists. Nice white cuffs. Made you feel neat and sharp. Like Willie Bauld, neat and deadly.

They lost the toss and changed ends, running through the oncoming Victoria team. The goalies shook hands, nobody else did. They looked a hard lot, sort of scruffy, too, they had Airdrie strips, white with the big red V down their chests. This way they'd face into the sun. In the second half it would be lower, better angle for dazzling them.

The ref looked round the two teams. People shouted. He watched the centre-forward's feet. The ref raised his whistle. Wait for it – the centre-forward had jumped the gun. The new ball, round and *lovely,* as bright as a Belisha beacon, was replaced on the spot. Then the whistle. God make me play a good game.

No wonder the first team hadn't lost since Christmas. They were fantastic. He hardly had any work to do. Victoria didn't have a hope. He took the ball off one of them easily, tackling the way you were taught, boot jammed in hard, knee over your boot, body over your knee, hit ball and man hard, bring it away, don't hold it too long, look for a man. Going up the left side of the field he saw Sammy and another of their forwards, but they were marked. A man came to tackle him. He cut in, switching to his right foot. Then he crossed it to the right wing. Had the scouts seen that? It went to their outside-right, McLatchie, all smooth and elusive. Nothing came of the cross. He fell back. Victoria must be *some* good or they wouldn't have reached the final. Most of the players had new laces on their boots, white on dark leather, the whole *thing* was neat and bright.

Victoria had a good inside-left, a very solid guy who could dribble like mad. Strong, too. After they'd seen two or three of his runs they began to tackle him in pairs, trying to crowd him off the ball.

In from the side, hook the ball away with the right foot. Missed! Going down on his left knee he curled his right leg round the guy's shins and hooked the feet from him. The ref shook his head when the Victoria guy raised his arms for a foul. Somebody else got the ball down field. The Victoria guy rubbed his knees.

"You try that again an' I'll kick yur face in," he said.

"You and what army?"

"Jist watch it."

Some guys thought they were very bigtime. Big mouths was more like it.

They scored the first from a corner, a header, easy as winky. While they all ran to clap their centre-forward on the back the Victoria defenders argued among themselves. Their goalie should have got it. That made you feel great. You were going to murder them. He could hardly believe it when the next came, a couple of minutes later. It was the first real thing Sammy Muir had done, flicking the ball over the right back's head, running round him, belting it from just inside the penalty box. When you saw it hitting the net you felt like screaming, as though a bright light had flashed in your head. They mobbed Sammy, hugging and kissing him. He wasn't nervous at all now. Then it was three, McLatchie dribbling right to the line and then cutting it back for Archie Kennedy to bang it in. Three up at half-time! Look at us, people! They ran into the wee tunnel, their studs clattering on concrete.

"No' bad, lads, you're doin' okay," said Baldy.

He sat on the bench that ran round the room, his head resting on somebody's jacket, panting slightly.

"Score another three and show these people," said Joe. "They're a load of rubbish."

Some guys shouted the odds and some combed their hair and some scratched their balls with both hands and some horsed about and some sat still and looked on. Baldy moved about, chatting quietly, a huge man in a pair of trousers that would've fitted an elephant. He made you feel you were somebody. You wanted him to speak to you, to give some sign he thought you were playing well. The lads said that if Cartneuk won the Scottish Cup Baldy would say "No' bad, lads" and then tell you off for not scoring another ten goals. McLatchie had once scored four goals for the first team and all Baldy had said was, "Pass it about more, lad, you're gettin' a bit selfish." It made you want to laugh. Or to do the impossible and see what Baldy said then.

"Don't get carried away," he said as they stood up to go out again. "Ye havenae won till the final whistle, remember that."

"What does he want, jam on it?" said somebody. They got a fair roar as they went out again.

This is what it would be like playing for Rangers, knowing you were in a *real* team, too good for anybody else, bigtime. He watched the inside-left. He thought he was a real hard man. Cheek of the rat, threatening *him*!

Up they came, Victoria must have had a real telling-off in their dressing-room. They looked angry. How about that then, he thought, as Jimmy Clark, their centre-half, shouldered the inside-left to the ground and cleared half the length of the pitch. He was near enough to hear the Victoria inside-left have a go at Jimmy.

"I'll do you," he was saying.

Jimmy spat and sniffed.

So that's what he was, a tough guy? Right then, let's get tore into them.

He went for the inside-left's ankles the next time he was near him, tapping the right heel so that his toe went on the wrong side of his left foot, sending him flying face first.

The ref gave a foul for that, although he put on an innocent face and held up his hands as though he couldn't believe it. The other Victoria forwards seemed like weak nonentities, not worth bothering about. Jimmy Clark had the same idea as he had. They both got near the inside-left and when the foul was taken they rammed him in the back as the ball came down.

The ref didn't give a foul. He was weak!

Victoria were getting bad-tempered. Their backs began to take fly-kicks at people. Faces were pushed together and fists clenched. Great fun. Beat them hollow then finish them off.

One of them got Sammy Muir in a two-footed tackle. Sammy went down so heavily they thought he was really injured. Joe Overend came running on to the field with his dripping sponge, his jacket flying at his side.

"Fuck me," said Sammy, lying on the grass, the rest of them looking down at him. "Is ma ankle broke?"

"They're asking for what they get," said Jimmy Clark. Joe gave Sammy a last rub and then walked back to the wee stand.

So they wanted a kicking match? Right. Let's get tore in

properly. Next time he'd tramp on the bastard's hands. All the people who watched him thought he was a coward. They all remembered him being frightened of the horses, of Blackie McCann, of guys at the dancing, of Telfer. There was only one way to show them.

It was the only way to play. To hate the other team. To want to destroy them. Jimmy Clark tripped a guy when the ball was at the other end of the park. Two of their forwards charged the Victoria goalie so hard he was actually crying. Two Victoria guys sandwiched McLatchie, almost breaking his ribs. The ref was hopeless, he ponced about and hardly saw anything. The crowd was going mad, especially the Victoria supporters. They were well beaten so they had to shout about something.

He hated the bloody lot of them.

The inside-left started another of his runs, this time moving out into the shadow of the stand, a thick-necked guy he was, very sure of himself, a hard man, thought he was Torry Gillick or somebody.

He beat one man, then hit the ball down the wing and started after it, quite fast. There wasn't much point in tackling him, the idea was to fall back and let him come to you, but what the hell, they were three up, he could take a chance.

He started out for the ball, body leaning forward, sprinting as hard as he knew how. The inside-left had his speed up now, going to make a dash down the wing.

Hit him, go on, hit the bastard.

There was a blinding sickness in his face and head. Everything went black. His stomach tried to heave up. The pain in his face made him want to vomit. He saw things but didn't understand what they were. People had a hold of his arms. He tried to say something, but they were miles away. He heaved up again. Shocks of agony went through his head. He couldn't hear what the voices were shouting. It was a dream. A dream. . . .

He woke up in a bed and thought for a moment it was still Saturday morning. A white bed, white blankets? Not at home. A big window. Where was he?

Then Joe Overend and his mother were coming towards him. They were looking at his face. He put up his hands. There was a bandage over half of his face. The game!

"How're ye feelin', Dunky?" Joe asked.

His mother looked as though she'd been crying.

"What happened?"

As he spoke he felt his mouth funny. His tongue was thick and sore. He ran it tenderly along his teeth. At the front he could only feel soft stuff. His mother leaned over him. Looking away from her he saw other men in white beds.

"Your nose is broken and you've lost two front teeth, oh Dunky, thank God you're all right."

"What happened?"

Joe patted his mother's back.

"You'll be all right, son," he said. "You should see the other guy. Huh, he'll no' be out of plaster for months."

He couldn't believe it at first. He didn't remember a thing about it. Joe said he'd charged the inside-left like a tank and sent him flying on to the wee wall, breaking his arm and two fingers. He must have broken his nose when he hit the guy, Joe said. Before anybody could get near enough one of the other Victoria guys had run up and booted him in the face, knocking out his front teeth. They'd run him to the Ayr hospital in Joe's van and then fetched his mother.

"The ref says he was sendin' you off anyway," said Joe. "You and the geezer that kickt you. Och, don't bother your head aboot it, Dunky, we'll claim proveycation, he was threatenin' quite a few o' the lads."

"Did we win?"

"Of course we did. We are the people, eh?"

They X-rayed him and found nothing worse and his mother came to collect him later that night. They got a bus from Ayr to Kilcaddie, folk looking at his bandaged face, his mother acting as if he'd broken his skull.

"I'm all right," he kept telling her.

When they got home he was still feeling chirpy, but suddenly he had another attack of vomiting and she put him to bed.

"I'll be all right, I'll be at my work on Monday no bother," he said.

At least it had saved him from having to decide what to do with himself. A great way to spend a Saturday night.

But it was his own fault, he knew that. He'd behaved like an animal and he'd got what he deserved. The big day all ruined, just because of sheer animalistic hate. He'd wear false teeth for the rest of his life, serve him right. And what about the other guy? Maybe his arm wouldn't set properly, or his fingers. What kind of job did he have? Christ, he'd behaved

233

no better than a criminal. His father had always been right, he *was* unnatural.

No, that was soft, to think like that. The other guy had asked for all he got. Bad luck, that's all it was. Or bad timing. He should've been more clever. If you were going to put the mockers on another player you had to do it the canny way. Learn to get away with murder, that was the motto. He'd been carried away. It was a lesson learned. Know better the next time.

Thinking about the next time made his stomach rise. The same sickening shock echoed through his brain, the breath-catching, heart-constricting shock you always got from a bang on the nose. He lay completely still, hands holding the blanket, eyes closed, trying to hold it down.

They thought he was finished. Aye, he knew. They weren't sorry. They wanted him out of the way. It would be theirs then, they thought. His land. His farm. No, damn ye, it's mine. I am Craig, the only Craig who counts.

Whatever they said was lies. They said he was to stay in bed. All of them, the woman, Willie, the doctor. Hangers-on. It is mine.

What was he doing on the floor?

Trousers.

Damn. He was weak.

Bed's for dying in. He wasn't dying.

Gey clever of them to keep him in bed. Weakening his legs.

Lying on his chest, face on the blankets, he pulled the trousers up and eased his arms into the braces. He pushed himself to his feet.

Boots.

Dam' it, he was that weak he could hardly stand. That was what they wanted. My memory's good as any, better than most. What do they know?

Jacket.

I'm coming, ye're gey clever laddies but have no fear, I'm coming. It's mine still. I'll shake ye.

Mary saw him as she came round the corner into the yard, the empty corn pail in her hand. He was at the end of the yard, walking like a man trying to cover ground before he fell, head down, back bent, arms at his sides, feet rushing to keep up with the forward fall of his body.

"Craig! Come back here!"

He was off down the track road. She let the pail fall on stones. She felt frightened. It was like something supernatural. Dying people were supposed to do strange things. She hurried to the stack yard to tell Telfer.

They were forking on to carts now, forking wheat, great brutes of sheaves, your gut tight with the strain of throwing them up on to the top of the load, working like demons to get it in before the forecast rain. Two prongs into the sheaf, brace yourself, take the weight, right hand at the bottom of the fork, left hand level with your chest. Up the side of straw, push it up, hold it up, feel Willie's fork jabbing in, got it, pull it away, bringing down your lead arms, into the next sheaf, get them two at a time, stagger under the weight, try to balance, shove them up, come on Willie, take the bloody things, arms bursting, take one next time, throw it up, bring it up to your hips, the fork held like a rifle with a bayonet, heave it up, watch it sail up, chaff flying about like snow, dust in your eyes, was it up? Another one, the cart going forward, another stook, hurry up, we havenae got all day down there, Logan, hurry it up, how much more? Want to eat something, shaking with hunger, stomach quivering, weakness in his arms, sickness in his throat, another two up to the top, arms stretched as high as they would go, take them, Willie, for Christ's sake, head feels like I'm going to faint, hot and sweaty, like a fever, starving of hunger, caught you suddenly sometimes, forehead sweaty, black spots before the eyes, shoulders wet, waves of fever, keep going, another sheaf, don't be a mammy's boy throw it up to the top, make it rain, hot and cold at the same time, my arms won't take it, isn't this load on yet, it's rolling forward like a great bloody sailing ship, Willie and McPhail on top, can hardly see them, they can't build it much higher, I'm shaking all over, Christ it's only half-past three, five hours yet at least, I'll never manage it, I'm sure the blood's lashing out of my nose, maybe the bandage has cut off the blood to the brain, I could pretend to pass out, they wouldn't laugh, they'd blame it on the nose. . . .

He saw McCann pointing across to the hedge. They were well into the middle of the wheatfield and he had to rub his eyes to spot what McCann was seeing. "It's Craig," McCann shouted, looking up the outward-sloping side of the load.

It was the face he remembered afterwards, the white, mysterious face peering out between gaps in the hedges, moving up the track road on the other side of the grassy bank, a strange white face much larger than it should have been, somehow, at that distance.

Willie let his feet dangle over the back of the load, layers of sheaves sagging under his weight. Then he let himself fall forward and down, a dark winged shape against the faded orange of the wheat stalks. He hit the ground with a thud and sprawled forward.

Picking up his cap he ran across the field towards his father. Dunky lay down on his back. He didn't understand it. Craig was supposed to be ready to kick the bucket. The white face had looked mad, somehow. He shut his eyes. Dazzling circles of light moved across his eyelids. Your eyes and your stomach seemed to go together. The moving lights were making him sick again. He opened his eyes and looked away from the sun. The whole sky was covered by grey cloud, except to the west where the sun came through a clear patch, making a strange, watery brilliance of light. Away to the east, over the hills, the sky was dark, gloomy, thunderous. He was a little bug lying all by himself in the middle of a huge field under a lightning sky. A stubble stalk cracked as he moved his head. It was the only sound he could hear. Everybody else was dead. He listened. Nothing.

He realised the fainting sensation had gone. Sitting up he looked for the others. McCann had been forking sheaves on the other side of the cart, but he was gone. Willie was gone. Was McPhail still up on top?

He stood up. For a moment he felt faint again, as the blood ran out of his head, but the giddiness passed.

"Hey, where are they all?" he shouted up the side of the load.

"At the gate," shouted back the unseen McPhail. "They've got the auld fella."

He waited at the horse's head, watching the small figures moving at the far end of the field.

"Ye'd better take this lot in," McPhail said.

The great load lurched across the field, cart wheels creaking and rumbling over the stubbly ground. Big Dick stamping his hooves, body straining forward against the weight, top sheaves bouncing as they crossed a rut.

Craig was still on his feet when they drew near to the gate. Willie had hold of one arm. McCann was at his other side, not too sure of whether he was supposed to grab hold, too.

Craig didn't seem to notice them. He was staring across the field at something they couldn't see.

It was downhill going out of the gate and there was no stopping Big Dick there, not with that load pushing at his back. He tried to slow him down, both hands pulling on the reins, but the horse was no match for the weight of wheat on the cart. He jammed his back hooves into the ground, body leaning backwards, but the horseshoes skidded forward on the grass and he had to keep going forward or fall between the shafts.

"Look out for fuck's sake!" Dunky shouted.

McCann and Willie pulled at the old man's arms but he stood his ground. They looked like two men holding on to a bull's horns. Dunky had to run to keep at the horse's head. Everybody was shouting.

Then McCann dived against the old man, knocking him out of the road of the horse, scrabbling to get clear of the wheels.

Dunky was still in front of the horse, running backwards, both hands on the reins, glancing over his shoulder to see the gate-posts, the horse snorting in his face, the load lurching from side to side.

The front right wheel hit the gate-post, which gave way with a rotten crack.

The load stayed on. He wheeled round and into the road and then he was able to bring the horse to a stop. He hung the reins on the shaft. At his back he heard the tractor. He saw Telfer standing behind the red bonnet, Willie's wife sitting on the empty cart.

He walked round the load, keeping as far into the ditch as possible in case it slipped off.

Willie was kneeling beside the old man, McCann standing over him.

"I couldnae stop at all," he said.

Willie looked up.

"We'll get him on the empty cart," he said. "We were lucky it didnae coup over on him."

They made a bed of sheaves for the old man, whose eyes were closed, and laid him on the back of the empty cart.

"I went to feed the chickens and he was away out the house before I knew anything about it," Willie's wife kept saying, as though she was being accused of something.

Telfer took it slowly along the back road, with Willie and

his wife and McCann holding the bed of sheaves steady against the bumps, the soles of the old man's boots forming a right angle, the patterns made by metal segs on the soles seeming to Dunky like dull bracelets.

He followed them leading Big Dick, with a tight grip on the bit-rope, left thumb stuck in the shoulder of his cotton vest. If you listened long enough to the tractor engine you thought you could hear voices speaking to you through the noise.

When they brought the two carts into the yard the grey clouds had blown over and in the sunshine the old farm looked as though it had been sleeping.

CHAPTER THIRTEEN

This was what it felt like to be a man!

Carrying the small leather cases with their football gear, Dunky and Billy Forsyth, the second-team goalkeeper, walked through the loosely-swinging doors of the public bar. There were men there already, lots of men, pressing against the chest-high bar counter, smoking, talking, drinking, ordering.

He put his case down beside the wall and loosened the belt of his gabardine raincoat. Billy went for the drinks. They always had the same to start with, a half of whisky and a dump.

"Cheers," said Billy, handing him the two glasses.

"Here's to Ne'erday," he said.

Whisky was for men. It went down inside you like a burning blow-lamp. Billy put his beer glass on the little shelf and got out his fags.

"Thanks," he said, taking a Capstan from the packet of ten. Fags were for men. They came out of the packet white and crisp between the nicotine stains of the first two fingers. It felt like a man, being a man, rolling the whiteness between the fingers. His nose looked horrible, his tongue never stopped licking round the sickening shape of his dental plate. He was repulsive, no use thinking of real love now. This was best, drinking with the real men.

The beer was cold. It was only half-past eleven in the morning and the beer seemed to make your stomach roll about inside you.

"Got your bottle for tonight?" asked Billy.

"I got a bottle awright, it's stuff called Old Maclean," he said. "You ever heard of it?"

"Nah," said Billy. "They sell anything at Ne'erday. You've got to order months in advance if you want a proprietary brand. Takes the enamel off your teeth a lot of what they give you at Ne'erday."

Men knew about whisky.

He unbuttoned his coat and put his left hand in his trousers pockets, his yellow wool scarf hanging down his shirt-front.

"I was lucky I wasn't working the day," he said. "The gaffer wanted us in this morning. We tellt him to go and boil his heid."

McCann had told Willie. Work on Hogmanay? Get lost, McCann had said. Telfer had joined in. Willie eventually said they could take the whole day off then and damn the lot of them. He'd sounded exactly the way Auld Craig used to sound. He'd changed, Willie. He was getting very miserable. McCann said it was because Mary was spending the Craig money as fast as the banker could cash the cheques. Or because their bairn had black hair. Ach, to hell with work. What good was Auld Craig's money doing him now he was rotting away in Kilcaddie Cemetery?

"I don't fancy this game at all," he said to Billy.

"Me neither. Is your mates coming?"

His new mates, Big Shanky and Jakie Reid – Springheel Jake. It was like a man to have mates like them. Big drinking mates.

"See me," said Billy. "I play better wi' a good bucket in me, so I do. Whisky makes you frisky!"

It was like a man to stand at the bar, nodding cheerily to the wee drinking fellas who let you up to the counter, giving your order to the barman in the white jacket, dropping your fag end on the floor and looking down as you wiped it flat with your toe, handing over the pound note, taking your change in an open palm, shoving it straight in your pocket without counting it, fingers knowing how to lift four glasses at once.

He had to laugh when he thought of the first time. Him and Alec on a Saturday night before the dancing just after the harvest. They'd walked up and down past the pub four times because Alec was scared one of his relatives might be passing, or somebody who knew him and would tell his father. But they'd been determined to do it, regardless. They'd walked into the crowded noise, Alec pretending to be blowing his nose into his hankie so that he could cover his face till they reached the far end of the bar and could stand with their faces to the wall. Then they didn't even know the names of any drinks! Luckily the man next to them had ordered. Two dumps. They'd ordered two dumps too, not knowing what dumps were, relieved to buggery when they turned out to be small bottled ales. A right pair they must have been!

Shanky and Jakie came in looking very gallus. They were both eighteen. Shanky had been a bigtime guy at the Academy, a right bad lot he was called because he nicked off school in the afternoons to play snooker in the billiard hall. Jakie was an electrician, a hard wee guy with red hair and fingernails chewed almost to the knuckles. Wee Springheel Jakie and Big Shanky, his gallus mates. He'd met them in a pub. Alec had stopped coming. He didn't like them.

"What's in the cases then, chief?" asked Jakie. "A cairy-oot for this afternoon?"

"Football boots," said Billy.

"Who're ye playing for, Alcoholics Unanimous?" said Shanky.

It was like a man to stand in a jam-packed pub on Hogmanay morning and tell dirty jokes with your gallus pals and drink whisky and beer and feel cheery. Wee Jakie always had new jokes.

"This bloke's wife is always having a kip in front of the fire when he comes home for his tea ..." *Uncle Charlie saying the boy's got the makings of a capitalist and his father, daddy, smiling* ... "he belts her across the chops and says if she's sleeping in front of the fire the next night he'll kick her teeth in ..." *it was for money you worked, not to show you were decent and steady, nobody thanked you for working till you almost dropped, they laughed at you* ... "so he comes home and there she is, snoozing away in front of the fire, her legs wide open ..." *it was women who told you to be respectable, women didn't know anything, what life had his mother seen, what did she know about pubs and men?* ... "so he says, you know what'll happen, you'll melt your guts sitting like that wi' your legs open ..." *the first time it tasted terrible but after that you began to like it, an acquired taste they called it, but it didn't matter about the taste, it made you feel better* ... "she's doing the same again, so he runs back down the stairs and goes to the butcher's shop and says give us a pound of offal ..." *it made you forget all the things you'd ever worried about, school, the belt, exam results, getting a job, getting a girl friend, speaking to your father, being called up to the army* ... "so he goes in quiet like and drops the raw, bloody, stinking offal on the carpet between her feet and nips out again, she's still sleeping ..." *nobody else knew how much you worried, nobody else knew anything about you, with a drink or two inside you it didn't matter* ... "and when he comes in again she's crying and his tea's on the table and she's begging him to forgive her and he says what happened? ..." *they were just nobodies, a family of nobodies, no better than anybody else, she had nothing to be snooty about, pubs or anything else . . .* "she says, oh John, you were right, my guts did melt and they fell out on the floor and I'd a helluva job getting them back in again. . . ." *you could laugh with your pals and put your hand on their shoulders and forget the whole bloody lot of it. Men didn't care if you were ugly.*

He and Billy Forsyth chewed gum on the way to the Corporation pitches but he was pretty sure, as they ran out of the dressing-room and across the mud, that Joe Overend knew they'd been in the pub.

The first half felt like a game played in a dream, where everything he did was perfect, where he ran quicker than anybody else and tackled harder than anyone else. He had a broken nose, he was a hard case, he could smash the lot of them. He even tried Charlie Tully's trick, raising his left arm and pointing to the wing as he dribbled the other way. It came off, the other team's right-half running the way he was pointing, chasing an imaginary ball.

At half-time his stomach felt full of gas. He sat on his hunkers and tried to belch the wind up. Maybe he'd got over his bad spell now. Maybe Joe had been right, he could play himself out of it.

"Awright, Dunky?" Joe asked, standing above him.

"Oh aye," he said, "I've got fuck'n indigestion or something."

"Ye could call it that."

He looked up at Joe, grinning. Joe grinned back. Joe didn't care if you had to be carried on to the pitch, as long as you got tore into them. The old Celtic stars, they always said, used to have a dram or two before the game.

But in the second half he knew it was no good. The drink had worn off and whenever he went for the ball he felt himself wincing, ready to cover his face with his arms in case he got a knock on the nose. His tackles were too late and too clumsy. If you had to screw up your courage before each tackle you might as well not bother. Why? He didn't feel afraid. Yet every time it was the same, as though his *face* remembered what had happened in the final, and was scared it would happen again. Reflexes, he supposed.

By the end of the game he was too winded to chase butterflies. Even off mud the ball seemed to bounce faster than he'd ever known a ball bounce before. A wee guy he should have tramped on gave him a right run-around and there was nothing he could do about it. His legs were weary. He could hear

Joe calling from the touchline. Joe would tell Baldy and Baldy would want to speak to him and he'd have to give Baldy some yarn and Baldy might give him another chance ... ach, tae hell with it! It was only a bloody game. It wasn't worth the effort. Drinking was better.

He waited till they were dressed and some of the lads had already gone. Joe was putting the ball into a string-net.

"Eh, Joe," he said, nodding for Billy to wait on him outside. "I don't think it's going to be any good, I'm chucking it in."

Joe put his shoe on the ball, rolling it backwards and forwards under the ball of his foot, the way all players always did.

"Och, I don't know, son, you'd quite a good first half."

Aye, I had a brilliant first half, but I was too drunk to care if I got my head knocked off.

"No, my mind's made up. I get sick when I go to head it. Here's my strip. Tell Baldy I'm sorry."

"All right, son, if that's how ye feel. Maybe if we're short some day ye'll give us a game? Pity to be giving it up altogether when you're only sixteen."

"Aye, maybe. See you then, Joe."

So that was that. A premature end to a promising career, as *Waverley* would say in the *Daily Record*. Ach, tae hell with it, he had a medal, he could always blow about that. It was only a rotten, stupid, stinking, lousy game.

"Come on," he said to Billy, "they'll be open afore we get to the Cross."

They drank beer till six o'clock, then he went home on the scheme bus for his tea. He washed his feet and legs in the sink basin, seeing his face in his mother's wee cracked mirror. Getting used to the twisted, flattened nose now. Not so much like a freak. He pushed out his dental plate on the end of his tongue. Two false teeth, two more medals to add to the list. He rubbed his tongue on the underside of the plate, tracing the rough stain left by cigarettes. Outside it was dark, the street-lights shining clear with haloes round the lamps in that way which told you it was freezing up.

Eating made you feel better. Warm tea.

"Your father'll think it's rotten you not going to see him on New Year's Day," said his mother. "If Senga can give up her friends for one day so can you."

"I'll go on Sunday," he said. She'd been moaning on about

243

the Ne'erday visit the whole week. "Tell him I'll see him on Sunday."

"Yes but it's Ne'erday, you should think of your father."

"I think of practically nothing else," he said, sticking his chin out at her. "The sooner he's walking again the better, I can get on wi' my own life."

His mother shook her head. Senga, as usual, had nothing to say. She'd put her hair up recently and had taken to wearing make-up. Not a bad-looking dish, for a sister. Sister? For all they ever said to each other they might as well be strangers.

"Will you be late?" his mother asked as he put on his good shoes, his sore feet crushing into the new, stiff leather.

"We're goin' first footin', I dunno how late I'll be."

He had the half bottle hidden under his clothes in the chest of drawers. He stood close to the drawer and slipped it into his raincoat pocket, leaving his coat unbelted so that she wouldn't see the bulge.

"Ta ta, Senga, darling," he said, "have a nice Hogmanay."

"I will if I don't see you," she said.

He blew her a big fart and left. As he closed the front door he could hear his mother talking, telling Senga to show respect to her big brother, no doubt. In the army, Shanky said, you could drink all you bloody wanted to, nobody gave a fuck. The army sounded good at times and hellish at others. Maybe it would be better to get in early and get the two years over with. It couldn't be any worse than working for Willie Craig now that he was the gaffer. Changed, just like that, snap, soon as his father was dead, snap, one day he was as daft as they make them, the next day shouting and bawling just like his father. The commies were right, it was a bloody swindle, you got seven quid a week and miserable bastards like the Craigs made a fortune.

He met Shanky and Jakie in the public bar of the Black Angus at half-past six. It was like something out of the Yukon gold-rush, Hogmanay and all the guys in Kilcaddie getting it down them as fast as it would come out of the bottles.

"So what's the big plans?" he asked.

Shanky had it all worked out. They'd stay in the Angus till closing at nine o'clock, making sure they bought the carry-out screwtops before they stopped serving in the wee off-sales cubicle. First they were going to the dance at the Caledonia ballroom, they could park the carry-out in Jakie's auntie's house in Tarbert Street. Then they were meeting a few other guys, Archie Hunter and his brother John, and their gang, and they were going to Chick Roy's house at Barskeddie.

"I'd like to call in at my pal Alec's house on the way to Barskeddie," he said. "He can't get out because he's getting engaged, poor mug. Let's drop in on the family gathering, eh?"

"You can but don't stay long," said Shanky. "It'll be hell on wheels at Chick's house, his folks are away. It'll be a riot, you know what Chick's like."

By half-past eight the men were six and seven deep at the bar and the six counterhands were practically running to keep pace with the orders. A wee drunk wandered up and down behind the tightly jammed backs, waving an empty glass. Shanky poured him a drop of beer from his pint.

"Ye're a gentleman, pal," said the drunk, his eyes like those of a dead fish, a dirty wee claw hand clutching Shanky's beltless blue raincoat, the shorty kind the Canadian ice-hockey players wore.

"Aye right, Jock," said Shanky. The wee man wouldn't leave them.

"Ye're a Chrustyin an' a gentleman, pal. Ah'll no' ferget yese, don't worry."

He put a finger to his lips and nodded.

Two young blokes started a fight, the crowd parting as their wild, wet faces glared at each other. Dunky shoved into the bar, holding up their glasses. If you didn't have your own glasses by now you'd had it.

"Three haufs an' three pints o' heavy," he shouted at the barman. It was so crowded everybody seemed to be leaning on everybody else. Men raised small glasses in neat finger holds and tossed back their whiskies. Some eyes were bright, some half-closed. Hands gripped shoulders, lips shouted into ears. The barman grabbed his pound note. Jakie was behind him and he ferried the glasses over the heads of the men, bumping a guy in the face with his elbow.

"Sorry, pal," he said.

" 'Sawright, Jimmy, 'sawright."

Big grins, thumbs raised. It could have been a fight. They gave Shanky ten bob each and he went for the screw-tops.

"It'll take him hours to get served," he said to Jakie.

"No' him, he's a fly boy, big Shanky."

Sure enough, he was back in no time with three carrier bags ull of pint bottles.

"We're drinkin' my rabbits now," Dunky said, lifting his pint. Shanky grinned, unbelievingly. "It's true, I got shot o' the lot o' them to some guy's brother. Five quid. No' bad, eh, for a bunch o' bloody rabbits."

He'd sold the lot to Laidlaw the greengrocer's brother. Now he had no rabbits, no ties, no responsibilities. Free to wander.

On the pavement men stood in groups, shaking hands, gripping biceps, swearing undying friendship. Everybody carried brown paper bags. Men. He felt like singing. His mates.

As they walked to Jakie's auntie's house he told Shanky why he'd given up the game. Shanky didn't believe him. He told him again. Shanky said he was showing the effects of the drink. He felt angry. Jakie stopped to shake hands with four or five men. They stopped. A man passed round a half bottle. The streets seemed packed with people, mostly men rushing from pubs to houses. He could hear shouts and singing.

"Jist keep quiet till we're in the house, okay pals?" said Jakie. "She's fed up wi' me fallin' at her feet when she opens the door."

It was up a tenement close. Shanky asked Jakie if there would be any decent wimmin. Jakie said his auntie went like a rattlesnake. He sounded a bit gone himself. They went into a living room. The men looked like uncles, cheery uncles, all with a good drop in them. They offered to give everybody a drink from their bottles, but the men said they ought to keep it, the night had a long way to go. Jakie's auntie gave them big whiskies.

"Here's tae us an' wha's like us," said the uncle-men. "Dam' few an' they're a' deid." He found himself talking to a man about football. A woman asked him if he'd like a sherry, he said sure, it tasted sweet but went down fine.

Shanky dragged them away to the dancing. The pavement was slippy with frost, unless you walked close to the tenement walls. They met some more people and shook hands. Gangs of guys shouted across the street. A man sat in a close entrance, ear pressed on the wall, his feet crossed cosily as though he was at his own fire, eyes half-closed, singing to himself.

There was a crowd at the entrance to the hall, it was an all-ticket do and scores of folk had turned up in hope of slipping in. Shanky had their tickets. One guy wasn't going to let them through.

"We've got tickets, chief," said Shanky. He could look very menacing when he wanted to. Bigtime.

"You lookin' for trouble, friend?" Jakie asked.

"Ach come on, Jakie, don't waste your energy."

There were girls outside, some of them carrying dancing shoes, wearing silk headscarves. It was like having a ticket for Scotland against England at Hampden Park, maybe somebody would jump you and grab the tickets, maybe they'd lock the gates ... in the cloakroom they gave their coats to a man. Boxing dead clever, he'd already transferred his half bottle to his inside jacket pocket.

He tapped it and winked as they went into the hall.

"We're awright for a wee drappie, don't worry,' he said.

"Keep it for later," said Shanky. "Let's view the talent first, I fancy lumbering a big piece to take to Chick's."

Dances were great if you had a good drink in you. Women. Bigtime. Easy meat. He danced a couple of times in the half-light, not hearing what they said, trying to shout against the noise of the band. It was hellish hot. He shoved about in the men's side till he saw Shanky talking to John Hunter. They were talking about where they'd meet before walking out to Barskeddie. It sounded hellish boring.

"Fancy a drop in the lavvy?" he said.

They got in a stall and snibbed the door behind them, knees jammed against the lavatory seat.

"Just one," said Shanky. "We want at least one bottle for the game the morra."

You needed a pal who could think ahead. They'd need a drink at the Rangers-Celtic game. He screwed the top on. Back in the dance he decided the hell with it he'd take a walk up the women's side and see what was going. Everybody was doing it. Every night should be Hogmanay, nobody cared what you did. He saw Magda Gemmell.

"Ye dancing, hen?" he asked her.

"Oh hallo, Duncan! My, you're a stranger."

Between dances he kept his arm round her waist, why bother splitting up? She was fast, dirty-minded. The ideal woman for a horror like himself.

"Hey, we're goin' to Chick Roy's house later on, you fancy comin'?"

She said she would try to slip away from her father and

mother. She was his sure thing. Bigtime. They were dancing cheek to cheek by eleven, when it was time to push off, her to get the Barskeddie bus, them off God knows where. They had a quick necking session in the corridor. She could get him steamed up any time.

"You'll be there, won't you? I'm countin' on it, Magda, you're the only decent woman I've ever known."

Honest. Cross my heart. They stood shouting after her and her pal, waving and whistling, then they went back to Jakie's auntie's house. He felt better after an hour or so without a drink. What the hell had he ever seen in bloody Elsa? It made him angry, just thinking about that love rubbish, keeping themselves pure! She was just a frigid wee bitch. Real women let you do *anything*. To get it from miserable hairies like Elsa you had to buy a ring and stick your head right into the noose. He'd escaped just in time. Poor bloody Telfer! He started laughing. He wanted to jump in the air and wave his arms about. To get Telfer annoyed these days all you had to do was ask him how the furniture-buying was going. Bigtime Donald Telfer, buying furniture! Talking about the rents of two-apartment houses! The nearest he'd ever get to Canada was at the pictures!

It was like a man, to have a good laugh about other people's hard luck. Hard lines, pal, as they said in Kilcaddie, eyes grinning, hard cheese, kid, hard cheddar, Jock, fuck your horrible luck bud. Guys like Shanky, laugh like a drain as they told you of some bloke's grim luck. Well, that's how it was, a hard world, laugh while you can.

Back at Jakie's auntie's house it all seemed a bit too grown-up. Men with red faces put their arms round each other. Women in corsets giggled as they took another drink, "Well, jist a wee wan mind, ye're no' tryin' tae get me merry, are ye?" Shanky gave Jakie's auntie a bit of patter, trust Shanky, how could anybody's *auntie* be game for a rattle? They turned up the wireless, Jimmy Shand, just before twelve, the accordion band blaring through the room, big rush to get glasses filled before the clock started chiming. He found it was easier just to grin at the people. Sooner they were away on their travels the better. Then a voice on the radio, some gabble, then silence, a woman telling her Bob to hold his wheesh, then the chimes, one, two, the end of the year. Like standing to attention for the National Anthem at the pictures. Then the last chime and the radio giving out the great roar from the

248

crowds at Glasgow Trongate and the people turning on each other, shaking hands, kissing, "A guid new year tae yin an' a'," they sounded like people imitating Scots people, they always did at New Year.

They were away up the road shortly afterwards, him and Shanky and Jakie. More groups on the streets now, the first-footers making fast time to the next house, shaking strangers' hands in the street, everybody was everybody's friend.

Great. So why did he suddenly feel peculiar? Alone and not really part of it.

On the way they passed St. Andrew's Church. The entrance was lit and people were coming out, shaking the elders' hands, the minister on the steps, the religious mob, decent folk, the men pulling on their heavy nap coats, women in furs and hats.

"Look at that lot," said Jakie. "Give ye the dry boke jist lookin' at them."

They stood across the road and had a pass round of Shanky's half-bottle, putting down the carrier bags. It seemed like a bit of fun, to show the toffs a bit of scruff carry-on. In the light of the church porch, his wife helping him on with his coat, he saw Nicol, the school teacher.

"That's my old teacher," he said.

"Which one?"

"Him putting on his coat."

"Him wi' the kilt on?"

"The kilt?" He screwed up his eyes. He could see thin legs below the coat. "So it is. Jesus Christ."

"Ah know whut to do wi' guys wearin' the kilt," said Jakie. "Chuck stones at them, stupid buggers."

"Come on," said Shanky. "We've to meet the Hunter mob at Meiklepark."

They meandered uphill towards the scheme. Shanky even *walked* bigtime, shoulders swinging, back straight, collar turned up, like Sterling Hayden in *The Asphalt Jungle*. Funny about him, parents dead respectable, yet he was snooker king of the Academy. Funny.

The Hunters had a small gang waiting at the corner which led into Meiklepark. They stood under a tall, concrete lamp post. They had a few women with them, too. Bigtime. He hoped Magda would turn up at Chick Roy's.

"I want to go to Alec's," he said. Jakie didn't want to go. Shanky said they'd wait for him. He said he would only be five minutes. He ran along the pavement, close to the hedge, eyes on the sparkling ground, right hand holding the half-bottle close to his chest.

"Welcome, happy New Year, you're our first foot," said Alec's father. "Got a piece of coal, have you?"

"Eh, no."

Alec's father took him round the back of the house and delved into the bunker.

"The first foot must have a lump of coal and a bottle," said Alec's father. He held it out as they went into the brightly-lit lobby. Alec came through a mob of aunts and uncles and whatnot, looking hellish glad to see him. Ethel Carruthers was there, too, banana legs! His cheeks burned after the chill outside. He had a couple of big drams. Neat. Down in a oncer.

"That's my big mate," said Alec, approvingly. "You can neck Ethel if you like, seein' how it's Ne'erday."

"Yippee," he heard himself shout. He got his arms round Big Ethel. She felt thin and cool and weak. No body at all. Hard lines, Alec. She didn't seem enthusiastic, either. A family party suited her. She looked like an auntie already. She didn't smile when he slashed a good drop from his own bottle into Alec's glass. Getting away was difficult, Alec couldn't come to Chick Roy's but he wanted him to stay, keep him company.

He ran down the sparkling pavement, the duty business over, let's get on with the big night! Yippee. Most of them had gone on, but Shanky and Jakie were still under the lamp post.

"Lead on MacDuff," Jakie yelled and they started on the five miles to Barskeddie. Along the road they met a gang of blokes. Jakie knew some of them.

"Come wi' us," he said, "Chick Roy's folks are away."

While they talked he sat down on the kerb and had a drag at one of the screwtops. Some guy in the other gang was miroculous. Suddenly he was shouting at Jakie and Jakie was lifting his fists to him. The other guy had a pint bottle in his hand. He ran across the road at Jakie, the bottle raised. Halfway across he slipped and sat down hard. The bottle broke. His mates seemed to think this was Jakie's fault.

"Ye fuck'n mug!" one of them roared.

"Come on," said Shanky, grabbing Jakie's elbow, dragging him away. "They're just a lot of shit."

They walked away, leaving the other mob to pick up their pal, who was lying on the road, crying. They walked to the next lamp post.

"I'll get them," Jakie kept saying.

Dunky hated them for being ignorant fighting animals. He had almost finished one screwtop. He swallowed what was left, turned back and hurled it at the other gang. They heard it breaking with a hard plop. Glass tinkled. They ran from the shouts. He was laughing. Shanky kept pulling him.

Walking five miles drunk was no bother at all. Like magic. He wanted to tell Shanky everything. Shanky was a bigtime guy, a real pal. Jakie fell into the hedge at the side of the road. They pulled him out, dragging him by the coat collar, forcing him to keep walking. People liked you when you were drunk.

"You like me, don't you, Shanky? Nobody likes me, Shanky. You like me, Shanky, don't you?"

"Yeah, sure," said Shanky.

"No, *really* like me?"

Jakie sat down between them. They dragged him up by the coat sleeves.

"Nobody likes me, Shanky, nobody in the whole world. They hate me."

He was sick. He stood for a few moments, head leaning forward, trying to keep it off his trousers. It came again, erupting out of his throat. Jakie sat down. He stepped round the vomit, shaking his head, blinking tears out of his eyes.

"That's better," he said. He made himself belch but there was nothing more to come up. "I'm awright now. Come on, Jakie, we'll never get there."

"People hate you," Shanky said. "And you hate people. Thank Christ you've stopped all that snivelling."

"I wasn't snivelling."

"I don't care what you call it. Let's get this drunken bastard moving again. Look, Jakie, I'm telling you for the last time, I'm getting to Chick Roy's whether you come or not. You want us to leave you in the ditch?"

"Leggoa me," said Jakie. He dug his heels in and shook their hands off his arms. Shanky took hold of him again. Jakie tried to punch him. Dunky got a fistful of Jakie's shoulder. Jakie, bent almost double, twisted round and tried to butt him in the stomach. Jakie always got a bit stupid when he was drunk. He couldn't tell his pals from his enemies. He called them a lot of dirty bastards.

"Awright," said Shanky, "if that's how you want it."

Jakie sat down in the middle of the road. His carrier bag

of screwtops lay across his leg. "Leave the bugger right there," said Shanky.

"What if a car comes? He'll get killed."

"To bad."

"We'll put him on the grass."

"On you go. I'm off."

"Ach, it's his own fault." He did, however, stop a few yards away and shout back for Jakie to get up. Jakie shouted something back. "Get killt then for all I care."

So it was just him and Shanky, walking like big hard men, under the moon, along the dark, icy road, trees on one side, a hedge on the other. The idea of Jake sitting there till a car's headlights lit him up suddenly seemed the height of hilarity. Shanky thought it was funny, too, although he wasn't the type to laugh out loud.

"We'll know what happened to him on the way back," he said. "If there's no big flat blob on the road we'll know he's awright."

"You're a cruel bastard, aren't you?"

"I've no time for nutters."

"But he's supposed to be your pal, you bastard."

"Ballocks to him. Look out for number one, that's the big motto. I'll tell you a story, kid. This English bloke's a Bevin boy down a mine in Fife, a right softy. He's shovelling for this big hard case of a miner who's on his back with his pick. The English bloke hears a rumbling up the tunnel but the big miner says nothing. It gets nearer. The miner keeps digging away into the seam. Then the English bloke looks up and sees a runaway bogie, weighing about a ton, crashing towards him down the line. He jumps for the side, it goes past like a rocket, it's so narrow in the tunnel it touches his back and whips the clothes off him and the skin off his shoulder blades. He's about ready to faint but he says to the miner, 'Christ, you musta known what that noise was, why the hell didn't you warn me?' The miner bloke looks up. 'Why shouldn't I?' he says. 'I'm no' your mammy,' he says."

"Is that what you believe in?"

"Yeah."

The detached bungalow had a little white wooden paling round its garden. They jumped the paling and ran across the grass. The door was open. Inside it was like V E night. He and Shanky did a tour of the various rooms, seeing what was what. They put their beer into the kitty but kept the half

252

bottles in their pockets. Chick Roy and the two Hunters and the main crowd were in the living room, guys sprawled on the floor, a couple necking on the couch, some drunk kneeling beside the gramophone, a girl trying to calm down her sobbing mate, some guy unconscious in an armchair. The drunk kept putting on Elvis Presley at the wrong speed, *Blue Suède Shoes* sounding like Mickey Mouse. Another guy kept shoving the drunk away and changing the gramophone to the normal speed.

"Hey come on an' I'll show you something," said Archie Hunter, thumbing them towards the door with big winks. "Chick's too far gone to care, they're wrecking the joint."

They followed him into the kitchen, drinking from screwtops. In the deeper of the two sinks, the big one used for steeping the washing, there was a bloke! Pissed to the world, his face on his knees, which were doubled up to his chest. The water was up to his elbows, the tap still running.

"That's Tommy Patterson," said Archie. "He's got gastric ulcers or something, he shouldnae drink at all. We put him in the sink for a laugh."

They roared. It was hilarious. Shanky passed round his half-bottle.

"That's no' half of it," said Archie. "The place is a wreck, Chick'll get murdered when his folks come back. Come on through the bedroom, hey, it's worse!"

It was one of those fancy bedrooms, the kind with a white rug and a brown silk bedcover and wee lace mats on the dressing-table. Archie pulled off the silk bedcover. There were two guys in the bed, wearing all their clothes, both unconscious.

"This one's just drunk," said Archie, pulling the guy's ear so that his face turned up, showing where he'd vomited on the pillow. He let him drop back into it. "This one hit his head falling off the dressing-table, he was dancing on it."

The second guy had dried blood on his forehead.

Other guys came in to inspect them. They rolled back to the living-room and joined in the hilarity. There was wine, too, bottles of VP. He tried that but it was too sweet to drink on its own. He poured some into his beer. There was dancing and jumping about. Some guy started shouting the odds about his whisky having been knocked. He wanted a fight, but Shanky and John Hunter got his arms up behind his back and shoved him face first out of the window, his legs slipping out of view.

He got up and went back through the kitchen, whisky in one hand, beer and wine in the other. The guy with ulcers was still unconscious in the sink. Water was now pouring onto the kitchen floor. He went through to the bedroom, singing. There were some dames in there being shown the two guys in bed. Holding the glasses above his head he tried to show them the sword dance. The rug slipped and he sat down on his spine. He lay on his back and laughed, the beer and wine pouring on his chest. A girl said something nasty about him.

He scrambled to his feet.

"I'm no' drunk, I havenae even startet yet," he shouted. "Yippee."

Magda was in the living-room. Nobody would listen when he said she was his big steady. He sat on the floor beside her and tried to hold her hand. People kept walking in and out in crowds. He had a whole bottle of V P. beside him, and his whisky in his breast pocket and a screwtop between his feet. Magda loved him. Singing. Magda talking. Magda on his lap. Laughing about Jakie. Laughing when a guy threw a bottle at the big mirror. Something about walking with Magda. Going to get married. Falling in a garden. Back in the house. Big rammy in the living-room. Shanky's my mate, he'll look after me. Falling down. Where's the bloody booze gone? I want a drink, thieving bastards, I want a drink. . . .

It was daylight. One of his eyes was closed up. His left leg had gone to sleep. It was over the arm of the chair. His neck had a crick. He tried to move and his head tried to burst through his skull. This was it, his first big hangover. It was worse than what they said it would be. He remembered all sorts of trouble. It was morning and he was still at Chick Roy's house. His mother would do her nut. He was a disgrace. She'd tell his father! His father was going to walk again and come back to the house. No, he couldn't stand all that again. Where would he go? Canada? No, that was just a big dream, a fancy notion for boys with their heads full of nonsense. There was no place for him at home. He was a disgrace. A drunkard. An ugly mug. Jesus would never help him now, God had given him plenty of chances. Maybe if he made it his New Year resolution, never again, not another drop . . . the hell with it, he was a disgrace, a bad lot. Maybe he'd been cursed.

What did it all mean? What were men, anyway? Why wasn't he a man himself? He was a nothing, a collection of poses. Easily led, his mother called it. Nobody knew anything about

254

you. You didn't know anything about anybody else. Telfer was getting married. McCann was talking about joining the police. Willie had become like his old man. Elsa had betrayed him. He hadn't cared, now he wanted to cry when he thought of her. You couldn't depend on other people, you couldn't depend on yourself.

If grown men could change so quickly how could you be sure of yourself? You wanted to be like other people but they did the dirty on you, one way or the other. You started off trying to be different, trying not to turn out like all the others. You ended up worse than them. You ended up knowing you were a disgrace, full of all the things you hated in other people.

He could never face them again, none of them. He wanted to run away. In the army they didn't care what you did. It was a hard life in the army. It was what he deserved. It would be his punishment. He wasn't fit for anything else. He was a waster. He might as well sign on for life. Never come back to Kilcaddie again, not ever.

Shanky came into Chick Roy's living-room, whistling, buttoning his shirt, his raincoat over his shoulder.

"Awright?" he said. "You look lousy. Come on, kid, on your feet, we don't want to be late for the train, let's beat it before Chick's folk come back, they'll go wild when they see this joint."

On the bus to Ayr and in the Glasgow train he kept wanting to be sick. It was madness to go all the way to Glasgow, but Shanky was determined to have his big day out.

They carried seven screwtops and an almost untouched half-bottle into Ibrox Park. He thought of his mother. She'd always said, since he was a tot, that the Rangers-Celtic crowd were the lowest of the low, drunken animals. A disgrace to Scotland. Who cared? He knew he was doing the wrong thing but he started drinking again all the same. What the hell did it all matter? Soon they were talking to some other men and bottles were being passed round. Rangers scored and they yelled themselves hoarse, banging each other on the back.

Somebody chucked a bottle on the pitch. They all laughed and had another drink.

"Kill they Fenian bastards," shouted one of their new pals.

"We are the people," shouted another.

He held his hands high above his head and roared and roared until his throat was sore.

AN AMERICAN DREAM   5/-

Norman Mailer

Author of *The Naked and the Dead*

There is nothing insubstantial or fairylike about *An American Dream*. It is a great powerhouse of a novel; a masterpiece of brutal realism; a blend of raw sex and tender love, hate and brutality, Good and Evil, with all the terrifying tension and pent-up violence of an awakening volcano.

With *An American Dream* Mailer reaffirms his towering stature as a novelist. Using the framework of a first-rate detective story, he has created much more—an epic of our own time, a triumphant return to the greatness which made *The Naked and the Dead* the outstanding novel of World War II.